AT ANY COST

ALSO BY ANDREA KANE

FORENSIC INSTINCTS NOVELS:

THE GIRL WHO DISAPPEARED TWICE
THE LINE BETWEEN HERE AND GONE
THE STRANGER YOU KNOW
THE SILENCE THAT SPEAKS
THE MURDER THAT NEVER WAS
A FACE TO DIE FOR
DEAD IN A WEEK
NO STONE UNTURNED

OTHER SUSPENSE THRILLERS:

RUN FOR YOUR LIFE
NO WAY OUT
SCENT OF DANGER
I'LL BE WATCHING YOU
WRONG PLACE, WRONG TIME
DARK ROOM
TWISTED
DRAWN IN BLOOD

HISTORICAL ROMANCES:

MY HEART'S DESIRE
DREAM CASTLE
MASQUE OF BETRAYAL
ECHOES IN THE MIST
SAMANTHA
THE LAST DUKE
EMERALD GARDEN
WISHES IN THE WIND
LEGACY OF THE DIAMOND
THE BLACK DIAMOND
THE MUSIC BOX
THE THEFT
THE GOLD COIN
THE SILVER COIN

AT ANY COST

ANDREA KANE

ISBN-13: 9781682320433 (Hardcover)
9781682320464 (Trade Paperback)
9781682320440 (ePub)
9781682320457 (Kindle)

LCCN: 2021944331

At Any Cost

For questions and comments about the quality of this book, please contact us at: CustomerService@bonniemeadowpublishing.com.

BonnieMeadowPublishing.com

Printed in USA

Publisher's Cataloging-In-Publication Data
(Prepared by The Donohue Group, Inc.)

Names: Kane, Andrea, author. | Kane, Andrea. Forensic Instincts novel ; 9.
Title: At any cost / Andrea Kane.
Description: Warren, NJ : Bonnie Meadow Publishing LLC, [2022]
Identifiers: ISBN 9781682320433 (hardcover) | ISBN 9781682320464 (trade paperback) | ISBN 9781682320440 (ePub) | ISBN 9781682320457 (Kindle)
Subjects: LCSH: Businesswomen--New York (State)--New York--Fiction. | Missing persons--New York (State)--New York--Fiction. | Private investigators--New York (State)--New York--Fiction. | Serial murders--New York (State)--New York--Fiction. | LCGFT: Detective and mystery fiction.
Classification: LCC PS3561.A463 A8 2022 (print) | LCC PS3561.A463 (ebook) | DDC 813/.54--dc23

With deepest gratitude, I dedicate *At Any Cost* to Angela Bell, Public Affairs Specialist, FBI National Press & Operations Unit, Office of Public Affairs (just retired), who has been there for me throughout my entire FBI experience and who helped me breathe the life of the bureau into my books. Thank you for being such a consummate professional, an amazing judge of people, a beyond-hardworking advisor, and—the best bonus of all—the most caring of friends. The bureau will miss you deeply, since no one will ever be able to fill your shoes!

PROLOGUE

Brightington University
Birchmont, Westchester County, New York
Eight years ago

A kill for a kill.

Weeks of watching and waiting. Plans devised. Soon to be meticulously executed. Mid-November. Football season nearing its peak. Thursday night. Nine p.m. Campus in early-weekend party mode. Undergrads drinking. Smoking up at the frat houses. Athletic building deserted.

Nearly deserted.

His target was there. Alone. Thursday night was his late night during football season. That's when he reviewed his game strategy and player weaknesses. That's when he targeted the next eager kid to torture until he broke.

The bastard wouldn't be breaking anyone ever again. Not the way he'd broken Hank.

As the star quarterback in high school, Hank had gotten a full-ride Division 1 scholarship. Since he'd come from a dirt-poor family, this was the opportunity of a lifetime. A first-rate college education with a shot at the NFL. It was supposed to be a life-changing event.

Instead it turned out to be a death sentence.

His executioner had been Pete Rice. Football coach? Bullshit. Rice hadn't coached Hank; he'd tortured him, driven him—until Hank had blown out his knee on a rain-soaked football field junior year, ending his college career, his dreams. And in the end, his life.

It was first down and goal.

Rice was about to find out the true meaning of payback.

The campus grounds were soggy, leftover patches of wet leaves and an endless span of slick grass, made worse by the cold, steady rainfall. The bare trees swayed as rain pounded their branches. A wet mess. Treacherous, like a wet football field.

Slugging through the debris, he approached the athletic building, pausing yards away to don the black ski mask. He then tugged his hood back into place. No point in taking chances. Security cameras were everywhere. He didn't need his face to be captured. Other than the mask, he could be any college student. A waterproof parka that swallowed up his body. Jeans and combat boots. Standard college garb.

He reached the building and slid Hank's ID card into the entry slot. The card still worked. Too soon for it to be deactivated.

He was in. He wriggled into his latex gloves.

The office door was unlocked. Rice was at his desk, files spread across it. He was scribbling something on one of them, brows knit in concentration, totally focused on his work.

Clueless that he was about to die.

In one fluid motion, he was inside the office, the door closed behind him. Rice leapt to his feet, snatching the heavy football trophy on his desk as he rounded the front of it to defend himself against the intruder.

Without a word, the killer whipped out a pistol and fired two bullets, one into each of Rice's kneecaps. Rice howled, collapsing to the floor in pain. The trophy hit the floor beside him with a thud.

The assailant moved quickly—four long strides until he was behind Rice, dragging him back to his chair and heaving him into it. He shoved a rag in the coach's mouth to stifle his screams, then moved behind him, wrapping a strong arm in a choke hold around Rice's throat. He pocketed his pistol, pulled out a zip tie, and leaned down to cinch the writhing man's ankles together. That done, he slapped a digital voice recorder on the desk, with the record feature on. He yanked the rag out of Rice's mouth, tossed it aside, and anchored his forearm against the left side of the coach's neck, using his free hand to pull as tight against the carotid artery as he chose to—for now.

A rush of power surged through him. He could taste victory.

But there was work to be done before the final play.

"You killed Hank Bishop," he growled. "I want details."

When he got no answer, only a violent trembling of Rice's body, he tightened the pressure around his neck. "Talk."

"Car crash…" the coach gasped. "I didn't…"

"Wrong answer." His grip tightened still more, enough so Rice was on the verge of losing consciousness. The coach struggled in vain, his attempts weak and fading.

His soon-to-be executioner eased the pressure the tiniest fraction. He knew just what it would take. And he wasn't ready. Not until he got what he wanted.

"Wanna die?" he asked in a flat tone that was chillingly devoid of emotion.

Terrified, blood oozing down his legs, Rice gave a feeble shake of his head.

"Good. Because this is what it will feel like."

He increased the pressure until Rice passed out. Slowly, he eased the choke hold until the scumbag came to.

"Now I'll ask my question again," he said calmly. "Why is Hank dead? Why was he in that car crash? This is your last chance. I want to hear it all—what you did, how you did it, what you drove him to."

Rice was drenched in sweat, his entire body shuddering, choking sounds coming from his throat.

No further coercion was necessary.

Between gasps for air, the coach spilled his guts, revealing everything he'd done, everything that had happened—plus a whole lot more that was happening still.

Interesting stuff. Some of which he knew about. Still more of which he didn't. It was even bigger than what he'd come here to learn. But frankly, he didn't give a shit. He'd originally planned to take the voice recorder with him to relive Rice's agonized confession whenever he chose to. But it really didn't matter. He'd committed the bastard's words to memory. So instead, he'd leave the recorder here, let the cops hear the entire confession, including the big-picture part that had nothing to do with Hank but that would send their investigation in the entirely wrong direction—a direction his employer wouldn't appreciate, but that was his problem.

His adrenaline pumping, he tightened his choke hold into a death grip, pressing against the carotid artery, closing it off and squeezing the life out of his victim.

A minute later, Rice was dead.

Luca Floris had been a security guard at Brightington University for a decade. The pay was shit. His other job paid a whole lot better. So when his boss instructed Floris to keep an eye on Pete Rice, he didn't ask questions. He just complied. Which meant he had a bird's-eye view of the masked guy who slipped outside the athletic building, glancing quickly around before pulling off his mask and disappearing into the night.

Floris pressed himself back into the wet bushes, waiting and watching until the guy was gone. Then he went inside the athletic building to take a look.

Five minutes later, he bolted out of the building, stuffing one item under his coat and another in his pocket. He glanced furtively around to make sure no one was nearby and then ducked back into the bushes to make his call.

"I need to see you—*now*," he said with rising hysteria.

The urgency was clear. No further clarification was necessary. "The usual spot," was the reply. "I'm on my way."

Floris weaved in and out of traffic, making the drive to Bayonne, New Jersey, in record time. He turned into the broken-down side street where these meetings took place and waited for the man parked in front of him to leave his car and join Floris in his.

A moment later, his boss was in the passenger seat, shutting the door behind him and turning to Floris. "What happened?"

"Rice is dead." Floris didn't mince words. "Strangled—there were choke marks all over his neck. There was blood on the floor and the smell of gunpowder, so I'm sure there was more that went on before he was finished off."

A hint of a pause. "Did you see the killer?"

"Yeah. On his way out." Sweat was pouring down Floris's back, and he raked both shaking hands through his hair. He'd never seen a murder victim in his life, nor had he ever had a desire to see one. "He was wearing a mask, but he took it off when he left the building."

"Recognize him?"

"I think so—yes."

"What does that mean?"

"It means that, if it's the guy I'm thinking of, I'm not sure if he actually goes to Brightington or just visits. But he's in the stands at almost every one of the school's football games. And he hung out with the star quarterback. They seemed really tight. That poor kid—the quarterback—tore up his knee and couldn't play anymore. Three weeks ago, he was killed in a car crash."

"Which his close friend might blame on the coach, for whatever reason. That would make sense. Revenge is a powerful motivator."

"That's what I figured." Floris still felt like he was going to puke. "So I rifled through Rice's files until I found the one belonging to the dead kid. Just in case you needed it. Also, there was a voice recorder on Rice's desk. Looks like he was talking when he died. So I grabbed that, too."

"Did you listen to it?"

"Hell no. I got out of there as fast as I could, called you, and drove here." Floris reached around back and snatched up the file and the digital recorder from the floor of the back seat. "Here." He practically shoved them at his boss.

The other man took the proffered items. "Did anyone see you?" he asked.

"No. And the area is deserted because all the kids are in party mode, mostly on the frat quad. But I'd better get back."

A nod. "Do that. And Floris? I'll take it from here. You forget this entire thing ever happened."

"It's forgotten." It was the most grateful, if impossible, promise Floris had ever made.

"Good." As he spoke, the man reached into his pocket and pulled out a wad of bills, folding them in half and handing them to the security guard. "Nice work."

Floris took the money on autopilot. He hadn't been sure what to expect, but this was sure as hell the best possible outcome. Freaked out or not, it felt good to be appreciated for something—and to be compensated for it.

"Thanks," he said.

He waited for his boss to head back to his own car before counting his bonus. Ten one-hundred-dollar bills. A thousand bucks. Double what he made in a week at the university.

Maybe finding a dead body wasn't so bad after all.

The other man slid behind the wheel of his sedan and slammed the door shut. This wasn't supposed to be the night. But the loose cannon had decided otherwise. Damn him.

He turned on the voice recorder and listened to the entire confession. Ironic. Floris had saved his own life by not doing the same.

He made a quick mental calculation. It had been too long since the murder had taken place. Time wasn't on his side.

Much as he disliked using the phone—even one as heavily encrypted as his—he'd have to make an exception. This needed to be taken care of ASAP.

He made the necessary call.

A voice answered on the first ring. "Yeah?"

"I need the sanitation crew for a black bag job," he said. "Athletic building at Brightington University. Second floor. Pete Rice. Send a cleaner. And some longshoremen to take care of his car. A silver Lexus SUV, parked outside in the lot. And I'd make sure the vehicle takes a long voyage to our friends overseas."

***

The deceased's office
Ten days later

Two local police detectives stood inside Pete Rice's office, arms folded across their chests as they dubiously eyeballed the young woman their chief had summoned to assist in the investigation. They didn't like the fact that she was here, and they made no attempt to disguise it. However, a week and a half had passed since Coach Rice had vanished, and the investigation had hit a brick wall. The university's bigwigs, together with the parents who paid their kids' tuitions, the alumni who cherished their football games—the whole college community and beyond—were up in arms. They were demanding answers—*now*. And the cops had nothing to give them, although not for lack of trying.

Despite an extensive search, no body had been found. The coach's car, which had been missing from the parking lot, had yet to be recovered, even in pieces. Other than the lingering smell of gunpowder and the small blood samples that Crime Scene had collected, bagged, and ultimately DNA-matched to Rice, the coach's office was devoid of evidence, and there was nothing personal about the coach himself.

The police hadn't stopped there. They'd thoroughly searched Rice's apartment. No signs of burglary. Nothing amiss. No indications of a man who had fled. Rice was single with no kids. But his neighbors had all been questioned, as had any other persons of interest. Not a shred of useful information had been uncovered.

Pete Rice had been a campus legend—a hard-core, win-at-all-costs coach. A hero. What he lacked in compassion, he made up for in skill. He was both hated and respected, feared yet sought-after by his players. The detectives had interviewed enough of his players, both past and present, to pick up on the undercurrents. But hating someone and doing them bodily harm were two entirely different things.

How much bodily harm? At least some, given the blood spatter and the residual smell of gunpowder. But more than that? No one knew. Certainly not the poor, terrified custodian who'd come in the morning after the incident to do his job and clean the coach's office only to walk into a frightful scene.

The lack of physical evidence caused the pressure from the community to reach a fevered pitch.

Which is why the chief of police had called in Claire Hedgleigh—quietly and with minimal media exposure.

"How long is this going to take?" one of the detectives asked her.

"I don't know," was her honest reply. "But I'll do my best."

"Yeah. Do that."

Ignoring the sarcasm, Claire tied back her long blond hair in a ponytail, freeing up her field of view. She'd learned to ignore the barbs and the scrutiny. She was used to it.

The truth was that no police force wanted to openly admit that they worked with psychics, even if Claire never billed herself as one. She explained time and time again that she was what was known as a claircognizant—someone who intuitively knew things, not someone who had bona fide spiritual connections to the past or the future.

The distinction never made a difference. To the authorities, what she did wasn't science. Therefore, it wasn't regarded. Still, more than a few Westchester County police departments had elicited Claire's help. And she'd proven her abilities time and again over the past three years, ever since her junior year in college when she'd been an integral part of solving a missing student crime at her own alma mater.

Word spread. Credibility was established. And Claire's consultations with law enforcement increased—under the radar but with a high success rate.

Now, she concentrated on the task at hand, starting with a brief perusal of Rice's office.

Barren. Metal file cabinets, a worn desk and chair, and a basic desktop computer and printer. Papers and file folders strewn around. Trophies on a shelf and a heavy one on his desk. Team photos on the wall. No personal touches, like family photos or indications of hobbies. Just exhibitions of the Brightington football teams.

With slow, deep breaths, Claire shut her eyes and channeled her energy. Nothing immediate. Then again, her insights came at their will, not hers. All she could do to help them along was to open her mind and let the energy flow.

The old-fashioned clock on the wall ticked away the minutes. Long minutes.

And suddenly, nothing became something.

Claire's eyes flew open, and her gaze settled on the missing coach's desk, a dark feeling of evil pervading her.

She stepped forward and pressed her palms firmly against the metal surface of the desk. Currents of death coursed through her.

Not just death. Murder.

She leaned forward and wrapped her fingers around the heavy football trophy that was planted on Rice's desk—something he frequently touched and always treasured. Something that would bring Claire closer to her insights.

Something that had been moved from the floor to the desk. Something the coach had been handling when fear had crept up his spine.

Something he'd planned to use as a weapon.

Filaments of awareness, fragments of certainty.

Vengeance, thoroughly planned and executed. Death, painful and sustained.

And a killer with a very sick, twisted mind.

1

CannaBD
Elmton, New York
Present day

Aimee Bregman left her office and hopped into her car, ready for the adventure du jour.

She loved her job.

When she was hired to be chief marketing officer of CannaBD, she felt as if she'd won the lottery. She'd never thought that being a party girl in college would be an asset in her job hunting—although, frat parties or not, she'd worked hard to earn her MBA in marketing. Still, this was a dream come true. She was being paid to take this exciting start-up beverage company and grow it into a household name. She'd already made great strides in getting the buzz going.

CannaBD, which boasted a unique line of CBD-infused beer, was the brainchild of Nick Colotti, a brilliant engineering grad student at Danforth University—Aimee's own alma mater. Nick had developed their core product through a combination of skill and luck. He was playing around in the university lab, trying to extract CBD oil from cannabis using supercritical CO2 and infusing it into a keg of beer for a frat house party he was throwing. The results were nothing short of spectacular. And CannaBD was born.

Nick, who Aimee had met at Danforth when she was still an undergrad, had hired her shortly after she'd gotten her MBA and he'd firmly launched the company—a launch made possible through the capital that his father had invested in his business. And Aimee had jumped in with both feet, ready to effectively market the product line.

Given the young demographic they were appealing to, Aimee joked that she was lucky enough to attend college all over again. She spent most of her time in and around colleges, meeting and talking with recent alumni, grad students, and current twenty-one-plus undergrads. She was smart enough to know that the largest consumption of alcoholic beverages was tied to Greek-life events. So she focused her efforts on schools with a large number of established and thriving fraternity and sorority chapters, all with active current and alumni members. And she worked very hard to build relationships with the student officers, members, faculty advisors, and alumni directors of those schools.

She didn't stop there. In order to drive word of mouth, she recruited young influencers in the alcoholic beverage space—not only officers, members, and young alumni of college fraternities and sororities but also socially active, attractive young people attending these colleges who knew how to showcase a highly spirited, coveted lifestyle via YouTube videos, Instagram, and Snapchat. She organized frequent product tastings right on campuses, which gave her yet another opportunity to chat with her target audience.

All in all, things were going great.

Until, abruptly, they weren't.

***

Danforth University
Office of the director of Alumni Relations
Manhattan, New York

Rita Edwell sat at her desk, staring at the printed sheet of paper in her hand, reading and rereading the factually imparted information. She didn't cry. The time for crying was over. She'd sobbed and sobbed when she got the initial diagnosis. This second opinion was a pie-in-the-sky attempt to mitigate the finality of her prognosis, a filament of hope that there could be some unknown treatment that could lengthen her life.

There wasn't. The cancer was too advanced. It had metastasized and was running rampant through all her organs. And this impersonal piece of paper in her hand slammed the door on her hopes.

She closed her eyes, numbly reflecting on the fact that she'd never see her fortieth birthday, that she'd never compile a bucket list, much less cross things off one, that she'd made such a mess of her life—a mess she'd been desperate to undo.

It was too late. A year from now, at most, she wouldn't be here.

And there was no way to clean things up by then, much less undo all the ugly things she'd done. All the material things that had mattered so much—her impeccable suede suit, her Louis Vuitton bag—now seemed meaningless and immorally obtained.

Her office phone rang, and she opened her eyes, staring blankly at the piece of equipment as if seeing it for the first time. She had to shake off this fog, to be in the present as long as she could.

She pressed the flashing button that was labeled with her secretary's name. "Yes, Marie?"

"Ms. Edwell, Aimee Bregman is here for her eleven-o'clock meeting," her secretary announced.

Rita blinked. Aimee. Yes. She'd made this appointment last week, when she'd still been hanging in medical limbo. She'd wanted to help her favorite protégé then, and she wanted to help her even more now. Maybe she could do a few good, decent things before she passed.

"Thank you, Marie," she replied, stuffing the sheet of paper in her desk drawer. "Tell Ms. Bregman to come right in."

A moment later, the door opened and Aimee's bright, smiling face greeted her. "Rita! Hi!" She hurried in, shutting the door behind her.

"Hi yourself." Rita couldn't help smiling back. Aimee had a natural, artless charm that drew people to her like flies to honey. It would serve her well in her new job. Just as it had made Rita notice her from the first, when Rita was working in the admissions office at Danforth and was representing the university at a college fair Aimee attended. Aimee had sought her out, asked a dozen questions in a way that had somehow not been annoying. Still, delightful or not, it'd been clear that Aimee was motivated and determined to get into Danforth's challenging undergraduate school and to move up to its even more rigorous graduate business school to earn her MBA.

Rita had found herself eager to make that dream a reality.

She'd become Aimee's point person in the admissions office, corresponding with her via email as Aimee worked through the applications process. She'd advocated for her when decision-making time came for potential matriculating freshmen. And she'd gone on to advise Aimee after she officially enrolled, as well as after Rita moved up to become the university's dean of undergraduate students.

Now, after transferring to the Office of Alumni Relations and rising quickly through its ranks to become director, she was in a unique position to continue advising and assisting Aimee at this point in the business world that Aimee had just stepped into. So when Aimee had asked for this meeting, Rita had been more than happy to agree.

She rose, reaching across her desk to give Aimee a quick hug.

"It's wonderful to see you." She gestured for her protégé to sit.

"You, too." The smile faded a bit from Aimee's face. "You look tired. Am I coming at a bad time?"

"It's never a bad time to see you," Rita assured her. "You're one of the few people who always brighten my day. Now…" She brought the conversation quickly to safe territory. "You said you needed an intro to a particular alum who'd be able to help grow sales for CannaBD. Who?"

"Chris Maher."

Rita felt her own smile grow cold. That was *not* the answer she'd been hoping for, although Lord knows, it was the answer she'd feared. Chris's father, Daniel Maher, was a household name—a longtime action-movie star whose earlier movies continued to be fan favorites a generation later and who was still getting roles even in his late fifties. Chris had inherited his father's good looks and charisma. Plus, he was smart—shrewd and smart. After graduation, he'd gotten a job at a New York steakhouse and worked his way swiftly up the ladder to become assistant manager—a job he no longer needed and had quit without a backward glance once the social media brand he'd created and launched back in college exploded into a major moneymaker. *Snacks for Sports* shared new ideas for what to eat while watching sporting events at home, including Chris's famous and innovative Super Bowl Bites. The number of hits he got on YouTube and Instagram were multiplying by the droves, and he was now an influencer with over a million followers. Those followers included an enormous number of millennials and even Gen Zers in their early twenties who fell into the same demographic as potential CannaBD customers.

Booze and bites. It was an ideal match.

It was also a fiasco for Rita.

Chris was trouble. Big trouble, on so many levels. And she had to be super careful about which levels she revealed to Aimee.

"Rita?"

Still lost in thought, Rita started when Aimee said her name.

"What's the matter?" Aimee was visibly puzzled. "I thought you'd think it was a great idea. If Chris would agree to market CannaBD side by side with his *Snacks for Sports*, we'd reach a gazillion people. The fit is perfect!"

"You're right, it is," Rita had to admit. "At least the products are. But the personality fit is another story entirely."

"What do you mean?"

Rita went for a truth that steered clear of the bigger, more dangerous one—a truth that Aimee could never know. “Chris isn't someone I'd be thrilled to have you team up with. He's reputedly into some questionable things.”

“Such as?”

“Drugs, for one,” she replied, unsurprised that Aimee was unaware of that fact. Chris was great about keeping his nasty habits under the radar. Well, Rita sure as hell knew about them. And there was no way she was sugarcoating this. “Rumor has it he's heavily into hard-core recreational drugs—coke, ecstasy, and meth—raging while under the influence, then driving recklessly and coming this close to wrapping his car around a tree too many times to count.”

“Oh.” Aimee frowned. “I had no idea.”

“There's more.” Rita pressed on, desperately trying to talk Aimee out of taking this avenue. “Chris allegedly had some ugly physical altercations with two of his previous girlfriends. No charges were ever filed, but a few people claimed to have witnessed the incidents. Not exactly a shining spokesperson for your company.”

Aimee considered all that for a moment, and then, despite being visibly conflicted, she opted for a sound business decision that was based in fact, not supposition. “I see your point. Except that nothing you just told me is more than a rumor—which isn't a surprise, given the way celebrity gossip works. Clearly, Chris's followers aren't buying into it. His numbers are sky-high. And my market research says that CannaBD's audience are avid followers. He's got it all—good looks, charm, and an uber-famous father. At least if I have a meeting, I'll have the ability to judge for myself.”

The sad part was that Rita couldn't argue with Aimee's logic.

“Nick is counting on me,” Aimee continued. “He was totally psyched when I told him I was seeing you about connecting me with Chris. CannaBD is his baby. He's determined to make it a raging success. And getting Chris on board would be a big leap toward that goal. Nick is willing to give him a top-tier influencer deal."

Aimee leaned forward in earnest. "Rita, I want to be the best marketing director I can be. I have to try to make this happen. It doesn't mean I condone any of the alleged activities you just ran by me. But given that no charges were ever filed and that I've seen no mention of these incidents anywhere, I have to assume that this is all just unsubstantiated gossip. And if Chris would push our product, he could open up doors that we, as a fledgling company, could never reach on our own. I have to ask—do you think you could convince him to meet with me?"

Rita was up against a wall and she knew it. She had no good reason to refuse Aimee's request. As for Chris, yeah, he'd get a real charge out of promoting a cool product like CannaBD beer. Not to mention the charge he'd get from being approached by a pretty girl who fed into his overinflated ego and the urgency her brand-new company felt over having his endorsement.

There was no way Rita could say no. All she could do was to make sure Aimee learned nothing dangerous from this meeting. Chris already suspected too much. Hell, he'd *been part* of too much. To add more fuel to the fire, he'd been in her office when she got one of *those* phone calls. She'd quickly postponed the conversation without mentioning names or specifics. Still, she had no idea how much, if anything, he'd pieced together. But she couldn't take a chance. She *had* to manage this meeting.

"I tell you what," she said to Aimee. "Let's compromise. I'll reach out to Chris. If he agrees to meet with you, it'll be the three of us, rather than just you and him. Okay?"

Aimee grinned. "You'd act as a kind of facilitator?"

"Something like that, yes."

A shrug. "It works for me. Anything that will give me the chance to make my pitch."

"Done." Rita rose from behind her desk. "Give me a day or two. I'll do my best to make this happen."

***

Fielding's Bar
Midtown Manhattan, New York
Two days later

Chris leaned back on his barstool, bent one long leg at the knee, and crossed it over the other. The bar was light on traffic and filled with more thirty-plus professionals in business attire than a young crowd in their twenties. Way too tame for his tastes, but he'd agreed to meet here anyway. He could have given Rita Edwell a hard time, but he was too intrigued to bother. Truth was, he was looking forward to this business pitch.

It was hard to keep the grin off his face as he watched Aimee Bregman play with her drink, gazing at him like he was some kind of superstar. Oh, he'd seen that look on many, many wistful faces, but it never got old, and it never stopped pumping his blood.

Rita Edwell was the only downer at the table. She was supervising them like a fucking chaperone at a high school dance. It irked him… but it wasn't about to stand in his way.

He angled his body toward Aimee, pointedly ignoring the university administrator. "I've actually heard of CannaBD," he said. "I remember reading about Nick Colotti's invention in the alumni news. Pretty brilliant on his part."

Aimee jumped on that positive reaction. "Nick is a genius, and CannaBD is a gold mine waiting to happen. We just need widespread awareness of our brand and our launch products—the initial line of CannaBD beer. If we get that, the beer will sell itself. Which brings me to a partnership with *Snacks for Sports*."

Chris chuckled. He liked this girl. She was less worldly than his usual type. Still, she was only a couple of years younger than he was, she was pretty, with just the right amount of makeup and trendy clothes to make her hot, and—the biggest turn-on of all—she had balls.

"Cutting right to the chase, huh?" he asked in a half-teasing, half-seductive voice.

Aimee didn't avert her gaze. "There's no point in pretending I don't have an agenda. Rita told you why I wanted this meeting. I'm hoping that the reason you're here is that you're interested in forming a business relationship with CannaBD. It would mean a top-tier influencer deal. And I truly believe that this would double your following."

"Only doubling?" Chris was really enjoying this banter—or he would be if Rita weren't glaring at him.

"Fine, maybe more." Aimee was visibly trying to figure out if she had him hooked. She sucked at hiding her thoughts. Then again, he read women's minds only too well. And this one was in *way* over her head with him.

He wondered what she'd be like in bed.

"That's a pretty lofty goal," he said. "Do you have marketing data to support that claim?"

Aimee reached for her portfolio. "I have quite a bit of marketing data to share with you. And while it can't promise exact numbers…"

"I believe you." Chris leaned forward and stilled her hand, gently pushing aside her portfolio. Subtly, he lowered his own hand beneath the table and gently caressed her thigh just beneath the hem of her dress. "I can already see the perks involved here."

"Cut it, Chris." Rita's words dumped a bucket of cold water on his intentions. She slammed her glass of sparkling water on the table and leaned forward, getting into his face before he could fully gauge Aimee's reaction. While she hadn't yet shoved his fingers away, Aimee had frozen on her barstool and was staring at him in stunned disbelief.

"This is why I was against this meeting," Rita said, her eyes blazing. "Your behavior, as always, is appalling. And *this* incident I didn't just hear about, I witnessed it myself—or did you think I missed your oh-so-subtle leg fondling?"

Chris was spitting bullets. "What I think is that you shouldn't be here to begin with," he snapped, jerking his head around to stare Rita down. "Aimee is a grown woman. She doesn't need a chaperone."

"This isn't a date." Aimee found her voice, her tone rife with anger. Simultaneously, she gripped his wrist and shoved his hand off of her thigh. "This is—*was*—a business meeting. I don't care *who* you are, it doesn't entitle you to act like a prick."

Chris's fingers clamped down on her wrist. "Who the hell do you think you're talking to, little girl? With one video, I could run your pathetic company into the ground."

"But you won't," Rita refuted furiously. "I think you've forgotten *who* made *you*—and it wasn't your daddy. I can unmake you like this." She snapped her fingers in his face. "So get your hands off of Aimee and get the hell out of here."

"Don't threaten me," Chris ground out between clenched teeth. He was literally vibrating with rage. "And don't even think of fucking with my life. I don't owe you shit. In fact, given what I know, I own you. Push me, and you'll find out just what I'm capable of." He pivoted to Aimee, his fingers tightening around her wrist. "If I were you, I'd forget this meeting ever happened. Don't even let the words *sexual harassment* come to mind, and don't remember a word of what was said. Otherwise, it'll be more than your new company you'll be worrying about."

With that, he jumped off his stool and strode out of the bar.

Aimee exhaled sharply as she watched Chris go, her heart pounding with fury and trepidation.

"Boy, am I gullible and inexperienced," she said. "One of the deficits of being raised in a small town and not moving to New York City until late in high school. I'm not exactly worldly. I've been in relationships before, but nothing much."

"Until now, and until Travis," Rita said, referring to Aimee's new boyfriend, who Aimee had happily mentioned the last time she and Rita had spoken.

"Yes, until Travis," Aimee agreed. "But I've never come up against an egocentric bully like Chris." A pause. "But he's not just a bully. He's abused women, you said. Rita, do you think he'd follow through on those threats he made to us?"

To Aimee's dismay, Rita's shoulders lifted, then fell. "Honestly? I don't know. I opened all the right doors for Chris when he got started. Had I known then what I know now, I wouldn't have. He's a loose cannon. Just to be on the safe side, I'd stick close to your friends for a while. Don't go out alone. And don't mention Chris's threats to anyone. When you go back to Nick, just tell him what a jerk Chris is, that he came on to you, and that he ridiculed CannaBD. That'll be enough to end any thought of a business alliance."

"Okay," Aimee said with a nod. "But what about you? He looked pretty damn scary when he told you what he'd do if you pushed him. You'd better steer clear of him, too."

"I plan to." Rita paused, took a deep swallow of her sparkling water as if it were hard liquor. Then, she set down her glass and met Aimee's gaze. "Aimee, I need to talk to you about something. I've put it off, but I'd rather tell you this when I'm still okay enough to be myself."

"Is this about whatever it is Chris meant when he said he owns you?"

Rita waved that away. "I don't know what the hell Chris was talking about. He doesn't know anything about my personal life. But it's important to me that you do."

"All right." Aimee felt a wave of unease. Whatever Rita was about to tell her, it wasn't good.

"The reason I'm so concerned about you toughening up a bit is that I won't be here to guide you for much longer." Rita swallowed hard, but she didn't weep.

"Are you transferring to another university?" Aimee knew in her heart that she was grasping at straws, but her heart was screaming a denial to what she was about to hear.

"No, Aimee. I'm not transferring. I'm dying. I have stage-four cancer. No treatment is possible; it's too far gone now to arrest. I have maybe a year to live. Maybe less if the cancer continues to spread at this rate." Rita swallowed hard. "I'm sorry to dump this on you. But I need to make sure you toughen up before I'm gone. Your family is far away. I know you're in a new relationship, but you don't know yet where it's going. And even if it turns out to be something solid, you still have to be self-sufficient. The world isn't always a wonderful place. I need to teach you that before it's too late."

Tears were streaming down Aimee's cheeks. "Oh God, Rita." She took her mentor's hands in hers. "How long have you known? Why didn't you tell me? And why are you worrying about me when the only thing that matters here is you?"

Rita's fingers trembled and she tightened her grip on Aimee's hands. "I suppose I was hoping for a miracle. Then I'd never have to tell you anything. But that miracle isn't happening. And I'm determined to help you for as long as I'm able."

"How can *I* help *you*?" Aimee asked through her tears.

"By listening to me. By not letting situations like this one happen again. By losing some of that naiveté of yours, no matter how endearing it is. It leaves you wide open for predators like Chris, and even for people who are going to try to screw you over in business. Please promise me you'll try."

Aimee nodded slowly. "All right. I'll try. If it means spending more time with you while I can, I'll do anything. But, Rita, I meant what I said. I want to be there for you. Please. Anything you need, just ask."

***

Rita returned to her office, depleted and still fuming. She'd had it. She was done. Done with creating animals like Chris Maher. Done with doing the wrong things for the wrong reasons. Done with it all.

At that moment her burner phone rang. She didn't need to glance at the number. She just pressed the answer button.

"Whatever it is, don't bother," she said. "I'm not living this way anymore. I'm opting out of our arrangement." She ignored the threatening voice at the other end of the line. "You're wrong. I can and I am resigning," she replied. "I'm no longer afraid of you. Why not? Because I'm dying. So I'm tying up loose ends—and you're one of them. What's more, if you make my walking away difficult, I'll tell the right things to the right people before I'm gone, and you'll be out of business and in jail where you belong. So leave me alone. Don't call me again."

2

Offices of Forensic Instincts
Tribeca, New York
Two days later, 8:45 a.m.

Casey Woods rolled her eyes in annoyance as she wove her way through the lingering yet persistent media hounds still hovering outside the Forensic Instincts brownstone. As president of FI, she'd answered enough questions about the case her team had just helped solve—a priceless Irish treasure that they'd discovered and assisted in restoring to its rightful place in the National Museum of Ireland. The official report had given full credit to the NYPD and the FBI. But FI's involvement and their near-miss with death had somehow leaked out, and the press was ever eager to hear the details of how Casey's renowned investigative company had factored into the dangerous and turbulent resolution.

She'd said as little as possible, once again stressing that it was law enforcement who deserved everyone's gratitude, but the reporters, historians, and bloggers weren't buying it. Forensic Instincts was too well known for its reputation in solving high-profile cases, using methods that were somewhat unorthodox but always successful. Plus their composite of team members was just too intriguing for the outside world to ignore—Casey herself a behaviorist, and her hires, two retired FBI agents, a technology genius, a claircognizant, a former pickpocket, and a former FBI human scent evidence dog. The notoriety Forensic Instincts had acquired had never been part of Casey's vision when she started the firm, but it sure as hell was part of it now.

Shielding the Hirsch pad that would gain her entry so as to avoid prying eyes, Casey punched in the code, pushed open the front door, and eased herself inside. She shut the automatically locking door behind her and leaned back against it, letting out an audible sigh.

"Dammit," she muttered.

"Are they still out there?" Marc Devereaux strolled down from his third-floor office to greet her. Marc had been with Casey from the beginning. He was former Navy SEAL, former FBI special agent, former FBI Behavioral Analysis Unit, and always Casey's right hand.

"They've thinned out, but it's getting to be a real pain in the ass," Casey informed him, shrugging out of her jacket. "It was easier when I lived here at the brownstone. Now I have to dodge this persistent stuff just like the rest of you. Whoever said that being president was an enviable job?"

Marc chuckled. "People who aren't president. Plus, it's one of the downsides for you about moving into your own place with Hutch. Now you have to be accosted outside the front door like the rest of us."

Casey nodded in frustration. She and FBI Supervisory Special Agent Kyle "Hutch" Hutchinson had just taken the significant step of moving into their own apartment in Battery Park City, after being a serious couple for several years. Until then, Casey had lived alone in her fourth-floor apartment at Forensic Instincts—an apartment she now used as a go-to location when she and the team were working on something that crossed a line Hutch found untenable. It was the deal they had struck when they moved in together. Despite his love for Casey, Hutch toed the line; Casey and Forensic Instincts did not. So the best solution was for Hutch to remain in the dark about the questionable elements of FI's cases. Still, more than once, he'd found himself walking a tightrope to keep Casey safe. Regardless, they were determined to make their relationship work. Thus, the new living arrangements and the new hassles Casey had to deal with when it came to avoiding the press.

With a sigh, Casey turned away from the coat rack. Simultaneously, she heard the rapid sound of padding canine paws, and a moment later, her bloodhound, Hero, appeared in the entranceway to greet her.

Casey squatted so he could lick her face. "I missed you, too, boy," she said with a grin.

"Sure you did." The sarcastic comment came from Ryan McKay, the team's way-too-good-looking-for-his-own-good tech whiz, as he came up from the basement level that was officially labeled his lair. "You and Hutch can thank me for your first night alone. Hero slept at my place, and he took up three-quarters of my bed."

"Leaving no room for Claire," Casey teased, referring to Claire Hedgleigh, the team's claircognizant, who was Ryan's girlfriend—a term that she and Ryan had only recently ascribed to their all-too-obvious relationship. "I get it. Thanks for my date night. I owe you one."

"Claire had some late-night yoga thing, so I wouldn't have seen her anyway," Ryan responded. "But you still owe me one. Hero snores. I got zero sleep. So *he* might be cheerful, but *I'm* not."

For the second time that morning, Casey rolled her eyes. "Yes, Ryan, we all know how you get when you're sleep-deprived. Fine. How about if I spring for a nice dinner out for you and Claire?"

That piqued Ryan's interest and his brows rose. "How nice?"

"Your choice of restaurants."

"Done. Consider us even."

Casey rose, running a hand through her shoulder-length red hair. "Who's here besides us?"

Marc tipped his head toward the staircase. "Patrick drove in early to beat the traffic and the media hounds. He's in the kitchen grabbing something to eat."

Patrick Lynch, retired FBI and now FI's head of security, was also the most grounded member of the team, the one who kept them from pushing the boundaries too far.

"Emma's been monitoring voice mails since she walked in," Marc continued, referring to the newest member of the team—a one-time street kid whose oh-so-innocent *Alice in Wonderland* looks contributed to her success as a former pickpocket. That same cunning mind and those deft fingers made her an invaluable member of the team. "So far the messages have been all bullshit. No new and exciting cases."

"Claire is having breakfast with Fiona," Ryan said, referring to his younger sister—*and* FI's most recent client. Fiona had been the target in a killer's hunt for the now-restored Irish treasure. Her skill as a goldsmith and jewelry designer, together with her deep interest in McKay family heirlooms, had made her walking prey. During the investigation, she'd developed a deep bond of friendship with the FI team, particularly with Claire. And not only because they both cared for Ryan but because they just connected.

Ryan glanced at his Apple Watch. "They met at Tribeca's Kitchen at seven thirty. They'll be wrapping up soon. After that, we'll have a full house."

Casey had no chance to respond before Emma came flying out of the reception alcove.

"Hi, Casey." She didn't wait for a response, just plunged right on in her usual exuberant way. "We got one repeat caller. Aimee Bregman. She sounds legit—and scared to death. She said it was urgent and that her life is in danger."

Casey arched a brow. "You're sure it wasn't just another member of the press looking to get a foot in the door for an interview?"

"Positive. This Aimee Bregman was as transparent as glass. She not only called, she emailed me her contact information and just about everything else about her, from her birthplace to where she went to school to her new job. Cool company and an equally cool job, by the way. Anyway, she was talking a mile a minute about fearing for her life."

"Did she give you any details?"

"She was too scared to do that on the phone. She begged me to set up a meeting so she could do that in person. But she did tell me the incident that's prompting all this hysteria. So I double-checked it—along with her background info, obviously—and it all rang true. The incident she's referring to did happen, just a little over a day ago. It made the news."

"What incident?" Marc asked patiently, trying to bring Emma down a notch.

It didn't do much good, although Emma did pause long enough to breathe.

"The director of Alumni Relations at Danforth University disappeared the night before last. The story's just leaking out now, but Aimee Bregman was apparently the last person to see the woman and is being questioned by the NYPD. She's convinced there was foul play involved."

Marc's lips twitched. "'Foul play'? Watching old detective movies, are we?"

"Marc, I'm serious and..."

"Emma's right," Casey interrupted. "I caught a news article about this disappearance before I left my apartment. The director's name was Rita Edwell. No official report is being released, but insiders are saying the NYPD is investigating and that Crime Scene was spotted on the campus grounds. Which means there's evidence of a crime having been committed, not just a woman who chose to vanish."

"Exactly." Emma bobbed her head up and down. "And our wannabe client obviously knows something. Trust me, she's really flipping out."

"Call her back," Casey replied without hesitation. "Set up a meeting for ten. If she's really afraid someone's coming after her, she'll be here in an hour."

***

Tribeca's Kitchen
Church Street
Manhattan, New York

Claire finished the last bite of her avocado and goat cheese omelet and pushed aside her plate.

"I'm officially stuffed," she said. "Not only do I talk more when you and I get together, I also eat more."

"But the food here is amazing," Fiona replied, sipping at her coffee and eyeing the remaining half of her last blueberry pancake. "At least you had a healthy omelet. I just scarfed down thousands of calories of carbs. I'll be running an extra five miles today." She tucked strands of her hair behind her ears to keep them safe from the messy syrup she was still using.

Her coloring was just like Ryan's—thick black hair, intensely dark blue eyes, and skin tone that looked as if it were perpetually tanned. And even though her features and body type were delicate while Ryan was solid and masculine, you couldn't miss the family resemblance.

Claire smiled. "We've talked about everything under the sun. But you never got the chance to tell me about the new jewelry pieces you're working on. A different collection?"

"Actually, yes." Fiona took another bite of her pancake. "I've never strayed from Celtic influences before. But for some reason, I had the urge to create something a little different—nature inspired this time. I'm happily creating leaves and flowers that look sculpted in gold and silver. You saw the technique in my cuff bracelet. The Light and Shadows collection is still a work in progress, but I'm spending a little time each day on these new pieces. I promise to show them to you as soon as the first few designs are done."

"I can't wait." As Claire spoke, her phone trilled, telling her she had a text message. She glanced down. "Ryan," she reported, clicking into the text. "Potentially a new case. I'm being summoned to the office ASAP."

She gave Fiona a rueful look as she dabbed at her mouth with her napkin and pulled out her credit card. "I'm sorry to cut this short."

Fiona waved away the apology and the credit card. "Duty calls. Go. This one's on me. We'll do breakfast again soon and it'll be your turn to pay." She put down her fork. "Now I have no excuse. I'm walking home to SoHo, changing into my running gear, and sprinting through the neighborhood like a track star to burn off my breakfast." Her eyes twinkled. "Give my brother a big hug for me."

3

Offices of Forensic Instincts
Main conference room, second floor
10:00 a.m.

Casey sat at the head of the expansive mahogany table, around which gathered the entire FI team—and their prospective client. Casey sipped her coffee, simultaneously studying Aimee Bregman.

The young woman was fiddling with her bracelet and gazing around the room with huge eyes. Casey felt bad that she was so nervous. Not long ago, this interview would have been conducted in the smaller, cozier first-floor conference room rather than in this far more formidable one. Unfortunately, FI's notoriety had grown to the point where a few phony clients, and even one shrewd, scummy blogger, had gotten by Emma's clever screening. Casey wasn't about to let that happen again. So even though her gut told her that Aimee was in real trouble, she wanted the young woman's guard to be down and for her to feel unsettled enough so Casey could pick up on all her tells and be thoroughly convinced of her sincerity.

This conference room was just the place to allow for that. It rivaled that of a Fortune 500 company. Decorated by Casey herself, it boasted polished hardwood floors, a plush Oriental rug, and a mahogany credenza that matched the table and that contained a state-of-the-art JURA Professional coffee station and built-in fridge and wine cooler. French doors led to a terrace that overlooked a small but professionally landscaped garden. A gigantic video wall covered the longest side of the room, allowing Ryan to assemble an overwhelming array of information into a large single image or several smaller simultaneous data feeds. Videoconferencing equipment, an elaborate phone system, and a personalized virtual workstation at each team member's station at the table completed the decor. And the rest—Ryan's crucial technology infrastructure—was all hidden from view.

Aimee had been announced at the front door by Yoda, Ryan's almost-human, almost-omniscient AI system, and then escorted by Emma directly to this room. Quick introductions to the accomplished team members, a cup of coffee, and a chair at the table had completed Aimee's arrival.

The whole experience was enough to intimidate even the savviest visitor. And Aimee was far from that. Even though she was in her late twenties, she seemed younger, greener than most women her age. Maybe it was because of the nature of her business, which exposed her mostly to a youthful audience. Or maybe it was just who she was—a small-town girl learning to survive in the Big Apple. In either case, she was definitely awestruck by FI.

Physically, she was more put together than pretty—"done," as Emma would say—her makeup carefully applied, her outfit trendy, her layered haircut equally so. Her "cool" job was an impressive title at a barely legal start-up company. True, the company had the potential of blowing it out of the water in terms of success. And it was located in a spot in Elmton that had room for physical expansion, no doubt chosen for that very reason. But right now, it was in its fledgling phase. As marketing director, Aimee obviously spent a good chunk of her life either on college campuses or schmoozing influencers who were barely adults. Yes, she was educated and intelligent. But Casey's scrutiny determined that she was far too guileless to be fabricating the situation she was now facing. No, she was every bit as terrified as Emma had described.

Time to put her at ease and to get down to the reason for her fear.

The team was poised, iPads on and ready, waiting for Casey to take the lead, which she now did.

"Start at the beginning and take us through everything, Aimee," she said.

Aimee's gaze snapped over to Casey. "Does that mean you believe me? That you're taking my case?"

"It means we're convinced enough to listen."

Aimee hesitated. "Is everything we discuss confidential, no matter what?"

"As long as you didn't commit a crime, yes, everything that's said here remains here, regardless of whether or not we end up taking you on as a client."

"Okay." Aimee paused for a second, anxiously gripping her purse and giving Casey a pleading look. "Your fee," she said, looking miserable. "I'm not sure how high it is. I make a decent salary, but I'm sure it's a far cry from what you charge. Please. I'll give you a credit card, and I'll pay out the full amount with interest…"

"Not to worry." Casey waved away that concern. "Our fees fluctuate depending upon so many variables. If we agree to work together, we'll have you sign our standard contract, and we'll settle on an estimated range we can all live with." A hint of a smile. "I promise, we won't bankrupt you. That's not the way we work."

A flash of relief crossed Aimee's face, although it did nothing to diminish the haunted look in her eyes or the strain that tightened her expression.

"I… Rita and I were friends," she said in a quavering voice. "I knew her for ten years."

A wave of compassion swept through Casey as she noted the fact that Aimee had said *were*, not *are*. It was clear she believed her friend was no longer alive. "How did that friendship come about? Rita's a good decade older than you. Did you meet at Danforth? I saw you attended school there."

"She was my mentor. I met her at a college fair when she was in the admissions department, and she guided me ever since." Aimee rested her hands on the table, staring at her fingers as she went on to relay her history with Rita. "So, when I started my job at CannaBD, I naturally turned to her for help and for the best alumni contacts she could recommend."

Casey nodded. "Makes sense. Go on."

"A few days ago, I asked Rita to connect me up with a Danforth alum who's a major influencer. She was really reluctant to do so, but she understood that he could have launched CannaBD big-time. He's—" Aimee broke off, twisting her fingers on the table. "He's famous. We all met for a drink. And what happened there…" She broke off, tears coming to her eyes.

"Famous how?" Casey asked that question first, before getting into the reasons why Rita was unhappy about making the introduction or about what had happened at the meeting. "As an influencer?"

"As in everything. It's Chris Maher." She spoke his name as if it were poison in her mouth.

Emma shot up in her seat. "Daniel Maher's son?" she demanded. "As in that gorgeous guy with a movie star for a father?"

"Yes."

"Wow," Ryan said. "Talk about a big name. Not only does he have a famous father, he's got a ginormous following on '*Snacks for Sports*'—myself included."

"Ginormous is right—his following is nearing two million," Aimee supplied. "And like I said, I was hoping to convince him to form a business alliance with my company."

"His products and yours are a great fit," Marc said. "And his promoting CannaBD would put your company on the map."

"That's *never* going to happen," Aimee said vehemently. "Not after that meeting. Not after... everything."

Casey sensed that whatever was about to be said would explain Rita's reluctance to make the introduction. And Aimee was on a roll, providing them with the information they needed. So she chose to remain silent and let Aimee answer the question on her own.

Sure enough, Aimee went on to fill the team in, first on the rumors Rita had shared with her and then on the details of what had happened at the bar—what was said and done, the threats that had been made.

"And the next thing you knew, Rita vanished and you were answering questions to the cops." Marc steepled his fingers together thoughtfully. "Not to mention Crime Scene being called in. That screams a violent incident."

"There's more," Aimee managed. "I could swear I saw Chris standing across the street from my apartment when I got home the night he'd threatened us. He stared me down and then turned his back and walked away. And the next day"—the tears came again—"Rita disappeared. But she didn't just disappear—she was hurt, or worse. I *know* it."

"It's clearly an open investigation," Patrick said. "What tone did the detectives take when they were questioning you?"

"They were firing questions at me, really grilling me. They said they'd checked Rita's calendar and our meeting was the last entry in it."

"Suggesting they believe you were the last person to have seen her," Claire murmured.

"What specifically did they ask?" Casey asked.

"How I knew Rita. Which one of us arranged our meeting for that day. The specifics of what we talked about. If she seemed upset or nervous in any way. If we made any future plans. And most telling of all, if I know anyone who might have held a grudge against her."

Marc and Casey exchanged glances.

"You gave them half answers," Casey said, a statement not a guess. "You didn't tell them about Chris Maher or about your suspicions."

"I was afraid to," Aimee admitted. "If Chris is a killer—which I believe he is—I'm his next target. I'm terrified to instigate him."

Yeah, Casey thought. *Plus if you'd breathed a word about his being at that meeting and about what happened there, he'd be dragged in for questioning. After which, your worries might very well have become reality.*

"That's why I came to Forensic Instincts," Aimee concluded. "I'm praying you'll take my case, investigate what happened to Rita, and put Chris away for life."

Marc continued where Casey had left off. "What answers *did* you supply to the detectives? You obviously let them believe it was just you and Rita who met for a drink. Did you say that meeting was purely social?"

Even as he asked the question, it was clear that Marc didn't think that was the entirety of it.

With a wealth of sadness, Aimee met his gaze. "No, I told them she needed to talk to me alone and in person—which is the truth, only it happened after Chris left." Tears filled Aimee's eyes again. "Rita was dying. She had cancer that was too far gone to treat. She had less than a year to live."

"How heartbreaking." Claire's gentle voice was a soothing balm, as it was to all their clients. Her heightened empathy level went hand in hand with her metaphysical gift.

"Yes, it is." Casey pursed her lips. "Which would ordinarily have given the police the motive they were looking for—that Rita had tied up loose ends and then disappeared to spare her loved ones from seeing her deteriorate. The fact that they weren't satisfied with that explanation only supports the theory that they believe someone either harmed or killed her."

"And if that someone was Chris..." Aimee shuddered, then gave Casey another pleading look. "Will you take my case? Please, I'm begging you."

Casey had long since made up her mind. But the FI rule was that taking on a new case had to be unanimous. So she glanced around the table and got the response she'd expected—all brief nods.

"Okay, Aimee," she said. "You're now our client."

Aimee literally sagged with relief. "Thank God. Where do we go from here?"

"First, we assign you a security detail." Casey glanced over at Patrick, who tipped his chin in acknowledgement and then rose and excused himself to get the process started. "That means twenty-four-seven protection. Chris Maher won't get near you again. If he tries to make contact with you—whether it's a phone call, a text, an email, anything—don't respond. Just hang up the phone or disregard the text or email. Call us immediately."

"I will," Aimee agreed without pause.

"Danforth University, Upper West Side of Manhattan," Ryan mused aloud. "Specifically, the twenty-sixth precinct. Did the detectives ask you to come in there for questioning? And how many detectives were there—one or two?"

"Yes, and two," Aimee responded. "Detective Graham and Detective Mullen. Detective Graham asked most of the questions."

"Good." Ryan looked cheerful. "I don't know them, so no ruffled feathers there. Still, that doesn't mean they don't know of FI. So don't tell them you hired us. Not yet. We need to stay a few steps ahead of them."

It was no secret that Ryan loved one-upping the NYPD detectives and that he got a kick out of being a thorn in their sides. The truth was that, no matter how many times Casey gave credit to the police for their case-solving skills, it was always the FI team who had the inside track and who ultimately solved their clients' cases.

"I agree." Despite her words, Casey shot Ryan a take-it-down-a-notch look. "Leave our names out of this—assuming the detectives even contact you again. Your story was innocent enough. I doubt it sparked much interest. My guess is they're off and running in a dozen other directions."

"But isn't withholding information a crime?" Aimee asked, fear lacing her tone. "Isn't it called lying by omission or some other legal term like that?"

"Technically, that's true," Casey replied. "But you're frightened for your life. Even if you do eventually tell the detectives the full story, they're not going to press charges. They'll be far more interested in what you have to say than the fact that you were too scared to say it right away. I'm not expecting them to call you with follow-up questions. But if I'm wrong, you won't be unprepared. Before you leave here this morning, we'll coach you on what to say."

"Thank you," Aimee said, visibly relieved.

"And in the meantime, we'll soon know more about Chris Maher than he knows about himself," Ryan assured her.

"How are you going to do that without interrogating him in person?"

"Let us worry about procedure," Casey replied, scooting around that question—especially since getting in Chris's face might very well be on the agenda. "You hired us because we're the best. Trust us to do our job. Suffice it to say that we're not bound by the same rules the police are, nor do we have to deal with the same red tape. Our sole priority is our client."

Marc interceded, shifting things in a different direction, partly to redirect Aimee's attention and partly to gather information. "Just so we're not blindsided, who have you told the actual truth to? Friends? Family? Significant other? Co-workers?"

"I told Nick, my boss," Aimee replied. "When I got back to work after that drink. Not all of it, just what Rita suggested. I said that she and I met with Chris. I said he was a jerk, that he came on to me and ridiculed CannaBD, and that he was definitely not our golden goose. Even though Nick was disappointed, he wasn't shocked. He didn't know Chris when they were undergrads at Danforth, but he certainly knew who Chris's father was, and he'd heard that Chris was a spoiled little rich boy. He just figured we'd take a shot at getting him on board, given how tight Rita and I were. But as I said, I gave Nick only the bare-bones facts. Is that a problem?"

"Just something we should know." Marc's forehead creased in thought. "If Nick weren't a Danforth grad, Rita wouldn't even be on his radar. Since he is, we have to assume he'll read about the police investigation in an alumni email. But since you didn't get into Chris's threats, Nick won't make the connection to your meeting. If he had, he would have called you before he opted to show up at the police precinct—*if* he opted to. Safe on that front."

"Anyone else you talked to about this?" Casey asked. "Partial or full truth?"

"I mentioned Chris's name to my boyfriend," Aimee replied. "But only to say how much I wanted to connect up with him for CannaBD. Travis Grady—my boyfriend—is a nurse. He's been working long shifts this week. So I never told him about the meeting or even that Rita had set it up."

"Are you and Travis close?" Casey asked. "Do you live together? Because I think that, for the time being, you should limit who knows about this to you and us. We don't need a jealous boyfriend charging at Chris and setting him off."

"Travis wouldn't do that, but I see where you're coming from. And, no, we don't live together. We've only been dating for three months. So I won't say anything."

Yeah, but your body language will, Casey thought, filing that away on an as-needed basis.

She sat forward, interlacing her fingers on the table. "When you were at the bar, you didn't run into anyone you knew?"

"Rita chose the place. I'd never been there before. But Chris made enough of a scene that I'm sure people noticed."

"I'm sure they did." Casey looked neither surprised nor fazed. "And given Chris Maher's public presence as Daniel Maher's son, I'm sure his outburst didn't go unnoticed. Not to mention the fact that the street cameras probably caught his exit. So if you eventually do come forward with the full truth, the detectives will check out Fielding's Bar and corroborate your story. No harm, no foul." Casey looked up as Patrick reentered the room, giving her a thumbs-up.

"John will be here in twenty minutes," he said, referring to John Nickels, who was one of the best and most qualified members of Patrick's security team.

Casey turned back to Aimee. "That gives us enough time to coach you on any follow-up you might have with the police. After that, we'll introduce you to your personal bodyguard and you can be on your way." A purposeful look. "Leave this in our hands. Do exactly what we've told you to do—nothing more, nothing less. We'll handle Chris Maher *and* keep you alive."

***

He lay on the bed, hands folded behind his head, watching droplets of rain splash against his window.

Less than two days had passed since he'd offed the administrator. He could already feel that familiar restlessness boiling in his gut. It was happening sooner than usual. Probably because Rita Edwell had been a boring, pathetically easy victim. She'd put up no fight. It was almost as if she were resigned to dying. That pissed him off. He preferred seeing the frantic look in his victims' eyes when they struggled for air right before he choked the last breath out of them. But with her—she'd been nothing more than a kill for hire. He hadn't even bothered using one of his creative tools. Just his hands. She was too listless to waste anything more on.

The next kill would be different. It would be *his* kill on *his* terms.

And he knew just who his victim would be.

Another step-in-shit scumbag who deserved to die.

4

After Aimee left the brownstone—with John Nickels following at a discreet distance behind the Uber they'd put her in—the FI team refilled their coffee mugs and got down to business, prepared to divvy up their roles in the investigation.

"This sucks." Emma held up the process long enough to make that assessment, looking as if the wind had been knocked out of her sails. "My whole celeb status fascination just took a huge hit. I mean, yeah, I've seen Daniel Maher's movies like three times each, but I've also followed Chris on social media. He's way hot. He's been seen with supermodels, actresses, and rich CEO's daughters on his arm. I've even tried some of his Super Bowl Bites. They rock. I thought he did, too. I'm so bummed." She took a long swallow of coffee, as if to console herself.

Ryan stared at her in disbelief. "I follow his blog and watch his YouTube videos. But if the guy is a killer, he's scum. Who cares what he looks like or who he dates? Forget it." He gave a dismissive wave with an I-don't-get-you expression. "Back to the issue at hand. I'll run a complete background check on Maher. I'll crawl through social media—Emma, you can help with that since you follow the guy and already know names and faces."

"No problem," Emma replied. "I can already tell you he lives somewhere here in Tribeca."

"Great." Ryan nodded. "Makes things easier. I'll find his address. I'll also get the names of the two women he *allegedly* assaulted. Shouldn't be hard. Bloggers everywhere probably posted the juicy details, maybe even photos of any altercations that occurred in public."

"According to Aimee, Rita told her there were witnesses," Casey reminded him.

"Yeah. And I'm sure there were also more than two incidents. With guys like Maher, where there's smoke, there's fire. I doubt he stopped at two victims to smack around. Who knows how many others there were who didn't get the same level of attention? They're out there. And I'll find them. As for witnesses, I'll locate them, too. Plus, I'll check out his daddy, since I'm sure he's footing the bill for his son's high living."

"Once you get his address, I'll put a tail on him," Patrick said. "I want to know where he goes, who he hangs out with, anything that tells us what he's up to. It could lead us to clues as to what he's *been* up to."

Marc took a calm belt of coffee. "I'll be the one paying him a visit later today or tomorrow. I'll wait until Ryan digs up enough dirt for me to rattle him with. No mention of FI, of course. But if he has an alibi, believe me, I'll get it. And if he doesn't—I'll get that, too."

No one argued that one. Marc had a way of being extremely intimidating. His height, rock-hard build, piercing stare, and unreadable expression—both innate and learned from his years as a Navy SEAL and, subsequently, as a member of the FBI's Behavioral Analysis Unit—combined with his unflappable demeanor, made him a formidable adversary. He kept his thoughts—and his Glock—well-hidden but at the ready.

"I'll make good use of the women's names Ryan comes up with," Casey said. "Hopefully, most of them will be local, so I can interview them in person, check out their body language, as well as listen to what they have to say. I want to know if any of them think their ex is capable of extreme violence. I'll stop short of using the word *murder*. At the same time, I'll see if there are any tells that signal memories of abuse—even if the women themselves won't admit that it happened."

"That's smart," Emma said.

Casey was still thinking. "I'll also wait for Marc's report and then check out anyone Chris Maher provides as his alibi. I might even pay his father a visit. The guy's a New Yorker when he's not filming a movie."

"Yes, but getting to him won't be easy." Claire spoke up for the first time. She was addressing Casey, but she looked faraway and surprisingly unsettled given the case was new and she was far removed from the victim and the crime. "Daniel Maher has a wall of security in place. Make sure to use key phrases implying his son is in some kind of trouble. If you do that, he'll see you. Chris is his weak spot."

Casey took that all in but eyed Claire pensively. "Claire, what is it?"

"I'm not sure." Claire's eyes slid shut, and she shivered at whatever it was she was picking up on. "Ever since Aimee sat down, I was swallowed up by a wall of dark energy... dark energy and death."

"Rita Edwell's?"

"Yes. She died painfully. The killer was trained. Skilled. And he's out there but…" She spread her hands in noncomprehension.

"Is it Chris Maher?"

"There's dark energy surrounding him, too. But there's something more, something terrifying. I just can't reach it… It's eluding me."

Ryan stared at her. "Wow. You sound more intense than usual when we're still at the starting gate."

"That's just it," she whispered. "I don't think we are still at the starting gate. It's like we've walked into the middle of something."

***

CannaBD headquarters
Elmton, New York

Aimee rode the Uber only as far as her Washington Heights apartment before hopping out and climbing behind the wheel of her own electric-blue Honda CR-V. Given the amount of time she spent either on the road or working at home, and the proximity between home and work—only forty minutes door to door—a car was a far better alternative than mass transit.

Her office at CannaBD was small, with most of the building's operating space taken up by the brewing and packing facilities, and just four offices—including hers and Nick's—separate and apart. Nick's office was larger than the others, with an alcove that functioned as a conference area. The other two offices belonged to Kimberley Perkins, CannaBD's CFO, and Oliver Steadman, the company's head of research and development.

Kimberley was tall and stick-thin, with a serious expression and a pair of stark black-framed glasses that made her look even more severe. Her hair was always pulled back off her face, which gave her an unimpeded view of her computer screen. She stared at that screen for hours on end, typing furiously as she produced spreadsheet after spreadsheet detailing all the monetary aspects of the company.

As for Oliver, he spent most of his time in his office or in the lab inside the beer production building, where he analyzed the prospects of expanding CannaBD's appeal and tested any promising results. At the top of his to-do list was finding a way to initiate Nick's latest big-picture vision—that being to apply Nick's formula to a wider range of alcoholic beverages. Nick was in and out of the lab, impatiently helping Oliver achieve results, and Oliver was always popping into Nick's office to pass along anything of substance.

Personally, Oliver was an affable enough guy, somewhere in his early thirties, committed to his job, and hardworking. He was a little socially awkward but in a way that was more endearing than offensive. He clearly realized he was different, because whenever he spoke to others, his gaze always darted around, rather than meeting the eyes of the person he was talking to. To Aimee's mind, his behavior was based on a combination of shyness and the awareness that his intellect and his IQ were somewhere in the stratosphere, making it near-impossible for him to fit in. She couldn't help but feel sorry for the guy. Actually, he reminded her of Sheldon Cooper from *The Big Bang Theory*. Sweet but weird, brilliant but quirky.

Aimee's own office was used for smaller meetings, mostly with people who inevitably wanted a tour and, more than anything else, free tastings. And since Nick was uber-private about his product development, those tours were minimal.

Today, she was a wreck, her hands shaking as she locked her car door and left the parking lot for the brewery, scanning the industrial area as she did. She half expected to see Chris Maher looming nearby. The only thing that kept her from going to pieces was the sight of John Nickels parked diagonally across the street.

He gave her a reassuring nod, and she managed a small smile in return. Then, she headed to the front door, opened it, and stepped inside. She would have locked the door behind her if she had her way, but Nick wouldn't know her reasons and he'd think she'd lost her mind.

She made her way to his office, hoping not to run into anyone else as she mentally prepped herself with what she had to say. Nick would either be in here, poring over profits, or in the brewery, overseeing the process. He was a genius at both.

As it turned out, he was at his desk, brow furrowed as he scoured whatever document he was reading. Nick's brow was furrowed a lot. He was a guy who concentrated deeply, whether he was in the lab or at his desk. He'd shove his dark hair off his face, narrow his equally dark eyes, and stare so intently at whatever he was doing, it was like he was trying to memorize every aspect of it.

Aimee had always viewed Nick as a walking phenomenon. He was a true scientific genius, one whose invention was like a prized child that he poured all his energies into. On the other hand, he still liked to party well into the night, the way he had in his fraternity days—and he had plenty of women who wanted to party with him. He wasn't into emotional attachments, but he was a good-looking guy, and he was ripped—his muscular body a major turn-on for women. And that was yet another layer of the complex guy behind CannaBD. He worked out in the gym for two hours before the sun rose each day—stress relief, he'd say. Frankly, Aimee couldn't fathom how he managed it all without splintering. But according to Nick, the thing he sacrificed was sleep. That, he'd say, he could do when he was dead. Now was the time to get things done and to enjoy doing them.

Aimee couldn't help but admire the guy. His crackling energy was part of what made her job so exciting.

She wasn't feeling that excitement now.

Fingers trembling, she knocked on Nick's partly opened door.

"Come in," he said absently.

She stepped into the office and shut the door behind her. "Hey," she greeted him in an unsteady voice, then crossed over and sank into the chair across from his desk.

Slowly, Nick tore his gaze away from his spreadsheet, taking a second to scribble a mark at the place where he'd left off. Then he turned his attention to Aimee. "You look like hell," he said. "What's wrong? You're not still upset about that asshole Chris Maher, are you? Forget him. You've already tapped into a strong bunch of influencers—young twenties who are living the high life. Traveling. Socializing. Tons of followers. You're on a roll. Host a few more of those tastings you're so good at. Anyone who tries our beer will be thrilled to endorse us in their YouTube videos in exchange for their own supply."

"I know." Normally, Aimee would have smiled at Nick's enthusiasm. But today wasn't a normal day. Although she did add, "I have more than a few ideas on who to approach. And it's not Chris I'm freaked out about." The last sentence tasted bitter as she lied her way through it. "Did you see the alumni email that just came through?"

"Huh?" Nick's expression was blank, and he was clearly as clueless about this as Aimee had expected. Catching up on routine Danforth news was low on his list, if not off it entirely. Still, he saw the strained expression on Aimee's face and heard the worry in her voice. "What email?"

Aimee didn't have to fake her distress. "Rita is missing. The police are involved. They think something might have happened to her." She went on to carefully fill in the blanks that FI had instructed her to.

Nick looked startled and upset. "Why would someone hurt Rita?" He turned to his computer, clicked on the email, and scanned the contents. "This says basically nothing except that she's missing and the NYPD is looking into it."

"The bloggers said a whole lot more. Including the fact that Crime Scene was involved in the investigation."

"You can't use bloggers as reliable sources."

"I'm not." A hard swallow. Even telling the partial truth that FI had allowed hurt deeply. "The detectives called me in for questioning. It seems that my drink with Rita was the last appointment in her calendar. I know it was routine—they were dotting their i's and crossing their t's—but the experience really freaked me out."

"Shit." Nick knew very well how tight Aimee and Rita were. "You must have totally lost it. What did they ask?"

"Basic facts. Why we were meeting. How she was acting. If she seemed off in any way. Or scared. All standard questions, but none of my answers could shed any light on their investigation. I told them we met because she was trying to help me in my new job at a start-up company. I said she acted normally. Other than that, I have no idea where she went afterwards or who she might have seen."

Nick didn't pick up on her glaring omission, and he gave a humorless laugh. "The minute the detectives finished talking to you, they must have called Chris Maher in for questioning. I'm sure he was infuriated by the negative press. He probably brought his lawyer with him through force of habit."

Aimee drew a slow breath, mentally running through FI's instructions for this part of the conversation. She pushed past the knot in her stomach and said what had to be said. "I didn't tell the detectives about Chris being at the meeting."

Nick's brows shot up in surprise. "Why not?"

"Because it would only dilute the investigation and have CannaBD thrown into the media coverage in an ugly light—which is the last thing we want." Aimee knew that would strike home with Nick. "Most important, I want the police to find Rita, not be distracted by an obnoxious pseudo-celebrity who fondled my leg and insulted our company. If the detectives had asked if anyone else was with us, I would have told them. But they didn't. So I kept quiet."

It took only a moment for Nick to process that. "I guess that makes sense," he said. "It wouldn't help Rita and it would screw up our rep. Bad news on both counts." He tapped his fingers on the desk, mulling things over. "Still, if the cops do somehow find out, it'll make us look like we have something to hide."

"No it won't." Aimee shook her head. "I'll explain that I was afraid of bringing Chris into the mix. If I had, he'd know right away who gave them his name. And if he got pissed and used his influence to hurt our company, CannaBD would be over before it began. Besides, his being at the bar with Rita and me really isn't relevant to the NYPD investigation."

Nick was visibly still on the fence. "All that's true, and I appreciate your trying to protect the company. But I think this whole situation is above my pay grade. I'm going to run it by my dad. He needs to know what's going on. Let's see what he says and if he thinks we need to give our attorneys a heads-up."

"Sure." Aimee wanted to kick herself for not anticipating this or mentioning it to FI. Nick's father was not only funding CannaBD but his liquor distribution company was getting it into bars, restaurants, and a slew of stores that sold alcoholic beverages. He was an influential businessman who ran several profitable companies and who'd worked long and hard to build them into highly successful endeavors. It was only natural that Nick would want to bring him into the loop.

She had to provide herself with some leverage.

"Please tell your dad that nobody but you even knows that Chris was at the bar with us that night. So I don't see how the police would find out."

That seemed to give Nick a little peace of mind. "You didn't mention it to anyone? Not even your friends or Travis?"

Aimee was beginning to feel as if she were back at the brownstone with the FI team. "No one," she assured him, just as she had them. "I've been so overloaded with work, I've barely texted anyone except Travis. And all he knows is that I was hoping to get connected with Chris. Nothing about the setup much less the meeting. His hours are as bad as mine. He's been at the hospital doing double shifts. I haven't seen him since last weekend."

"That'll take my dad down a notch." Nick looked more than a little relieved. "My guess is, he'll say to sit tight and do nothing. But at least he'll be up to speed, just in case."

"I understand." Aimee felt her eyes tear up again. The pain over Rita and the stress of the past few days were starting to pull her under. She was at her breaking point.

Nick must have heard her sniffle or caught her stricken expression, because guilt flashed across his face. "I'm really sorry, Aimee. Rita is a lot more important than damage control. We have to hope that she's okay and that there's another explanation for this."

Aimee was aware that, in his own way, Nick was trying to comfort her. They both knew that things looked bleak if the NYPD and Crime Scene were involved. Nick wasn't an emotionally expressive guy. So Aimee realized that this conversation was way uncomfortable for him.

"Do you need some time off?" he asked.

"Thanks, but no." Aimee shook her head. "If I do that, I'll go crazy. I've got to stay busy. I'll get on the task of finding new influencers. I've got a few college seniors and grad students on my list already. And

I've done a lot of online research. I'll contact the names I think will work for us." She paused, well aware that travel was not in the cards for her right now. "I will contact the right people and set up future university tastings. Just not right now. I want to stick close to home in case there are any developments..."

"I agree."

It was obvious he was thinking beyond her mental health and to the possibility that she might have to go to the cops and give them the full truth.

Aimee pushed back her chair. "If it's okay with you, I'll head home now. It goes without saying that, should your dad want to talk to me, I'm available."

"Thanks." Nick fiddled nervously with a pen on his desk. "And call me if you hear anything."

"I will."

Aimee walked out of the office and almost collided with Oliver, who was just outside Nick's door, holding what appeared to be sheets of paper containing product updates.

Aimee was barely holding it together. Making conversation, even brief and impersonal, was almost more than she could bear. But she couldn't very well avoid it, not with Oliver standing a foot away, looking startled by Aimee's sudden appearance.

"Hi, Oliver," Aimee said. "I guess you're here to see Nick. He and I just finished up, so he's all yours."

Oliver shifted uneasily from one foot to the other. "I didn't realize you were in there. Did I interrupt a scheduled meeting? It must have been back to back with mine, because I'm slotted in at two thirty."

Aimee shook her head. "No, actually I just needed a quick consult with Nick. Sorry if I cut into your time."

With a quick glance at his Apple Watch, Oliver looked relieved. "No problem. I'm two minutes early."

Aimee had to get out of there. Oliver's gaze was already flickering over her head at Nick's door, and she was more than happy to let their meeting start at the dot of two thirty.

"Great." She'd already taken two steps and was determined to get to the front door. "I won't keep you."

Oliver made it easy by sidestepping her to get to Nick's door. As he knocked, he looked back at Aimee, his expression odd—almost as if he had more to say. But Nick called out: "Come on in," so whatever it was remained unsaid.

He vanished into Nick's office, the door shutting behind him.

5

Offices of Forensic Instincts
6:15 p.m.

Ryan swore under his breath, shoved back his chair, and rose, pausing only to take a swig of cold coffee before starting to pace around his lair.

A whole day wasted on bullshit.

He'd been holed up in his lair since leaving the conference room, peeling back the layers that made up Chris Maher. At first, it had been an absorbing challenge, given what an interesting subject Maher was to delve into. Publicly, the guy was everywhere, on social media, in articles, blogs, anywhere and everywhere—where it came to *Snacks for Sports* and Super Bowl Bites.

But Chris Maher the guy? Now that was another matter entirely.

Bottom line, it had been nearly impossible to find anything personal on him other than the barest of specs. His profiles were spotty and what there was of them made him sound like a squeaky-clean Boy Scout. They had definitely been scrubbed by a pro. Oh, Ryan had done enough back-door work to get the names of the women Maher had publicly abused. He could pass those on to Casey. Unsurprisingly, neither of the victims lived anywhere near the Big Apple. They had once but had conveniently relocated—or *had been* relocated—after the incidents occurred.

There was a gold mine of information on Maher that was missing—information that Ryan was determined to get.

He wasn't about to waste any more time on the conventional route.

Time to go the unconventional one.

Ryan loped up the steps and knocked on the conference room door. Huge though it was, it was the room of choice for Casey when she was in investigative mode. She could breathe in here, she claimed, and so could her brain.

"Come in," she called.

Ryan walked in, surprised to see his boss standing at the panorama of windows, looking out, rather than at the head of the oval table, pounding away on her iPad keyboard.

"Hey," he greeted her. "You okay?"

Casey turned and shrugged. "Claire's reaction has been bugging me all day," she said. "What's more, I don't have any metaphysical gift, and I have the same sense that we're walking into something bigger than it seems. I trust my instincts. I'm just not sure how to utilize them right now."

"Well, if you'll give me the okay, I can help."

He held up one of his favorite self-constructed robotic incarnations—a gadget he'd employed many times before but had updated as the years had passed.

A small smile curved Casey's lips. "Ah, Gecko," she said. "I haven't seen him in a while."

"The little critter was being updated with the latest and greatest," Ryan replied, admiring his own handiwork as he spoke.

Gecko, as the team affectionately called him, was a small robot with suction-cup-like attachments on its feet—attachments made of a special rubber compound that adhered to everything. Not quite the size of a paperback book, Gecko was capable of walking up walls and inside ductwork. The "little critter," as Ryan dubbed him, sported miniature video cameras that could scan places and built-in microphones that could communicate back to Ryan via his trusty iPad. Gecko was, in effect, a robo-lookout or collector of digital information.

"We need hard-core answers fast," Ryan continued. "After wasting way too many hours, I've come up with next to shit on Maher." He tipped his head toward Casey's iPad. "I sent you the names and specs of the two women he publicly attacked. Both lived in Manhattan when the incidents occurred. Now, one is in Dallas and the other in Chicago. Very convenient. Needless to say, I could have kept digging until I found more of Maher's victims, but I'm sure they've been settled in equally faraway locations, and that would have just chewed up more time we don't have. Bottom line, someone's gone to a lot of trouble to clean up Chris Maher and make his transgressions vanish."

"So much for my interviewing Maher's victims," Casey said with a frown. "A close reading of body language isn't doable on Zoom."

"Yeah, I guess that's a dead end," Ryan agreed. "Sorry, boss."

Casey arched a brow. "So we ditch that approach. New approach on digging up dirt on Maher—Gecko?"

"Yup. The little critter is just the one to shine the true spotlight on that scumbag—in more ways than one." Ryan grinned as he thought of just how accurate his own assessment was. He couldn't wait to test the new capabilities he'd added to Gecko. Thanks to the infrared scanner he'd installed in the little critter, Ryan would be able to find exactly what he needed to know.

"What are you smiling about?" Casey inquired, clearly already having the answer to her own question. "New upgrades to Gecko for you to try?"

"Oh, yeah." Ryan's grin broadened. "And he's all set to use them."

"What if Maher is home?"

"I'm counting on it."

"You want him there? Isn't that taking a huge risk?"

"Nope. Gecko's never detected. As for Maher, I need him home to ensure his computer network is up and running. We're lucky. He's obsessive about working on *Snacks for Sports*. And it's Monday, a dead night for partying. So he'll be home, making new YouTube videos and blogging away."

"Makes sense." Casey didn't ask how Ryan knew all this or why it was necessary. This was his arena and she trusted him. "Was Emma right?" she asked instead. "Does Maher live here in Tribeca?"

"What do you think?" Ryan answered dryly. "Has Emma ever been wrong when it comes to celeb statuses?"

Casey's lips curved. "Good point."

"He's a spit's throw from here. Low-rise apartment, right across from the park. Another plus—there's a narrow alleyway alongside his building. With a modicum of luck, that will provide great visibility for both the little critter and me. Everything we get will be transmitted back to Yoda for analysis. I just need your okay."

"You've got it." Casey raised her head, speaking to Ryan's near-omniscient AI system. "Yoda, we need you on standby."

"Yes, Casey," Yoda replied. "Whatever data Ryan transports will be instantly analyzed."

***

Beach Street
Tribeca, New York
6:55 p.m.

Ryan strolled up and down Chris Maher's street, his iPad tucked beneath his arm. Ostensibly, he was chatting on his iPhone, when, in fact, he was watching the stream of pedestrians and waiting for them to slow down to a trickle.

Once they had, he made his way to the building and eased down the alley alongside it, Gecko nestled securely in his jacket pocket. He scrutinized the area carefully, ensuring that no one was in the vicinity. That done, he pulled Gecko out and placed his super-suction-cup appendages against the brick wall. Another quick look around.

All secure.

Ryan turned on his iPad, opened a custom app, and used it to employ the robot's built-in cameras and control his ascent. Up he went. One story. Two. Three. Four. Five. Stop. Only the best for Daniel Maher's kid—the top floor with a great view of the park.

Carefully, Ryan maneuvered Gecko between two large windows in Maher's apartment. Having done that, he went into the menu of tasks that the little robot could perform and selected Scan.

Gecko responded immediately by extending his legs and pressing his belly against the exterior wall of the building. Once he was in position, the infrared scanner he was now equipped with activated, giving Ryan a view of the apartment's interior. Sources of heat—people, animals, and especially computers—any or all of those would glow brightly.

Excellent. It was an open loft—lots of space, very few walls.

Still, the view through the first window was a bust. It accessed Maher's sleeping area, which was in an alcove. There was no one present and nothing of import to see. But the heat sources glowing from window two told Ryan he'd hit pay dirt. The wide-open focus of the loft. Maher's home office, complete with an elaborate computer station and Chris Maher himself hunched over the keyboard.

Ryan eased Gecko over and parked him just below that window.

Step one—in place.

Leaving Gecko just where he was, Ryan crossed the street and settled himself on a park bench that gave him a direct line of sight. Manipulating his iPad, he started the Wi-Fi-sniffing tool encoded in

Gecko's onboard computer. Short minutes later, he found the SSID of the Wi-Fi router and determined its make and model number. A couple of probes and he found that Maher had never patched its firmware.

Easy-peasy.

Ryan hacked his way past the router security and established credentials on Chris's network. From there it was simple to identify all the local devices and exploit the vulnerabilities in each.

Ryan deployed a malware script that disabled the antivirus software on Chris's Windows 10 computer and started to scan his SSD for anything useful. The script found all his online accounts: banking, email, and social media, along with the passwords to those accounts. Ryan transmitted all of those directly to Yoda, who started the process of mining every communication Chris had made and assembling the raw information into a series of threads that the FI team could analyze.

While Yoda was doing his thing, Ryan turned his hacking arsenal to Chris's mobile devices. That was a bit more difficult. But knowing what social media platforms he used gave Ryan a clue as to where he could leverage a vulnerability in an app. This was the fun part. It was always a game of Whac-a-Mole. A vulnerability would be found by the hacking community. That was the mole popping its head out of the hole. Some hackers would share it—for profit or fun. Other hackers would exploit it until a security researcher found the same flaw and reported it to the app's creator. It might take them some time to fix it. Then it was up to each user to upgrade to the latest version. When that happened, it was like whacking the mole back into his hole.

So Ryan went down the list of apps that Chris used until he found an entry point into his phone. From there, he deployed some malware, which extracted the critical phone information that would allow Ryan to SIM jack his phone. Then, he exported all the text messages on the phone and sent them to Yoda.

Thirty minutes later, Ryan was done… and Maher was still hunched over his computer, without a clue that all this had happened.

Using his app, Ryan skillfully maneuvered Gecko down the wall. He then shut his laptop, crossed the street, and plucked the little critter from the wall with a gentle tug that broke the vacuum suction on Gecko's "paws"—those same paws that allowed him to climb any surface with ease.

"Job well done," he muttered, tucking Gecko back into his pocket. "Time to bring you home, plug you into a USB charger, and restore you to full power. By the time Yoda and I are halfway done with our analysis, Marc will have more than enough to scare the shit out of Maher. Oh, and for the record, you're exceptional and I'm a genius."

6

NYPD twenty-sixth precinct
520 West 126th Street
Manhattan, New York
7:35 p.m.

Detective Karen Graham tossed aside the file she'd been reading and shoved loose strands of hair back into her hairband. Deciding it was a lost cause and her hair was going to remain a disaster, she gave in to the migraine that had been pounding at her head all day and massaged her eye sockets with her fingertips.

This whole Rita Edwell case was really getting to her.

It should have been a simple disappearance. Especially given the medical diagnostic report they'd found in the woman's desk, relaying the most dire news a human being could receive. She was dying. She had friends, both on and off campus, who cared about her and whom she'd want to spare watching her deterioration. It would be a classic reason for her to make herself vanish.

Except none of those pieces overrode the evidence.

Edwell's apartment was elegantly decorated, but nothing in it was gone—not her upscale clothes, her luggage, her personal items, or even her medications. None of her credit cards had been used since the night she'd gone missing. Her car was still in its assigned spot in the parking lot of her building.

None of that smacked of a woman who'd run away.

In addition to all that had been the state her office was in when the police had arrived on the scene, prompted by a call from her worried assistant. The young woman had come back to pick up a few things she'd forgotten to take home with her that night and spotted the light behind Edwell's half-shut door, the sight of which caused her to poke her head in and then call the police.

Edwell's desk chair had been toppled, her desk drawers rifled through. Crime Scene had found strands of her hair—not just in her comb but scattered all over her desk and chair. And even if that was attributable to the cancer, it didn't explain the clothing fibers that had been recovered, in a jagged weaving pattern across the office floor and to the door in a way that suggested she'd been dragged from the room.

Something had happened here, something that took place after Edwell's drink with her protégé, Aimee Bregman.

But what? And why?

Edwell was well-liked—her colleagues, her superiors, her friends, her neighbors. Not one of them could think of someone who would want to harm her.

Except someone had.

But the leads were running dry.

"You look as lousy as I do," a nearby voice proclaimed.

Karen glanced up, unsurprised to see her partner, Jerry Mullen, standing at her cubicle, looking as tired and frustrated as she did. Twelve years her senior, Jerry was one of the best detectives Karen had ever worked with. And even though she'd taken the lead in questioning women like Aimee Bregman, who were closer to her age and female, Karen looked to Jerry to head up the investigation. She could and had been lead detective on other cases. But this one smacked of homicide, something Jerry was far more seasoned with than she was. This wasn't about gender. It was about experience.

Coming up on fifty, with graying temples and a hint of a belly, Jerry had seen and done it all. He was a workhorse, old-school and dedicated, and he worked each case with the same all-in effort. His three kids were in college now, and he was incredibly compassionate about Karen's situation of having a husband who traveled for business and two elementary-school-aged kids who needed either their mom or dad at home, especially since at-home childcare was unaffordable. Often, Jerry would stay late, while Karen took her work with her, just so she could be there for her five-year-old and six-year-old boys. Jerry was a godsend, and there weren't enough words for Karen to express her gratitude.

She thanked Jerry in little ways—showing up in the morning with a venti-sized cup of Starbucks coffee and a slice of his beloved lemon loaf, sending him links to classic cars websites since she knew that one of his greatest dreams was to own one, getting him gift cards on his birthday and anniversary so that he and his wife could go out for a few well-deserved dinners.

It was the least she could do.

Right now, Jerry didn't look like he wanted thanks. What he wanted was to catch a criminal.

Still, he paused when he saw Karen rubbing her eyes. In fatherly fashion, he propped his hip against Karen's desk and frowned at her. "When was the last time you put anything in your stomach besides Snickers bars and stale coffee?"

"Don't knock it," Karen replied, attempting a smile. "Caffeine and sugar are a cop's best friends. Keeps you from falling asleep on the job."

Jerry snorted. "When have you ever fallen asleep on the job?"

"I've been known to doze during a lengthy stakeout."

"Yeah. Right." Jerry rolled his eyes. "Karen, you're already so thin you're about to disappear yourself. You're pale, you've been here since six a.m., and you've got to get home to your kids. As it is, you've paid for a babysitter three nights in a row with money you don't have, and you've checked your texts a hundred times. Get out of here. The Edwell case will be here in the morning."

Karen arched a brow. "Like you're leaving any time soon? I can see the bulldog look all over your face. You want to solve this case as much as I do. Something happened to Rita Edwell. And you and I are going to figure out what. And who. Before this becomes an official homicide and Manhattan North steps in."

With a resigned sigh, Jerry pulled his chair over to her desk. "All right. One more hour. Let's use it to revisit every name on our list. Maybe something one of them said will jump out at us."

Even as he spoke, they both suspected the tactic would lead to nothing but more aggravation.

"We need Edwell's damn cell phone records ASAP," Karen said in annoyance. "Sometimes I hate the system."

"Yeah, join the club."

***

Beach Street
Tribeca, New York
10:55 p.m.

The street was quiet. Residents were either in for the night or grouped together inside the local restaurants. Other than a few passers-by, Marc was pretty much alone—except for Larry Sanders, the member of Patrick's security team who was now situated diagonally across the street. Larry had notified the FI team that Chris Maher was still at home and had not left his apartment since Ryan's visit.

Thanks to Ryan, Marc had exactly the ammunition he needed to throw Maher off-balance and, together with a little physical persuasion, to get Maher to blurt out something incriminating. Maher's phone records showed payments made from his Venmo account to the accounts of the "relocated" women who'd made noise about filing harassment charges. Ryan had supplied Marc with the printed data—now tucked away in Marc's pocket—to shove the tangible proof in Maher's face.

In the interim, Marc had done his own homework.

Chris Maher's building had tons of amenities, but luckily one of those amenities was *not* a twenty-four-hour doorman. That meant one less keen pair of eyes spotting Marc as he passed by. Not that he had any intention of breaking in through the front door, since, even with his skill set, it would take him longer than it would take a resident to get in. That would call unwanted attention to him. Especially because, in a building as cozy as this, all the tenants doubtless knew each other. One of them would spy a stranger hovering at the entranceway in a nanosecond.

He zipped his leather jacket up to his neck and hunched into its upturned collar. Too early in the season for a hooded parka. Still, the late-autumn night was cool, so he didn't look out of place.

With a quick glance around, he turned the far corner of the building and eased his way down the alley alongside it. He continued past where Ryan and Gecko had done their thing, made his way around back, and stopped at the basement door.

He worked fast, slipping on his latex gloves and pulling out his lock-picking tools.

It was a standard lock. Marc had guessed that, since dead bolts were a fire safety hazard. This would be easy.

His fingers were poised to do their job when something odd caught his eye. There were scratch marks on the lock, few but distinct.

Someone had attempted to break in here before. Surprising. This section of Tribeca didn't have a high crime rate. And the attempt had to have failed, or there'd be a lot more security in place.

There was no time to ponder the discovery.

Without further delay, Marc went to work.

Forty-five seconds later, he was inside the building.

He used the stairs rather than the elevator, pausing every few seconds to listen for footsteps that would tell him he wasn't alone. He'd memorized the names of the tenants, all of whom Ryan had given him. If need be, he'd say he was visiting one of them. But the building was quiet and Marc's ascent went unnoticed.

Reaching Maher's apartment, Marc prepared to knock and then shove his way past the guy to get in.

Instead, he found the door slightly ajar.

Warning bells went off in Marc's head, and instinctively, he slid his hand into his pocket, his fingers closing around the handle of his Glock. Then he elbowed open the door and stepped inside. Shutting the door with his foot, he pulled out his weapon and swept the place, which was essentially one large room with an alcove that held a bed and a dresser.

His gaze went directly to the computer station.

There, tied to his desk chair, was Chris Maher. He had a gag stuffed in his mouth, and his head was hanging forward at an unnatural angle. Marc inched closer and he could see the cord from a phone charger tied tightly around Maher's neck. His jeans and T-shirt still clung to his body in a drenched sweat, indicating that whoever had attacked him had done so recently.

Marc's check for a pulse told him what he already knew.

Maher was dead.

And not just dead. Maher's thigh had been impaled by a butcher knife, one that was still protruding from his body. A black and white college football player's glove had been stabbed through and was now adhered to Maher's jeans. Blood was oozing out, staining the glove and the jeans and seeping down to the floor.

Marc stayed just seconds, long enough for him to whip out his cell phone and snap a few photos.

Then, after carefully checking the hall, he got out of the apartment—leaving the door ajar exactly as it had been when he arrived. He retraced his steps and exited the building and the alley.

With quick strides, he made his way up the street. The NYPD's first precinct was way too close for comfort. He had to gain some distance before he made his call.

Two blocks away, he pulled out a burner phone and made the anonymous call. Then he broke it in half, tossed the phone in the trash, and headed straight back to FI's offices.

7

Offices of Forensic Instincts
11:40 p.m.

The entire team had been hastily summoned and now gathered around the conference table.

"Pretty gruesome," Ryan said, looking at the photos that Yoda had expanded to full size and were now displayed on the screen on the far wall of the room. "And talk about coming out of left field. This murder blows our theory about Chris Maher out of the water."

Patrick's brow was furrowed in annoyance. "I spoke to Larry. He said the only person who went down that alley during the interval between when Ryan left and Marc showed up was a guy in a black hoodie. The guy was visibly drunk, and Larry could hear him hurling in the alleyway. As a result, Larry didn't focus on him. He was watching the street and the front of the apartment." A pause. "I'm not happy. Larry's not usually careless. And this one cost us."

Casey was accustomed to Patrick's perfectionism. "Don't be too hard on Larry," she said. "Remember, Maher was supposedly the killer. Our job was to watch him and his activities. Aimee is the one we're protecting—against the very guy who was killed. Larry's focus was right where it should have been."

"That's true." Patrick looked slightly mollified. "Still, anything unusual should have been reported. I'll be speaking to Larry."

None of the team doubted that.

"Whoever the killer was, this was personal." Marc was studying the screen, seeing his photos more thoroughly. "Personal and angry. Obviously, this wasn't random, nor was it a coincidence that it happened days after Rita Edwell's disappearance."

"Rita's body hasn't been found," Casey pointed out, knowing exactly where Marc's head was. "So technically there's more than one possible explanation for how these two incidents are connected."

"Yup."

"What are you two talking about?" Emma demanded, turning her palms up in noncomprehension. "We're obviously looking at two related murders that were carried out in different ways."

"Maybe." Marc gazed patiently at her. "Or maybe Rita disappeared long enough to return and kill Chris Maher before vanishing for good."

Emma's jaw dropped. "Do you really believe that?"

"No," Marc replied. "The theory is weak—and that's without taking into account the fact that Claire is certain Rita was murdered. Maher was a tall guy with a relatively large build. Rita was an average-sized woman with no tactical skills. Overpowering him long enough to wrap that cord around his neck and choke him to death without him putting up a fight—which there was no evidence of—seems dubious. All that having been said, I'm sure the police will consider the possibility that she's the killer."

"That glove." Claire was staring white-faced at the screen, her gaze locked on the knife protruding from Chris Maher's thigh. "It was chosen for a reason."

"Certainly to be found," Marc said. "The killer is being very specific. In the process, he's leaving behind a clue. He expects it to be found, but he thinks he's too smart for anyone to figure out what it means." A pause. "That speaks to a certain kind of psychological profile."

"Yeah," Emma muttered. "A psycho."

"A sick, twisted mind," Claire murmured. "But an intelligent one. An experienced one."

Marc inclined his head, eyeing Claire thoughtfully. "All that is obvious from a behavioral standpoint. Are you sensing more? A repeat offender, I suspect?"

"Yes." Claire's fingers closed into her palms. "But one I..." She broke off, gave a frustrated shake of her head. "My mental connection to this is getting stronger now that we're looking at actual photos of Chris Maher's murder. But what I'm grasping for—it's still out of reach."

"Something specific about the killer?" Ryan asked.

"The kill*er* or the kill*ings*. I'm not sure which. But either way, what I'm missing is significant. I might need something tangible to hold—something that gives off perceptible energy."

"Something of the killer's?"

"Or the victims." Again, Claire gave a frustrated shake of her head. "I won't know until I have personal items to handle. But studying these photos, I'm even more certain than I was before. We're walking into the middle of something. And whatever that something is, it's terrifying. The killer is terrifying."

"The glove is probably from a college football team." Ryan was studying the photos as Claire spoke. "I don't know if it's team specific, since lots of teams wear black and white gloves. Yoda zoomed in already and there's no insignia."

"Then it's not tied to the school itself." Marc's eyes were narrowed as he tapped his pen on the table. "As we just determined, this is a smart, seasoned killer with a personal agenda. If he wanted the cops' attention drawn to a particular university, he'd have chosen the exact glove he wanted. This is more symbolic. We just don't know of what."

"Does Danforth's football team wear black and white gloves?" Emma asked.

"They do," Casey replied. "But, as Ryan said, so do many other college teams. It's true that Marc is right about the killer's not choosing an exact match to a specific university. Still, we can't ignore the fact that Danforth was Maher's alma mater. And that it's also where Rita Edwell worked and where she came up the ranks."

"It's Aimee's alma mater, too," Claire said softly. "The three of them had drinks. A few days later, two of them are dead."

"And then there was one," Ryan muttered. "Shit."

Casey turned to Patrick. "I'm calling Aimee now and telling her to pack an overnight bag. I'll keep the conversation calm. I'll just say we need to fill her in on our investigation and that it's late enough for her to crash on our futon. No other details. Please give John a heads-up that he'll be driving her here right away."

"Done." Patrick was already whipping out his phone.

"The entire focus of our investigation has now changed," Casey continued. "Although we have to keep probing into Chris Maher's life. He plays a part in this, even as a victim."

"Totally agree," Ryan said. "I also have to start digging deeper into Rita Edwell's life, to see if I can find connections between her and Maher." He paused, rolling his eyes. "Maher's murder took place here in Tribeca. That means we'll be dealing with the first precinct. And you know how much they love us. Same for Manhattan South's Homicide Division."

"We'll worry about that later," Casey said. "Aimee's questioning came from the detectives in the twenty-sixth. Manhattan North probably isn't in the equation yet, since there's no solid proof that Rita Edwell was murdered. So the twenty-sixth is where Aimee will go back to—as soon as word of Chris Maher's death gets out in an official capacity."

“As in not through us,” Emma muttered.

“Exactly. But given who Maher was, news of his murder will be center stage in everyone’s morning newsfeed. Once that happens, Aimee has to set up a meeting with the detectives who questioned her and fill them in on what she knows. They’ll coordinate their investigation with the first precinct and with both homicide divisions.” Casey drew in a breath. “But that’s not what I’m worried about.”

“No,” Marc agreed. “As of now, Aimee’s life could be in grave danger.”

***

Offices of Forensic Instincts
First-floor conference room
Tuesday, 12:35 a.m.

The warm, soothing décor of the smaller conference room did nothing to settle the sick feeling in Aimee’s gut. She perched at the edge of the settee, her back ramrod straight. She gripped her coffee cup with both hands, and her gaze darted from one FI team member to the other. She looked as if she were waiting for a fatal blow.

“What’s happened?” she asked. “You must have learned something crucial or I wouldn’t be here in the middle of the night.” She swallowed hard. “Just tell me. No sugarcoating. I need to know everything about a man who might be trying to kill me.”

Casey took the helm, relaying the news frankly but gently. “Chris Maher is dead, Aimee. He was murdered a few hours ago in his apartment.”

Aimee’s mug crashed to the floor. “*What*?”

“I can’t get into any details. Not yet. The official report hasn’t even been released by the police. Which means this news stays within these walls until they go public with it. But trust me, it’s true. Whatever threat Maher represented—if he ever represented one at all—is over.”

Aimee was taking shallow breaths as she tried to assimilate what she was being told. "How do you know?"

"That's not important," Casey replied. "What is important is that the two people you had drinks with the other night are either dead or presumed dead. It's up to us to figure out what the two of them had in common—and if that commonality extended to you, which would put you at risk."

"Oh God." Aimee pressed the heels of her hands against her eyes. "I was so sure… And now the real killer is still walking around out there. With both Rita and Chris dead, there's even more reason now to believe I'm his next target." She looked up. "Where do we start?"

Marc was the one who replied. "We start with the threats Chris made at the bar. We try to figure out if he knew something that would get him killed and if Rita was aware of it, as well. You might have just been in the wrong place, wrong time. But if those threats mean you unknowingly learned something dangerous… we have to establish that."

Aimee gave a helpless shrug. "I already told you about that conversation. Chris was furious at Rita for calling him out about hitting on me. She was equally furious."

Marc nodded. "Tell us exactly what was said. I know you did that at our first meeting, but a little time has passed. Sometimes a new detail will pop into your head."

Aimee swallowed. "It's not the kind of fight you forget. Rita reminded Chris that it was she, not his father, who'd made him who he was and that she could unmake him just as quickly. He warned her that she'd better not threaten him, that he knew things about her that were damning. His exact words were *I own you.* He said if she pushed him, she'd find out what he was capable of." Aimee shuddered. "Then he told me to forget all about the meeting we were having and that if I ever accused him of sexual harassment, he'd retaliate in some horrible way."

"He said *I own you*?" Casey asked. "That's new information."

Aimee blinked. "I'm sorry. I thought I… I guess I…"

"Don't apologize. In stressful situations, thoughts get diluted and then, as Marc said, resurface later. Clearly, Maher had something to blackmail Rita with."

The frown lines on Marc's forehead deepened. "It's possible he's not the only one who had damning information on Rita, or vice versa. Whatever Maher knew, and whatever Rita did to establish Maher in some major way, it seems likely that someone else was threatened by it. Someone who killed them both."

Aimee was still shaking. "Do you think it was someone at the bar? Someone who was listening in? As I told you, the fight was loud and ugly. Anyone who wanted to hear it wouldn't have to strain his ears."

"We don't know," Casey interjected. "But we're going to find out." She held up her hand to halt Aimee's oncoming question. "You've told us everything you can. Now the ball's in our court. Right now, we have two immediate goals. One is to double up our protection of you. The other is to review what you're going to tell the detectives you spoke with."

"That's right." Aimee looked ill. "I really have to go back now, don't I?"

"Yes. Right after you hear the news of Chris's murder through official channels." Leaning forward, Casey placed a soothing hand on Aimee's arm. "By tomorrow morning, the news will be out. The NYPD will be forced to hold a press conference. And you'll be forced to go back to the twenty-sixth precinct to fill in the blanks you left out the last time you were there."

"I know we coached you on what to say," Patrick added. "But this is a whole new ball game. You're going to have to walk a fine line. Tell them that, given who Chris is, given his high profile and extensive monetary resources, you were worried that he might go after you legally. Stress *legally*. Don't get into fear for your safety." Patrick broke off, looking distinctly uncomfortable.

Casey knew that look. Patrick's ethics and discomfort about bending the law were two of the things she most respected about him.

"You have to soften the details of Maher's argument with Rita," she said, taking over the reins. "Skip the intensity and the drama and certainly the specifics you just told us. Stick to the basics. Chris made a pass at you, and he and Rita had words over it. She ordered him to get his hand off your leg. He told her to stay out of it because it was none of her business. Act more embarrassed than frightened. Like you felt objectified."

"You want me to omit things," Aimee said. "Why? Because you don't want police interference in connecting the two murders?"

"No, because you're our client and we want to protect you."

"I don't understand."

Marc took a swallow of coffee and provided the answer. "You're going to end up filling in all the blanks once they question you anyway. But it's the way you initially come across that matters. We need the detectives to see you as a victim. Not a suspect."

"A suspect?" Aimee whispered.

"Yes. No matter how you spin it, you're the common denominator here, the person who was with both Rita and Maher not long before they either vanished under suspicious circumstances or were killed. Which means the detectives are going to investigate you. That's protocol given the situation. It's up to you to convince them you have nothing to hide."

"But I *don't* have anything to hide." Aimee paused and then gazed quizzically at Casey. "Except for the fact that I hired you."

"Yeah, leave that part out," Ryan said immediately.

"No." Casey shook her head. "If you do that, it will invalidate everything Patrick and Marc just instructed you to say and make it look as if you're dodging the police for suspicious reasons. Bad idea. They have to know we're in the picture. Remember, you hadn't hired us yet when they first interviewed you. Now you have. It's why you did so that has to be tweaked."

Without hesitation, Casey went on. "Tell them you hired us to help investigate Rita's disappearance because you weren't sure the police were viewing it as a homicide. Say you knew Rita so well that you knew she'd never just vanish. So you paid us to pursue that avenue and that avenue only. No digressing to figure out if she ran off. No red tape. No trying to amass enough resources. Just figure out who killed your friend, how he or she did it, and what the motive was. And then to make sure that killer is put away for life."

Aimee digested that, chewing her lip worriedly. "I hope I can pull this off. I'm a nervous wreck."

"Use those nerves to your advantage," Casey said. "Two people you met for a drink a few days ago were murdered or are presumed dead. Anyone in your position would be unhinged. That will be noted by the detectives and work well toward eliminating you as a suspect."

"Should I have a lawyer with me?"

"Definitely not," Ryan spoke up again. "That screams guilt. You have to look as scared and green as possible—even though we've just fully prepped you."

Claire stepped in to take Aimee's panic down a notch. "This is the only interview you'll have to handle alone from here on," she said. "Once you've spoken your piece, the detectives will be on our front doorstep in a nanosecond. And we'll tell them we've already done a thorough background check on you."

"Which, of course, we have," Ryan added. "That's standard operating procedure when we take on a client."

"Oh." Aimee was still processing everything she'd heard tonight.

"What Claire is saying is that, once you tell the detectives your story, we'll step in," Casey said. "We'll be in the forefront if they have any more questions for you. Which, honestly, I doubt they will. At least not as a suspect. As a prospective victim, yes. And in that arena, they'll be an asset, not a liability. They'll do drive-bys of your apartment.

They'll keep you apprised if they learn you're in danger. And they'll do their best to be one step ahead of us."

"Which they won't be," Ryan said. "They never are."

"Camp out here tonight." Casey rose from the settee, bringing the conversation to a close. "We'll all be here, doing our homework. By midmorning we'll be watching a police news conference. After that, all systems will be go."

8

Colts River, New Jersey
Tuesday, 7:35 a.m.

As was always his routine, Victor woke up at six thirty and made his way down the circular staircase and out back to the heated Olympic-sized swimming pool on his seven-acre estate. He did his laps for exactly thirty minutes before toweling off and returning to the master bedroom suite of his eight-thousand-square-foot mansion, after which he showered and dressed in an open-necked collared shirt and a neatly pressed pair of slacks.

Neither the laps nor the shower did much to invigorate him. He'd had a lousy night's sleep. That was becoming the rule rather than the exception. Now that his fifty-fifth birthday had come and gone, he tended to dwell on the future. And given the life he'd chosen, that meant lots of dwelling to intrude on his sleep. No regrets, just more planning and less vicarious living.

His wife, Frances, was still asleep as he quietly left the bedroom and headed back down the stairs, this time to the state-of-the-art kitchen with its marble counters, lacquered cabinets, and stainless-steel appliances. He went directly to the island at the center of the room and brewed his first cup of dark roast coffee.

His and Frances's routine was that she would join him for her first cup and his second, after he'd replied to his early-morning texts and emails, returned his phone calls, and completed his pressing must-do work. At that point, he was ready to concentrate on a conversation in which they caught up on the previous day. Usually, she talked and he listened. News about the kids, social updates, and healthy recipes she was eager to try. World events and the economy. Sometimes he brought up his businesses, usually to assure her that they were thriving and occasionally to gripe about an annoying or under-performing employee. She always listened attentively, expressing what she knew he needed to hear at the time.

She didn't know everything about his life. For many reasons, he made sure to keep it that way. But she knew enough, more than enough to understand that she had to keep her mouth shut. She was a good woman, and a smart one. She also liked the finer things in life. And he provided her with more than enough of those. So she was content. And when she wasn't, she bought herself a new piece of jewelry and looked the other way.

Victor popped the pod into the coffeemaker and pressed brew. The machine whirred to life and did its job. He stood beside it and waited for its loud hiss of a finale. Then he removed the used pod and tossed it in the trash. He added a splash of milk to his drink, frowning as he did so. He missed his cream like hell. But his cholesterol had gone up, and Frances had made low-fat milk a staple in the house. It was a sound if aggravating decision, one he accepted with minimal grumbling since it had been made out of love and concern, both of which he valued highly.

Gripping the handle of his mug in one hand and his cell phone in the other, he sat down in a leather chair at the kitchen nook. He took a healthy swallow of coffee and simultaneously began scanning his morning newsfeed before reviewing his checklist on the party he was catering this weekend.

He scrolled down once, twice, and his thumb froze on the screen.

Chris Maher, son of Hollywood star Daniel Maher, was dead. No comment from law enforcement, no official details being released at this time. But rag reporters and social media were all over it, claiming it was murder.

No official details being released yet? Well, Victor was about to get around that bullshit.

He called his longtime contact at the NYPD, Detective Stefano Bellone. Stefano worked in the Organized Crime Investigative Division at One Police Plaza. He handled active cases in the OCID and had access to both case files and intel files. In order to ensure Stefano's continued loyalty and cooperation, Victor provided him with generous monthly payments. As a result, Stefano provided him with whatever information he needed.

In this case, Victor explained what he wanted, and Stefano went off to make discreet inquiries. Not twenty minutes later, he called Victor back with the details—details that confirmed Victor's worst suspicions. The MO was there. So was the victim type. And most of all, the signature calling card was there. A knife plunged through an athletic glove into Maher's thigh. That single detail gave Victor a modicum of relief, since he knew that that ritual was reserved for his guy's personal kills, not those sanctioned by Victor. Swift and clean were Victor's instructions. No fanfare or added touches. With a modicum of luck, the knife and the glove—which had been used in several recent homicides—would send the detectives down the path of a probable serial killer.

Still, an investigation into Chris Maher was a given. And that made Victor's gut clench. He had no idea where the investigation would lead or what would be uncovered in the process. An overlap like this had happened only once before, and that first one was an easy fix. But this? It could never happen again. It could jeopardize Victor's entire operation.

He had to take steps to ensure this fiasco was a one-time error—an error that never repeated itself. And he had to do it *now*.

***

NYPD twenty-sixth precinct
520 West 126th Street
Manhattan, New York
Tuesday, 11:15 a.m.

Detectives Karen Graham and Jerry Mullen remained side by side in their chairs in the interviewing room, elbows propped on the table, listening to the clicking of Aimee Bregman's heels as she headed away from them and toward the front door of the precinct.

When more than enough time had passed, they turned to face each other and talked.

"That sure as hell came out of left field," Jerry began, abandoning his deceptively relaxed Q-and-A mode and resuming his normal get-it-done demeanor. "She must have rushed over here as soon as the NYPD press conference ended and news broke about Chris Maher's murder."

Karen rolled her empty Styrofoam cup between her palms. "To set the record straight and to fill in her earlier omissions—of which there were many." Her brows knit in a frown. "I don't doubt that, during Bregman's first visit here, she left out the entire part about Maher being at the bar because she was scared. As for this morning, my gut tells me she wasn't lying, just skewing the story to present it in a certain light."

"I'm sure she had help doing that."

"Forensic Instincts."

Jerry nodded. "Yup. By hiring them, she tapped into all their skills, including managing what she shared with the police." He fiddled with his pen. "And while that sucks, it also suggests she didn't kill anyone.

Forensic Instincts has a rep for overstepping boundaries, but they don't take on guilty clients. And for the record, I don't think Aimee Bregman killed anyone, either. Her hysteria over the Maher murder is genuine, as is her worry over what happened to Rita Edwell. Not to mention the fear for her own life."

"I agree," Karen said. "When she did tell us that Maher was at the bar with her and Edwell that night, she downplayed the argument between them—until we started pressing hard. After that, she didn't skirt our questions. I think she wound up giving us a pretty comprehensive picture of what went down. As you said, I see Forensic Instincts' laying the groundwork for her. They didn't want us to view her as a suspect. A smart strategy. Also, not without merit. You and I just agreed that she was guilty only of being too scared to tell us everything the first time and letting us draw the answers out of her the second time."

Pausing, Karen blew out a breath. "We'll have to contact the first precinct right away, as well as the homicide teams at both Manhattan North and South. These two cases have to be coordinated. It can't be a coincidence that Maher and Edwell had a drink and then were either harmed or killed within two days of each other. We have to do some digging into both their lives, see what we can come up with that links them."

"Yeah. And deal with Forensic Instincts up close and personal for the first time."

***

Washington Heights, New York
11:55 a.m.

Aimee let herself into her apartment, locked the door, and promptly burst into tears.

The morning had been brutal. First, a grueling hour at the police precinct, answering countless questions and giving the best explanation possible for her silence. Next, a follow-up phone call to Casey to fill her in on the interview. And last, listening to Nick's three voice mails and reading his six text messages.

She hadn't had to fake her hysteria when both Detective Graham and Detective Mullen grilled her. Given the events of the past few days—aggravated by zero sleep—she'd more than reached her breaking point.

The detectives had seemed sympathetic, but they'd kept their expressions unreadable as they emphasized that she should be available for additional questioning. Conversely, she'd been relieved when they hadn't commented, negatively or otherwise, on the fact that she'd hired Forensic Instincts to investigate what she believed to be Rita's murder. They'd simply nodded. And they'd assured her that, from their end, they'd have a police car do periodic drive-bys of her apartment.

It was as much as she could ask for.

Casey had been calm and supportive when Aimee relayed the details of her meeting with the detectives, clearly unsurprised by anything she was hearing. She praised Aimee for a job well done and told her to go ahead and call Nick to fill him in. She also suggested that, since there was no more need for secrecy, Aimee should call her boyfriend, spend some quality time with him, and share what she chose to.

In other words, find a way to distract herself, to calm down, and to let the FI team do its job.

That wasn't happening until she dealt with Nick.

She waited only as long as it took to change into sweats and curl up on the comfy sofa of her studio apartment with a cup of herbal tea. One extra second to remind herself to edit out the severity of Chris's threats. She'd given that information to the detectives. It was part of a police investigation now—as well as Forensic Instincts'. No need to extend that circle of knowledge to Nick.

With that, she pulled her phone out of her pouch pocket, pressed his number, and steeled herself.

Nick answered in a nanosecond, blasting into the conversation before she'd said hello.

"Why didn't you return my calls?" he demanded. "My texts? Shit, Aimee, Chris Maher was killed. Where have you been?"

"Not killing Chris, if that's what you're asking." She had no idea why she'd retaliated with that response. She knew that's not where Nick's head was. But, dammit, she was on emotional overload.

"*Killing Chris*?" Nick sounded shocked and horrified. "Why would I be asking that?"

"Maybe it crossed your mind. It sure crossed the detectives' minds. That's where I was when you were texting and calling me. I went to the precinct as soon as I saw the news conference about Chris's murder. I told them about Chris being at the bar with Rita and me that night, about how he came on to me, and about the fight he and Rita had. So there are no more secrets, Nick." Aimee's voice quavered. "I didn't mean to blast you that way. It's just that I've had about all I can take. So please go easy on me."

"I'm sorry." He blew out a breath, although Aimee suspected it did little to calm him down. "Are you saying the cops actually view you as a suspect? Why?"

Aimee reached over and grabbed a blanket, throwing it over herself. She couldn't shake the internal chills, and she wondered if she ever would. "I effectively lied to them the first time. And since I'm convinced Rita was killed, I'm the only one left alive of the three people at that meeting. I can't blame them for considering the possibility, although I don't think it's high on their list."

"Were you with Travis? Can he vouch for you?"

"Nope. He was at the hospital. I was alone in my apartment at the time of the murder. So no alibi." She gave a humorless laugh. "I guess my security detail can vouch for the fact that he didn't see me leave. But if I were a truly cunning murderess, I could find a way to get past him. Isn't that how it works in the movies?"

"Security detail?" Nick asked bewilderedly.

"Oh, yes, that's the one thing I haven't told you. After my first round of questioning, I hired Forensic Instincts. I'm sure you've heard of them. As I said, the police aren't totally convinced that Rita was murdered. I am and have been from the start. I needed investigators who could prove it and who could find Rita's killer—and now probably Chris's killer, too, if it's the same person."

Now Nick sounded intrigued. "Forensic Instincts? Wow. They've got an unbelievable rep. How could you afford them? Maybe I'm paying you too much."

For the first time, Aimee smiled. It felt good.

"They gave me a break. They probably felt sorry for me; I was such a wreck when I met with them. And I kind of think they were intrigued by the case."

"And they were obviously concerned for your safety. Why?"

Careful, Aimee, she cautioned herself. *Stick to the basics.*

"Chris Maher is—was—a public figure with a high profile and a rich daddy. He threatened me if I went to the police about his come-on. Now I'd been interviewed by the police. If he heard about that and drew the wrong conclusion…"

"He might retaliate." Nick processed that in a way that made Aimee believe she'd been convincing enough. "Makes sense. So you've got a real live bodyguard?"

"Right outside my building."

"Very cool."

"Please keep that quiet," Aimee requested. "That's what Forensic Instincts wants."

"Understood."

Aimee didn't want the answer to her next question. But she had to know where things stood. "How did your dad react when you spoke to him? Was he really pissed at me?"

"More pensive than pissed. He appreciated your trying to protect CannaBD. But he was concerned about any fallout that might occur. No surprise there. I'm pretty sure he put his lawyer on standby the minute I left. And he insisted that I keep him informed. Again, no surprise. He's got his distribution company and his own rep to protect. I'm sure he'll be relieved that you followed up with the detectives, even if it was because Chris was killed."

"I'm sure." Aimee took a fortifying swallow of tea. "Please tell him how sorry I am. What I did was stupid, no matter how good my intentions were."

"I'll pass that along," Nick replied. "Although I wouldn't worry. If you were really on my dad's shit list, I'd know it and so would you."

A rueful smile. "In other words, I'd be looking for a new job."

"That's not happening, so let's not dwell on it. I'm more worried about you. Instead of viewing you as a suspect, the police should be viewing you as a potential victim. You're the only one from that meeting who's still alive."

"I know. So do the police. More importantly, so does Forensic Instincts."

"You must be scared shitless."

"I am. But I'm desperately trying to think rationally. And when I manage to do so, I can't see a connection. I never even met Chris Maher until the other night. Obviously, Rita is another story; she's been in my life for years. I was the odd man out at that meeting since Rita and Chris knew each other through Danforth—although I'm not sure how well. Still, when the irrational voices in my head take over…" Aimee broke off, massaging her temples. "I'm going to hang up, take a shower, and try to sleep for a while. But first, I'm texting Travis. I could really use some normalcy—downtime with pizza and beer."

"As long as it's CannaBD beer," Nick quipped, striving for a joke that fell flat. Trying for a more serious, comforting note, he added, "If you need anything, I'm here."

"Thanks, Nick." Aimee knew how awkward this whole soothing thing was to Nick, and she was touched by his efforts. "I appreciate it. I need all the emotional support I can get."

9

Offices of Forensic Instincts
Tribeca, New York
Tuesday, 1:15 p.m.

Ryan was downstairs in his lair, staring at his computer monitor as he continued his analysis of the data he'd acquired on Chris Maher. The guy was a total scumbag. He used and abused women, then relocated them and paid them off for their silence. It was all a game to him. He spent a fortune keeping these women happy and out of the picture—a lot more money than even he was making. No problem there. Enter daddy. Chris was a bloodsucker when it came to his father, hitting him up not only for the payoff money but for thousands more every few weeks. He blew it all on sports cars he didn't drive and electronic toys he barely used. Just to have them. Just to be the little shit he was.

Ryan knew there was more. Something dirty that was tied to Rita Edwell. Based on the details of their argument, it involved blackmail, from his side and maybe from hers, as well. But without access to Edwell's data, Ryan's hands were semi-tied. He could keep at it from the Maher angle. But he was flying blind from the Edwell angle. And it was driving him crazy.

The NYPD had confiscated her cell phone, her computer, and her personal calendar—all of which Ryan needed to begin unraveling her life story and seeing where it crisscrossed with Maher's. None of which he had a prayer of gaining access to.

Never one to be thwarted, Ryan had taken his own less-than-legal route.

He'd SSHed into a server he maintained in Russia just for these purposes. Once logged in, he'd launched the cyberattack from overseas, first commandeering some US-based assets, who, in turn, were used to access the target systems. He'd launched two hacks—one targeting T-Mobile in order to obtain the call record details from Edwell's phone and the other aimed at Wells Fargo, Edwell's bank, to pull her bank statements for the past few years. Identifying T-Mobile as Edwell's provider had been as easy as using the cell phone number Aimee had provided and accessing mobilephonelookup.com. And getting the name of Edwell's bank had been the sheer luck of Aimee having been with her twice when she'd run into a Wells Fargo bank to make withdrawals.

It would take a little time for the infiltration to be successful. Security teams were always looking for frontal assaults on their firewalls. So Ryan had to be careful. His procedure would take finesse and patience.

Finesse he had. Patience was another story entirely. He needed that data and he needed it now, not only because of his personality but because FI was in the middle of an active investigation that necessitated it.

In the interim, he'd started with the one commonality he knew that Edwell and Maher had: Danforth University.

Maher had graduated from his alma mater seven years ago with a decent-but-not-fabulous GPA and an interest in the food industry. Thus, his old job at the steakhouse, as well as the enthusiasm with which he'd amped up his sports food blog, started way back in college.

Ryan planned to dissect every single aspect of Maher's education. He'd do the same with what he knew of Edwell's career path. And maybe he'd get lucky and find an overlap, one that could be confirmed by his hacks. It was all he could do until those were complete.

As he contemplated the next step in his strategy, the "all call" sound chirped from his cell phone. The whole team was being summoned for a meeting. Casey probably wanted to play catch-up. Well, it was just as well. Ryan could use the break. This way he'd get back to work with a fresh eye.

He pushed back his chair, rose, and headed up to the second floor and the main conference room.

All the FI team members filed in, grabbed some coffee or, in Claire's case, herbal tea, and gathered around the conference room table. Hero stretched out on the Oriental carpet, head held high, looking like a vigilant attendee, ready for a call to action.

Casey stroked his head and took her seat at the head of the table.

"No mind-blowing revelations, I just wanted us all on the same page," she began. "As expected, I've already received calls from both the twenty-sixth and the first precincts. The detectives asked a slew of leading questions, basically trying to figure out if we knew more than they did. I was as gracious as can be, but of course, I gave them nothing. They, in return, made it quite clear that they expected to be kept up to speed, and even clearer that they were *not* happy to have us in the mix. They expect full access to Aimee, which I assured them they would have—*with* one or two of us present."

"Did they refuse that?" Marc asked.

Casey shook her head. "No. As I said, they're not pleased. But they didn't say that the only person Aimee could have with her if questioned is a lawyer, either."

"Which means they're not about to bring her up on charges." Marc swallowed some coffee. "She's obviously a person of interest but nothing more. There's no evidence implicating her, because none exists. Still, they want her on their side because she might be able to provide some relevant information."

A corner of Ryan's mouth lifted. "And how annoying for them that we'll be in their faces whenever they seek her out."

"Yeah, there's that, too," Marc responded, ignoring Ryan's sarcasm and addressing the situation with his customary pragmatism. "I suggest I back Casey up with the NYPD. I'm former law enforcement. So is Patrick, but he's tied up managing the security detail on Aimee. I can establish a connection with the detectives that will, hopefully, keep things from getting too unpleasant. Especially when the two Homicide teams step in."

"I agree," Casey said with a nod. "Plus, you have a very calming presence, which will be necessary. Not only for Aimee's sake but to put the detectives at ease. The less we provoke them, the better. So you and I will be the police contacts, Marc."

Claire sighed. "I have no update yet. I'm at an impasse right now."

"I'm sorry I couldn't get you something personal from Maher's apartment," Marc said. "I know it would give you something to connect to, but I couldn't risk contaminating the crime scene."

"Definitely not," Patrick agreed. "Not only would that potentially interfere with the police investigation but, if it ever came out that you had done that, the NYPD would cheerfully charge us with evidence tampering."

Ryan arched a brow. "They'd love that, wouldn't they? Well, we're way too smart to implicate ourselves. But speaking of not-so-kosher activities, here's what I've been up to." He filled the team in, leaving out the more intricate technical details that no one understood but giving them the overview of what he hoped to accomplish.

"How long will that take?" Casey asked.

"A few days, if we're lucky." Ryan made an impatient gesture. "It sucks, I know. But if I accelerated the process..."

"You might get caught. Which can't happen."

"Right. In the meantime, I'm digging into the Danforth connection between Maher and Edwell. Given the threatening words they flung at each other, it's a strong lead to run with."

"I agree." Casey turned to Patrick. "John is still watching Aimee?"

"John and Gary." Patrick was referring to Garrison Miles, a newer FI hire with an impressive resume. He'd worked FBI for twenty years in the New York field office's organized crime division. He and Patrick had handled multiple cases together, but Garrison had only recently retired from the bureau. Soon after, he'd contacted Patrick and expressed an interest in working security for FI. And Patrick had hired him five minutes after running it by Casey.

"John and Gary are relieving each other as needed," Patrick said. "But more often than not, they're both on duty. Two murders, double protection, just as the team discussed. Plus, I have additional backup at the ready."

"Good." Casey slanted a glance at Claire, who was looking utterly miserable at being stuck in neutral. "You need a physical object to hold in your hands in order to gain insights. I have an idea. How about if Emma and I set up a meeting with Daniel Maher? He'll know us by reputation. Which means he'll not only know we don't fail, he'll also know we have better, more unorthodox resources than law enforcement does. Once he hears that we're working on a case that overlaps with his son's murder, he'll see us. We'll all have the same goal—the hope that something he says can lead us to Chris's killer. And while we're talking—"

"I can find something of Chris's that I'll pocket and bring home to Claire." Emma looked positively ebullient. "It's a great idea. I know a lot about Chris Maher, his interests, his hobbies. Like he builds model cars—expensive sports cars—and then he goes out and buys the real things. I bet he has a few of those models lying around his father's place. Or maybe Daniel Maher will point out gifts Chris gave him or things he left at his father's place. Or maybe—"

"Okay, okay." Casey held up her hands, laughing as she did. "We all get the picture. I knew you'd love this opportunity to play the Artful Dodger."

Claire's relief was palpable. "That would be wonderful," she said. "Anything personal you can bring me, anything Chris Maher might have touched and that meant something to him—at least I'd have a chance of picking up energy that could help us."

"Then leave it to Emma and me." Casey glanced around the table. "Are we all caught up here?"

A series of nods.

"Good. Then I'll make the call to Daniel Maher."

***

Washington Heights
1:55 p.m.

Aimee peered through the peephole at her front door, double- and triple-checking that it was indeed Travis who stood there. Her entire body sagged with relief. There was no mistaking the close-cropped hair, dark blue eyes, and light-up-the-room smile that had won her over the day they'd met, both of them ordering a CannaBD beer at the counter of a local bar.

That brilliant smile faded a bit, and his brows drew together in puzzlement. "Aimee? It's me." He was clearly baffled by the wait time given the fact that he'd heard her on the other side of the door.

Aimee pulled it open. "I'm so glad you're here." She gave him as grateful a hug as she could, given the box of steaming pizza that was separating them.

"So am I. Give me a minute and I'll show you how glad." Travis strode into the apartment and set the pizza box down on the coffee table and the six-pack of CannaBD beer on the floor beside it. "I know you've got plenty of this on hand, but I wanted it to be my treat. It's part of my apology for being so unavailable this week."

He turned, started back to Aimee, and came to a dead halt, his smile totally vanishing as he watched her quickly and shakily double-locking the door. "Aimee, what is it? You're a wreck."

"Worse than that, if it's possible. I'm on total meltdown."

"What's going on?" Travis studied her face. "I thought your text was your way of telling me you feel neglected because I've been working ridiculous hours. Clearly, it's more."

Aimee's eyes slid shut, and she nodded. "A lot more. These past few days"—she opened her eyes, which were bright with unshed tears—"they've been hell."

Travis crossed over, took Aimee's hand, and led her to the sofa, where he eased her down beside him. He tipped up her chin so he could meet her gaze. "Talk to me."

Aimee hadn't realized how much she'd needed this. Part of her wanted to just fling herself into his arms, to feel the warmth of human contact. The other part was reticent given how new their relationship was. The sex between them was great. But that was a far cry from wrapping herself around him like a clinging piece of ivy.

"How much time do we have?" she settled for asking. "Because this isn't a one-slice-of-pizza story. Are you coming or going from a shift?"

"Coming. I worked the night shift and stayed on through the morning because we had a slew of emergencies. I fell asleep before I hit the sheets. I saw your text as soon as I woke up. I showered, got dressed, and answered your plea for pizza and company. At least I thought that's what you were asking for. Obviously, it was more. What is it?"

"I take it you haven't scanned the news," Aimee responded. She saw the blank expression on Travis's face as he shook his head. So she continued. "Chris Maher was murdered last night."

"Murdered?" Travis did a double take. "Was it a robbery?"

"No." Aimee didn't mince words. "And he's not the only victim I suspect was killed." With that, she blurted out the whole story—from her upsetting meeting with Rita and Chris, where he'd hit on her, to Rita's suspicious disappearance, to the questioning she'd gone through with the NYPD—both before and after Chris's murder—to her fear for her own life, to her hiring of Forensic Instincts.

Travis's expression went from shock to anger to worry to surprise and then back to worry again.

"I don't believe this," he said when she was finally finished. "You're telling me that whoever killed Rita Edwell and Chris Maher could also be after you?"

Aimee dragged her fingers through her hair. "There were three of us. Now there's just me. I don't know what the killer's motive is, and neither do the police, which scares me all the more. When I first went to Forensic Instincts, it was all about Rita and figuring out what happened to her. Now..." Her voice trailed off. "The coincidence just seems too close to be a fluke."

Travis had gone very still and he looked grim. "It doesn't sound like a coincidence to me. What does Forensic Instincts think? I've seen them in the news. They have a great success rate."

"They're on the same page as we are. They put security detail on me. Round-the-clock. And they're looking into everyone and everything. My guess is they're starting with Danforth. It's the only thing I know of that the three of us had in common."

Travis interlaced his fingers with Aimee's. "Why didn't you tell me about this sooner? All I knew was that you were asking Rita to set up a meeting with Chris Maher."

Aimee stared down at their joined hands. "Two reasons. One, you were overwhelmed at work and practically unreachable. You lost a patient this week. When you texted, you sounded drained. And two, we're still pretty new. I wasn't sure you wanted all this dumped on you."

"We might be new, but I care about you. Of course I'd want to know. I'm pissed enough that Maher not only grabbed your leg but threatened you if you spoke the words *sexual harassment*."

"I was afraid he'd killed Rita and was coming after me next. I was wrong. It's someone entirely different." Aimee sighed. "There's no point in rehashing this. It's in the detectives' and Forensic Instincts' hands. Can we just eat, drink, and talk about normal things that couples talk about? That's really what I need."

"Done." Travis flipped open the pizza box, put two slices on a wide paper plate, and handed it to Aimee, along with a bottle of beer. "We'll talk about normal things couples talk about." A corner of his mouth lifted as he served. "And after that, we'll *do* the normal things couples do—only better. I'll make sure to divert you for hours. I promise."

10

East 84th Street
Manhattan, New York
Tuesday, 3:25 p.m.

Daniel Maher lived in a four-bedroom apartment of a modern, jaw-dropping Upper East Side high-rise. Its fifty-story elegance rose over the quietly residential neighborhood close to both Central Park and Museum Mile, offering its residents open space, unparalleled beauty, and numerous cultural attractions. Upscale boutiques and corner coffee shops lined the streets, giving the neighborhood almost a suburban feel, separate and apart from the pounding intensity of Midtown Manhattan.

The customarily peaceful neighborhood was anything but that when Casey and Emma arrived.

The periphery of Maher's building was swarming with members of the media, crowding close and hoping to catch a glimpse of Daniel Maher, maybe even to get a few words from him about his son's murder. That wasn't about to happen—not just because the poor man was undoubtedly locked away, inside his apartment grieving—but because he had an army-sized team of security lining the street and posted inside the building's white marble lobby. Three police officers were also posted strategically at the front of the building, clearly assigned to protect the peace. The doorman himself looked like a bouncer, his powerful arms folded across his chest, his stance wide and threatening, and his features set in a just-try-me scowl.

No one was getting near the place, much less inside.

"These vultures suck," Emma muttered under her breath as she and Casey wove their way through the crowd. "The poor guy just lost his son. Can't they just leave him alone?"

"Not in this century," Casey replied, jostling her way along. "You know the media. We've dealt with them enough." She grabbed Emma's arm and pulled her forward, up to the bouncer-doorman who stared them down like an angry bull.

"Casey Woods and Emma Stirling," Casey said without preamble. "From Forensic Instincts. We have a three-thirty appointment with Daniel Maher." She kept her voice calm and low. "Please feel free to check with him."

The bouncer blinked twice, the only indication that he'd even heard Casey. He didn't call upstairs to verify the information Casey had just provided. But after looking them up and down, he said, "ID."

They both produced their driver's licenses, which the bouncer scanned, and then he nodded. "Mr. Maher's expecting you." He gestured at one of the security guys, who eased aside so the bouncer could open the entranceway door just wide enough for Casey and Emma to pass.

"Get in—now," he ordered.

The order wasn't necessary. Casey and Emma were practically propelled into the lobby by the media mongers who crushed forward the instant they saw the door ajar and smelled an opportunity.

The opportunity was slammed in their faces, and the bouncer resumed his position.

"Geez," Emma said, catching her breath and regaining her balance. "I'll have black-and-blue marks for a week from that."

"Um-hum." Casey acknowledged the comment, but she was too busy sizing up their surroundings. The lobby was like a white marble sculpture with chrome accents and a sweeping horseshoe-shaped reception desk. Behind the desk sat two attendees—one man and one woman—both in their mid-thirties, both impeccably dressed, and both, even while working on their laptops, poised like seated sentries. The tenants here paid for their privacy. It was up to these two to ensure that they got it.

Casey tipped her head at Emma and walked straight to the desk. The man—Drew, according to what his gold nameplate read—appeared to be grappling with a computer issue of some kind. The woman—with the engraved word *Melissa* on her nameplate—was focused on her work but in a much less agitated state than her coworker.

As a result, Casey turned to her. "Good afternoon."

Melissa looked up and adjusted her designer eyeglasses with fingertips that boasted a flawless French manicure. "May I help you?" she asked with a cordial smile.

Casey indicated herself and then Emma. "I'm Casey Woods and this is Emma Stirling. We have a three-thirty appointment with Daniel Maher."

"Let me check." Melissa's fingers tapped on her keyboard, and she scanned her monitor. Then, she nodded and looked back up at Casey and Emma. There was a spark of interest in her eyes, which told Casey that, along with their names, their company name was also listed in the appointment entry.

"May I see some form of ID, please?" Although she stayed very professional, Melissa looked more than a little impressed.

Once again, both Casey and Emma produced their driver's licenses.

"Thank you." Melissa studied the licenses and then handed them back, after which she pointed to a side corridor a little way down the hall. "The elevators are located there. Take the second one on your left. You'll be going to the thirty-seventh floor, apartment D."

Casey nodded. "Thank you for your time."

Emma followed Casey to the appropriate elevator, which responded to their page in under a minute. They stepped inside, pressed the number thirty-seven, and waited. The doors slid shut soundlessly and the car began its ascent.

"Wow," Emma said, exhaling in a rush. "This place is amazing. How much do you think it costs to live here?"

Casey's lips curved. "Why? Are you thinking of putting in an application?"

"Right." Emma grinned. "I couldn't even afford to rent the elevator, although it's big enough to turn into a studio apartment. Besides, this part of the city isn't my thing. Too old and farty, too boring and quiet. But seeing it up close like this, knowing we're about to meet a famous movie star—that's pretty awesome."

"Remember why we're here." Casey's words pulled Emma down from the clouds. "We're not fawning over a famous Hollywood legend, we're interviewing a grieving father. Our job is to learn something that will help keep Aimee safe, which means figuring out who killed Rita Edwell and Chris Maher and why."

"You forgot the fun part." Emma looked like the cat who was about to swallow the canary. "I get to lift something of Chris Maher's from his father's palace so we can give it to Claire."

"Carefully," Casey cautioned. "Very, very carefully. We'll choose the object together. And you'll make it happen without landing us in jail."

"That's what I do best." Emma wasn't the slightest bit perturbed. In fact, she looked more and more excited as the elevator floor numbers that were lighting up got closer to thirty-seven.

The *bing* announced they'd reached their destination. The door slid open.

Casey and Emma both stepped out, noting the arrows that pointed them in the right direction. They veered right and followed the apartment letters that led them to D.

Casey put her finger on the doorbell. "Remember the rules."

"Always."

"Good. Then let's make this happen."

A fortyish-year-old man, medium height but built like a brick shithouse, opened the apartment door, stepping aside to admit Casey and Emma.

"Ms. Woods, Ms. Stirling, I'm Malcolm Evans, Mr. Maher's personal assistant." He shook both their hands, and, given the strength of his grip and the size of his biceps, Casey deduced he was more a bodyguard than an assistant. Not particularly surprising. Daniel Maher was a household name. It was logical that he'd want a muscle man to ward off eager fans and persistent media.

"Please have a seat." Evans led them into a sunken living room with contemporary furnishings, walls of modern—and Casey suspected genuine—paintings, and a panorama of windows overlooking Central Park. The view was lovely and would be stunning at night. On the glass coffee table were a few ceramic pieces, an indelible marker, and a stack of photos that had been in the process of being autographed.

Not a lot to work with in terms of pickpocketing. Emma was going to have to get creative. Or else they were going to have to find a way to access other rooms in the apartment. Either way, this was going to be a challenge.

"Would either of you like a cup of coffee or tea?" Evans asked politely.

"Thank you, no," Casey replied. "We're fine."

"Then Mr. Maher will be right with you."

"I'm here." Daniel Maher walked into the room, hands shoved in his pockets, looking like a beaten man. His rugged features were drawn, his eyes were red-rimmed, and his shoulders were slumped. He looked ten years older than his publicity shots, but Casey had the feeling it had less to do with the lack of makeup than it did the tragedy that had just smacked him between the eyes.

Casey and Emma both rose as he approached them.

"I'm so very sorry for your loss, Mr. Maher," Casey said, shaking his hand.

"So am I." Emma was staring, as only Emma would. Investigation or not, cautious words from Casey or not, she was still star-struck about being in the same room as *the* Daniel Maher. "I've seen all your movies," she blurted out. "You're amazing. I can't believe I'm meeting you in person, even if it is under such tragic circumstances..." Her voice trailed off as she caught herself, and she flushed. "I apologize. Sometimes my mouth moves faster than my brain."

A tired hint of a smile. "Thank you," he said. "I appreciate the compliment. I, too, wish the circumstances were different. And please, both of you call me Daniel." He gestured for them to reseat themselves on the sofa, and he followed suit, perching at the edge of a matching chair. "I know your company's reputation. I'm praying you can help find the animal who killed my son."

"We'll do everything we can," Casey said.

"Whatever you're currently being paid, I'll double it. Triple it. I'll pay any amount you name."

"That won't be necessary. As I told you, we're currently representing a client whose life is also threatened by whoever killed your son. That client is paying our fee. No additional compensation is required."

"And you can't give me your client's name or explain the overlap to me because it would violate confidentiality," Daniel surmised aloud.

"Exactly." Casey flipped open her portfolio and took out her pen. In interviews such as this one, she found it far more effective to take notes by hand rather than typing into a tablet. People responded better to the personal feel of talking to her face rather than to the back of her iPad and, as a result, were far more open to her questions—and more relaxed about supplying their answers.

"Our questions will probably be similar to the ones the detectives asked you," she said with another swift perusal of the room. Her surveillance confirmed her original worry. The place was devoid of knickknacks. Emma was going to have a hell of a job finding something to lift for Claire. Well, they'd have to improvise—later.

"Please be patient," Casey continued. "We have a way of running with ideas as they strike us."

Daniel nodded. "Go ahead."

"What was your relationship like with Chris? Were you close? Did you spend much time together?"

Daniel blew out a harsh breath, clearly pained by repeating this answer. "Sadly, no we weren't very close. Chris's mother died when he was young and my career was just beginning to skyrocket. So I substituted the time I didn't have with the money that I did. I regret that decision and have for so many years. But you can't undo life. Chris was raised by nannies and driven to after-school activities by chauffeurs."

"In Los Angeles?" Casey asked.

"Initially, yes. But I've always had dual residences. Chris loved Manhattan. So he lived most of his life here, with staff members I hired. He was adept at eluding authority figures, and he wasn't much about adhering to rules. In short, he managed to do whatever he wanted, whenever he wanted, despite the attempts at supervision."

"No summer or after-school jobs?" Casey asked tactfully.

Maher gave a humorless laugh, steepling his fingers on his lap as he spoke. "Money was never an issue for him, so no. I gave him everything he wanted and more. He was your stereotypical poor little rich boy. Lacking in attention, overindulged financially. And nothing changed when he became a man. I continue—*continued*," he painfully corrected himself, "to transfer large sums of money to him on a regular basis. I also helped him when he found himself in… need of investment capital."

Casey looked up from the notes she'd been taking. "You gave him the money he required to pay off the women he'd harassed and to relocate them elsewhere."

Daniel's brows shot up. "You know about that?"

"We do."

"Nothing was ever proven." Daniel was instantly on the defensive.

Casey defused the defensiveness right away. "Whether or not the allegations were true is not part of our investigation, Daniel," she said. "Not unless you think any of those women was furious enough to kill your son."

"Quite the contrary. They were all delighted with their arrangements—lovely apartments, good jobs, and an exorbitant amount of spending money. Given that, plus the lack of evidence to any harassment claims they might make, I'm quite sure they'd have no desire to kill off their cash cow."

"So no threats or blackmail attempts?"

"None. And that's something Chris *would* have come to me about."

"Since he was getting all his make-it-go-away money from you."

"Yes." Daniel gave a rueful sigh. "I'm not proud of any of this. But Chris was my son. I had to help him. Even at the risk of my own reputation. If word of my paying people off leaked out, there'd be a media frenzy and my career would take a huge hit. But I'd let Chris down in so many ways over the years. Who he'd become was very much my fault and my failure. And if any of those allegations were indeed true, my actions could also make some amends to the women who were hurt by Chris."

Casey couldn't help but feel sorry for Daniel Maher. He might have screwed up with Chris, but he wasn't a bad man. And he'd loved his son. No one deserved to lose a child.

She had one more area to probe before steering the conversation in a meatier direction. At the same time, she was still worrying about what Emma could get her hands on for Claire.

She had to buy time, come up with a reason to visit other parts of the apartment.

"Did you know that Chris was heavily into drugs, enough so that he was probably an addict?" she asked.

Daniel cast his gaze downward. "I didn't before today. The detectives told me. I can't say I was shocked. Saddened but not shocked. I never understood Chris's wild lifestyle nor the fact that he was always at the helm of organizing over-the-top parties."

"He probably liked living on the edge," Casey replied tactfully. "Plus enjoying the strong sense of power it gave him."

"I suppose." Daniel regarded them thoughtfully. "You're very insightful. And you're probably right. Chris loved to be in the limelight and to come across as bigger than life."

"I'd say that's a good assessment." Casey paused, having gotten everything she needed from the routine questions.

On to the more pertinent subject.

"You said that Chris loved Manhattan. Is that why he chose to attend Danforth University?"

Was it Casey's imagination or did Daniel shift ever so slightly in his chair?

"That was part of it," he said. "But Chris also knew how prestigious a school Danforth is. He got a first-rate education."

"And his college experience as a whole? Was he happy there?"

Another shift in his seat. “Chris didn’t confide in me. As I told you, we weren’t close. But he seemed happy. And he never told me otherwise. The detectives asked me about Danforth, as well. They were curious as to whether or not Chris attended alumni events—to which I don’t know the answer. They said the questions were routine. But now I’m beginning to wonder. Maybe you’ll be more forthright than they were. Why is everyone so interested in Chris’s education?”

“I can’t speak for the detectives,” Casey replied, lying through her teeth. “In my case, I’m thinking about how much the other students might have resented him for having such a famous father and how easily things came to him. Danforth is a pressure cooker and is super competitive. That kind of culture breeds a lot of bitterness when it comes to privileged kids—especially privileged kids who have established themselves as bigger than life all on their own.”

“You think Chris made enemies that far back?” Daniel asked in surprise.

“It’s possible.”

“Then why wait all these years to kill him?”

“He’s even more renowned now, thanks to his blog. Millions of followers. People hanging on his every word and trying his recipes while watching their favorite teams compete. Another major coup. Another reason to increase already existing resentment.”

“I never thought of that.”

“So back to his college days. Do you know if he retained any relationships from then? Friends? Professors? Advisors? Anyone we could speak to who might fill in the blanks?”

Daniel spread his hands wide, looking utterly frustrated. “I can’t help you. I wish I could. I can authorize Danforth to release any records that might assist you. I made the same offer to the police. Would that help?”

“That would give us something to work with, so yes. I’d appreciate that.”

"I'll take care of it right away. You'll have those records within a day." Daniel looked utterly miserable. "And now you're going to ask me about his current friends. I don't even know their names. Have you spoken to the owner or employees of the steakhouse he used to work in? They might be able to fill in some blanks. Plus, as you said, Chris had millions of followers on that blog of his. I'm not computer savvy, but maybe you could find a way to reach out to them? Maybe through social media? I wouldn't begin to know how to help you on that score. That's one thing Chris did do for me—handled my social media accounts and my online presence. I can do basic things like emails, but overall, I'm technology illiterate."

Casey felt the almost imperceptible stiffening of Emma's body beside her. She'd thought of something. And whatever it was, it was essential that it happened now. Because this interview was over and there was no way to prolong it or ask for a tour.

Casey shut her portfolio and responded to Daniel's suggestion. "We're already working on the things and the contacts you mentioned. I'm sure the police are, as well. The NYPD is exceptional. But we have more targeted resources than they do, budgets and manpower being what they are. So we'll blow through your ideas ASAP. Please contact Danforth for us so we can probe that avenue. And if you think of anything else pertinent, please let us know. Anything we can do to bring the killer to justice, we will." She took out a business card and handed it to Daniel.

"I most certainly will," he said.

He came to his feet. So did Casey and Emma.

Emma hung back, looking wistfully down at the coffee table. "Your publicity photos are really cool. Do you get lots of requests for them?"

A small smile curved Daniel's lips. "Believe it or not, yes. Even in this modern computer age, there are fans who want the real thing. I try to accommodate them to the best of my ability. Chris had some software that produced the photos and a printer that took glossy paper. I haven't a clue how any of it worked. He just got the finished photos to me, I signed them, and my secretary sent them out."

Emma shuffled around, her cheeks pink as she spoke. "You must have a limited supply. Would you... I mean could you… sign one for me? Like I said, I'm a *huge* fan. My roommates would be totally jealous if I showed up with an autographed picture of you." She continued to gaze longingly at the stack of photos. "Unless you don't have enough."

Daniel was already bending down, reaching for his marker and one of the photos. "You don't have to ask twice. It would be my pleasure. I assume you spell your name E-M-M-A?"

"Yes! Oh, thank you!" Emma beamed as he presented the personally autographed picture to her. She held it by the edges, as if even one smudge would mar its beauty.

Casey bit back a smile as she watched Emma in action. FI's Artful Dodger should never be underestimated.

They made their exit, and three minutes later, they were back in the elevator, descending to the ground floor, with Emma groping in her tote bag. She pulled out a few Ziplocs, each a different size. Fumbling with them, she settled on the gallon-sized bag and shoved the rest of the bags back into her tote. Then, she opened the larger bag, slid the photo inside, and sealed it shut.

"Almost no new fingerprints," she said triumphantly. "And definitely handled by Chris. Mission accomplished—and legally, I might add."

Casey chuckled. "You're one-of-a-kind, Emma."

"That was partially dumb luck—with some added smarts." Emma was beaming ear to ear. "I saw Daniel's office diagonally across the hall, and I was racking my brain, trying to come up with a reason to see it. Then—pay dirt. Daniel told us Chris had formatted and printed those photos. That means he'd handled them. And that means Claire has what she needs."

"I'm proud of you."

"Actually, so am I."

11

Colts River, New Jersey
5:25 p.m.

Victor was closeted in his home office, fingers steepled on his desk, as his mind raced over the past days' disruptive events together with the holes he had yet to plug. On some vague level, he remembered Frances poking her head in a short while ago, announcing that dinner would be ready at six. Given their empty nest, Victor did his best not to disappoint her by letting business cut into their evening meal. But he had a lot more to think through before he left this room.

He'd started damage control by arranging a brief meeting with Chris Maher's killer. They'd met in a deserted section of woods far away from Victor's home. Victor had made sure to keep his voice calm, non-accusatory as he presented the situation. It was the only way to resolve the matter, given who he was dealing with. He had to put a stop to any future overlap kills, but he had to do it in a way that didn't incite violence. His tactics had worked, and his questions had been answered. As he suspected, the guy had gone rogue, carrying out the hit for reasons of his own. Victor had explained the problem to him and strongly requested that he not go after someone who could jeopardize Victor's operation—which might, in turn, curtail the lucrative payments Victor was able to provide.

His message had struck home, as he knew it would. The lust for killing was only tempered by the lust for money.

Hopefully, he'd done enough to prevent any future problems.

Once home, Victor had called Stefano's private line and asked for an update on the Chris Maher investigation. There was nothing much new, other than the fact that Homicide had called in additional resources on this high-profile case. Daniel Maher had made sure of that.

Victor took the only recourse he could. He asked Stefano to arrange for any incriminating information found in Chris Maher's Danforth University files to vanish, including any and all ties Maher had to Rita Edwell. Stefano had the access to take care of it, but his computer skills weren't sophisticated enough to do what Victor required. Victor assured him that he'd immediately get him the help he needed and that that help would contact him right away. This whole procedure had to be completed ASAP so the information would look like it never existed.

He made the urgent phone call. Voice mail. He swore, hanging up the phone and making a mental note to call back in a half hour.

That was as much damage control as he could do for now. He would also have to rebuild his resources and expedite the acquisition of his candidate.

Victor blew out a sharp breath and rubbed his temples, suddenly aware of the crushing headache that was pounding at his skull. Stress and lack of food. Bad combination.

The loss of Rita Edwell left a gaping hole that needed to be filled. Why did she have to be at death's door? With that knowledge, she just didn't give a shit anymore. She'd openly threatened him. That had forced his hand. It had also left him without one of his key inside people—someone who could do what was necessary, both before and after the process was complete.

He had others. But he wanted another Rita. She was sharp, well-connected, and hooked on the hefty fees she was receiving. Finding a replacement wasn't going to be easy. And in the interim, he needed to find new blood.

It was time to call Linc again.

***

This time, Linc answered on the second ring.

"I figured I'd be hearing from you soon," he said. "The past few days must have been eventful."

"They've been tough. I've had my hands full."

"I'll bet. That's why I left you alone. I knew you'd bring me in when you were ready."

"I'm ready. I need you to work your magic on some Danforth files." Victor went on to explain. "You'll have Stefano to assist you with the non-techno-work."

"I assume you need this done now."

"I needed this done yesterday. But now will work."

"I'll take care of it. That'll erase any tie between Rita and Chris Maher, much less his murder."

"Hopefully, yeah," Victor replied. "I'd feel a lot better if his father wasn't a famous movie star with enough money to dig deep."

"If that were the case, Chris wouldn't be a Danforth alum at all. A Catch-22."

Victor blew out a breath, wishing his damned headache would go away. "The timing of all this sucks. With Rita Edwell's disappearance, the last thing I needed was for Chris Maher to be murdered. And the link between them, naturally, is Danforth University."

"We'll just have to nudge the cops in a different direction."

"That's the plan. Meanwhile, Stefano is shredding as fast as he can."

"I'll take over wherever he leaves off, including deleting Rita Edwell's log-in data."

"I'm counting on that. Stefano is good, but you're a pro. I need everything scrubbed clean."

"No problem." Linc was quiet and thoughtful for a moment. "Do you think it's a coincidence or did the same person kill Edwell and Maher? Or do you think Edwell just dropped out of sight and then came back and killed Maher herself?"

"From what I heard, the cops have no idea and no suspects. And I really don't care—as long as the investigation doesn't focus on Chris's relationship to Danforth." Victor wasn't letting this conversation get out of hand. He had the utmost faith and trust in Linc. Still, in this case, he was keeping all shared info on a need-to-know basis. "Let's concentrate on where we go from here."

"You want me to find a replacement for Edwell," Linc said.

"At least get the ball rolling," Victor replied. "It's going to take months to get this done. Use your contacts. Find a good candidate who's currently working at a high-level position at another top school we do business with. Someone who'll do what we need and, if they want to transfer schools to move up, find someone who the hiring committee at that college or university will have no problem saying yes to."

"I'll handle it. And, yeah, it's not going to be easy. But I started checking out possibilities since Edwell disappeared. I'll eventually find someone and then turn him or her over to you."

"Good." Victor liked what he was hearing, and he could feel the pounding in his head begin to ease. "And speaking of other schools we do business with, how's it going with new recruits?"

"I have one definite prospect and three more I'm still vetting. I need to check out some of the financials to make sure that it's a fit."

Victor opened his mouth to reply just as Frances poked her head into his office and gave him a hurt look.

"It's six fifteen," she said. "Can you finish up your business tomorrow? Dinner is getting cold."

"Sure." Victor wasn't pissed. He'd finished up the pressing parts of his business with Linc anyway. "Pour us each a glass of wine," he told Frances, pushing back his chair. "I'll be in by then." Into the phone, he said, "Give me a call when you have things in place."

"No problem. Enjoy dinner."

***

Offices of Forensic Instincts, third floor
Tribeca, New York
6:30 p.m.

Dusk was still settling over the brownstone, and Claire's yoga room was quiet still. The curtains were drawn over the two small windows, shutting out the last filaments of daylight. The lamps were dimmed, and the door was carefully locked.

Claire herself—the room's sole occupant—sat in lotus position on the soothing lime and turquoise area rug. Her eyes were shut. The photo of Daniel Maher lay on the rug right above her knees.

She took a few deep, cleansing breaths, clearing her mind and opening it up to the unique energy flow necessary to accomplish her goal.

Once she felt ready, she placed her fingertips lightly on the photo—not the edges the way Emma had done but directly on Daniel Maher's face.

Slices of emotional pain lanced through her. Daniel's pain. His sense of loss. So heart-wrenching that it was almost too much to withstand. A devastated man who'd lost his son. Parental guilt over anything he might have done to prevent this from happening. Deep-seated regret at the time lost during Chris's childhood. More regret at the time they'd never share in the years to come. Anger at whoever had taken his child away and how brutally it had been done. Determination to get at the truth and see the killer punished to the max.

With another slow inward breath, Claire eased her fingers away from Daniel's face and toward the sides of the photo—the logical spots where Chris had held the picture.

Abruptly, Daniel's anguish vanished, replaced by the tortured onslaught of Chris's last moments of life. Jolts of agonizing pain scorched Claire's fingertips, shot through her body like wildfire. She gasped, fighting the primal instinct that screamed for her to pull away. She wouldn't give in. She had to stay with this, open up and let the sensations flow.

Choking. A sharp object breaking the skin around his neck, drawing blood and suffocating the life out of him. He fought—hard—gripping the strand that was wrapped around his neck and pulling with all his might. But the pressure intensified. Panic rose in his chest, and he flailed about until all the breath had left his lungs and his body succumbed. Life slipped away into nothingness.

The killer was shrouded in darkness. He leaned over to check his handiwork, ensured there was no pulse. Then he pulled out a glove and a heavy knife and stuck the knife through the glove, nearly tearing it in two. In one violent motion, he brought down his arm, stabbing the glove into Chris's thigh, and leaned back to admire his handiwork.

Dammit. Why couldn't Claire see his face? His build? Anything that could help identify him?

He half turned, his profile cast in shadows, and smiled at the blood oozing out of Chris's thigh. Then he slipped out of the apartment.

As he left, an eerie feeling came over Claire. Something that slithered through her like a lethal snake.

Her skin began to crawl.

She was familiar with this man. Somehow she'd encountered him before. He was brutal, seasoned, and emotionless. He enjoyed killing, got off on the thrill of it.

How did she know him? Had they met? No. But she recognized his aura, the evil inside him. She'd come up against him in the past—another time, another place.

It was imperative that she remembered.

12

Offices of Forensic Instincts
Ryan's lair
7:45 p.m.

Ryan had spent the entire afternoon and evening digging as deeply as he could into Rita Edwell's life, hacking into the Danforth University database, and accessing everything he could.

Professionally, the woman appeared to have been a paragon of virtue throughout her dozen years at Danforth. From the Office of Undergraduate Admissions to the dean of Student Affairs to her current—and final—role as director of Alumni Relations, she'd seemingly done it all right. Her promotions were justifiable. She'd worked her way up by being exceptional. No red flags to suggest nepotism or shady dealings in her climb to the top. Judging from the scope of her job and the professional correspondence Ryan had managed to find, she'd clearly built a widespread contact list that included everyone from the students and faculty at Danforth to colleagues at other top-tier universities. Ryan was itching to get a bigger picture of that contact list, along with any and all phone calls Rita had made. But as he'd told Casey, getting the data from Rita's cell phone would be another day or two in coming. Much as he'd love to just hack the T-Mobile system, it was too risky. Too obvious and too easy for the carrier's IT team to discover. No, he had to wait for the route he'd taken to provide him with his answers.

Back to what he could access on Rita Edwell.

She appeared to be primarily a loner, with some casual friends from Danforth and a few fellow educators she grabbed drinks with from time to time. Ryan couldn't find any serious romantic involvements in the recent past. Other than excelling at her job, all her energies had been targeted on fighting a losing health battle.

Time to check out where her life and Maher's crisscrossed.

Ryan pulled up the Danforth files Daniel Maher had supplied, along with the ones Ryan had hacked from the university's database. The former didn't yield more than the bare-bones facts. But the latter most definitely did. Rita had been a key deciding factor in Chris Maher's admission to Danforth. She'd lobbied hard for him, despite the fact that his grades weren't that outstanding. She'd stressed his potential, although she never specified what that potential was, other than to point out the sophisticated marketing work he'd done for his celebrity father—a claim that was quite a stretch, in Ryan's opinion—as well as a germ of an idea for a blog that had promise. Interesting. Chris had been playing around with "*Snacks for Sports*" even then.

Also interesting was that Rita's hard sell barely touched on Daniel Maher's superstardom and his staggering wealth. Fame and money were huge motivators to a college admissions committee. Documented or not, they had to have factored into Rita's push for Chris's matriculation. And yet it was just a mere mention in Rita's emails to the rest of the admissions committee. Very odd. To further compound things, Aimee's recollection of Rita's threat to Chris at the bar was that she'd made him and she could unmake him. Had there been a financial incentive offered to Rita by Daniel Maher and had she taken it—*and* buried it? Was that why Chris had come back at her saying that he owned her? Did he know about the bribe and was holding it over her head, even though, by revealing it, his father would be implicated, as well?

On the flipside, did Rita anticipate that Chris was a loose cannon and might say something unfavorable about her to Aimee? Was that the reason she'd insisted on attending the meeting at the bar? To make sure Maher didn't let something snarky and incriminating slip?

Ryan muttered under his breath. He knew in his gut that he'd just touched the tip of the iceberg. There were a lot more unknowns and specifics that he had to dig up and analyze. He was just getting started on the good stuff.

There was a tentative knock at his partially open door, and Claire leaned around it.

"Hi," she said quietly. "I know you're working, but I—" Her voice broke a little. "I wondered if we could talk, just for a few minutes."

Ryan knew Claire well enough to recognize that tone. He swiveled around in his chair and came to his feet.

"Are you okay?" he asked.

"Not really. I'm a mess. I wouldn't be bothering you otherwise."

"You're never bothering me." Ryan walked over, took Claire's hand, and drew her into his lair, reaching behind her to shut and lock the door. "What happened?"

"I took the photo of Daniel Maher into my yoga room." Her breath was coming quickly and her face was bathed in perspiration. "And all the images and energy that came through nearly brought me down. I don't know what to do, I'm so freaked out."

Ryan frowned. Claire looked like hell, and her reaction was more extreme than usual. "Sit down." He gestured at the futon across the room. "I'll make you some herbal tea and we can talk."

"I can't sit." Claire began pacing around. "I'm not even sure I can talk."

"Try." Ryan put a mug of hot water in his microwave and brought it to a boil. Then he dunked a bag of herbal tea into it and brought it over to Claire. "This will help. It always does."

She took it, staring dazedly into the cup as the tea darkened the water. "This wasn't just a wave of stimuli smothering me all at once," she said. "There was more. It was the same taunting evil I keep feeling—only stronger. There's a sense of unbearable awareness that I know this killer."

Ryan blinked. "As in personally?"

Claire's shoulders lifted and fell, and she took a sip of tea on autopilot. "I don't know. I can't see his face. So I can't link him to anyone I've met. And yet I know our paths have crossed." She raised her head to meet Ryan's gaze. "I sat in my yoga room and racked my brain until I started seeing little black spots. Still, nothing." A pained sigh. "So, as has become a habit, I came to you. I'm not sure how I thought you could help. Maybe you could add something scientific to the equation. Doubtful, right? Then maybe you could just say something that would calm me down."

A corner of Ryan's mouth lifted. "That's not how I usually accomplish that."

"Yes, I know." Clare was still vibrating. "But I wasn't thinking about sex when I ran down those steps."

"Then think about it now." Ryan took the teacup away and set it down on the nearest table. He placed his hands on Claire's shoulders, rubbed them up and down her arms in a gentle, soothing motion until he felt her trembling ease, then turn into something else.

"Come here," he said softly, giving her the chance to show him if she was ready.

Claire didn't hesitate. She took the single step that separated them, simultaneously tugging off her T-shirt.

That was all Ryan needed. He had them both naked and on the futon in mere seconds.

Hours later, Claire wriggled onto her side and sank limply against Ryan, burying her face in his chest. She couldn't move, nor did she have any desire to. Ryan was lying flat on his back, one arm thrown over his eyes, his breathing ragged and rough. With great effort, he groped for the blanket that was crumpled on the floor and pulled it over them.

Claire gave a grateful sigh. "Umm," she mumbled.

"What inspired that happy sound, the blanket or me?" Ryan murmured into the crown of her hair.

"You know the answer to that."

"True. But I still like to hear it."

"Okay, then five percent the blanket and the rest you."

Ryan chuckled. "I'll try to soothe my ego about the lost five percent."

"Like your ego ever needs soothing." Claire shifted a bit. "Has this futon always been so lumpy?"

"It gets lumpier every time." Ryan's grin broadened. "Should I replace it?"

"I don't think so. It's kind of like an old friend. Lots of memories."

"Such a sentimentalist," Ryan teased. "Although I *am* partial to this lumpy thing myself."

"Guess I'm rubbing off on you."

"I like that image."

Claire had to smile. "So do I."

Ryan's fingers trailed up and down her spine. "Better now?"

Claire didn't pretend to misunderstand. "Much. You've held the monsters at bay."

"Good." Ryan yawned, lifting his arm long enough to glance at his Apple Watch. "Ten forty-five," he announced. "I should get back to work. But you wrecked me. I can barely lift my head."

"I'm not doing much better." Claire's eyelids were drooping. "Maybe a couple of hours' sleep?"

"Sounds good. We need some recoup time."

"Recoup time from our recoup time."

"Exactly." Ryan wrapped his arms around her. "Sleep."

"Okay." Claire snuggled closer and drifted off.

Ryan was close behind. His last coherent thought was that he doubted they'd be awake before sunrise.

***

He sat, hunched over his laptop, rewatching, for the umpteenth time, the You Tube video he'd saved on the NYPD channel of the press conference. He felt the same adrenaline rush shoot through him. The police were stumped. No leads. No motive. Nothing but a bunch of NYPD detectives scrambling around and soliciting help from the public. How pathetic. And how blood-pumping was the amount of publicity his kill was receiving? One-point-two million views and still going strong. The victim was an entitled rich boy with a superstar of a father—every news show, talk show, and entertainment show wanted a piece of it. That meant countless more hours of new YouTube footage and media entertainment for him. He might even put off planning his next kill while he soaked up the fame that was anonymous to everyone but him.

Him and one other.

He'd been warned not to mix business with pleasure. Okay, fine. The business assignments paid the bills and a whole lot more, but they were routine and fairly uninspiring. The other kills—his personal kills—they were creative and exciting. They eased the perpetual anger that raged in his gut and quieted his thirst for vengeance.

He'd pick his next victim soon enough.

For now, it was time to replay the video and watch it again.

13

NYPD first precinct
16 Ericsson Place
Manhattan, New York
Wednesday, 10:15 a.m.

Aimee exhaled sharply as she walked out of the precinct doors, with Casey and Marc flanking her on either side. It hadn't been as bad as she'd expected, thanks to their easing her way. They'd made it clear to the questioning detectives that Aimee was their client. Simultaneously, Casey assured the detectives that FI wanted to keep a low profile, so as not to give the media more ammo to ignite this investigation and blow it out of the water.

Mixed reaction. Annoyance at having to deal with the Forensic Instincts team. Relief that FI's role was going to be kept quiet.

As a result, no argument was voiced.

Aimee tried to be as forthcoming as possible. She'd only met Chris Maher one time, that night at the bar. She had no idea who his friends and enemies were, nor who might have had a motive to kill him. As for Chris's relationship with Rita, she knew just as little. Rita had never spoken about him before the meeting she'd arranged, other than to warn Aimee of his vices—vices that weren't exactly a secret. And, yes, there was clearly hostility between Rita and Chris. Aimee had felt it. But Rita had never elaborated on it, and Aimee had felt uncomfortable asking.

She freely explained her own one-time interaction with Chris—and she didn't hide her fear that he'd harm her in some way, either physically or reputation-wise. She'd been angry and scared, but she'd also felt sick when she heard about his murder. The detectives had nodded and seemed to accept her reactions.

Occasionally, the pressure exerted on her to "remember" things she never knew got intense. Each time that happened, Casey and Marc put a quick halt to it, making it clear that the detectives were overstepping their bounds and that Aimee had already told them all she knew. And pissed off or not, they'd backed off.

Finally, Casey had leaned forward and shut the lid on her iPad—a clear message that this interview was over. "I'm sure you can confirm the answers Ms. Bregman gave you with those she provided to the twenty-sixth," she said.

Marc pushed back his chair and rose. "We'll be available for any further questions you have. But I don't think our client can give you any more than she already has."

"I really can't," Aimee had said in a shaky voice. "But as Marc said, I'll make myself available if I'm needed."

The three of them exited the room.

Now Aimee walked on shaky legs, glancing from Casey to Marc and back. "Did I do okay?"

"You were great," Casey assured her. "You told them everything you could. If they think of something else, they'll let you know. But I'm pretty sure they realize you're a dead end."

"I hope so." Aimee raked her fingers through her hair. "I'm not sure how much more of this I can take. I'm not holding anything back. I just don't have any answers to their questions."

"We know that," Marc said. "Just stay calm. Let us do the digging. If there's something to be found, we'll find it."

Aimee opened her mouth to reply, when her cell phone began ringing. She glanced down at it. "It's Nick. Can I take this call?"

"Of course," Casey replied. "Do you need privacy?"

"Not at all." She held up her index finger. "I'll just be a sec." She pressed the accept button. "Hi, boss."

"Bad time?" Nick asked.

"Nope. I just finished another round of police questioning. I feel like I'm filming an episode of *Law and Order*. Nothing about CannaBD," she quickly assured him. "Just if I had any ideas who killed Chris Maher. Which, of course, I don't."

"This really sucks," Nick replied. "I'm sorry." He paused. "I'm sure this is the last thing you need right now, but I'm calling an all-staff meeting for four p.m. today. We've got a potential major investor, and I want all of us there for an open discussion and expert opinions. I've already talked to Kimberley and Oliver and they're coming. Kimberley will paint an upbeat—and factual—picture of our growing stream of income and our increasing number of investors. Oliver will explain our processing, quality control, and the high demand for our product. I need you to discuss our marketing strategy and how we're building our brand and our audience. Can you come?"

"Of course," Aimee said without hesitation. "I'll be there at three thirty so we can discuss our strategy."

"Great. We're all doing the same. Come directly to my office."

"Done. See you then."

***

Offices of Forensic Instincts
2:20 p.m.

Ryan perched on a chair at the small kitchen table and wolfed down his second chili dog, bought on the fly after his midday run with Hero. He was ravenous, and his morning protein bar had barely made a dent.

Hero had been in rare form, his paws racing along as if his goal was to be the first bloodhound to win a greyhound race. That had been fine with Ryan. He'd more than needed that exercise since he'd never gotten to the gym for his regular grueling workout. Just before seven a.m., when he and Claire had finally, and reluctantly, left the futon and the lair, they'd each gone home to shower, change, and get back to work. By eight, Ryan was at his desk, fingers on the keyboard, wishing like hell that Rita Edwell's cell phone and bank records would arrive.

His lunch break and run had been necessary diversions. But it was time to get back to work. He glanced down at Hero, who was stretched out on the floor beside him, snoring at the top of his lungs, and grinned.

"It's a dog's life, right, guy?"

Hero's eyelids opened a crack and then slid back down.

"Ryan?" Yoda's voice echoed through the brownstone.

Ryan shot up in his chair. "Yes, Yoda. What do you have?"

"The call logs from Russia have arrived," the AI system informed him. "I assumed you wanted me to format them in an Excel spreadsheet. I am opening it up on your laptop. It should now be visible on your second monitor."

"Let me get to the lair." Ryan was already moving, racing down the three flights of steps at warp speed. He burst into his lair, launched himself into his desk chair, and scrutinized the monitor.

Basics. Number called, date, time, and duration of call, organized from oldest to most recent.

Just the shell of what Ryan needed.

"Yoda," he instructed. "Please sort the records by the column marked outgoing with a secondary sort on the date and time of the call, reversing the order of calls from most recent to oldest. Add a column called *name*. It will be blank for now. Fill in the names of the numbers we know, like Aimee's and Chris Maher's. We'll be filling in more names later. Indicate the most frequently called numbers. Once that's completed, do the same thing for a column marked *incoming*. For all unknown numbers, create a Python script and use the Twilio API to cross-reference the phone number with a carrier and determine which of those numbers is assigned to a mobile phone and which to a landline. For those numbers that are landlines, see if you can use the search engines and identity lookup services to cross-reference phone numbers and companies."

"Of course, Ryan," Yoda replied. A minute passed, followed by Yoda's announcement: "Your spreadsheets have been updated as requested."

"Great. Now please Slack the whole team, posting a link to the folder containing the spreadsheets. Ask them to review it and be ready to analyze it together at our five-thirty-p.m. meeting today."

"I've also downloaded PDFs of Rita Edwell's bank statements for the past twelve months from Wells Fargo online and placed them in our private file server in the cloud. One of the PDFs is about to appear on your screen. When I Slack the team, should I post links to the individual PDFs or just the folder?"

"Just the link to the folder." Ryan scrutinized the PDF. "This process—linking the right phone calls to the right bank deposits—is going to take the team days to analyze. Let's get them started."

14

CannaBD
4:05 p.m.

The atmosphere in CannaBD's cozy conference room was electric.

The whole team was excited. Jason Williams—a thirtysomething guy with money to invest from a recent inheritance—was very interested in CannaBD. He'd made no secret about the fact that this investment deal was theirs to lose—something that Nick, Aimee, Oliver, and Kimberley had no intention of doing.

Nick kicked things off by welcoming Jason and then getting into the history of the company.

"I created CannaBD, but it was hardly what you'd expect. I didn't develop the formula while being buried in a lab for months." Nick grinned, providing the truth. "I was a grad student playing around in the university lab, infusing CBD into a keg of beer for a party. The particular mix—with an added ingredient or two—turned out to be fantastic. And CannaBD was born."

Jason grinned back.

"After that, I hired this amazing team"—Nick gestured toward Kimberley, Oliver, and Aimee—"and CannaBD just took off. It's been only three years, and we've already sold five million dollars of product, with serious distribution in the tristate area. We're poised to expand first to the entire Northeast and then to go nationwide."

Jason was perched at the edge of his chair. "That sounds promising. But tasting is believing. I see that your food cart contains a lot more than coffee and cookies. I see bottles of CannaBD beer." He tipped his head toward the rear wall, where Nick had set things up in anticipation of this request.

Chuckling, Nick said, "I agree." He then walked over to the cart, picked up a bottle, twisted off the cap, and handed it to Jason. "Enjoy."

Jason took a swallow and his brows rose. "You're right. This is great. And the buzz has yet to come."

"We think so. As do our customers." Nick addressed Jason, while simultaneously nodding at Oliver. "As I told you when we sat down, Oliver is our manufacturing guru. I'm going to turn the reins over to him now, so he can describe our current operation and highlight potential opportunities for expansion."

Oliver straightened in his chair and woke up his iPad, pulling up the slide deck he had created. He was in his element now, which was the only time he spoke and acted like a regular person.

"Can everyone please open the app called DriveIn?" he began. "Jason, you can use the loaner iPad we set up for you." Oliver handed him the extra device. "Once you're in the app, please accept the invitation I've sent you. It will say CannaBD Confidential. Then we'll be ready to get started."

Oliver swiped a few times, and suddenly everyone else's iPad displayed what was on his screen, too—the beginning of the presentation.

"What you're seeing is a simple block diagram explaining how CannaBD beer is made," he began.

Seeing Jason nod in understanding, Oliver continued with his presentation. He switched screens to a video of the packaging line, and as it played silently, he described how that was a major choke point limiting their production. "We have three infusion tanks, and with the addition of three more, we could double our capacity. There's enough room for the tanks and ancillary equipment, but the packaging line would need a building expansion. We have enough space, and zoning isn't an issue, but the reconfiguration of the plant will be challenging."

"And how do you intend to meet that challenge?" Jason asked, ignoring his coffee to take another swig of beer. "The process itself, not the monetary funds necessary to carry it out."

Oliver cleared his throat, ready to show just how thorough his planning was. "We would need to run twenty-four seven for about a month to build enough inventory to satisfy demand while the plant shuts down to relocate the packaging lines. Once the existing packaging lines are moved, new packaging equipment can be installed and the three new tanks installed in the old packaging area that's freed up. Phase One, the building expansion, will take a year. Adding the packaging lines and infusion tanks will take another six months. In less than two years, we could double our output running only one shift. If we added a second shift, the capacity could double again."

Aimee caught Nick's eye in a pointed look that said that Jason had heard enough and that anything more would be overkill.

Nick nodded. "Thank you, Oliver," he said. "Jason, part of why we need this expansion is because I'm determined to add new products to our already-thriving beer, namely wine and spirits."

Oliver's lips narrowed into a thin line. He was clearly pissed at being cut off. He didn't say another word.

Jason, on the other hand, was on the edge of his seat with enthusiasm. "Awesome idea. You'll appeal to an even broader audience, leverage the distribution relationships you already have, which will boost your sales and make it easier to expand nationally."

"Exactly." Nick was beaming now as he spoke about the potential of his "baby." "And on that note", he said, "I'll turn things over to Aimee so she can give you an overview of the sales, marketing, and distribution success we've achieved."

Aimee took the initiative, elaborating on Nick's segue. Then she continued, "However, in order to reach national status, we need more and bigger distributors—ones that can help us go national. We need to invest more money in building the brand, including upping and targeting our digital advertising campaigns, increasing awareness through influencers with higher status and bigger followings." A heartbeat of a pause as the name Chris Maher erupted in her mind. "Even finding someone famous as our spokesperson." She wasn't going to let her memories get in the way of her job. "All these campaigns and initiatives will obviously take some investment to ensure the right people are aware of the product and keep coming back for more."

Aimee wrapped up her presentation by sharing demographic data of their target customers and taste test results.

Her eyes twinkled. "Seventy-five percent of all those who participated in their wide-range samplings of the survey preferred CannaBD beer over all other beers simply because it tasted better. When they find out it contains CBD oil, they are truly amazed."

"That comes as no surprise," Jason said, polishing off his beer.

Finally, Kimberley took the reins, transferring the screen-share to her hosted slide deck file and guiding Jason through the financials. Given that this was the area in which he had the most questions, she provided him with more detailed analyses, demonstrating the product cost drivers and major marketing expenditures.

"Your growth projections are optimistic," Jason noted. "What if the actual results fall short?"

Kimberley had anticipated Jason's question. "I've constructed several sensitivity analyses to address that contingency. Even under the worst-case scenarios, CannaBD would be free cash flow positive, and we would not require a subsequent cash infusion."

Jason's knit brows relaxed. "So my investment wouldn't be diluted by another round of equity."

"Exactly."

"And there you have it," Nick closed. "A snapshot of our company and the compelling reasons to invest in its future."

"I'm impressed," Jason said. "Thank you all for your detailed presentations."

"How about you and I talk privately for a few minutes," Nick suggested.

"Works for me," Jason replied.

On that note, the rest of the team rose, exchanged handshakes with Jason, and filed out.

Aimee shot a quick backward glance as she followed Kimberley into her office to wait. The two women didn't hang out much, but this was a team moment, and she wanted to share it.

"I wish we could hear what's going on in there," she said, fighting the urge to retrace her steps and peer into the conference room, where she could try to read their lips.

Kimberley gave her a rare smile. "We can't be huddling out there when Jason finally exits. Not only would we look like a team of desperate employees, we'd look like a bunch of groupies."

Aimee gave a reluctant sigh. "I know."

"Where's Oliver?" Kimberley asked, glancing around. "I thought he was right behind you."

"He was." Aimee rolled her eyes. "He veered off, probably to sulk in his office. He was angry that Nick didn't let him get into a lengthy technical explanation. But you know what would happen if he got started. He'd get into every minute detail. And Jason was already shifting in his seat. I'm the one who shot Nick a heads-up look to bring Oliver to a halt. He clearly agreed. I'm just sorry that Oliver's feelings are now hurt and he feels less valued."

"That happens a lot," Kimberley replied. "He's one weird guy."

"But brilliant."

"Yeah, there's that. Professionally, he's right on point. But personally"—Kimberley wiggled her hand—"not so much." She paused, visibly torn about whether or not she should continue.

She made her decision, tilting her head toward Aimee. "Right before you came on board at CannaBD, Oliver asked me out. Since he definitely wasn't my type, I made up some excuse and got out of it. He said he understood, but he was *not* happy. He tried again, several times. His persistence and his arrogance were real turn-offs. I was starting to feel uneasy. Then, you joined the team. And he backed off. I wondered if he'd decided to turn his attention on you."

Aimee shook her head. "Not really. I mean, he hung around me at the beginning, and I got the feeling he wanted to ask me out. Then, his focus seemed to shift to being CannaBD's number one. He spent more time with Nick than with anyone else."

"Yeah, he's very insecure. He needs to be recognized and respected all the time."

Aimee glanced down the hall. "Thus, the sulking. He's probably pissed off at me."

"Too bad," Kimberley replied. "Winning over a new, rich investor comes first. He'll get over it."

As Kimberley spoke, the door to Nick's office opened, and he and Jason stepped into the hallway.

"Okay, then, I'll call my lawyer and get the ball rolling," Nick was saying. He stuck out his hand. "I look forward to a long and profitable working relationship."

Jason gripped Nick's hand in a solid handshake. "As do I."

Inside Kimberley's office, the two women gave each other a high five.

Down the hall in his office, Oliver brooded.

15

Offices of Forensic Instincts
Tribeca, New York
Wednesday, 5:20 p.m.

Ryan had just pushed his most current information out to the team's laptops and was about to head upstairs to the conference room when Yoda said, "I updated the spreadsheet tabs outlining both the incoming and outgoing phone call records, Ryan."

"Great." Ryan planted his hands on the computer table and stared at the screen, quickly taking in the new tables of completed data.

"These calls appear to be primarily to and from cell phones, not landlines—other than a bunch to other universities," he noted aloud. "No surprise." His gaze paused, and he mentally counted off a bunch of numbers that appeared multiple times, mostly on the incoming list. "There are eight repeat callers who show up on both the incoming and outgoing tables, with no information attached to them. Dig deeper into those numbers." Ryan read the phone numbers aloud.

Yoda replied, "I saw just what you saw, and I will, Ryan—while you're meeting with the team." A pointed pause. "A meeting that begins in three minutes."

Ryan grinned at the reminder. "Never fear. I'm on my way."

***

Forensic Instincts' main conference room
5:30 p.m.

The entire FI team converged, taking their regular seats around the table.

"We've all read the information you forwarded to us, Ryan," Casey began. "Rita's calls were primarily cell calls, plus a bunch of landline calls to other universities. Nothing odd there."

"Nope," Ryan agreed. "All the calls are to colleges and universities on par with Danforth. Delver University. Malhart College. Both on Long Island. Baring University in Bergen County, New Jersey. Birchmont University and Brightington University, both in Westchester County, New York. Lakely College in Boston. Two more in Connecticut—Arborley College and Wheatley University. And one in Pennsylvania—Cameron College. Calls to colleagues. No red flags."

"Agreed," Casey said. "So, given the complexity of what you forwarded to us, I think you should run this part of the meeting."

Ryan didn't have to be asked twice.

"Okay. For starters, before Yoda brought all this data to me, I thoroughly researched all I could on Rita Edwell. She definitely lobbied for Chris to get into Danforth, and the odd thing is that her recommendation said nothing about the prestige angle—that he's the son of Daniel Maher. That's a red flag unto itself. The son of a movie star? That's gold to a prestigious university. Yet it's almost as if she left that out on purpose." Ryan glanced around the room and continued. "It got me wondering if Daniel and Rita had some sort of private arrangement, maybe a payoff to get his son into Danforth."

Casey pursed her lips. "That sounds like a distinct possibility. It certainly would explain the threats Rita and Chris hurled at each other in the bar that night."

"Let me add another inconsistency to that hypothesis," Marc said, leaning forward in his chair as he spoke. "I examined all the

Danforth records that Daniel had requested the university forward to us, together with the data Ryan's initial hacking produced. I noticed the same thing Ryan did, plus the obvious fact that Chris's grades were subpar, not to mention his extracurricular activities, which, incidentally, were weak, too."

"Right." Ryan clearly wanted something new.

Marc's lips twitched at Ryan's customary impatience. "A short while later, I went back to Chris's admission file. And everything about Rita's connection to Chris was gone, including her letter of recommendation."

Ryan shot up in his seat. "But I saw that letter, plus all the data supporting it. I even took screenshots."

"I'm sure you did. But trust me, it now looks as if Rita had nothing to do with Chris's admission to Danforth, nor his years spent there. There's literally no trace of a connection between the two of them."

"Shit." Ryan sank back down, rubbing the back of his neck. "Someone wiped all that information during the time you were looking elsewhere. How much time passed before each of your reviews?"

"Maybe a half hour," Marc said.

"That was quick. It means that whoever did this has both access to the Danforth computer system and the skills to manipulate it. This whole thing gets seedier by the minute."

Casey looked pensive. "Yes it does. It also raises the question of the motive behind the tampering. Who would do this? Rita is, by all accounts, dead. As is Chris Maher. Daniel has less than zero tech skills, according to him. And even if he's lying about that, he wouldn't wait to delete anything incriminating in Chris's college records. He'd do so immediately, before the university sent the files to the police and to us."

Marc nodded. "Total agreement from my end."

"So who did this and why?" Emma spread her hands in non-comprehension.

"Someone who's obviously very much alive and threatened by the connection between Rita and Chris," Patrick replied. "And to me, that suggests Rita wasn't doing this on her own. Someone else was pulling strings and trying to cover up everything illegal."

"Which means this is a whole lot bigger than just a one-time bribe," Casey said. "Maybe this string-puller paid Rita off on a regular basis—for a lot more than getting Chris admitted to Danforth. Maybe Rita was doing him other favors, maybe even ones that had nothing to do with Danforth."

"The theory that Rita is reporting to a higher-up would certainly explain the frequency of phone calls from the block of phantom numbers I just asked Yoda to check out," Ryan put in, tapping his fingers pensively on his thigh. "Interesting that the owner of one of those numbers called Rita the day she disappeared-slash-died. That's no coincidence, in my mind. So if that number belongs to whoever was yanking Rita's chain, it would tell us a lot."

Claire hadn't spoken a word since the beginning of the meeting, nor had she absorbed any of what was said. She was being swallowed up by white noise, crushed by the claws of a growing panic. Sweat was pouring down her back, her gut was tight, and chills shivered through her. She drew a deep breath and allowed her energies to go where they would. The landline calls. To the colleges and universities. What schools had Ryan mentioned?

She let out a sharp cry, interrupting Ryan's verbal analysis.

The whole team whipped around to look at her. It was clear she was suffering.

"Claire?" Ryan asked, his brow furrowed in worry.

She didn't answer, not at first. Then she whispered, "That's the connection. I never even thought of it. But it's real. Oh my God." She wrapped her arms around herself for warmth, and all the color drained from her face.

"Tell us," Casey said quietly. "What connection?"

Claire was still staring into space, seeing something that none of them could see.

Her trembling intensified. From some faraway place, she was aware of Ryan wrapping his sweatshirt around her shoulders. She burrowed into it, besieged by horrible memories.

A moment passed, the team silent, waiting.

Finally, Casey stood and grabbed a bottle of water from their coffee station. She returned to the table, twisting open the bottle cap as she walked, then placing the water in front of Claire. She leaned forward to touch her forearm, keeping the contact light but constant. It was one of the ways Casey brought Claire back to them under circumstances such as these, guiding but not spooking her.

"Claire?" she said very quietly.

Claire's eyelids closed and then lifted. Her gaze was clear, and she was definitely present, although she was still clinging to Ryan's sweatshirt as if it were a lifeline as chills continued to rack her body.

"Drink." Casey indicated the water.

Claire gratefully picked up the bottle and took a series of deep swallows before placing it back on the table. "Thank you," she whispered.

"Can you talk to us?" Casey asked.

"Yes." Claire took a few deep breaths and then refocused on the team. "I consulted on a homicide investigation at Brightington eight years ago." She swallowed as a flood of memories came back. "A football coach was killed in his office at the university. The body had been removed, but I could sense details of the murder and the murder*er* that no one else could." She went on to elaborate, wincing at the images that were engrained in her mind.

"I was very new at channeling my gift," she added. "But the pervasive sense of evil, the sick, twisted mind—they were the exact same images and aura that I felt at Chris Maher's murder scene. It was him. I know it."

Ryan did a double take. "You're saying that the one who killed your victim eight years ago is the same person who killed Chris Maher?"

A nod. "Yes. And Rita, too, I believe. It's why I couldn't get past the feeling that I knew the animal who committed all three crimes. I never met him, couldn't visualize him, but I felt the connection." Claire wrapped her arms around herself, trying to stem the shaking.

"Did Rita know him?" Marc asked. "Was she a source in this eight-year-old murder?"

Clare shook her head. "I'm not feeling that. No. The old homicide had nothing to do with her. The only commonality between the three murders is the killer."

"Interesting," Marc noted aloud. "The killer's MO with this football coach was more like Rita's than like Chris Maher's." He ticked off on his fingers. "No dead body. Lots of signs of violence. And no proof of the murder. Quite the opposite with Chris. It's almost as if the killer had two distinctly different kill methods."

"I suppose." Claire gave a tremulous sigh. "But what I know in my gut is that if we find the original killer, all these cases can be solved."

Emma's eyes were huge. "How do we find him?"

"We start at the beginning," Casey said. She looked at Claire. "Who called you in on the case?"

"Birchmont's chief of police, Carlos Molina. I think he retired a few years ago."

"Better still." Casey was visibly pleased. "He'll be able to talk more freely as a private citizen. Either Yoda or I will get his personal cell number. I'll give him a call tonight, telling him just enough but not too much—only that we're investigating a crime that's similar in nature to an old, unsolved case of his and that anything he can do to help us would be greatly appreciated. Hopefully, he'll be cooperative."

"He will be," Claire reassured her. "He's a fine person as well as a dedicated police chief."

"That's good. I'll see if he has any free time tomorrow to talk to us. You and I will drive up and have a serious conversation with him. Let's find out where his investigation on the football coach's case was going and what evidence the police had." A quick glance at Claire. "Can you handle that?"

"I'll make it my business to handle it," Claire replied.

Ryan shot Claire a worried look, then continued. "In the meantime, the rest of us have a shitload more analysis to do on these Wells Fargo bank records. Since we have so little data to work with, this is where we have to compare the bank deposit dates with the phone call dates. There's a story here—one that phone call records and banking information tells. I need everyone but Casey and Claire working to figure it out."

"Emma won't be able to help out, either," Casey added, pivoting to face Emma, who looked more intrigued than surprised.

"Sure. I'm not much of a heavyweight where it comes to financial analysis," she replied. "What do you have in mind?"

"I need you to stay close to Aimee. No need to keep track of her whereabouts; we have Patrick's guys to do that. But reach out to her for a drink, a lunch, anything to keep her engaged. Waiting is probably driving her crazy. And that's what she'll have to do for the next few days."

"No problem. I can serve as a distraction," Emma replied. She gave Casey a quizzical look. "Somehow I sense there's more to my role."

"There is." Casey nodded her approval at Emma's blossoming sense of awareness. "I didn't want to freak Aimee out even more than she already is, at least not right away. But it's time we examine her personal life, in the event that she really is a target. Once she calms down, she'll be relieved to help you. Use your social time together to go over her social media accounts. Also, review her emails and texts, to Rita and to anyone else who's connected to Rita. Keep it light and calm, and don't divulge anything of consequence. Our team needs to all be on the same page before we start filling Aimee in on our conclusions."

Emma took all that in. "No problem. Do you want me to check out her boyfriend and her colleagues at CannaBD?"

Casey shook her head. "Leave that to Ryan. He'll go at it quickly and objectively, not through Aimee's eyes. But should it come to scrutinizing her CannaBD social media accounts, I'll ask you to step in again. That's low priority right now. We have no reason to believe there's a link between the two homicides and CannaBD."

Emma gave Casey a thumbs-up. "I'm on it."

"Good," Casey replied, her gaze sweeping the room. "Time for all of us to get busy."

16

Aimee's apartment
Washington Heights, New York
Wednesday, 8:05 p.m.

Aimee wrapped the sheets more tightly around her and leaned back against her plumped pillows. It felt so good to be happy, even if it was just for one night. The investigation and the fear would be back. But for now, it was held at bay. She took another sip of champagne and gave a contented sigh.

Beside her, Travis grinned and rolled over to pick up the bottle from the nightstand, refilling both their flutes before he shifted onto his side to watch Aimee's face.

"And here I thought you'd be pissed because I didn't bring CannaBD," he teased.

Aimee's lips curved. "This girl never turns down a bottle of Veuve Clicquot," she said. "Besides, given our victory today, CannaBD will soon have its own better-than-anyone-else's brand of champagne."

Travis started to laugh. "Smug, huh? Well, you should be. Your new investor has deep pockets and tons of enthusiasm. Your company will be rolling in money before you know it."

"It sure feels that way." Aimee leaned over to kiss Travis's mouth. "Thank you for doing this—the champagne, the flowers, even the takeout Thai. You really made this day complete."

He pulled her closer, deepening the kiss and taking the flute from her hand. He held the kiss even as he placed both their glasses on the nightstand.

"You left something out," he murmured against her mouth. "Or did I not do as good a job as I thought?"

Aimee slid down in the bed until their bodies pressed together just so. "You did an amazing job," she whispered. "But I'm a little woozy from the champagne. Maybe you should remind me again?"

"With pleasure."

Talk about pleasure. The next hour was hot and wild and exciting. When Travis finally let her rest, Aimee felt as if she'd run a marathon and was now collapsed in a heap at the finish line. Travis was a tireless and inventive lover, and being with him made her come alive in a way that she'd never before imagined nor experienced.

With her eyes still shut, she held up one hand and waved it. "Consider that to be my white flag of surrender. I can't move."

A satisfied grin curved Travis's lips. "Does that mean I outdid the flowers, the champagne, and the Thai food?"

"By leaps and bounds." Aimee yawned. "I need sleep. When I wake up, you'll tell me about your day. I'd much rather discuss that than the chaos that's my life."

Travis frowned. "Has something else happened?"

"Other than another police interrogation, no. The Forensic Instincts team has upped the investigation, and I've been instructed to sit tight."

"Until when?"

"Until they have something to share with me. It sucks, but I trust them. So I'm following their rules."

Travis didn't argue that point. "But your bodyguard is still outside, right?"

"He's stuck to me like glue." Aimee paused. "Let's drop this. I don't want to ruin the magic of the night."

"I agree. But before we drop the subject, do you want me to make an appointment to talk to Forensic Instincts? They'll probably want to meet with everyone who's significant in your life. Maybe I could be helpful and also bypass the need for them to reach out to me."

Aimee turned her head to face him, visibly touched by the offer. "I never thought of that. But you're right. So, yes, I'd appreciate that very much."

"I'll email them as soon as you fall asleep. No time like the present."

Aimee reached over to the nightstand and picked up her phone. "I'll text you their contact info." She did just that.

A moment later, Travis's ringtone sounded. He glanced at his phone. "Got it."

Satisfied to be actively *doing* something rather than just comforting Aimee, Travis wrapped one arm around her and waited as she pillowed her head on his chest.

"Rest," he said softly.

"Um-hmm…" She was already drifting off.

Once she was asleep, Travis eased his arm away from her so he could use two hands to compose the email. He hit send and felt some of the tension ease from his body. From what Aimee had said, Forensic Instincts was all action, on top of things every minute.

Hopefully, they'd get back to him by morning.

***

Home of retired Chief of Police Carlos Molina
Birchmont, Westchester County, New York
Thursday, 10:35 a.m.

Casey and Claire turned into the driveway their GPS indicated they should. Like all the other houses on this tree-lined street, Molina's was a well-kept split level, probably built in the 1960s, with a fresh coat of ivory paint accented by dark gray shutters. The bushes, the walkway to the house, everything was in pristine condition.

"I have a feeling I know what Chief Molina has been doing since his retirement," Claire said, glancing around as Casey parked. "I recall that home improvement was always a hobby of his. Now it looks as if it's expanded into a major retirement routine." Claire waited for the car to come to a halt and then unbuckled her seat belt. "I'm willing to bet he's still tangentially involved in the police department, as well."

Casey was already climbing out of the driver's seat. "That would be very helpful to us. So let's find out."

The front door opened as they reached the short flight of stairs leading inside, and a muscular man with thinning hair and a welcoming smile stepped out.

"Hello, Claire," he said, extending his hand. "It's great to see you again. You've certainly fine-tuned your gift and applied it effectively and with far greater acceptance than you had eight years ago."

Claire smiled, met his handshake. "Thank you, Chief Molina. I've always been grateful to you for believing in me. You were one of the first."

"But far from the last. Forensic Instincts. Quite a talented and successful company. I'm proud of you."

He pivoted slightly, his hand still outstretched. "And you're Casey Woods, the company's president and a very impressive woman. I've seen and read about your team's accomplishments. And I'm eager to hear about your current case and how it connects with one of ours. You were very cryptic on the phone."

Casey shook his hand. "Thank you for seeing us on such short notice, Chief Molina. We'll try not to take up too much of your time."

"You can both start out by calling me Carlos. I'm a very informal person—especially now that I'm retired." He gestured for them to come in. "Let's talk in the living room," he said, closing the door behind them and leading the way.

The living room was very traditional, with its sweeping upholstered couch and matching chairs, its round mahogany coffee table, and its hand-made vases and figurines displayed on the side tables. A polished mahogany piano was positioned against one wall. Other than that, the room was uncluttered, with an open, airy feel.

"Your home is lovely," Casey said.

"That's my wife's touch. I can do all the big jobs, but when it comes to decorating and making this place feel special, that's all Elena."

"Is she home?" Claire asked. "I'd love to meet her."

"Nope. She teaches fifth grade and loves it. I doubt she'll ever retire." He chuckled. "She also thinks it's best for our marriage. Having individual days means more to talk about at night and much less time to disagree and get on each other's nerves."

"Sounds like a healthy formula." Casey found herself smiling. She liked this down-to-earth, straightforward guy.

He gestured at the couch. "Anyway, have a seat. I've got coffee and tea and a plate of Elena's famous coffee rolls. Eat one and I promise you'll never go back to a bakery."

Once Carlos had left the room, the two women settled themselves on the couch, and Casey shot Claire a quizzical look. "He's nothing like the way you described him."

Claire's shoulders lifted in a baffled shrug. "He was always serious and professional with me. And remember, I didn't know him all that well. I'm as surprised as you are."

"I guess retirement agrees with him."

"I guess," Claire agreed. A pause. "Meanwhile, I think you should set the tone of this meeting. You're the boss and the one with more objectivity."

Casey gave a thoughtful nod. "Okay. I'll provide a quick overview. But this interview is going to move into your ballpark fairly quickly. I can address the present. You have to connect it with the past."

"I know."

Hearing the anxious note in Claire's voice, Casey studied her expression. "You're sure you're okay with all this?"

"Very sure." The anxious note was gone.

A moment later, Carlos returned to the living room, carrying their refreshment. The highlight of the tray was a plate of Elena's coffee rolls, which looked and smelled like a piece of heaven. He bent to place the tray in the center of the table and then walked over to sit on one upholstered chair.

"I should have asked who prefers coffee and who prefers tea," he said.

Casey was leaning forward, admiring the coffee rolls. "We could skip both and just eat. Wow. These look amazing."

"They are," he assured her. He shot a questioning look at Claire. "I seem to recall that you're a fan of herbal tea. So I brought in a few packets for you to choose from."

"Thank you," Claire replied, genuinely touched.

She and Casey each tasted Elena's coffee rolls with a chorus of *ums* and *aahs*. Then, they got down to business.

"Our current investigation has led us to two homicides," Casey told Carlos, taking a sip of coffee and then setting the cup back in its saucer. "We're chasing down every possible lead, in order to protect our client, who could be in danger. Claire has a strong sense that the murders are somehow linked to a case she assisted you with."

Carlos shot a curious glance at Claire. "There were three, all of which are now cold cases. Which one are you referring to?"

"The football coach," Claire replied.

"Somehow I'm not surprised. Excuse me for a moment." Carlos left the room, returning with a thin file in his hands. "I visited the precinct this morning before you arrived. I borrowed the cold case files on all three of the investigations you consulted on." He sat, putting one manila folder on his lap. "This is the one you're referring to. Football coach Pete Rice."

Claire was eyeing the folder with trepidation. "That's the right one."

"What makes you think the homicides are somehow connected?" Carlos asked. "Rice's murder happened eight years ago."

"I know." Claire raked a hand through her hair. "All my instincts—everything I'm sensing… I believe the same killer committed all three crimes."

The police chief did a double take. "Are you sure?"

"As sure as I can be without physical evidence." Claire was still staring at the case file on his lap. "The same twisted mind. The same overwhelming sense of evil. Eight years ago. And now. Probably more murders that we know nothing about."

"A serial killer?"

"I think so, yes. A warped killer who has different motivations for killing different people."

"And different MOs?" Carlos asked. "Because, if that's the case, it explains why the police never linked the three cases."

Claire nodded and spread her hands wide. "There are still holes to fill in. That's why we're here." She unfolded her clenched hands. "May I see the file?"

Carlos hesitated for a moment. "I have a theory about Rice's murder. Even after the case became cold, I poked around. Which would help you more—reading the file after I've given you my thoughts or before?"

"I'd rather hear them first," Claire responded. "The more information I have before trying to make a metaphysical connection to the object I'm holding, the better."

"Very well." Carlos steepled his fingers beneath his chin, his elbows resting on his knees. "I don't like cold cases. I'm all about closure. So I reviewed the case multiple times—the methodology, the lack of a body despite an obvious show of violence, and the fact that Rice vanished from that point on—a pretty sure sign that he's dead. I also did some digging into his bank accounts once they became available to me. He was a wealthy guy. His lifestyle reflected it. He lived way beyond his means—way beyond the salary of a college football coach."

"You think he was getting the rest of his income illegally," Casey stated.

"I do. And the more I probed, the more convinced I was that he was getting payoffs from a professional, not a parent or student."

"Organized crime," Claire breathed, certainty lacing her tone. "Rice was working for the mob. And he was targeted for execution by them. I don't know why, but I'm sure of the rest." She reached her hand out to Carlos. "Unless you have more to tell us, I'd like to see Rice's file now."

Wordlessly, he handed it over.

Claire opened it, staring at the few sparse pages that were inside.

Her fingers just brushed them and she got that faraway look in her eyes. "Rice was a mob middleman," she said, her inner voice guiding her. "I'm not sure why he was on their payroll. But I am sure that he was becoming a problem to them—a problem that outweighed his usefulness." She paused, staring at the file as she tried to establish a deeper connection. "He was pressuring his employer for more money," she said at last. "That's what prompted the hit order."

Claire brow furrowed, and for a moment, she stopped speaking.

Both Casey and Carlos remained silent, not wanting to break her concentration.

"Wait," she said. "A targeted hit. Yes, by the mob. But it's more complicated than that. Another reason. Another… No, the same killer." She squeezed her eyes shut, reaching for clarification. "I'm feeling his aura. I'm sensing the mob. I'm sensing more. I don't understand. At least not yet."

Claire paused again, flattening her right palm against the police pages. Just as quickly, she yanked it away, looking as if she'd been burned. "It's the same killer," she said. "All three crimes—it's him." She shuddered. "I can't even absorb this level of depravity. He's a sick, evil man, capable of inflicting torture and pain and enjoying every minute of it."

"And he's a mob hire," Carlos said. "This wasn't the same MO as the ones in either of your other two homicides?"

"Yes and no," Claire replied. "One of two MOs was close to identical. The other was different. The body was left in place, mutilated, and proudly displayed for the police. I wish I knew why."

Carlos took a thoughtful sip of coffee. "He's a serial killer. My guess would be that he has two, maybe more, types of killing. One is as a mob hire. In those cases, there's no corpse to be found. And it's those cases that pay the bills. The other murders are independent kills, done in any way he chooses and with as much flair as possible."

"Those are his prize kills," Casey murmured, mentally reviewing everything Hutch had taught her about the psychological components of a serial killer. "They fuel his fire like drugs do for a junkie." A pause. "Now our job is twofold. We have to dig deep to find the reason for the mob hits and why they chose the targets they did. We also have to figure out why this sicko chooses the victims he does for his personal kills."

Claire nodded, still clutching the file.

Carlos studied her, clearly contemplating something. "Take the file with you, Claire. It's buried in dust at the precinct, and there might be something inside to help you along the way."

"Thank you," Claire replied, looking both relieved and frightened. "I need the file for future insights. We've just touched the tip of the iceberg. There's so much more here, so much we still have to learn about this killer." Her voice lowered to a whisper. "We're on a dangerous path."

"But one we have to take," Casey said. "We have a client to protect and a case to solve." She rose, giving Carlos an appreciative look. "We really appreciate your help. Clearly, we have a lot of territory to cover. But I promise to keep you in the loop and fill you in on the details once we're ethically able to."

"Fair enough." Carlos stood, as did Claire. "I never expected retirement to be so eventful, nor did I expect to enjoy keeping my foot in the door. Who knows? I might consult for you one day."

Casey smiled. "And I might take you up on that."

17

Sarabeth's Restaurant
Upper West Side, Manhattan, New York
Thursday, 11:10 a.m.

Aimee was sipping her Four Flowers Smoothie, savoring the combined flavors of orange, fresh pineapple, banana, and pomegranate juice. She and Emma had been seated, as per Emma's request, on the outside terrace, at a corner table near the surrounding fence. Enough space between tables to ensure some measure of privacy. Between that, the warm decor, and the tantalizing smells coming from the kitchen, it was the ideal setting to talk.

Emma twirled the straw in her own smoothie, watching Aimee as she unwound visibly. Emma had chosen this restaurant for two reasons: one, its ambience, and two, it was partway between Washington Heights and Tribeca. Less time to travel, more time to talk.

"I'm really glad we're doing this," Aimee said. "I feel like a rat in a cage. I never leave my apartment, and other than a few visits from Travis, it's just me and my laptop. I was already freaked out. Now I'm worse. All I do is fixate on who killed Rita and Chris and if that killer is coming after me. I realize I'm overreacting, especially since John is parked right outside, but that's what happens when you're alone with nothing but your imagination for company. It feels like an eternity. As I said, Travis has visited a few times, but he works crazy and long hours. So I'm almost always alone. Alone and terrified."

Emma reached across the table and squeezed Aimee's hand. "FI is all over this. We'll solve this case and you'll be free to live your life again."

"Thanks for the pep talk." Aimee arched a knowing brow. "And you can tell Casey I see her hand in all this. She wants you to keep me from imploding. Tell her she's doing a good job."

Their breakfast arrived, and Emma didn't respond until the waiter had placed their omelets on the table in front of them, ensured that they didn't need anything else, and then hurried off to pick up his next order.

Emma leaned forward in her chair and replied, "Yes, Casey did think this would be a good idea on a few fronts. But I jumped all over the chance. I like you. I want to help you. Hopefully, this is one way I can."

Aimee tasted her omelet, murmured in pleasure, and then glanced up, her brows knit in question.

"You said this would be a good idea on a few fronts. What does that mean? Other than sharing a great breakfast and good conversation with me, what else did you plan for this impromptu meal?"

Emma was as blunt as Aimee. "I'm hoping we can run through your social media accounts. To check on your followers, as well as those you follow. Maybe how those networks branched out to others. We want to know if there's anyone in your life who might have a grievance. Although we still don't have any evidence that you're tied to either Rita's or Chris's death," she added hastily. "We're just covering all our bases."

Aimee chewed her lip thoughtfully. "Only my personal accounts or CannaBD's, as well?"

"Tough question to answer. Let's start with the personal. If we find a lot of overlap, we can move on to cover your marketing role at CannaBD. One step at a time." Emma indicated the iPad in her tote bag. "The Wi-Fi here is great. I checked as soon as I got here. So, would you prefer eating and chatting about normal stuff first, or would you prefer getting right down to work? I'm okay either way."

Aimee didn't miss a beat. "The omelets look delicious. But I think we can manage doing both at the same time. I'm really on edge."

"Done." After taking a bite or two of her breakfast, Emma whipped out her laptop. "What are your go-to accounts?"

"Facebook, Instagram, and YouTube. I have thousands of Facebook friends, some recent and others going back to my high school days. Some are real friends, others are just users who friended me. Some are connections I've made through other friends. And some are through mutual interests we share—like traveling and reading good books. Even though you and I aren't getting into work today, everyone at CannaBD is a Facebook friend—although I doubt you'll find anything interesting on that scope. We're all work colleagues, so we tend to communicate more on my business page. As for Instagram, that's even more extensive. That's where my personal and work life overlap."

Emma nodded. Nothing unexpected there. "I'm sure that's the same with your YouTube account. Personal videos you posted or work ones—guaranteed to drum up business for Canna BD. Overall, we have a lot of ground to cover. Let's start with your Facebook profile account. Give me your log-in info. We can start things rolling from there."

***

Offices of Forensic Instincts
Tribeca, New York
Thursday, 12:45 p.m.

Marc, Patrick, and Ryan were gathered in the War Room, heads bent over their work, when Casey and Claire walked in, Emma at their heels. It was fortuitous timing since they all needed to be updated from every angle.

Casey took in the men's rumpled appearances and irked demeanors. "You haven't budged since we left," she said. "Judging by your glum expressions, I'm guessing there are no updates."

"You guessed right." Ryan took another swallow of coffee.

Casey frowned. "Have any of you eaten today? Breakfast? Lunch? Because you all look like hell."

Marc glanced up. "And we feel like hell. Staring at numbers for half a day and not making any sense of them. And, yeah, I ordered a couple of pizzas. The delivery guy should be here soon. I ordered extra. There's more than enough for you and Claire."

Hero woofed and wagged his tail. Marc grinned, squatting down and scratching the bloodhound's ears. "Easy, boy. You'll be getting lots of crust."

Hero's ears perked up. He was a big fan of the crunchy pieces of crust he received when the team ordered in pizza.

At that moment, Yoda's voice sounded through the room.

"Ryan, the phantom numbers you indicated all lead to a prepaid carrier."

"Shit," Ryan said, a scowl darkening his face. "That means they're probably tied to burner phones that the contact used to remain anonymous. Not that I'm shocked. But still—shit. Eight burner phones—that's a solid block. It means this is going to take some time to figure out. Now I'm going to have to hack into cell phone tower data and exfiltrate a lot of information. It's going to need to be a slow, patient, and stealthy process in order to avoid detection."

Casey blew out a breath. "Not good. Time is not our friend."

"Tell me about it," Ryan muttered, his entire body coiled with tension.

"Hey," Casey said, softening her reaction in order to keep Ryan from losing it. "Do what you have to, for as long as you have to. Don't let pressure and impatience get in the way. As you said, we have to avoid detection."

He gave a reluctant nod.

"Time for us to be filled in," Patrick said. He turned his attention to Emma. "Anything at your end?"

Emma's shoulders lifted then fell. "Not enough. Aimee and I ate our breakfast and got better acquainted. But she's a nervous wreck and was eager to get down to business. She and I went through her personal Facebook and Instagram accounts. We checked her followers and the people she was following. Nothing jumped out at me. That doesn't mean it isn't there. I just touched the tip of the iceberg. Not only do I need more time and access but I have to examine her CannaBD profile. There's a pretty wide overlap in her personal and professional lives. I don't think we can separate the two."

"So how did you handle it?" Marc asked.

"I explained all that to her, along with the fact that I needed more time to get it done. I asked for her log-in names and passwords for Facebook, Instagram, and YouTube. She gave them to me. By then, she was pretty wiped. I doubt she's sleeping much these days. So I turned the conversation to movies, music, and food. She was definitely more relaxed when we went our separate ways."

With that, Emma held up her tote bag and tapped her laptop. "I have all the names and passwords saved on our Box account, so we all have access to them. I can get started whenever you give me the word."

"Good job, Emma," Casey praised, struck by how much FI's Artful Dodger had grown. "You can start after this meeting. But right now, it's crucial that Claire and I tell the whole team about our morning."

"I get the distinct impression that your meeting with the former chief of police was a big success," Marc said.

"Yes," Casey replied. "We left with answers and more questions." She paused. "This is a long and complex story—one that I'm going to turn over to Claire to share. But first, one quick tidbit. Aimee's boyfriend, Travis Grady, emailed me last night. Aimee obviously told him as much as she knows, and he's worried about her. He offered to come to the brownstone to talk to me after his night shift at the hospital ends early tomorrow morning. He's a smart guy. He realizes we're going to reach out to everyone Aimee knows, particularly those closest to her, to try to learn even the smallest detail that Aimee might have forgotten."

"Proactive move," Marc replied. "Good. And knowing you, you responded a minute later."

"Guilty as charged," Casey said. "I set something up for nine thirty tomorrow morning. I think I should take this one alone. Travis is very upset, and I don't want to overwhelm him by having the team march in en masse. I'll chat with him in one of the downstairs meeting rooms—small and unintimidating. I'll put out some muffins and fruit. And I'll record the convo so we can all listen to it together after he leaves."

The whole team murmured their agreement.

Casey turned to look at Claire, trying to assess her state of mind. She'd been quiet on the car ride home, lost in her own thoughts or memories or both. "Go ahead, Claire," she said. "You have the floor." She raised her brows in question. "If you're up for it?"

"I have to be." Claire took a few deep breaths before relaying the entirety of what had happened during their trip to Carlos's house. She didn't skip a detail, not one she'd learned nor one she'd recalled.

By the end, she was trembling again. She wet her lips with the tip of her tongue and finished with, "So that's where things stand. We're looking for a single sociopathic killer—one who's connected to the mob and, in addition, one who kills for his own sick reasons and has been doing so for years." She held up the file on Coach Rice. "Carlos loaned this to me. It will help me channel my energy where it's needed."

The entire team was staring at her, looking both stunned and worried.

Ryan was the first to speak. "Shit." He took a step toward Claire and then checked himself. He and Claire had both agreed that, other than their private time in the lair, they'd keep their personal relationship separate and apart from their professional one.

"You look like you're about to collapse," Ryan said instead. "Are you okay?"

Claire met his worried gaze and nodded. "I'm fine. Just still overwhelmed. That'll pass. The important thing is that I've given us a lot more to go on."

"Hell yes," Ryan agreed. "The mob. They weren't even on my radar."

"Nor the rest of ours," Marc said. "But all this? Not a coincidence."

"Definitely not," Casey agreed. "The mob and this serial killer are integral parts of this case—of all these cases," Claire said. "This psycho has been doing this for at least eight years. I'm sure there are many more bodies than the various police departments realize are connected. Our serial killer is smart. He covers his tracks well. And he gets away with all of it."

Marc pursed his lips. "He's obviously a lot more dangerous and a lot more seasoned than we originally thought."

Ryan's wheels were turning. "Let me jump on this immediately. It could be a game changer." He rose from his chair. "Would one of you mind bringing half a pie down to the lair? Preferably the one with sausage and peppers. I want to get started ASAP. This could narrow down my research."

"No problem." Marc was studying Casey's face. She was obviously deep in thought. And he knew just what those thoughts were about.

Sure enough, she asked, "Do you guys mind if I go out for a while? I have a quick research trip to make—assuming I can make it happen right away."

"You want Hutch's take on this," Marc said.

Casey was unsurprised by Marc's insight. He was her right hand and had been since the inception of Forensic Instincts. At this point, they could almost always read each other's thoughts when it came to a case.

"If he's available, yes," she replied. "First, I'll get Aimee's permission to bring him into the fold. If so, I'll lay out the whole situation, minus the parts where we treaded outside the law. I want to get Hutch's input on this serial killer." Casey's brows knit in question. "I hope that doesn't offend you, Marc."

Marc waved away that notion. "It's been years since I worked for the bureau, much less the BAU. Hutch is still in the game and is the best there is."

Casey couldn't argue that. Hutch was special and brilliant. He was squad supervisor of the FBI's New York field office's NCAVC—the National Center for the Analysis of Violent Crime. He'd transferred from Quantico, where he'd first worked the BAU's crimes against children, then crimes against adults. And he was now the BAU coordinator and head of all the New York field office's Violent Crimes squads. It was a high-level, coveted leadership job, which Hutch handled with the same expertise and commitment he'd handled being a BAU agent and, before joining the bureau, a DC police detective.

A corner of Marc's mouth lifted. "Why do you think I introduced you two?"

Casey grinned. "Fair enough. Let me make some phone calls and hopefully head out of here now."

18

Casey and Hutch's apartment
Battery Park City, New York
3:45 p.m.

Hutch stepped out of the shower, wrapped a towel around his waist, and returned to the bedroom. He had to chuckle at the sight of Casey, barely able to prop herself on the pillows and struggling to focus on the slim file she'd brought with her to their "meeting."

"I guess I didn't distract you enough," he said. "You recovered way too soon. Usually, you bathe in the afterglow for a long time."

She looked up and smiled back. "To the contrary, you distracted me so much I can barely move. I didn't expect this impromptu marathon, but I loved every minute of it." She yawned. "The better question is, how am I going to get back to work after this?"

Hutch sat down on the bed and settled himself, wrapping an arm around Casey. "Our work hours suck. We barely see each other. We're going to have to change that. Otherwise I can't be held responsible for my actions once I get you under me."

"I like that thought. Can't we have both—more time together and extra time in bed?"

"Sounds like a plan." He kissed her tenderly. "We'll work it out like we do everything else. But in the meantime, I doubt this was the only reason you wanted me home in the middle of the day—especially since you have a file lying beside you."

"Guilty as charged, although I loved the prelude to our talk."

Hutch chuckled and glanced at his Apple Watch. "I've got to get back soon. And from the sound of your voice when you called me, so do you. So let's get down to what you need."

Since Aimee had gratefully given her permission to bring Hutch into the fold, Casey described the whole investigation—sans the not-so-legal steps they'd taken. She concluded with Claire's certainty that they were dealing with not only the mob but a long-term serial killer.

Hutch scowled. "Don't think for a minute that I'm not noting the glaring blanks in this story. I'm just choosing to ignore them, since I know why you're skipping over them." He tipped Casey's chin up so she could meet his gaze. "Be careful," he said. "What you're describing—and *not* describing—is dangerous territory. I love you. And I worry."

Casey laid a hand on his jaw. "I love you, too. And I'll be careful. Promise."

Hutch arched a brow. "Yeah. Like always." He waved away her protest. "You want my take on things, assuming your theories are all fact. Okay, here it is, starting with the mob. Whatever their operation is here, it doesn't sound like it has tentacles that spread further than a few members of the family. It sounds like a very straightforward and targeted plan, one that's probably being run by a capo or a smart soldier who wants to get rich and to impress his boss. I'd need a lot more to figure out the exact details of their operation and what it's yielding them. But with regard to how your alleged serial killer fits in, my guess is that he's a kill-for-hire and that his boss either stumbled upon or was referred to him."

"Sounds like a lucky break."

"Yes and no. This guy knows what he's doing. But according to what you're claiming, his kills fall into two categories—his mob hits and his personal kills. The latter are the ones that fire his blood but piss off and intimidate the mob. He doesn't give a shit what they think, and they know it. But they're afraid enough of him that they ignore what he does on his own time. His work for them is perfectly executed, so they look the other way. As for him, he toes the line just enough to pay the bills. After that, it's his victims, his way." Hutch frowned thoughtfully. "I'm willing to bet that he's at the end of the ASPD spectrum."

Seeing Casey's brows knit in question, Hutch supplied the answer. "ASPD is antisocial personality disorder. The person who has it could fall anywhere on the spectrum—from someone who exhibits occasional bad behavior to the end of the spectrum where you find a high-functioning sociopath."

Hutch didn't look happy with his own explanation. "To analyze a killer like that, you need to see a pattern of behavior, a link between crimes, along with physical evidence. You have none of that. You only have one personal kill to go on right now—that being Chris Maher. Rita and that Coach Rice would definitely fall into the mob hits category. No body. Little evidence. And no personal touches. Chris Maher is another story entirely."

"High-profile," Casey murmured. "A body at the scene. And an openly displayed signature touch. A college football glove stabbed through the victim's thigh."

Hutch arched a brow in her direction. "I saw the press conferences. The police never disclosed those specifics. Nor would I expect them to. Details like that would be part of a tight-lipped investigation. And yet, you're aware of them. Do I want to know how?"

"Definitely not."

"Yeah. Right." Hutch's lips tightened, but he didn't push. "The killer's choice of victims is one of the reasons I went for the high-functioning sociopath. I don't know why he chose Maher, but it's obvious he's a high-profile target. Low-functioning sociopaths go for more random victims, like prostitutes or drug dealers. Not your killer. I'm guessing his victims are all pretty high-profile. Oh, and judging by Chris Maher's murder, I'd say that he's also narcissistic. Displaying a body is uncommon. He relishes his work and likes to show it off, complete with his personal touches."

This time it was Casey who arched a brow. "Should I ask how *you* knew the details that were never revealed?"

Hutch chuckled. "Sure. I'm as transparent as glass. We live together now. I notice when you're intently researching a particular crime. So I made a quick phone call before I came home."

"And the NYPD was more than happy to share their findings with you." Casey shook her head. "I'll have to learn to be more covert. But in this case, no harm, no foul."

"And no illegal actions taken," Hutch said pointedly.

"I get it. Can we move on now?"

"Sure. Although I doubt you're going to like what I'm about to say."

"I know what you're about to say," Casey replied. "So speak your mind and let's get past it."

A terse nod. "Now that I've played out this entire scenario with you, the whole thing is pure conjecture. You have only three homicides—two that might suggest mob hits and one gruesome one that you believe was committed by the same guy, just with his own personal touches. Even if all that's true, there's no evidence that he's a serial killer. This entire line of thought was generated by Claire's insights."

"They're not just insights. They're realities. This is *Claire*. And that's proof enough for me." Casey met Hutch's gaze, absolute certainty in hers, less so in his. Not a first. Hutch was always on the fence with regard to Claire's claircognizance. Still, he'd seen it firsthand. So, he couldn't just dismiss it.

"Stop looking so dubious," Casey said. "Her gift might not be scientific enough for you, but it is real. As for the killer's mob connection, Claire isn't the only one who's sure about that." Casey handed Hutch Coach Rice's file. "The former police chief who handled that coach's murder eight years ago is equally sure. Hutch, please, I need your help. So I need you on board."

Hutch relented. "Okay, let's use everything you just said as a starting point. The first thing you need to do is to figure out who some of the other victims were. Let Ryan research that, and fast. It's essential that he comes up with what you need. Because, since you know very little about the killer, you need to study the victimology of the people he's killed."

"Go at it backwards, you mean."

Hutch nodded. "You need all you can get on each victim. Who were they—everything from their names and addresses to more in-depth factors? Who were the people closest to them? Their outside interests? Any prison record and for what? Any bad habits, like gambling or drugs? And then obviously, if the method used to kill them was identical all ways around, right down to the football glove stabbed into their thigh."

Casey's wheels were turning. "Ryan's research will tell us more about this sociopath's signature kills. What about his mob kills?"

Hutch opened the file Casey had handed him and glanced through it. "There's some decent evidence in here, especially the fact that Rice was living way beyond his means. The problem is that this crime happened eight years ago. The trail is cold. It's going to be hard to link it to Rita's murder. That being said, if you find she was also living well above her means, you'll have more commonality between victims. In that case, these crimes would warrant further investigation to see if they're related."

"Marc and Patrick are working hard on analyzing Rita's bank records. The task is a lot more cumbersome than anyone expected."

"Well, what they turn up could change your ability to link the two cases. If the mob operation has been in place long-term and you're dealing with a serial killer, the link is not out of the realm of possibility. So go with it."

"How?"

"Start with the obvious. Both Rita and Rice worked for universities. Different schools and different types of jobs. Still, I'd look for evidence of payoffs. Ryan has already opened the door by getting Rita's bank records. Her phone records might also lead you in a specific direction. All you need to do is find one suspicious contact, and you're good to go. Marc and Patrick will know exactly how to proceed from there. And since I do believe this is a one- or two-man operation, it shouldn't take long to get to your source. The harder part will be the why—what's the scheme the mob is running?"

Casey gave a deep sigh. "There are a lot of open threads here and very few certainties."

"You'll find them. I have faith. Your goal is to close in on both types of crimes and hopefully link them together."

Casey nodded. "Easier said than done. But we'll get on it right away." She gave Hutch a quick kiss and took back the file. "Thank you."

"You're very welcome." Hutch glanced down at his watch again.

"Yes, I know," Casey said, scrambling to collect her clothes. "My team is going to send out a search party for me, too." She gestured for Hutch to do what he had to. "You get going. I'm going to jump in the shower and put on an outfit that isn't wrinkled and doesn't scream sex."

19

Franklin Lane
Hartsville, Westchester County, New York
Thursday, 7:20 p.m.

He drove slowly up the street, that familiar bloodlust pulsing through his veins. He'd been wrong. Watching those YouTube videos hadn't kept the demons at bay. They'd made them worse. Bad enough the cops had gone silent. But the fucking media were useless. Spouting unimportant bullshit about Chris Maher—his life and his enemies. Not even one leak that would shock the world and bring the gory murder back to center stage. The focus was all wrong. This should be about *him*, not some spoiled, patronizing pseudo-celebrity. He was so sick of people ignoring his superior abilities and intellect. He wanted photos. Good ones. Zooming in on the mutilated body and focusing on the artistic skills of the killer.

Instead, all the media was yammering about were theories on who would have it in for Chris Maher. Who cared? The talking heads wouldn't shut up. Especially that bitchy blond commentator, Karly Listor, who was a big-mouth know-it-all with a vile, condescending attitude. Everywhere he looked, she was there: TV, blog posts, social media sites. Spewing on and on about possible motives. Jealousy, vengeance, and the one that pushed him over the edge today—a pissed-off groupie.

No one reduced him to that. No one.

His hand automatically closed around the handle of his butcher knife. One block more and he'd be there. He'd already canvassed the neighborhood. Just as he'd expected. A quiet suburban community, with most people already settled in their home for the night and only the occasional dog owner outside, taking their dog for a stroll and traveling only as far as it took for their pet to do its business before returning to the comfort of their home.

His blood was pumping. His hatred had grown to the point that he wasn't wasting an instant looking around her place for a cable to choke the life out of her. He'd brought his own murder weapon—a piano string that he could squeeze until it broke her skin, cut into her throat, and drew pools of blood as the wire sank more deeply into her flesh. He'd inflict as much pain as possible, easing and tightening his grip to hear her chortling sounds, her gasping, her begging. Once he had enough, he'd allow himself the sheer triumph of watching the panicked realization in her eyes and the sheer agony contorting her face as he yanked with all his might, cut the life out of her.

Anticipation made his heart pound faster, and he rounded the curve to reach his destination.

The house came into view, and he froze, his rage mixing with disbelief. There were a handful of cars parked in her driveway and on the street. He double-checked to make sure he was staring at the right house. He was.

He slammed his fists so hard against the dashboard that the car shook.

"Fuck," he got out between clenched teeth. "Fuck, fuck, fuck."

The bitch was having a party. Not huge, maybe ten or twelve people. But it was enough to wipe out any chance he had of getting to her tonight.

He took a minute to compose himself enough to function. Then, he swerved the car around and tore back in the direction he'd come. His tires screeched their protest. He barely heard the sound. His chest was pounding, his palms were slipping on the wheel from his sweat, and there was a wild haze clouding his mind.

He'd get her another day, and it would be even more brutal. He'd torture her longer and more savagely. And rather than strangulation, he'd impale her again and again on his butcher knife. No clean death like Maher's. And nothing done postmortem. He'd slice her up while she was wide awake.

Still filled with untapped rage, he swerved onto the parkway and headed back toward the city, weaving from one lane to the other, leaving all the other cars in his wake. One by one, they slowed down, fell far behind him, some out of fear, some out of caution. He didn't even notice. He just pressed harder on the gas pedal, twisting the steering wheel more violently as he left the other drivers behind.

Jake Flanders pulled out of the rest stop he'd been brooding in. He had his own anger issues to face as he cut off traffic to reach the left lane and slammed his foot on the gas pedal, half hoping to wrap himself around a tree. He'd worked for that packaging company for fifteen years. And now, all of a sudden, they were downsizing and it was bye-bye, Jake. Jake, who had a two-year-old daughter, a very pregnant wife, and a house with a mortgage being paid off by the skin of his teeth. He was drowning in debt, worry, and resentment. And the resentment was starting to claw at his insides.

Vaguely, he realized all the other cars had fallen back. An instant later, he saw why. Some crazy was bursting along like a rocket, lurching from lane to lane at a speed that far exceeded Jake's 90 mph. He had to be doing 120.

For a moment, Jake slowed down, letting the lunatic fly farther ahead.

Then, that over-the-top anger resurged, gripping everything inside him.

Before he could even think about it, he floored the gas pedal, closing the gap between himself and the lunatic ahead. Maybe he was a lunatic, too, but he didn't care. Somehow he had to challenge that guy, to beat him, and to savor the win that would make his life less worthless.

He raced up the left lane until he was just behind the coupe. He tried to see who was behind the wheel, but it was too dark to make out anything except a shadow, one that looked like a man. Jake zigzagged in front of him, a quick glance telling him that it was indeed a guy. He was buried in a ski coat, his shoulders hunched up as he swerved the wheel back and forth, tires squealing from the strain.

As Jake cut him off, the guy realized what was happening. And clearly, this was a war he intended to win. He lurched ahead, sharply cutting Jake off and passing him in a flash.

Jake was equally determined. He accelerated again, keeping up with the other car, then blasting ahead to cut him off—not once, not twice, but repeatedly.

His competitor had obviously reached his limit. When Jake made the mistake of crossing over to the right lane, the other guy edged over until he was right beside him. Seizing his advantage, he took care of Jake, pushing his own car relentlessly until it forced Jake off the road and into the side rail. The sounds of twisted metal accompanied the motion, and Jake looked over helplessly at the other driver, making eye contact and begging with his eyes.

It was only then that he realized he'd made a huge mistake.

***

Thursday, 11:45 p.m.

He let himself into his apartment and closed and locked the door. His adrenaline was starting to drop, and fatigue was setting in. So was hunger, which warred with the fatigue for first place. But getting clean stepped in and won the battle.

The night had gone a lot longer than expected. He'd scrubbed up pretty well in the car, but not to his satisfaction. So he tossed his clothes and parka into the washer and let it do the rest while he jumped in the shower and scrubbed away anything he'd missed. Not too bad, considering what he'd looked like before. Between the dirt and mud caked on him from the filth of the warehouse he'd transferred his victim to and the fresh blood all over him, he'd had a major job making himself look human once the deed was done. But he always kept cleaning supplies and a change of clothes on hand for that very reason.

Then came the additional job of getting rid of his car, rented under an assumed name. A few drivers—the one or two who were close enough to have seen his license plate—might have called it in. Especially if they'd spotted him shoving an unconscious body into his trunk. He'd done it quickly and cautiously, having knocked the guy out beforehand. Still, he couldn't take the risk of leaving physical evidence behind. So, after finishing off his kill, he'd driven the car far enough into the woods and away from a populated area and then torched it. Bye-bye, fingerprints and blood spatter. The coupe was burned to a crisp.

He'd walked a ways after that, finally emerging along the parkway in a rest area. He'd swung himself over the divider, stuck out his thumb, and waited. Lady Luck had shined down on him when a couple of college kids pulled over and offered him a ride. Putting on his most grateful expression, he hopped in and asked if they were going anywhere near Tuckstown, a neighborhood that was a two-mile walk to his place.

They'd said no problem and delivered him to the address he provided—and to a strange house he'd never seen before. With a thank-you and a wave, he sent them on their way.

The instant they disappeared from view, he'd begun his trek.

He'd made it home in forty minutes, taking back roads and moving at a healthy stride, his adrenaline still pumping enough to carry him along.

The shower helped take him down several notches. Relaxed but more alert, he weighed his fatigue against his hunger.

His bed could wait another half hour.

He checked the fridge, saw that there was a hunk of strawberry pie left over from a few days ago, and sliced a piece. He put it on a plate, took a fork, and then paused to grab himself a beer.

He plunked down in his favorite chair, ready to savor his snack. He was always hungry after a kill. It was as if he'd done a full workout at the gym, only much more satisfying.

He ate a few bites of pie, then twisted off the cap of the beer and took a healthy swallow. He was thirstier than he'd thought. He might need another before going to bed. His gaze fell on his laptop, sitting on the table beside him. Nope. Too soon. Besides, the guy had been a nobody, so the news reports would be minimal—just the name of the victim he'd used his piano string on, who'd begged for his life and who'd died in his own blood. Name, place of residence, occupation, and the family he'd left behind. The social media posts would be more interesting and satisfying. The wailing of those close to him as they posted their hardship on Facebook and tweeted it on Twitter.

In the end, none of it really mattered. What mattered was that the pathetic loser had served his purpose.

That didn't mean he wouldn't go back as soon as possible, mutilate, and kill that bitchy reporter.

20

Offices of Forensic Instincts
Tribeca, New York
First-floor meeting room
Friday, 9:30 a.m.

Casey had chosen this particular room in which to chat with Travis Grady because it was even cozier than their small conference room and looked more like a den in someone's home than an office space. Pale lime walls—a soothing background, as per Claire—a multicolored pastel area rug that accented the walls, a light oak coffee table, and both a settee and matching tub chairs completed the decor. The coffee table, which curved into the seating arrangement so guests could reach their food easily, now brandished the muffin basket and fruit platter that Casey had had delivered. At Casey's urging, Travis had helped himself to a muffin and fruit, along with the cup of dark roast coffee Casey had poured.

He was now settled on the settee, sipping his coffee and munching on a corn muffin that he'd politely sliced into quarters. Casey sat on the tub chair to his right, drinking her coffee and nibbling at some fruit. She wasn't really hungry, but it was imperative that Travis felt relaxed.

She assessed him quickly over the edge of her mug. A good-looking guy with close-cropped hair and a ready smile. Neatly dressed in a cable-knit sweater and crisp jeans. His entire demeanor—his posture and his expression—wasn't strained, which told Casey he wasn't nervous about this interview. But the look in his eyes—that spoke a different story. Worry. Frustration. Those were tells Casey recognized. Travis was apprehensive, not about what he might say but about what he might hear. Just how much danger was Aimee really in?

Casey knew he wanted answers. She'd do what she could. But it was the answers he gave her that were top priority right now.

With that in mind, she began.

"I'd like to record this conversation," she said. "FI works as a team, and I want to make sure everyone has access to your insights, just in case something you say prompts a new avenue to pursue that I overlooked."

"No problem." Travis gestured for her to go ahead, and she complied by pressing the record feature on her iPhone and setting it down beside her.

"I really appreciate your reaching out to me," Casey said. "We'll obviously be trying to interview everyone close to Aimee, and you were about to be our first phone call."

Travis nodded. "I'll help any way I can. Aimee's told me what's going on. The threat to her life is terrifying. So I'm at your disposal."

"Great," Casey replied. "Before we begin, would you mind telling me exactly what Aimee said? I want to make sure there's nothing more I need to fill you in about."

Travis went on to relay all of what Casey had expected. Which was everything except the details of FI's research, some of which Aimee knew and some of which she didn't.

"You're totally up-to-date," Casey said when Travis finished. "So let's start by talking about you. You're a nurse and you work at Manhattan Hospital."

Travis nodded. "For four years now. I've always wanted to work in the medical field. The military made that possible. I enlisted in the army right out of high school, became a Green Beret, and was lucky enough to get highly specialized training in medicine."

Casey's brows lifted in respect. "Wow, a Green Beret. That's impressive. And a medic?"

"Yes. So the transition to civilian nursing involved only a few courses and I was hired right away."

"That's quite a resume," Casey said.

"Thank you."

"Next, let's talk about you and Aimee. You've been together three months?"

"A little more, but yes. We met at a bar where we were both getting a CannaBD beer. It was a great jumping-off point." Travis's lips curved slightly. "Aimee is passionate about her company's product. But after talking half the night, we found out we had a lot more in common than just the beer we drank. We started seeing each other whenever we could and texted in between. It was kind of fast and furious. It still is."

"You care about her a lot," Casey responded.

"A lot. I also worry about her. It doesn't matter how long she's lived here, she's not a diehard New Yorker. She's way too trusting and even a little fragile. Which is why I felt so relieved when she told me you were handling this case. Although I can't imagine anyone who'd want to hurt her. She's warm and kind and incredibly positive and upbeat. People gravitate to her and she never blows anyone off. She doesn't have an enemy in the world that I know of. Obviously, I don't know enough."

Casey walked that line carefully. "Remember, we're still not sure Aimee is an intended victim. Only that she was with the other two victims right before they either died or disappeared."

"That doesn't sound like a coincidence to me," Travis replied.

"That's something we intend to find out—while keeping Aimee safe in the process." That was as much as Casey wanted to elaborate on, so she shifted the conversation. "Do you and Aimee have any mutual friends or couples you go out with?"

Travis looked rueful. "I'm sorry to say, no. We both work so many hours a week that we're lucky to see each other, much less other couples. The only people I interact with are co-workers at the hospital, and that's true of Aimee with regard to CannaBD. I know she's kept in touch with college friends, but they only see each other once in a while."

"Have you met them?"

"Unfortunately, no. I haven't even met her family because they live halfway across the country. The only one I *have* met is her boss, Nick Colotti, who seems like a really nice guy. Demanding, but that's because his business is his life. He's hired the best of the best, and that includes Aimee."

"I can relate to your situation," Casey said. "My boyfriend and I live together and we still barely see each other. We work until we drop, and our hours rarely coincide. It's a tough path to navigate."

"Yeah, tell me about it." Travis grimaced. "We don't know the words *recreational time*. Actually, that's not entirely true, not for Aimee. The trips to college campuses and taste test parties are a big part of her job. They're technically work, but they are fun and give her a bit of an outlet."

Casey studied Travis's expression. She saw no overt jealousy or anger about the perks of Aimee's job. Still, she probed a bit.

"I never thought of it that way, but you're right. College campuses, Greek life, and organized collegiate events. To my mind, that can be either an enjoyable outlet or totally exhausting."

"Both," Travis replied. "And to be honest, it makes me feel a little less guilty during the weeks when I have mostly night and weekend shifts. I'm glad she has more to her life than the regular work routine."

Admirable, Casey thought. But there was one more subject she wanted to explore, and she wanted it to come out of left field.

"Had you ever met Rita Edwell?"

Travis looked sadder than he did startled. "I wish I had. Aimee speaks—*spoke*—the world of her. Rita mentored Aimee from her pre-college days. There was a special bond between them. Rita was more like a friend than a business contact. Aimee fell completely to pieces when she was killed."

"That hasn't been proven yet," Casey reminded him.

"To Aimee, it has. Besides being afraid for her own life, Aimee is mourning the loss of Rita's."

"I know," Casey agreed. "Plus, she's not thinking ahead yet, but once this nightmare is over, she'll have to. Rita's death leaves a gaping hole in Aimee's close contacts. She'll have to build a new relationship with whomever Danforth hires to replace Rita. It's going to be a hard transition. Aimee will have to pick up the slack on her own, seek out the right college grads to promote CannaBD, at least at Danforth. And she'll have to turn to other universities' staffs for help."

Travis nodded. "But as you said, Rita had a lot of contacts. Not just campus kids but administrators."

"True." Casey nodded. "Let's hope they offer her help."

"Knowing Aimee? What a pleasure she is to work with? She'll make it happen."

A small smile curved Casey's lips. "Having someone who believes in her like you do? I don't doubt it."

Travis paused, visibly unsure if he should ask his next question. He took a chance. "I realize you can't give me updated details, and I won't even ask for them, but can you at least tell me if you—or the police—have made any progress?"

"I wish I could address that," Casey replied. "But it's all confidential information. The NYPD would tell you the same. This is an ongoing investigation. Until it's closed, we can't discuss it."

Travis sighed. "I suppose I expected that answer. I just feel so helpless..."

"I understand," Casey said. "Please trust us. Not only with the case but with Aimee's well-being. We know what we're doing. I know how hard it is to sit on the sidelines and not be an active player. But when we take on a client, we solve their case."

Travis blew out a breath and nodded. "I'll do my best."

Once Travis had gone, Casey mulled over the interview. Travis obviously cared deeply about Aimee. He also saw the naivete in her that Casey had from their first meeting. She couldn't blame him for his questions or for his protectiveness.

However, he'd given her an idea. It was true that almost no one knew about Aimee's situation.

But Nick Colotti did.

***

CannaBD headquarters
Elmton, New York
10:45 a.m.

Nick was in a fine mood.

He leaned back in his office chair, locked his fingers behind his head, and decided he would go out and eat some real food for lunch today, not just scarf down one or two random granola bars that were stuffed in his desk drawer. It might not yet be time for an all-out celebration, but his instincts told him that he'd be scheduling a victory dinner for the team quite soon.

He'd just hung up with his attorney. The contract sealing the deal on Jason Williams becoming a CannaBD investor was going faster and more smoothly than expected. It had only been a few days, and already things were rolling along. Several more document exchanges, a week's worth of reviewing and tweaking, and they would be on the verge of having its largest investor ever—other than his dad.

His cell phone rang, indicating it was his office number being transferred over, and he punched the accept button.

"Nick Colotti speaking."

"Good morning, Mr. Colotti," a woman's voice greeted him. "This is Casey Woods of Forensic Instincts. I hope I haven't called at a bad time."

Nick's good mood vanished.

"Mr. Colotti?"

Nick found his tongue. "Yes, sorry. I was in the middle of something with my attorney."

"I apologize. Shall I call back?"

"No, it's fine. We just wrapped up."

"Good." Casey Woods sounded just as she did on camera—professional, outgoing, and a little intimidating. "I'll only take a moment of your time—at least for now."

Nick wet his lips with the tip of his tongue. "I guess this is about Aimee."

"Yes. She told me she confided in you about our representing her, first, to discover what really happened to Rita Edwell, and second, to safeguard her, especially since Chris Maher was murdered."

Nick was feeling more unsettled by the minute. Still, he wasn't stupid enough to lie about something Forensic Instincts already knew firsthand. "She did. I was really upset about Rita Edwell. And Aimee was a mess. She was also scared to death that Chris Maher was going to kill her. But now he's dead, too. That's all I know."

"That's quite a bit."

Nick blew out a breath. "Aimee's worked for me pretty much since I started CannaBD. She's incredibly sharp and a huge part of why we're so successful. I'm her boss. She felt I needed to know what was going on. But it's not as if we're tight friends. It's all business. Period."

"And yet, aside from Aimee's boyfriend, Travis, you're the only one she's talked to about her situation."

"As you just said, Travis is her boyfriend. It's natural that she go to him. In my case, she told me out of respect."

Casey wasn't letting up. "I'm sure that's true. Still, I'd like your take on what Aimee did say. Can you free up some time to talk to me? I'd, of course, come to your office. And I promise to stay only a half hour."

Nick felt himself freaking out. An in-person meeting? What was she looking for? He knew very well that she was a trained behaviorist. Would she be able to see right through him?

In the end, he really had no choice.

"If it would help Aimee, I'd be happy to talk to you," he said. "When were you thinking?"

"I was hoping you had some free time this afternoon. Say, about one? Or does that interrupt a meeting or cut into your lunch?"

Today. Shit.

Stalling would do nothing except make him appear to be hiding something. "One o'clock would be fine."

Casey sounded pleased. "Great. I'll be there. Thanks so much for your time." She disconnected the call.

Nick continued to grip his cell. He had a little over two hours to prepare. What should he say? What should he *not* say?

He had to reach his father—*now*.

Oliver backed away from Nick's door, leaving it as it was—slightly ajar. He was livid. This was news to him—and not good news.

He had to nip it in the bud.

21

Formen's Diner
Woodfield, New Jersey
Friday, 3:15 p.m.

It was between the lunch and dinner rush, so the diner was quiet.

Victor sat in the usual booth, fiddling with the large envelope he'd brought with him, now placed close to his side. There were four smaller envelopes in it, all bulging with cash.

He watched the door, his stomach churning with that familiar sense of stress.

His stomach was always restless when he met with his captain, passing along the various percentages of profit. It wasn't as if he ever screwed the family. Still, money was money and volatility was volatility. If things weren't handled just right, the consequences could be dire. Following the rules kept him protected, respected, and alive. He was allowed the freedom to run his operation independently, assisted by an occasional soldier and associate. But when he needed the top guys, they were there. It was an equitable relationship, and Victor had no intention of rocking the boat.

The payoffs he had to make were always the same. Fifteen percent to his captain. Twenty percent each to the consigliere and underboss.

And thirty-five percent to the boss. True, Victor only kept about ten percent, but ten percent of a fortune was still a fortune.

The front door swung open and Salvatore Orsatti walked in. He wasn't a particularly imposing man—medium height, stocky, with an expression that could switch from solemn to smiling in the blink of an eye. His aspirations were high; it was no secret that he didn't want to stay a captain forever. But word was he was loyal to the family and therefore ready to wait until it was his time.

With a quick wave at their regular waitress, he made an automatic left and headed to the booth Victor was seated in.

"Hey, Sal," Victor greeted him as he sat down. "Good to see you."

Sal signaled their waitress, indicating with a few gestures that they would have their usual, and then turned back to Victor.

"Good to see you, too, Vic. You look good. Your business looks even better."

"No complaints." Victor gave him a half smile.

"There shouldn't be. Your profits are increasing. Make them increase even more. Raise your prices. These rich bastards can afford it. I'm going to be keeping a closer eye on you *and* upping my cut."

Victor swallowed. "Whatever you decide, Sal."

Sal grunted his agreement, then waited while their food was served. He took a belt of his black coffee and remained silent until their waitress had scurried off. She knew the routine. When these two men were having a meeting, they wanted speedy service and privacy. She gave them both.

Once they were alone, Sal asked, "Are you on top of that nosy investigation company?"

Victor nodded, although his gut tightened further. "I've got everything under control. They have no clue who I am or what I'm doing. Plus, even if they were to check me out—which they won't—I've made sure there are no bread crumbs whatsoever leading to you or the family. Forensic Instincts is my problem, if they even become one."

"And your wack job?"

"Still proving useful. But I put him in his place the other day. He's under control."

Sal patted Victor's hand. "Smart."

There was a long silence—one that always occurred at this point in their meetings, once the pleasantries and the inquiries were over. Victor knew what was expected of him.

He glanced around to make sure no one was nearby and then handed the envelopes of cash quickly under the table. Sal had already scooped up his jacket. He took the large envelope and stuffed it inside his inner pocket, laying the jacket on the bench beside him.

"Now we can eat and catch up," he said with a smile, almost simultaneously with the arrival of their food.

Forty minutes, two cups of coffee, and a plate of eggs later, Sal collected his jacket and bid Victor goodbye. "I'll let you know when our next meeting will be."

"Of course. Be well."

"You, too. Stay good," Sal responded.

He slapped down some bills on the table and, with another wave at the waitress, made his way out of the diner.

Victor blew out his breath in a relieved sigh. Thank the good Lord. Everything was copasetic. Additional financial pressure didn't come close to what he'd been fearing—what he always feared.

He could actually feel his stomach unclench.

He pushed away his plate, yanked on his own jacket, and nodded at the waitress as he left. He crossed the parking lot and slid behind the wheel of his new Mercedes-Maybach.

As was always his custom before heading home, he checked the messages on his personal phone, as well as his various burners. Nothing on his personal line; his wife rarely bothered him when he was doing business, and all their friends called her to schedule plans.

But his most worrisome burner phone was filled with voice mails. Lots of them. Left by a man who was on the edge.

His hired killer's voice was vibrating with rage—the kind of rage that set off alarm bells in Victor's head. It was clear he'd uncovered some threat to the operation—one that endangered him.

Victor didn't turn over his engine. He glanced in his rearview mirror and made sure Sal had driven away. Then he made the return phone call.

"What's going on?"

"Forensic Instincts and Aimee Bregman—that's what's going on," the angry voice shot back. There was a fine line of control in his tone, and Victor had the distinct feeling he was holding on to his self-control by a thread. "She's smarter than you think. She's moving forward, and so is Forensic Instincts. This is getting too close. And I don't plan to wait around for a bomb to explode in my face."

Victor tried to stay calm. He wanted all the details without having them clouded by a raging lunatic with his own agenda.

"Tell me everything you know."

The more Victor heard, the more worried he got. The guy at the other end of the phone might be unstable, but he was also smart. And he was right. Liaisons were strengthening, potentially dangerous information was being sought, and if all this continued, it could become a major threat.

"Are you still there?" his killer demanded.

"Yes. I'm thinking."

"Don't. I'll be taking care of this one."

"What the hell does *that* mean?"

"It means it's time for people to worry about their lives, not about our business."

Victor's chest began to pound. "Tell me what you're planning."

"I'll surprise you. But you'll like the results."

The line went dead.

Victor stared at his phone, the pounding in his chest intensified. What was that damn loose cannon going to do? What should *he* do? He'd just told Sal that everything was being managed. Clearly it wasn't. And this wasn't one of those times when he could force the psycho to meet with him so he could talk him down. The guy was already in motion.

What the hell was he going to do?

Victor's mind was all over the place, from the bomb that would now explode to how he was going to deal with the mob to the more mundane but important issues gnawing at his gut.

He was going to have to put his life—and his income—on hold for the foreseeable future. There were going to be a shitload of events coming up he'd have to cancel. He already had two this week, ones it was too late to call a halt to.

There was the wealthy house party he was catering tomorrow night, one that would culminate with a fat check from the host and hostess. He'd hoped to find some additional opportunities there. Okay, well, he could accomplish all that in a modified version. He'd arrive late. His company guys would have already delivered and set up the food and booze. He'd then show up, and rather than stay for the party, he'd stay for just a half hour to make sure everything was just so, to schmooze the host and hostess, and to get as many introductions as he could in that short amount of time. He'd leave, only to return to the party when it was wrapping up to make pleasantries and to pick up his money.

All equating to about forty-five minutes of exposure.

The next event, scheduled for Wednesday night, would be trickier. It was a high-scale catering gig at a top-tier university's New York City alumni event, set at the university's Midtown location. The setup was perfect for mingling, moneymaking, and seeking out new parental prospects. But he'd have to truncate—show up along with the food and booze, circle the room to say his hellos, and then leave, letting Joe Giulio, his most trusted and experienced guy, run the show. He'd get much less out of it—prospects and money, but he couldn't take any further risks. Until he knew just how much Forensic Instincts knew about him *and* what insane act his sicko employee was about to commit, he'd have to go radio silent.

He'd use the time to nurture ongoing relationships and issues from within and keep clear of establishing new liaisons—at least for a time. After that, hopefully, the situation would be under control and his life could resume.

Hopefully.

Trembling, Victor pressed the brake pedal and dash-mounted button, using his Mercedes's KEYLESS GO to start his drive. He pulled away from his meeting place and headed home.

Lord help him if Sal or anyone else in the family learned about any of this before it was contained.

His life wouldn't be worth shit.

***

Battery Park City, New York
10:45 p.m.

Casey walked into her apartment, flipped the lock shut behind her, and placed the tote bag that held her laptop on the living room sofa. She went straight into the kitchen and poured herself a glass of wine, perching against the kitchen nook to sip it.

She'd left the office earlier than planned, given her new and totally unnerving concern, which added to the amount of interview analysis she still had left to do. But she needed a fresh eye and a change of scene to continue her work. Hutch was heading up a big case and wasn't due home for hours, which would give her time to review the day's meetings and get a firm handle on where things stood.

She glanced at her wine goblet, realized the cabernet wasn't doing the trick to calm her racing mind, and set it down, choosing instead to take a hot shower to unwind.

Twenty minutes later, she emerged, clean if not unwound, and shrugged into one of Hutch's comfy T-shirts. She tied back her damp, shoulder-length red hair, stopped in the kitchen to collect her wine, and headed into her home office.

She sat at her desk chair, massaging her temples, her laptop still unopened.

The meeting with Travis. The meeting with Nick. They'd taken a backseat to her latest and most prominent concern. Her instincts were rarely wrong. And when she and Nick had met at CannaBD, she'd had the nagging feeling they were being watched.

But by whom? And why? And was the person inside the building or outside, with a bird's-eye view of Nick's office?

Something definitely wasn't right. And whatever it was, it didn't bode well for Aimee.

Frowning, Casey realized she hadn't even had the chance to report this new development to the team, nor about the interviews themselves, because everyone had been scattered and inundated all afternoon and evening. She'd tell them first thing in the morning. For now, it was time to stop fixating on this unknown and to plunge into a review of her notes regarding the meetings themselves.

Before she could begin, her iPhone binged. It was the phone on which Ryan had installed a sophisticated and high-tech security software—a phone whose number and software all the FI team members shared. Glancing down, she saw that she had an email and a link from Marc.

She opened the email on her laptop.

Read this, it said. *Then let's talk.*

Casey clicked on the link, which led to a reputable Westchester County news source. It was a small piece, and it read:

A man was found dead in the woods in southern Hartsville. The death is being considered suspicious and is being investigated by the Hartsville police. They've released no name and no details, saying only that the immediate family has been contacted and that it is an open investigation.

Casey reread the short piece twice, her forehead creased in question.

Then she picked up her iPhone and punched Marc's contact button.

"Hey," he greeted her. "Did you read it?"

"Yes," Casey replied. "I'm sorry for the guy. But is it meaningful to us?"

"Yup. One of my friends works for the Hartsville Police Department. He gave me a call. He said he shouldn't be telling me this, but he'd already contacted the NYPD, and since he knows we're investigating the Chris Maher murder, he's bending the rules in the hopes that we can solve this case—fast."

"Go on," Casey urged.

"The guy was identified as Jake Flanders, a former employee of a packaging company. And when I say former, I mean until yesterday. He'd just been laid off."

"Suicide?"

"Definitely not." Marc squelched that theory in a hurry. "He was bound and brutally choked with a cable. There was a butcher knife protruding from his thigh. Impaled on it was a college football glove."

Casey's eyes widened. "Our psycho killer."

"None other."

"Do we know his connection to Jake Flanders? Because, based on the signature kill, this was not a mob hit. It was one of the sociopath's sick personal assassinations. Did your friend have any more information?"

"He was limited in what he could say," Marc replied. "He did tell me what led them to Flanders's body. A bunch of local residents called in to report seeing a cracked-up Subaru on the side of the parkway just a couple of miles from where the body was found. They took photos of the license plate number and the vehicle itself. They transmitted it all to the detective handling the case."

"And the car belonged to Flanders."

"Right. But there's more. Two couples who were on the parkway that night saw Flanders get into a major road rage competition with another driver. The wild man was driving a Camaro and was moving too fast for anyone to catch the plates. Whatever happened must have been bad, because Flanders's car was pretty crunched up. So the police started a search. That area is heavily wooded. But they found the body."

"Was there any trace evidence in Flanders's car?" Casey asked. "Blood splatter? Fingerprints?"

"Nothing. The whole car was either wiped clean or the killer wore gloves."

"Family? Friends? Anyone who's suspicious in Flanders's life?"

"So far the police haven't established any suspicious relationships in Flanders's life. He was a family man, with a solid marriage, a little girl, and a new baby on the way. Given he was just laid off, I'd buy the suicide theory. But this was murder, grotesque and personal."

"And it doesn't help us with the victimology angle we're taking." Casey's tone was rife with frustration. "What could he and Chris Maher possibly have in common? Chris was a wealthy, high-profile victim. Unless Flanders has a private stash that the police have yet to find, his job would indicate a modest income and a low-profile life."

"Maybe our investigation will tell us more," Marc said. "It could be that he and our sociopath knew each other in some different way. Again, our answers to find."

"First, we have to rule out any connection to Aimee. Although I can't imagine there is one. Still, she's our priority. When we spread our tentacles in order to learn more, I want to check out CannaBD, too."

"I'm not following." Marc sounded puzzled. "Flanders didn't work for CannaBD. What ties are you looking for?"

"I don't know. But I have a strong feeling that CannaBD is in some way a key factor in Aimee's case." Casey went on to tell Marc about the feeling of being watched she'd had while interviewing Nick.

Marc listened intently. "Rita and Chris weren't involved in the company."

"Maybe the killer thought otherwise. Because the discussion taking place between them and Aimee at the bar that night was all about CannaBD." Casey's shoulders lifted, then fell. "I know I'm reaching."

"You rarely reach. We have to check this out, as well. And let's remember, this could be a lucky break. Flanders is the first body whose murder specs match Chris Maher's."

"Agreed," Casey said. "Go get some sleep. I'm Slacking the whole team. We'll meet at eight a.m."

22

Offices of Forensic Instincts
Ryan's lair
Saturday, 6:45 a.m.

When Ryan left his apartment at five thirty, Claire was still fast asleep in his bed. Leaving her was a tough call. But he had limited time before the team meeting Casey had called. And he had a shitload to do, including continuing to track down other possible victims of their psycho killer. Also, he'd been reading and rereading the cell phone records they already had. And something about the university landline calls was bugging him. He planned on reviewing those ASAP.

Most of all, he was eager to get going on the next step of tracking the phantom phone numbers. He'd activated the bots several days ago. Time for step two—a step that would be even riskier and would take longer to complete.

He'd stopped for a quick workout at the gym, then bought a protein shake and took it straight to his lair. The office was quiet, but that would be changing soon. Marc and Patrick were probably squeezing in a quick breakfast with their wives, after which they'd show up at the office pronto. Emma liked to sleep in over the weekend, unless she was summoned, at which point sleep was forgotten and she was at the office in record time. That would be the case this morning.

And Claire… well, she was normally a crack-of-dawn riser and often the first to arrive. But since he hadn't let her go to sleep until after three in the morning, today was an exception. However, she'd gotten Casey's Slack message. And there was no way she'd be a moment late for this meeting.

"Good morning, Ryan," Yoda greeted him cordially.

"Hey, Yoda." Ryan was already getting settled at his desk. "I've got some human intelligence to kick off. It's going to be a long wait—could be up to a week. Hopefully sooner rather than later. After that, I'll be turning the results over to you."

"Very good, Ryan. In the interim, I'll be ready to do whatever tasks you need of me."

"Great." Ryan woke up his computer and perched at the edge of his seat, poised and ready to go.

It would take quite some time to trace the phone calls emanating from a series of random burner phones. Gaining access to a shitload of cell tower records was a delicate process. Carriers had sophisticated systems to detect hacking attempts. Querying the database containing cell tower records for one phone number might not draw attention from the hacking prevention systems, but investigating eight burner phones simultaneously would.

Ryan would need to design strategies to make the queries look random and unconnected. That would take time, deployment of cloud resources, and creation of custom scripts to appear isolated and different, not the concentrated efforts of a criminal enterprise or a nation-state hacking group.

The computer whirred to life. Ryan logged in using one of his dark web aliases. A few more clicks. Then, he began typing furiously into the keyboard. He paused, waited for a response, and entered his commands. In order to carefully extract the data he was seeking without being discovered, he intended to wake up one of the sleeper bots he had inside the T-Mobile network. He'd send it little bits of information, erasing his tracks along the way.

A few more entries into the computer.

The bot was awake and ready to go.

***

Offices of Forensic Instincts
Second-floor main conference room
Saturday, 8:00 a.m.

Everyone had grabbed their respective coffee or herbal tea and was gathered around the table, waiting to begin.

Casey didn't waste any time. She filled the team in on her interviews with both Travis and Nick, plus the unshakable awareness that, during the latter meeting, she and/or Nick were being watched. Before the team had even had the chance to digest all that, Marc told everyone about Flanders's murder and the specifics surrounding it.

Afterwards, you could have heard a pin drop in the room.

Emma broke the silence. "I don't even know which topic to ask questions about first..."

"I'll start with the practical," Ryan said, angling his head in Marc's direction. "Can you send me all the specifics you just relayed about Jake Flanders? I initiated an in-depth search for any victims I could find who were murdered with that same signature kill. No luck yet. But this is a real connection. It'll give me a great starting point."

Marc nodded. "Done. I'll get it to you as soon as this meeting breaks up."

"What about whoever was watching you?" Claire asked Casey. "Why? It doesn't sound as if you were having an inflammatory or revealing conversation with Nick. You weren't exposing any secrets. So what was the point of the surveillance? Or am I missing something?"

"No, but yes," Casey replied. "There was nothing inflammatory that I'm aware of. That doesn't mean there isn't someone who's very interested or concerned about what Nick and I were discussing. Or even the fact that I was there to begin with."

"Which leads back to Aimee," Patrick said with a frown. "If CannaBD is somehow involved in this mess, then the threat to Aimee is most likely linked to her job."

"I agree," Casey replied. "Which makes me want to alter our original plan to question only people who had direct knowledge of Aimee's situation. I think we should expand our interviews to include other CannaBD employees. I'll start with the rest of the management team: Kimberley Perkins, the company's accountant, and Oliver Steadman, the head of production."

"There are also warehouse and distillery workers," Marc pointed out. "You can't handle them all. I'll cover this one with you." He paused. "If anyone there is dirty, my presence—coupled with yours—will freak them out. Some revelation could come from this. And we'll keep the tone light and the questions nonthreatening and non-informative so those who are innocent won't suspect a thing. In the meantime, we can also sharpen our instincts to see if we can get a clue as to who was watching you during your last meeting there."

"That's great. We'll talk through our lines of questioning as we drive to CannaBD." Casey's lips curved. "I can't wait to tell Nick Colotti that we'd like to return and talk to his people."

***

CannaBD headquarters
Elmton, New York
Saturday, 11:30 a.m.

Nick was pacing around his desk, sweating profusely, when Aimee eased open his office door and poked her head in.

"Nick?" she asked. "You wanted to see me. You sounded pretty urgent."

Nick whipped around. "Come in and close the door."

Aimee complied. She wasn't stunned by Nick's mood. Casey had called to prepare her, just as she had when she'd scheduled her initial meeting with Nick. Casey's gut feeling was that she and Marc should chat with the rest of the CannaBD team, just in case Nick had inadvertently said something that could impact Aimee. Frankly, Aimee didn't see the purpose of it, but on the other hand, she had the feeling that FI had its reasons. So she'd given Casey the go-ahead.

And this was the result.

Nick wasn't mincing words. "Why is Forensic Instincts making daily trips here?" he demanded. "What did you tell them? How am I—or anyone employed by CannaBD—part of their investigation?"

Aimee tipped her head in question, ostensibly unsure why Nick was so upset. "It's no big deal. Truthfully, I think Casey was making sure I didn't spill my guts to you, rather than just lay out the facts. They know I'm coming apart. So they probably checked with you and are now doubling back to speak to the staff to ensure I wasn't blabbing details and putting myself in more danger. But as you know, I didn't. They just want to ensure that fact for themselves."

Nick settled down a bit. "Is that what Casey Woods told you?"

"Not in so many words, but yes. It's the only reason I gave them permission to contact you." Aimee's eyes widened. "Why? Did they offend you in some way?"

"No, no, nothing like that." Nick waved away her question, the sweat beginning to dry on his forehead. "It's just that they… Never mind. I was overreacting. Before you came on board, I was sued by a competitor claiming formula infringement—which, of course, was complete bullshit. But I was bombarded by investigators. I don't like them. So when a renowned investigative firm comes in to 'talk with you' two days in a row, you worry. At least I do. I was concerned that they thought someone at CannaBD was part of what you're going through."

Aimee waved away that notion. "Hardly. And just to ease your mind, FI is making great progress. I'm not telling you a single detail other than that, so I keep my information flow to you exactly as it was. But for the first time, I feel like there's a chance I'll be able to live normally again."

"That's great." Nick sounded a lot more curious than he appeared to be. Instead of pursuing the subject, he shot a quick glance at his Apple Watch and then made a one-eighty.

"Let me take you to lunch," he said. "It's the least I can do to make up for bellowing at you."

Aimee forced a smile. She had the distinct impression that Nick was trying to buy time. "You didn't bellow—well, maybe a little. So I'll take you up on that lunch."

Nick's grin was one of relief. "You pick the place."

23

CannaBD headquarters parking lot
Elmton, New York
Saturday, 2:10 p.m.

Aimee turned over her engine and pulled out of the lot. She turned onto the main road and checked her rearview mirror to ensure that she was alone—which she was, other than John, who was already positioned to follow her home.

She gave him a quick wave and then called Casey.

"Hi," Casey answered immediately. "How did things go?"

"Pretty well, I think," Aimee replied. "I never imagined I could be such a good actress."

A chuckle. "I never doubted you."

"The important thing is I think I calmed Nick down enough to clear your path." Aimee paused. "Although he seemed to have some kind of time agenda. Once he was at ease, he made it a point to take me to lunch—an unexpectedly long lunch."

"Interesting," Casey replied. "So you think he was buying time for something or someone?"

"I'm not trained like you guys are, but it definitely seemed that way to me." Another pause. "I'm still pretty much in the dark about why you're talking to Nick and the others. Are they suspects?"

"I'm not sure," Casey answered honestly. "I didn't think so. But the way Nick is acting, and the vibes I picked up when we were talking… it's possible. I'll see what happens when Marc and I go back to CannaBD later this afternoon. I'll keep you posted if I learn anything."

"Okay." Aimee disconnected the call, wishing FI would tell her more. After all, it was *her* life. On the other hand, they were the ones saving it. So she'd follow the rules, knowing they'd fill her in with anything important.

Aimee's apartment
Washington Heights, New York
Saturday, 2:50 p.m.

Traffic was light, and Aimee pretty much flew home.

That was a relief, since the meeting and lunch had taken a lot out of her. Making small talk and enthusiastically downing a burger and fries—plus a dessert she hadn't asked for and really didn't want—with a boss who she no longer fully trusted and who was turning this impromptu lunch into a major meal… The whole thing was almost impossible for her to pull off.

Whether she'd succeeded or not, she was very glad to be home.

She jumped out of her car, took the outdoor steps and then the elevator, and was already pulling off her jacket when she reached the front door of her apartment.

Abruptly, she froze.

The door was open a crack and there were scratch marks on the outer lock. Someone had broken in and might or might not still be in there.

Aimee began to shake uncontrollably. She considered running full speed out of the building, but that might alert the intruder and give him time to grab her or to get away.

Instead, she retraced her steps, turned the corner, and pulled out her phone with trembling hands. One press of a button, and John's voice answered.

"John," Aimee whispered. "Someone broke into my place. I don't know what to do. I don't know if they're still inside..."

"I'm already halfway to the elevator," John replied, his quickened breath telling her he was moving at a dead run. "Where are you?"

"Around the corner from my apartment."

"Stay there. And keep the line open."

Moments later, John blew out of the elevator and strode down to where Aimee stood white-faced. The corridors were all clear.

"Let me go in first," he instructed, whipping out his harnessed pistol and pausing only to put on plastic gloves.

Aimee nodded, wrapping her arms around herself.

John disappeared inside, and, while there were no gunshots, he was gone for what seemed to be ages.

At last, he emerged, a dark expression on his face. "The intruder is gone. But we have to call the police. I'd like you to check out the place first, but I have to be blunt. It's bad. Really bad."

"I'm going in," Aimee said.

John nodded. "I'm right behind you."

Aimee steeled herself, then walked through the door.

Bad was an understatement.

The place was totally and violently trashed. Furniture overturned, her sofa sliced to ribbons, her tables and chairs shattered to bits. Following the chaos into the bathroom, Aimee saw that drawers had been dumped, and the contents of the medicine cabinet were everywhere.

Her heart filled with dread, she turned and walked into her bedroom. This time she couldn't hide her horrified gasp, her hands flying to her face.

The bed had been slashed repeatedly, and feathers had been flung around. The feathers were all covered with droplets of blood. In the center of what remained of the bed was a huge pool of blood, large enough that it seemed to represent a person.

Aimee let out a small whimper, her gaze frozen on the spot.

"It's not blood," John said quickly. "It's red paint."

Red paint. That reality swirled around in Aimee's frozen mind. *Red paint, not blood.*

She tore away her gaze. More droplets of paint were splattered on the dresser and nightstand and dribbled on the carpet. All the drawers were overturned, and her clothing and intimate undergarments were torn to shreds, left on top of the red-stained carpet.

She pivoted, finding herself face-to-face with the mirror hanging over what had been her dresser.

Across the glass, written in bold strokes of red paint, were the words:

Silence or violence.

"It's a lot to take in," John murmured, laying a gentle hand on Aimee's shoulder. "Are you all right?"

"No," she whispered.

"Can you hold up for a few minutes? I want to dust the place for fingerprints and do whatever else I can before the police show up, tape off the place, and declare it a crime scene." John paused, clearly upset about what he was about to ask. "Once I'm done, do you think you can check to see if anything is missing? I know it's a lot to ask, but the police are going to ask this same question, plus a whole lot more, and I'd like us to be prepared."

Mutely, Aimee nodded.

"Good. Stay just inside the apartment. It'll take me only a few minutes. Then, I'll get you."

"Okay." Aimee wondered how much longer her legs were going to support her. She didn't budge or even look around. She just waited dazedly for John to issue further instructions.

He returned to her side. "I wish I didn't have to ask this of you."

"I know. But it's something I have to do." Aimee's hands balled into fists at her sides, as anger began to filter in, mixing with the other emotions she was experiencing. "I want to catch this psycho."

With John's calming presence at her side, she slowly examined the apartment for missing items, moving from the living room and kitchen to the bathroom and finally to the bedroom.

She found her jewelry box, which was cracked into pieces, with jewelry strewn around. She rifled through everything, finally lifting her head.

"Two things are gone," she said in a voice she didn't recognize. "A pair of diamond studs and a gold pendant with three stones in a heart. It represented my family. Our birthstones." She started to cry, then broke completely down, sinking to the bedroom floor, her shoulders shaking with sobs.

John squeezed her arm. After a moment, he asked, "Anything else?"

She raised her head, looked at the remnants of her nightstand. "The emergency cash I keep in that drawer—maybe a couple of hundred dollars," she continued on autopilot. "And I think the prescription drugs that were in my medicine cabinet. There were only three bottles. But I didn't stay long enough to count the number of pills..."

"That's enough." John eased her to her feet. "I'll call Casey, give her a head start. Then I'll call 9-1-1. Let's step into the hall and wait."

Casey and Marc arrived a few minutes before the police. Marc yanked on gloves and walked the floors with John, both men quietly talking as they scanned the inside of the apartment. They stayed inside only as long as necessary, since neither of them wanted to risk being where they shouldn't be when the cops showed up.

Casey stayed in the hall with Aimee. She gave her a hard hug, seeing the state of shock she was in. And judging from what Casey could see inside the apartment, Aimee's reaction was justified.

Aimee drew back, wiped her eyes with the backs of her hands. She told Casey about the bed, as well as what the message on the mirror had said.

"Are they're coming back to kill me?" she asked. "Is that what all this means?"

"No." Casey gave an adamant shake of her head. "This is a scare tactic. They want you to panic and shut down."

"Why?" Aimee spread her arms wide. "I don't know anything—at least I think I don't." She gave Casey a quizzical look.

"There's a lot we need to talk about." Casey answered the puzzled expression on Aimee's face. "It wasn't necessary for us to freak you out even more yet. But now it is. We have more facts. We need to be up-front with you. In the meantime, let's just say that they think you're on the verge of figuring out things they want hidden."

"Who are 'they'?"

"That's part of what we need to tell you." Casey's eyes darted around. "This isn't the time or the place. The cops will be here any minute. Once you've answered yet another batch of their questions, we'll go to the brownstone. We'll talk there."

Aimee nodded. She averted her gaze, digesting what she did know and letting it all sink in. When she turned back to Casey, her eyes were flashing with the same anger that had flared when she reentered the apartment.

"I'm not bowing out," she stated flatly. "This is my life. I'll find another apartment. And once I know everything we're dealing with,

I'll be on board with you, help in any way I can. I'm sick and tired of being a victim. I'm terrified of this psycho, but I'm not letting him win."

Casey gave Aimee's hands a hard squeeze. "Good for you. And we'll be right there by your side. We'll put together all the pieces. I'm certain."

Before Casey could say more, two NYPD detectives from the thirty-fourth precinct blew out of the elevator and straight to Aimee's apartment.

Another interrogation was about to begin.

24

Aimee's apartment
Washington Heights, New York
Saturday, 4:10 p.m.

Aimee had learned a lot from FI about what truths to reveal and what truths to conceal when it came to the NYPD.

It was two female detectives this time, and they seemed to be a little more empathetic than the detectives Aimee had met at Manhattan Homicide South. Then again, these two detectives probably didn't see as many murder cases, either. Plus, they were here on a B and E, not a homicide.

Casey and Marc offered to drive Aimee to the station for her Q and A, while John stood by to answer the detectives' questions. He knew the drill. He waited until after they'd swept the place for DNA evidence and then taped off the apartment as a crime scene before they talked.

John provided direct answers to straightforward questions. The intensive part, he knew, was for Aimee to handle.

***

As they drove, Casey and Marc prepped Aimee once again.

This time she was a lot stronger and much less naïve than she'd been the first time she was interviewed by the NYPD. The only clarifications she sought from Casey and Marc were how much to tell these new detectives about the previous crimes, about the other police precincts that were involved, and the full extent of what she knew.

Casey answered. "You don't know much more than you knew when Chris was killed. You were afraid for your life both when Rita was allegedly killed and when Chris was murdered. What just happened at your apartment only serves to reemphasize that fear. Tell them about the first and twenty-sixth precincts' involvement, as well as that of Manhattan Homicide North and South. Also, tell them that you've met with all those precincts repeatedly and that they have all the facts up to this point. That'll spur action. Coordinating efforts will take the cops endless hours of red tape as they try to fit pieces together."

"Leave out any speculation and just stick to the facts," Marc said. "The destruction to your apartment is self-evident. Your panic and state of shock are to be expected. You have no idea who committed this violent act. Let the police work this. I'm sure you'll be asked for a return visit, probably from a newly formed task force. But that will take a while to put into place. For now, answer only what you've been asked."

"That's no problem," Aimee said with a sigh. "I have nothing else to tell them—*yet*." she stressed. "But all that will change when we have our meeting afterwards. Then I'll be chock full of information, right?"

"Yes," Casey said. "Right."

***

Victor's house
Colts River, New Jersey
Saturday, 5:35 p.m.

Victor poured himself another glass of bourbon. He had no idea how many that made, nor did he care. Being drunk was the only way he could cope with this waiting.

He'd paced his office floor for so many hours since yesterday afternoon when the lunatic had called that the area rug was compressed and the oak floors were scuffed.

Several times during the night, Frances had come down to ask if he was okay and if he wanted something to eat. He'd answered her as pleasantly as he could. But she knew him, and she knew what it meant when he behaved this way. So she didn't press him to come to bed or even to stop drinking. She just gave him a quick peck on the cheek and made herself scarce, leaving with a frightened look in her eyes.

Victor barely noticed any of it. Sleep was out of the question, as was eating. All he wanted was for that damn phone to ring.

As if the heavens had heard him, the correct burner phone trilled.

He snatched it up. "Stefano? Please tell me you have something."

Stefano blew out a breath. "Yeah, I have something. But it's nothing you're going to like."

"It's something I have to hear."

"The report just came over from the thirty-fourth."

"The thirty-fourth?" Victor felt bile rise in his throat. "That's Washington Heights."

"Sure is. And before you ask, yeah, it was Aimee Bregman's apartment. The place was mutilated."

"Her *apartment*?" Victor jumped on that. "Not *her*? She's not dead?"

"That's about the only good news I've got. She's alive."

"Thank the Lord." Victor sank into a chair, rubbing his now drenched forehead. "What did the lunatic do?"

"A lot." Stefano went on to read Victor the report he'd printed out, detail by detail. By the time he finished, Victor was close to vomiting.

"That's almost as bad as if he'd killed her," he managed. "In some ways, worse. She's alive and talking to the cops. If she were dead, she'd stay silent. But either way, the spotlight will shine just as brightly on the fact that she's a target. And being that she's already linked to the other two murders, plus the fact that she has Forensic Instincts investigating for her—I don't see how I'm going to stop this from snowballing out of control."

Stefano grunted his agreement. "While you're figuring that out, what do you want me to do at my end?"

"Stay on top of every single detail you can get."

"Yeah," Stefano said. "There's gonna be a lot. Three separate precincts plus both homicide divisions. Expect a task force to be formed so all information and efforts can be combined. I'll stay plugged in."

"And stay in constant contact with me," Victor replied. "I've got my work cut out for me."

***

Offices of Forensic Instincts
First-floor small conference room
Tribeca, New York
Saturday, 7:35 p.m.

The whole FI team, plus Aimee and John, were settled on the various tub chairs and settees, eating slices of the pizzas Emma had ordered in. Everyone had agreed that the first topic of discussion would be the invasion of Aimee's apartment. All the team members, other than Casey and Marc, needed to be updated. Once that part of the meeting was over, John would head home for a much-needed break, and Garrison Miles, John's counterpart, would take over Aimee's security detail.

At which time, Casey would fill Aimee in on as much as she felt their client should know at this point.

"You were excellent in your police interview," Casey praised Aimee before they got into the nitty-gritty. "Calm, cooperative, and just forthright enough."

Aimee sighed. "Part of me is still in shock."

"And part of you is angry. That'll work well in moving forward. The shock will fade. And by the way, as for your living arrangements, you'll be staying at the brownstone for the immediate future. We'll worry about finding you a new apartment later."

"Thank you," Aimee said with a shudder. "It's going to be a while before I feel safe anywhere. And I'm certainly not walking back into that mutilated apartment. Even after it's been sanitized from top to bottom, all I'll ever see is the scene I walked away from."

"What scene?" Emma demanded. "I feel like I just walked into the end of a movie."

"Sorry," Casey said. "Aimee, why don't you and John tell us the whole story. Marc and I only know secondhand."

Aimee turned her palms up in an unsure gesture. "I found the door open and the lock picked. I ran into the hall and called John. He was there in a heartbeat." She glanced up, looked directly at John. "Can you please take it from there? You're the pro and I'm just the exhausted prey."

"No problem," he said. He started at the beginning and left nothing out.

"Shit," Ryan muttered when John was finished.

"You poor thing," Claire said, facing Aimee. "What a horrifying experience. I'm so sorry."

"Thank you," Aimee replied.

John then got into some FBI-type observations. "The intruder tried some ridiculous tactics to throw off the cops. Taking jewelry and money to try to suggest that this was just an over-the-top burglary. Stealing some random prescription meds to try to convince them he was an addict—which was totally absurd given that what he stole were allergy meds and mild sleeping pills. The sick bastard couldn't conceal that this was a very violent and very personal attack against Aimee. This will be treated as a violent crime even before all the precincts are brought up to speed."

"The threat to Aimee is very real and is now escalating," Casey said. "And she's right. She's entitled to know where things stand in the investigation." A quick glance at the team—one they all recognized to mean *information given with moderation.*

John pushed back his chair and rose. "Do you still need me here?"

"No." Casey gestured toward the door. "Thanks for everything. Go get some rest."

Aimee gave him a grateful look. "I can't tell you how much I appreciate what you did tonight. Thank you."

John gave Aimee and Casey each a mock salute. "Just doing my job." He yawned. "I'll be back on duty tomorrow night." He left the room, closing the door behind him.

25

Aimee didn't waste an instant.

The minute the door closed behind John, she sat up taller in her chair, having barely eaten half a slice of pizza. "Fill me in."

"Okay," Casey replied. "But let me touch on one last point before we do. Was Rita into money? Did she dress expensively? Was her apartment way bigger and professionally decorated in a way that her salary could never cover? Did she take lots of lavish vacations? Stuff like that."

Aimee blinked. "She always wore classy outfits, and, yeah, I guess they were expensive. Oh, and she had a Louis Vuitton bag. I always complimented her on it. As for her apartment, I never saw it. And vacations? Rarely ones I know of. We were close but not *that* close. More like mentor-mentee. Why?"

"Because it affects what we're going to tell you now. Did she use her credit card for large amounts?" Casey pressed.

"She paid cash at Fielding's Bar the night she and I met with Chris. It wasn't a university expense." Aimee pursed her lips thoughtfully. "The other times we went out, it depended on whether our meetings were Danforth related or personal get-togethers. For the former, she used her university AmEx card. For the latter, she used cash."

Aimee considered the question further. "She always had a full wallet, if that's what you're asking. I guess it was important to her to differentiate work and play. Remember I told you that that's how I knew Wells Fargo was her bank? She ran in a few times for withdrawals. Now please tell me why you're asking me these questions and what's going on?"

The team, led by Casey, did their job. They told Aimee about the calls Rita had received from unknown burner phones and how FI was tracking them. They told her that they were analyzing payments made to Rita's bank accounts. And they told her that they were working to get more data on Rita and Chris Maher's killer—the same killer they believed had trashed Aimee's apartment and painted the threat on her bedroom mirror. Gently, they explained that they believed the murderer was a serial killer, and they were digging to find any previous victims whose murder method matched that of Chris Maher. The description of that method they limited to violent strangulation, along with a football glove left at the scene of the crime.

They omitted any mention of the mob and about Casey's suspicions that she was being watched during the time that she was meeting with Nick at CannaBD. Also omitted were specific details of what Ryan was doing and how he was breaking the law in doing it.

When they'd finished talking, Aimee was very pale and her eyes were huge.

"A serial killer?" It was the natural thing to zero in on. "In other words, Rita and Chris were far from his first victims. How many preceded them?"

"We still don't know," Casey reiterated. "But we intend to find out. It'll give us a pattern by which we'll find him—and we *will* find him."

"How long has he been doing this?"

"Not sure yet," Ryan answered. "But it looks like it's been close to a decade. Maybe more."

Aimee swallowed hard. "Do we have a motive in each of these crimes? Are they all linked?"

"That we don't know," Patrick said carefully. "As for motives, there could be several. Money is a huge motivator. So is the thrill of the kill."

"The *kill*..." Aimee stared down at the floor for a long moment. When her head came up, so did her chin. "I'm not shocked. And I'm not resting till this bastard is caught and punished."

"Nor are we," Casey replied, inwardly proud of Aimee's newfound strength. Her cooperation would be of real help to them.

Aimee turned her attention to the matter Casey had been alluding to. "You're suggesting that Rita was accepting bribes, which I find very hard to believe. But let's say I'm wrong and that what you're saying is true. What would she be promising in exchange for her payments?"

Marc answered that one. "Our guess is that she was helping unqualified students get into Danforth."

"And their parents were paying her to do it?"

"Yes. That was the case with Chris Maher," Marc replied. "We interviewed his father and learned enough to come to that conclusion."

"You spoke with Daniel Maher?" Aimee asked incredulously. "How on earth did you manage..." She waved away her own question. "Never mind. You move mountains. So let's not waste time discussing how you make things happen." Another pause. "The parents are calling her from burner phones?"

"That's what we're in the process of figuring out," Ryan said. "There's a lot of red tape when you're dealing with phone companies. Banks, as well."

Aimee seemed to accept that. "Do you actually think this serial killer was working with Rita? It makes no sense. Rita would never hurt anyone. And no parent would pay to kill, no matter how desperate they were to get their child enrolled at Danforth. No, this killer and Rita had to be working for someone else. Do you know who?"

Now they were treading in murky waters—waters that Casey did *not* want to navigate in front of their client.

"We don't know who hired them or why. But we don't think Rita was pulling the strings," Casey replied. "Again, we're trying to dig up more information to give us clarity. There's still a lot we don't know."

"So many moving parts," Aimee murmured. "And nothing solid."

"*Yet*," Casey emphasized. "We're not only trying to figure out the answers to your questions but also where you fit into this equation. Why are they targeting you? It's essential that we figure that out."

"Which is why you decided to talk to those I've spoken to about the situation and about the fact that I hired you."

"Exactly. That's why I asked your permission to talk to Nick Colotti and, of course, to Travis."

"Travis came to you before you had the chance to approach him," Aimee reminded her.

"That's true. He emailed me and then came in to help. He was great and very forthcoming." Casey lightened the mood for a moment. "He's crazy about you, you know."

Aimee smiled softly. "The feeling is mutual." Her smile faded. "Anyone else you need to speak to?"

"Probably the other employees at CannaBD." On this subject, Casey was honest while omitting her sense of being watched. "Nick was jumping out of his skin when I interviewed him. He couldn't wait to get rid of me. He was definitely nervous about something. And that something could be protecting one of his hires."

"I can't imagine who, although Nick is fiercely protective of his staff."

"So I gathered. As a result, getting them to cooperate isn't going to be pretty. Especially if one of them has something to hide. We need a little more to go on." Casey glanced at Aimee. "Not tonight, because you need to eat that pizza you haven't touched and get some sleep. But tomorrow, when you're feeling more yourself, I need you to tell me all you know about your other two counterparts—Kimberley Perkins and Oliver Steadman."

"I'm perfectly fine," Aimee assured her. "Food and sleep can wait a few minutes, because frankly, there's not a lot to tell. Kimberley is CannaBD's CFO and Oliver is its head of R and D. Kimberley is super focused, kind of an introvert, but very nice when you get to know her. Oliver is… weird. He's as dedicated to CannaBD as the rest of us, but he's different."

"Different how?" Casey prompted.

"He doesn't quite fit in. I don't mean just at CannaBD but as a person. I guess you'd call it socially awkward. He's uncomfortable around people and spends most of his time in the lab facilities or locked away in his office. He's shy—he never quite meets your eyes when he speaks. His intellect and his IQ are off the charts. I'm sure that's the reason he expects so much of himself and why he needs constant recognition and ego boosting."

"And if he doesn't get it?" Patrick asked.

"Nothing dire. He just gets grumpy and withdrawn. But it's short-lived." Aimee waved away the direction they were headed in. "He's never violent and never feels like a threat. So if you interview him, do it with an open mind. Oliver is Oliver. But he's certainly no killer."

The team exchanged subtle glances but refrained from pursuing the subject. Casey and Marc would find out the real deal when they visited CannaBD again.

"That's really helpful," Casey said. "It's always great to have a personality sketch before you interview someone."

"You're going to be very busy," Aimee added. "There are a large group of warehouse employees there. Maybe ask Nick for some introductions?"

"Good idea. After that, it'll be our problem—unless you're friendly with any of them, enough so you have solid info to pass on to us."

Aimee shook her head. "I wave at them when I pass by, and I know their names from our Christmas parties. But I'm not tight with any of them, and I certainly wouldn't confide in them about something as important as this."

"Which brings me to one last point before we call it a day," Casey said, meeting Aimee's gaze directly. "This conversation, and from here on in, *all* case-related information, is confidential, and limited only to the people in this room. That, unfortunately, means no updates to Travis."

Aimee inclined her head. "He's a suspect?"

"No, but he's your boyfriend. Whatever happens, he'll either decide to insert himself into this investigation or to intercede if your life is in danger. We can't risk either of those things. We need to do our jobs—meticulously and alone. No obstacles. I'm sorry, but that's just the way it is."

"Okay," Aimee agreed reluctantly. "One problem. I already texted Travis about the break-in at my apartment. I told him I'd give him all the details when we see each other. He's working a hospital shift now, so he hasn't yet responded."

"That's not a major roadblock," Marc replied. "Law enforcement is involved, which means the media will be front and center. I'm sure descriptions and photos will be leaked. So tell Travis what you need to. Stay strong, rather than falling to pieces. It'll defuse the situation rather than exacerbating it. And after this, no sharing of information."

"Even what you are telling him, insist that he keeps this between the two of you," Casey added. "He'll understand. And it'll make him feel like he's involved, part of the solution. That'll calm him, as well. He'll certainly understand why you're not going back to your apartment. But you might have your hands full anyway, making him understand why you'll be staying at the brownstone."

"I know Travis a lot better than I did before this nightmare began," Aimee said. "We've grown a lot closer this past week. He's going to insist I move in with him until I find a new place to live."

Casey nodded her understanding. "Tell him you need a short time here, under the full protection we've provided. It'll stall the process. Once Patrick can put a tight security plan into place that'll allow full surveillance around and into Travis's apartment, you can readdress the issue."

"I can manage that." Aimee yawned, reaching for her slice of pizza. "I'm suddenly hungry and tired. I'll manage to swallow a few slices of pizza and then go to my usual guest room. Is that okay?"

"Perfect," Casey replied. "Get some rest."

She didn't add the phrase *while you still can.* But she knew the whole team was thinking it.

26

Victor's home office
Colts River, New Jersey
Saturday, 10:45 p.m.

Victor was sitting at his desk, head down, lying cross-armed on the cool surface. The near-empty bottle of bourbon sat beside him, even though he'd already made the change from booze to coffee a half hour ago. He had to be alert. The psycho was bound to call him, boasting about his prowess and looking for accolades.

Well, that's not what he was going to get.

Victor's personal, security-protected cell phone rang. His head came up and he checked out the number. Hopefully, this would be good news. He sure as hell needed some.

"Hi, Linc," he answered.

"You sound beat. I saw a bunch of photos on my feed, so I more than get why. Do you want me to call back tomorrow?"

"No, tonight is fine." Victor rose and poured himself a tall mug of coffee.

"Do you want to talk about it?"

"Not even a little."

"Okay, well, before I get into my updates, I want to put your mind at ease. I took care of tonight's party. It's still going strong and as smooth as silk."

Victor nearly dropped his mug. "Shit," he ground out. "The party. I forgot all about..."

"It's going fine," Linc assured him again. "I contacted Joe Giulio, your go-to guy. He's a pro, handling the gala just as you would while singing your praises to make sure everyone remembers who's at the helm. He's ready to handle Wednesday night's gig, too. So, maybe tonight's party isn't quite as lucrative as it would be if you yourself were there, but, hey, it's pretty damn successful. Joe's last text said that he's got at least three couples who want in. That's a nice take—too big to sneer at and too small to attract attention."

Victor's shoulders sagged with relief. "You're the best," he told Linc. "I don't know what I'd do if I didn't have your level head to count on."

"Maybe if you told me everything, rather than need-to-know fragments, I could do more."

"I'm protecting you, not me," Victor replied. "You know more than enough. Details I leave out are intentional. It'll keep you safe if things go wrong."

Linc snorted. "Give me a break. I've done enough illegal shit already to be locked up."

"But not for crimes that would make you *stay* locked up." Victor wasn't budging. "Why don't we move on to your follow-ups?"

"Fine." Linc gave up, at least for now. "You said you had to lie low and do behind-the-scenes work to generate income. So I did some poking around regarding currently enrolled students you got into the top schools and who might not be living up to expectations. I found three of them, all at different schools, none of those schools being Danforth. I'm sure you agree it's best to stay far away from Danforth right now."

Victor's lips curved a bit—as close to a smile as he'd had in days. "I more than agree. You and my coffee are really starting to improve my night."

He knew where Linc was headed. There were two parts to this process: getting the kids enrolled and then keeping them there. The top schools always fought to keep their retention rate sky-high. Sometimes, they just needed some help.

"All three of the candidates fit the bill," Linc continued. "Two sophomores and one freshman. A combination of plummeting grades, documented disciplinary actions filed for frat house ruckuses involving booze and drugs—you get the picture. And their rich parents, who paid you once, will freak out when things get bad enough for the colleges to contact them. They'll doubtless be ready to write you a blank check." A pause. "The one snag you have is that Rita Edwell is gone."

"Yeah, that's our long-term complication." Victor's wheels were turning as he thought about ways to circumvent what was going to be a missing piece of the puzzle for a long time—until a suitable successor could be found and put into place.

Rita had been the lynchpin to all his hires. Her job had involved working with them all. It also involved not just manipulating the process so the kids got into the right schools but keeping them there even when they were teetering on the verge of expulsion. She'd made disciplinary action go away, tutoring and counseling services available, and other equally successful interventions that turned things around.

"I'm on the hunt for a Rita replacement," Linc assured Victor. "It's not going to be fast or easy."

"I know," Victor agreed. "And we can't jump the gun. It has to be the right replacement. So let's stick with slow and methodical. I'll work around it in the interim. For starters, text me the contact info on those three kids. I'll reach out to their parents and get the ball rolling."

"Texting now," Linc replied. "And once all three sets of parents beg you to make everything go away, I'll do the necessary record tweaking to make it happen."

A moment later, the text appeared on Victor's screen. As always, Linc had been thorough. Name, school, year enrolled, parents' contact info, and a link to what he'd hacked: the students' college records and indiscretions.

"Perfect," Victor said. "I can get on this first thing tomorrow. Tonight, I'll check in with Joe and verify Wednesday night's event. You don't have to middleman this anymore. My lapse in efficiency is over. I'm back. I have to be, behind-the-scenes or not."

"Cut yourself some slack. You had a hell of a night. I can only guess how bad it was."

"Bad," Victor said. "And it's not over yet."

***

Victor's home office
Colts River, New Jersey
Saturday, 11:59 p.m.

Unsurprisingly, on the brink of midnight, Victor's most-hated phone rang.

"Yeah," he answered.

"Have you seen my handiwork yet?" The killer's voice was chilling. "Or is it too soon to pop the champagne?"

"There won't be any champagne."

A pause. "Why the hell not? I made a huge splash *and* took care of an equally huge problem."

"Creating an even huger problem." Victor walked the careful line he'd established the minute he hired this lunatic. He had to reel him in. On the other hand, he didn't want to wake up with a horse's head on his bedpost.

"You might very well have scared the shit out of Aimee Bregman, enough so that she'll keep her mouth shut and stay out of our way," Victor said. "But at what cost? The NYPD is probably going to form a task force to try tying all the recent crimes together. If they come to the right conclusion, we're all dead in the water."

"You're so dramatic—and such a downer," the killer replied, talking to Victor as if he were a small child who needed educating from the master—him. "So I added salt to the fire. The cops aren't nearly as adept as you think they are. They'll be chasing their tails forever. And with Aimee scared into silence, she won't stay the center of attention." He paused. "Understand?"

Yeah, you sick sadist. I understand a whole lot more than you do. But I'll play your ego-stroking game.

"I understand," he replied.

"Great. Now that we've gotten that bullshit out of the way, it's time for you to admit that what I did was brilliant."

Careful, Victor. You can't push him over the edge.

"What you did was creative and definitely grandiose," he replied. "For that I congratulate you. And at least Aimee Bregman wasn't one of my recruits, the way Chris Maher was. So I won't be losing any money over her being removed from the operation."

"*Grandiose*. I like that word." The psycho was more than pleased with himself.

Victor had to drive home the destructive results these actions could cause. "Let me reiterate, after this, no more going after targets that relate to my project, unless instructed by me. Keep in mind that, if this all burns to ashes, so does your cash supply."

"Yeah, yeah, I know."

"Then do as I say. I don't want to end up poor and in prison. Neither do you."

"Fine. I hear you."

"Good. Aside from your work for me, use your creativity in any way you choose. That's your call, not mine." Victor intentionally swapped their positions of power.

"You're right." The killer considered that and sounded even more pleased, his ego properly stroked. "Now, since we're not popping champagne, I'm off to celebrate on my own."

He disconnected the call.

27

Offices of Forensic Instincts
Ryan's lair
Sunday, 3:25 a.m.

Ryan had gone home and tried to sleep. He'd tossed and turned for an hour and then given in to the fact that his mind was too cluttered to relax.

The team had disbanded just after midnight, all of them going home to get some rest before tackling the challenges of the new day. Claire had taken one look at Ryan, given him a soft smile, and then headed home to her own place. Thankfully, she always seemed to sense his state of mind. And tonight, her instincts had told her he needed to be alone.

His alone time had proved futile. He'd flopped down on his home sofa and shut his eyes. But sleeping or even unwinding just wasn't in the cards.

He'd given up. He'd showered, jumped into some comfortable sweats, and ridden the subway back to the office, going straight down to his lair, where he brewed his own muddy but effective mug of coffee.

"Hey, Yoda," he said, sitting down at his desk and waking up his AI system.

"Ryan, I didn't realize you were returning tonight."

"Neither did I. Please stay on standby. I might have something I need you to handle."

"Of course." Yoda fell silent, letting Ryan do what he needed to before giving Yoda his assignment.

Ryan turned on his laptop and called up the spreadsheets that showed Rita Edwell's phone calls, both sent and received. There were still way too many blanks to suit him, but that would be rectified as soon as he could compile all the data he was fishing for.

He and the team were totally zeroed in on the calls between Rita and the burner phones. And, yeah, that was key.

But why were the landline calls bothering him so much?

Ryan scrutinized the spreadsheets, looking for a pattern to those particular calls. He felt as if he were working a crossword puzzle whose key was just out of reach.

He gave an impatient shake of his head. He was going about this ass-backward. He knew it. Those calls might mean something, but the calls to and from the burner phones meant a whole lot more.

FI had been thinking small, until they realized Rita was working for someone, turning the money over to them, and getting a chunk of change in the process.

Time to think bigger.

Cash. Rita only used cash. Well, so did the mob.

Ryan's chin came up. It wasn't a leap. FI had already deduced that the mob was involved in the three murders they were investigating in order to catch their sociopath. They now also knew that Rita had been living well above her means, was working for someone in order to collect the money that provided her with that lifestyle. The team had just been looking at it the wrong way, seeing these facts as two separate entities. Well, what if that weren't the case and the two parts were linked?

Ryan's mind raced as he pressed his theory forward.

Those outstanding burner numbers stood out like a sore thumb. Rita was in constant touch with whoever owned them. And who most likely to use burners if not the mob?

It was more than possible that Rita was working for them doing what she'd clearly done with Chris Maher—getting undeserving kids with rich, desperate parents into Danforth.

And if she were pulling this off so successfully, why would the mob stop at Danforth? Why wouldn't they let Rita work her magic at other prestigious schools, as well? What if the landline calls to and from those other colleges—the ones that were gnawing away at Ryan—had nothing to do with educational discussions? What if Rita was connecting up with faculty members who were actually direct reports of hers, keeping her hands dirty and the mob's hands clean? What if those college faculty members weren't paid nearly as much as they thought they were worth and so were happy to deal dirty to get rich by helping Rita get unqualified students into their respective schools? The MO would be the same: rich parents, desirable college admissions arranged, big payoffs to the mob to make that a reality. The mob, in turn, would hand over cash payments to Rita. She'd be in charge of passing along the agreed-upon cuts to her reports while keeping a hefty wad for herself.

Maybe she'd gotten greedy. Maybe that's why they'd offed her. She'd been a valuable mob asset. It must have taken a lot for them to get rid of her. Money or threats of retaliation would be the only motives severe enough for the mob to hire their psycho killer to murder her, after which the mob would make the body go away.

Ryan paused, remembering what Aimee had said at their original meeting. Rita was dying—soon. Had she grown a conscience, decided to opt out of her arrangement or even threaten her boss with making the truth public?

That would give him no choice but to get rid of her.

At one time, Ryan would have thought this entire theory was a weak, unprovable reach.

Not anymore. Not with the mob involved, Ryan's gut feeling about the landline calls being shady, and Rita clearly accepting bribes. FI had determined that Rita was working for someone. So the bribe money the team had assumed was going directly to her was, instead, going to her boss. The mob liked big-scale operations. Well, involving a large cluster of colleges in this process could yield a friggin' fortune.

With that in mind, Ryan leaned over his computer and zeroed in on the calls made to and from all colleges and universities. He bolded those lines on both the *to* and the *from* pages, and then sat back in his seat to view his handiwork.

Interesting. Some of the calls were made to and from what looked to be the colleges' main lines. Not long after, return calls were initiated, this time from direct extensions. Ryan recognized that by noting Rita's extension and Danforth's main number.

All the college-related calls fell into that same pattern.

"Yoda," he said. "I've just bolded specific landline numbers on both of Rita Edwell's call lists. Omitting Danforth, which we already know, please re-identify all the numbers that are the universities' and colleges' main lines. Then, go back and check out the numbers with the same area code and first three digits as the original call. The last four digits will be the faculty members' direct extensions."

"I understand, Ryan," Yoda replied. "What would you like me to do with that information?"

"Using FI's blocked number, call those direct extensions," Ryan replied. "Do it ASAP, while it's the middle of the night. That way, you'll get voice mail, which will provide us with what we need: the names and departments of each person tied to those extensions. Compile a list of that data and forward it to me. Then use that list to target each of those faculty members. Find out everything you can about them. Focus on their monetary statuses. See if they live bigger lifestyles than their salaries would afford."

"I'll start immediately," Yoda responded.

"Good." Ryan felt his blood pumping as he whipped out his cell and texted Casey to contact him as soon as she woke up. He needed to bandy this theory around, first with her, then with the team. And if he was right, it would mean a tristate road trip for Marc and Emma.

He *knew* he was right.

A smug grin curved his lips as he quickly Slacked the entire team to schedule a seven-a.m. meeting.

"Yoda," he said. "I think we're on to something."

***

Casey and Hutch's apartment
Battery Park City, New York
3:55 a.m.

Casey and Hutch were still intertwined on the bed, their breathing unsteady as they slowly recovered from the past hours' lovemaking marathon. Neither of them had gotten any sleep tonight, but it had definitely been worth it.

Casey wriggled a bit, and Hutch smiled in the darkness. He could read Casey like a book.

"Catch your breath first, beautiful," he said into her hair. "Then you can check your messages."

Casey tipped up her chin, shaking her head in amazement. "You knew?"

"I heard your phone bing a few times a little while ago. My mind was fuzzy and absorbed with you and only you. But, yeah, I heard it." Hutch saw the rueful look on Casey's face and tenderly tucked a loose strand of red hair behind her ear. "Not to worry. Unless those messages are urgent, I plan on dragging you back for another round."

Casey twisted slightly around, staying in the circle of Hutch's arms as she reached for her phone. "I'll make it easy for you. I won't budge."

She glanced down at what she'd received. "One text from Ryan saying to contact him as soon as I wake up. Well, that's easy enough to ignore for a while since I never went to sleep. The other bing is a Slack message from him to the whole team calling for a seven o'clock meeting. Whatever this is, he's pretty psyched about it."

Hutch slid his hand up her leg. "What's the verdict?"

Casey put down her phone and turned back to him. "Another hour for us, then a quick catnap, then a callback to Ryan while we get ready to shower and head back to work."

"Done." Hutch pulled Casey under him and kissed her as he made all thoughts of work disappear.

The catnap was forgotten.

***

Victor's home office
Colts River, New Jersey
6:50 a.m.

Victor had allowed himself the luxury of a few hours' sleep, a shower, and a change of clothes. But after brewing a pot of coffee and pouring himself a tall mug, he knew that no further procrastinating would work.

He picked up the encrypted phone. There was no escaping this dreaded conversation.

He took a few deep breaths and pressed the number.

"It's early," Sal answered. "Got something on your mind?"

"Yes. And it's important. Otherwise I would have waited until a decent hour. But there's something you need to know."

Sal grunted. "You mean about your maniac's latest hatchet job? I already know. In fact, if you hadn't been man enough to call me yourself, you'd probably be offed by ten. So you're spared. Now, I'll give you a chance to explain and to then make me believe that he's worth allowing to live, much less work for us."

Victor had scalded the inside of his mouth with gulps of blistering hot coffee. He didn't even notice.

"Thank you," he said, also thanking the Good Lord for sparing his life. He went on to explain what had happened and why. "Do what you have to, Sal. But I've been thinking about this all night, and I can't get past the fact that he makes our operation run smoothly. When we need someone gone, they're gone. Fast and clean, leaving the cops chasing their own tails. He craves the money we give him, which is how I keep him in line. Yeah, we could probably get someone else, but who besides a sicko kills people for a living?" Victor blew out his breath. "We knew what he was about going in. And you and I accepted the risk because we believed the gains were bigger."

"I'm starting to question that decision," Sal replied. "I have guys who could handle this."

"You're right, you do. And if you think they're as good, then we'll go that route. It's totally up to you."

There was a long silence at the other end of the phone.

"Have you talked to him since he destroyed Aimee Bregman's apartment?" Sal asked.

"He called last night, seeking accolades for his great accomplishment. My response wasn't pretty. He listened to my orders—for now. It's my job to come up with a long-term solution. If not and he pulls this shit again"—Victor paused and shrugged—"then he's gotta go. And it'll be my job to find a replacement."

"*My* job," Sal corrected. "I might also be finding a replacement for you."

28

Offices of Forensic Instincts
Second floor, main conference room
Tribeca, New York
Sunday, 7:00 a.m.

The team was all there and ready. Emma had even stopped to pick up donuts to go with their coffee. She put them out, grabbed a donut and her own piping-hot mug, and slid into her seat at the conference room table.

The whole team thanked her and, after a sip and a bite, turned to the head of the table, where Casey sat, Hero at her side. Alert as always, Hero had jumped awake when Casey and Hutch sprang out of the bed and into action. He'd jogged the one-mile walk to the brownstone with Casey and was now happily chomping on a donut.

Aimee, despite her protests, had been barred from the meeting, regardless of the fact that she was staying right there at the brownstone.

"Standard protocol with all our clients," Casey had explained. "FI team meetings are closed to everyone, including our client."

"That even applied to my sister," Ryan added. "So it's not personal."

"Trust us to get things done," Marc had said. "When we have something solid, you'll be the first one to know."

"Okay," Aimee had reluctantly agreed.

Now, Casey cleared her throat and began.

"I spoke to Ryan a little while ago. This is a pretty big theory and, if it's correct, a huge leap in our investigation. I only got a quick overview, so I'm turning the meeting over to him."

For once, Ryan looked more excited than he did arrogant.

"Yoda and I spent the night researching." He took a visual sweep of the group. "I know this is a real reach, but hear me and out and keep your minds open. Because so far all this checks out."

Everyone nodded.

"Good." Ryan went on to explain his theory in the same two parts as he'd tackled them. First, the mob being Rita's financial connection, after which he paused to let that sink in.

"That's… Wow," Claire said. "I knew the mob was connected to our serial killer, but to Rita, not as a victim but as an employee? I assumed she was getting kickbacks from someone, maybe the parents who were paying to get their kids into Danforth. But this…"

"We all assumed Rita was working for someone. We never considered the mob. But this new theory makes sense," Patrick said after careful consideration. "Especially in light of Rita's communications with whoever owns those burner phones."

"I agree with all of this," Casey said. "As you both said, we knew Rita was getting payoffs. We believed they were coming directly from parents, and only parents at Danforth. But then, we also deduced that she was working for someone and that she was living way over the top. Spending wads of cash. Putting together everything Ryan said, I'm ready to accept his theory."

A murmur of assents.

"But how can we know that this bribery scheme extends to colleges outside of Danforth?" Emma asked, still looking incredulous.

"That brings me to part two of my theory—evidence to support it." Ryan gestured to them all. "Open your laptops and look at the highlighted lines on the spreadsheets."

"Rita's call log again," Emma said with a sigh. "I think I've memorized it."

Marc arched a brow at her. "You've barely seen it. That's Ryan's, Patrick's, and my job. Oh, and Yoda's. So stop complaining."

"Sorry," Emma muttered. "I just want something solid to do."

"And you'll have it." Ryan was itching to get back to the topic at hand. "Just let me finish here. Then you'll get your marching orders."

Emma sat up straighter.

"Back to the highlighted lines on my spreadsheets," Ryan said in a pointed tone, primarily meant for Emma. He then went on to specify what each line meant. "Every one of those calls follows the exact same pattern. General number followed by a same-locale personal extension, and vice versa. I asked Yoda to use that information to gather more data. We already knew the main number of each college. But he called all the extension numbers and learned names and departments of each contact."

"And?" Marc asked, leaning forward with anticipation.

"And further investigating determined that every one of those staff members—from athletic directors to admissions officers to other heads of alumni relations—have all got fairly lavish lifestyles and average university salaries."

"That can't be a coincidence," Casey said. "Especially given what an eclectic group you've compiled."

"All at different pay grades," Patrick agreed. "Ryan's theory applies to every one of them."

"Exactly." Now Ryan sounded a little smug and totally pleased with himself. No one took a sarcastic jab at him. He deserved every ounce of his self-congratulations.

Marc was still studying the spreadsheet. "We're talking about a hell of a lot of schools, now examining the calls made to them from a different vantage point. As I said before—Delver University and Malhart College, both on Long Island. Baring University in Bergen County, New

Jersey. Birchmont University and, of course, Brightington University, both in Westchester County, New York. Lakely College in Boston. Two more in Connecticut—Arborley College and Wheatley University. And one in Pennsylvania—Cameron College. All top schools."

"Making this a big-scale money-making operation." Patrick was nodding as he, too, rescanned the spreadsheet data. "And targeting these top-tier schools is the only way of ensuring the operation's success. Speaking as a father of college-aged kids, many of today's seventeen- and eighteen-year-olds don't automatically choose a college education as the way to go. Not when there are so many other avenues that result in lucrative careers. The exceptions are the Ivies, the Little Ivies, and the other top-tier schools. Diplomas from any one of those institutions still raise eyebrows and open doors, meaning that there's a long line of high school seniors—and their parents—clamoring to get in."

"It's ridiculous but true," Ryan responded with a dismissive wave of his hand. "I'm an MIT dropout and I'm… well, me."

"And there's that humility again." Claire sat back and shook her head. "We know you're a genius. Let's get back on point."

Casey stifled a smile. "Even though I'm completely on board with this theory, we still need to solidify it with concrete proof before we use it as a jumping-off point. Patrick, can you do anything with the banking PDFs?"

"With time-specific information like this, I can go through the PDFs and see if Rita made cash deposits soon after a number of her phone call exchanges. It'll be a long and tedious process given the extensive banking records we have, but it can be done. That would strengthen our theory."

"Good idea." Casey tapped the table with one fingertip. "If we could just get something a little more absolute…?"

"I'm one step ahead of you, boss," Ryan replied. "With your approval, I'd like to send Marc and Emma on a road trip."

"To visit all the college staff members on our list," Casey deduced. "How do we get proof without showing our hand? And how do we get in their doors to begin with?"

"We make Emma a superstar pupil who's visiting top-tier schools and specific individuals—those who'd be significant in her decision—in order for them to convince her to attend their college or university."

Emma was already grinning. "Meaning you'll be creating a whole new me, complete with stellar academic and athletic skills."

"The whole new you is Emily Waring."

"Nice name. Close to mine, so easy to remember." Emma was already embracing her alternate persona.

"Yup. Emily will also have recommendations from impressive people," Ryan added. "Believe me, when I'm done creating you, every school will be begging for you to choose them."

"And where do I fit in?" Marc asked.

"Ah." Ryan's eyes were twinkling as he replied. "Emily will have been orphaned at a very young age and was raised by her devoted uncle Zachary, attorney extraordinaire, whose bio is already in the works. Her very rich, very devoted uncle Zachary will ensure that Emily has everything she wants, and would pay a king's ransom to get her into the college of her choice."

Marc practically spit out his donut. "You're kidding."

"Nope." Ryan continued to look cheerful. "Hey, look at the bright side. I could have made you her father. But the age spread is way too tight for that."

"Gee, thanks."

By this time, the entire team was laughing.

"I can't wait to hear the rest of this plan," Claire said.

"Then I won't keep you waiting. I never do." Ryan shot her a wicked grin and was rewarded with a withering stare.

All innuendo gone, Ryan got down to business, laying out the plan.

As Casey had surmised, "Zachary" and "Emily" would be visiting every school on the list and keeping prearranged appointments with every name Yoda had provided. For each person, Emily would have a tailor-made reason for her visit.

"So much for getting them in the door," Ryan said, answering one of Casey's questions. "Once they're inside and Emily is involved in the pluses of her matriculation there, she'll make sure to create an opportunity to gush over her visit to Danforth—which was her mother's alma mater—saying how gracious Rita Edwell had been and how awful her disappearance was. No doubt, all the staffers will keep a poker face, and when she casually asks them if they'd known Rita, they'll, of course, say no."

"So far, so good," Casey said.

"Also, as an extra precaution, I'll make sure to enter Emily's mother's name and a short dated record into the Danforth database, just in case anyone checks. Storing records electronically wasn't as thorough and sophisticated then as it is now, so there's less to fake. So we'll be cool on that front." Ryan went on with certainty. "But I doubt anyone will check. Rita was their contact and now she's gone. There's no one to check in with, and they'll be too scared to try."

"Is that everything?" Marc asked.

"No, there's more. Just to be sure, we'll do an in-person double check of their names and extension numbers." Ryan held up a small gizmo that looked like a mini-microphone. "Marc, you'll have this on you."

"For what?"

"Once you've heard their denials, excuse yourself and go use the bathroom. While you're in there, dial the guilty party's direct extension. He or she will answer, which will confirm the link between their phone number and the person assigned to it. To eliminate any suspicion, don't just hang up. Press the button on this device and hold it up to the phone." Ryan demonstrated, following his own instructions.

A loud, rhythmic set of high-pitched beeps sounded.

"A fax machine," Casey said over the blare. "That simulates one."

"Exactly." Ryan released the button, and the room, thankfully, quieted. "The noise will obviously be loud enough for Emily to hear it through the phone, double confirming my theory—that the number belongs to the guilty party. They'll, of course, hang up, annoyed but accepting it as another caller screwup. During the time that this is going on—"

"I can pocket anything I can that could help Claire," Emma finished. "Brilliant."

"I think so," Ryan replied with a broad grin.

"Exit, ego," Claire muttered.

"Not this time," Ryan told her. "This is all just too good."

Casey nodded. "It actually is. It would be all the proof I need that these staff members, who've had multiple conversations with Rita, are doing something illegal that pays well and involves her. Plus, Rita's burner phone contacts that we have yet to identify. Go with it."

"Great. Then let's get this show on the road," Ryan said with great anticipation. "Once Yoda and I have finished our part in this, and Zachary has set up the various meetings, I'll go back to finding other victims of our sociopath. All in all, a hopefully win-win few days."

29

Victor's home
Colts River, New Jersey
Monday, 1:20 p.m.

Victor sat out on the veranda, nursing a drink and breathing in the fresh air. Thanks to Sal's threat, he'd barely stepped out of his office all weekend, much less relaxed or been outdoors. Doing so felt good, especially now that he'd successfully accomplished the first steps of what he needed to.

It had been a royal pain in the ass, making all those phone calls and getting things back on track.

He'd tackled the stress-free part first. Calling the parents Linc had told him about—those who needed to get their kids' heads back in the game. Easy-peasy. They'd all been mortified that their teens were faltering. The fact that they had no idea what was happening was thanks to the joy of their kids being over eighteen, supposedly adults, and therefore having no parental communication from the college—not until expulsion became a real possibility. Now the parents begged Victor for help and offered him additional small fortunes to make the issues go away. He assured them he would, pleased by the fact that he'd be filling his slightly depleted coffers.

After contacting Linc and giving him the go-ahead, Victor moved on to the wide-scale, exhausting task of calling all Rita's counterparts.

None of them was Rita.

His business relationship with her had started out over a decade ago as a very personal one. He'd wanted to get his kid into Danforth. And just like the parents he dealt with now, he'd do just about anything to make that happen. He'd done his homework. Rita's job and her personality fit the bill as just the type he was looking for. Back then, she was dean of Student Affairs. She'd liked the finer things in life, and her job wasn't about to afford them to her. She was primarily a loner, which would make it easier for him to get her to keep her mouth shut. And it turned out, Victor's research found out about the bribe paid to her by Daniel Maher to get his high-profile son into Danforth.

What could be a better combination?

He'd made his business proposal on the spot, offering her a substantial enough sum that he knew she wouldn't, or couldn't, refuse. Probably both. He'd thrown in the fact that he knew about Chris Maher's matriculation and her part in it. He hadn't exactly phrased it as a threat. But the fact that she'd perceived it as such was just as he wanted.

She'd pondered her options, barely hesitating before accepting his offer. They'd then worked together to figure out the right technique to use and the right way to go about using it. Ultimately, Rita's scenario had worked, and in record time. The following calendar year, Victor's kid had become part of the Danforth community.

Victor had paid Rita a small fortune, adding that there'd be more to come if his kid had any problems or indiscretions that needed to go away. She'd said she had access to counseling and tutoring services, so that wouldn't be a problem.

After seeing her thoroughness and success, he'd made his wide-scale decision. He'd gone to Sal with his concept and his choice. And given that the risk factor for him was low and the profits high, Sal had given him the go-ahead.

He'd contacted Rita and laid out the job opportunity. She'd listened, quickly guessing what he was and what she was committing herself to. Playing a significant role in a mob-based operation was a huge leap from gaining admission for one student. But Victor had sweetened the pot, offering her a truly staggering sum of money, with more to come if she moved up the academic ladder and, therefore, had more influence. He also told her that he'd be hiring counterparts of her in other schools—and would make them her direct reports—meaning she'd also be earning a cut of the profits they delivered.

It was enough.

Rita had accepted the job. She'd immediately brought him a list of hopeful high school seniors and their rich parents who were potential takers. And she'd performed magic to make things happen.

Victor was duly impressed, especially when he watched her grow into her job at a remarkable pace. And when she was promoted to be Danforth's director of Alumni Relations, she'd really soared. Now her career involved traveling and wining and dining affluent alumni in an effort to convince them to make lavish contributions to Danforth. And as she soon discovered, many of the fortysomething alums had college-aged kids of their own now who they were dying to have admitted in order to extend their legacy.

Rita had recognized a gold mine and came to Victor with it. He'd been thrilled, instructing her to limit her efforts to those schools in the tristate, Pennsylvania, and New England areas. It was the specific region he wanted to concentrate his efforts on—for now. If this took off as he thought it would, he'd go national as quickly as possible.

That had been kicked off some time ago.

Now, Rita was dead, as was her policy of working with her counterparts to come up with the right names, issuing the right instructions, and arranging for the meetings where she handed them their payoffs after bringing the majority of the cash to Victor and taking her healthy cut.

It was now up to Victor to get things moving in the right direction ASAP. Especially since this was prime time in the calendar year for the admissions cycle to start cranking up.

He made his calls. None of the recipients had ever spoken to him directly. They had a good idea who and what he was, so they were a little meek and very obliging.

Victor took care of that, keeping the phone calls positive and promising. Each staff member he spoke to worked in different schools and had different jobs and different opportunities to open the necessary doors for eager-to-matriculate students. Victor knew the ins and outs well, so he laid out plans, improvising on some of the techniques to widen the field of rich prospects seeking admission for each of their respective schools.

They were irritated, yes, but they were also relieved. Help was being offered. Since Rita's disappearance, they hadn't known what to do or who to contact. They needed the guidance she provided. But they all got the bigger picture now. For the immediate future, they'd be reporting directly to Victor. He'd provide the necessary leadership, starting by providing them with one another's contact information so they could all be in touch as needed—a step that had never before been necessary but now was. They could bandy around ideas and support each other. He had no intention of becoming their parent.

He also sweetened the pot by increasing their financial rewards. More money was always an incentive.

When he finally hung up, he was totally spent but convinced he had the filaments of a network in place. Hopefully, that would be enough, at least until a new Rita could be found and trained, which wasn't happening any time soon.

So the whole operation was entirely in his hands—running it while *also* controlling the lunatic he'd hired.

He'd better pull both of them off.

Otherwise, his life wouldn't be worth a damn.

***

Offices of Forensic Instincts
Ryan's lair
Tribeca, New York
Tuesday, 9:15 a.m.

Ryan was cranky. He hadn't had a full night alone with Claire for what to him seemed to be a millennium. He'd spent the entire weekend, plus some, here at FI, finishing up "Emily's" stellar educational and extracurricular portfolio and "Zachary's" impressive legal and educational background.

The exchange of emails to set up appointments had been completed, and finally, the investigative trip had begun.

Emily and Zachary had left early this morning, traveling in the town car Ryan had rented for them from the FI account. Yeah, it was an expense, as were the two nights of hotel accommodations Ryan had booked once he'd planned their route. But he'd gotten Casey's okay first. Besides, that's what a portion of FI's coffers were for.

Now, Ryan was resettled in his lair, intent on finding other victims of their serial killer. He'd been at this for nearly a week, and he was frustrated and pissed that he'd turned up nothing.

Well, today he had a new plan. Up till now, he'd made his search comprehensive—seeking out incidents that took place over the entire country as well as the entire eight years from when Coach Rice was murdered.

That sweeping plan had fallen flat.

This time, he was narrowing the length of time as well as the breadth of his search. Rather than the full eight years, he was limiting his probe to the most recent two. And instead of exploring the entire country, he was now setting his parameters only in and around the tristate area. Just as before, he was applying his unique software application to access all related blog and social media posts in the data collection process so he could learn when the killer's signature kill was utilized—something that would be suppressed in any statements by law enforcement.

Ryan felt a surge of positive energy and renewed anticipation as he embarked on this new, more focused approach. Small towns would now be flagged as frequently as larger cities. And those small towns' newspaper articles, blogs, social media posts, and investigation details would show up, rather than be buried too far down to be captured. It was like zooming in on a tighter range, rather than zooming out and losing the detail.

Serial killers as warped as the one they were dealing with left mangled bodies. Clearly, there were other victims—victims who'd exhibited this guy's signature kill. Step one was to find them. Step two was to figure out a connection between those new victims, Jake Flanders, and Chris Maher.

Ryan inputted all his amended data. His computer whirred and whirred as it started a search for what he was looking for.

"This is going to take time, Yoda," he said. "I assume you see what I'm doing?"

"Yes, Ryan. And I understand the logic of it. However, you're still searching a large area over a period of two years."

"I know." Ryan sighed. "I'm going to have to turn my attention elsewhere, or I'll lose my mind."

He didn't have to consider his diversion options. He walked straight out of his lair and up the stairs until he reached the third floor. There was a buzz of activity coming from the War Room, but the door was shut and the hall was empty. So was their makeshift guest room.

He could hear clinking plates and silverware in the kitchen, which he assumed was Aimee making herself something to eat.

Which meant the coast was clear.

Ryan went directly to the yoga room. The door was partially ajar, which meant Claire wasn't in a deep meditative state. He knocked, simultaneously walking into the room.

Claire looked up. She was sitting on her yoga mat, sipping herbal tea, and eating some unappealing kale-like stuff. Seeing the expression on his face, her brows lifted in surprise. They both knew he was breaking the rules. Personal encounters were meant to be infrequent and were limited to the lair.

"Can I come in?" Ryan asked.

"It looks like you're already in."

"Yeah, I am." Ryan shut and locked the door behind him. "Fuck the rules. This is an official booty call."

Laughter bubbled up in Claire's throat. "Is there an *unofficial* booty call?"

"Yup. It's used by nonurgent people who aren't going insane with lust."

"Insane with lust." Claire pushed her cup and plate off to a side and leaned back on her elbows. "That sounds pretty serious."

"It is." Ryan was stripping as he spoke. "Get naked."

Claire didn't argue with the command. Ryan knew that meant she was going crazy, too. Normally, she'd rip him a new one for overstepping their agreed-upon limits. Not so now.

She wriggled out of her clothes, then lay back on the mat, her blond hair splaying out around her.

Ryan's eyes darkened, but he didn't speak. He just crossed the room, lowered himself beside her, and pulled her into his arms. "I hope you've got hours of free time. Because I'm not unlocking that door until you can't move."

"And if Yoda calls?"

"Yoda who?"

Hours later, Ryan rolled onto his back and lazily stretched his arms over his head.

"Feel better?" Claire teased, propping herself on her elbows, as totally replete as he.

"Like a new man," Ryan answered her with a broad grin. "How about you?"

"Incredible. Although I hesitate to say so when you have that cocky grin on your face. Don't be so proud of yourself. I'm as impressive as you are."

Ryan threw back his head and laughed. "No arguments, Claire-voyant." He reverted to his longstanding nickname for her. "You absolutely wreck me. As soon as we solve this case, I'm asking Casey for vacation time for us both. Some tropical location. No work. Just us. We deserve it."

"Sounds perfect." Claire reached forward and grabbed her hand-knit quilt from the chair. Together, she and Ryan managed to cover themselves. As they did, Claire studied Ryan's profile.

"As happy and sated as you are, there's something on your mind," she said. "Something that's making you super agitated and even more frantic than usual. It's about the case and, I'm guessing, about your attempts to find other victims of this serial killer. Do you want to talk about it?"

Ryan sighed, sitting up and letting his anchored hands carry his weight. He wasn't surprised about Claire's insights. It wasn't only her natural gift, it was about knowing him so well. Sometimes it scared him just *how* well.

"You're right. I'm busting my ass to find other victims who had our sociopath's signature kill. So far, nothing. I researched Jake Flanders down to his childhood. His upbringing. His education. His marriage. His role as a father. His monetary status."

"And there's no commonality between him and Chris Maher."

"Nope. Not even a hint of one. And as I said, I'm digging deep to find other victims. So far nothing. Yoda is researching a narrower field for me. Narrower but with a more intense focus. If that makes any sense."

Claire sat up, too, and wrapped her arms around her knees. "It does." She fell silent, deep in thought. "While you're hunting down similar victims, maybe you should also delve into the mob hits. I know the scenarios are very different, but the same killer committed all the crimes. Maybe you can find a more subtle connection there."

Ryan's brows knit in question. "Is that a practical or a metaphysical suggestion?"

"Actually, both," Claire replied. "It makes logical sense, based on what we know. Also, I can't explain why, but I feel as if there might be something there. There's no signature kill and no body, but Coach Rice was strangled to death, and for all we know, Rita was, too." A pause. "I've always sensed that she was. So part of the MO is the same." Claire chewed her lip. "I need to think about this. My instincts tell me I'm missing something."

"You don't miss things."

"Sometimes they elude me," Claire amended. She twisted around to look up at Ryan. "You give that theory a whirl. Meanwhile, I'll continue to reexamine the things Patrick and John took from Aimee's apartment. Maybe I can sense something more about the killer. So far, no luck, but that doesn't mean it won't come. Also, in a few days, I'll have whatever Emma brings home to enhance my process."

Ryan brushed his knuckles across Claire's cheek. "We make a good team, don't we?"

Claire reached up and squeezed his fingers. "Most of the time, yes. A great team."

Ryan felt an odd tug inside him. He had an uneasy sense of free-falling, and it scared the shit out of him. He wanted to say something, but he wasn't sure what.

As it turned out, he didn't have to figure it out—at least not yet.

"Ryan?" Yoda's voice rang out. "I think some data just came in."

Ryan leaned forward to give Claire a gentle kiss, then rose and grabbed his clothes. "On my way, Yoda."

30

12:45 p.m.

Ryan strode into the lair and sat down at his desk. "Talk to me, Yoda."

"Two incidents that match your search just appeared—one right after the other," Yoda apprised him. "They're stored in my database. I've put them up on your screen, complete with details."

Ryan scanned the screen. "Yes," he said, pumping the air. "Finally." He scrutinized the data more closely.

The first victim was Roger Clarke, a psychiatrist who practiced in a high-crime area of Pauliston, New York. Pauliston was way north, almost in Canada. Being that it had one of the highest violent crime rates in the country, it would be easy for a local incident—one in which the cops let nothing of substance leak—to get lost amid a wave of crimes. As a result, it could slip through the cracks of Ryan's first, more widespread search.

Not this time.

Dr. Clarke had been choked to death, his body left in his office. Ryan's software program tapped into a slew of news commentator and blog posts, all of which leaked that the doctor had been viciously strangled, stabbed in the thigh with a butcher knife, and was impaled in that same thigh with a college football glove.

The murder had happened a year and a half ago. Time to find out everything about Dr. Clarke, right down to his shoe size.

Ryan was about to jump on that when his eye was caught by the name of the second victim.

Karly Listor.

Karly Listor? Ryan's head shot up. Listor was a well-known New York City news commentator who was a media maven. She spoke on television news shows, had her own blog—which had millions of followers—and made frequent comments on social media. She wasn't shy, sharing her opinion of politics, entertainment gossip, and hard-core news events. And the only reason she hadn't showed up in Ryan's initial search was because she'd been killed last night, in the dead of the night, in her Hartsville home.

"Shit," Ryan said, shifting screens so he could delve into all the news circuits, starting with a brief statement from the Hartsville police. From there, he visited the usual blogs that were always one step ahead and eerily correct in their info. The strangulation. The signature kill. The viciousness of the crime.

Even as Ryan read, his mind kept leaping back to the obvious—Hartsville. The same town in which Jake Flanders had been killed.

Hartsville was a pleasant suburban area. Very little crime. So why two violent crimes in a week? Crimes whose victims were totally dissimilar? What was the link?

On the other hand, there were plenty of links between Karly Listor and Chris Maher. They were both public figures, with high visibility and lots of money. Their names were big enough that their murders would be spotlighted until their killer was found. If the sociopath FI was hunting down was narcissistic, as Hutch had told Casey, these were good reasons for him to bask in the limelight.

Limelight, however, had two sides.

Karly Listor had been very vocal about Maher's murder. She'd spun possible motives such as jealousy and vengeance. And she'd driven home the notion Ryan remembered her harping on most—that the killer could very well be a pissed-off groupie.

What a slap to an overinflated ego.

Ryan propped his elbows on his desk, wondering if people of power triggered their particular psycho's hatred. And if condescension pushed him over the edge. Did the killer know these victims or were they complete strangers?

No point in spinning his wheels. Ryan was in well over his head. He knew zip about psychopathology.

But he knew just where to turn.

Casey was on a call when Ryan knocked at the half-open conference room door and poked his head inside. She gestured for him to come in.

Ryan stepped inside and shut the door, watching Casey and itching for her to hang up.

For the umpteenth time, he noted that very few people could pull off such a powerful presence at the head of that massive table. But Casey was unique and thrived here. There were several rooms in the brownstone that would have nicely served as an office for her. But she had chosen this space in which to work. As she frequently told the team, she loved the panorama of windows—it cleared her mind and helped her think, just as the openness of the room did. If she needed a smaller, more private space in which to work, she had her old bedroom on the fourth floor. Ryan, who worked in perpetual clutter, didn't get it. But he didn't have to. Casey was the heart of FI. Whatever worked for her was fine with him.

Now, she concluded her conversation and disconnected the call.

"What's up?" she asked.

"Sorry to interrupt," Ryan replied, walking over to the table. "I wish I could say I'll come back later, but this is pretty urgent."

Casey waved away his apology and gestured for him to sit. "I was talking to Nick Colotti, making arrangements to return to CannaBD tomorrow to talk to the rest of his staff. He was as jumpy as last time, trying hard not to trip over his words. I guess he'd hoped I forgot about my decision to come back. Anyway, with Marc out of town, I thought I'd ask Claire to come with me. It'll be a different scenario than divide and conquer. But Claire's insights will be great to have."

"Yeah, that makes sense." Ryan shifted impatiently in his seat.

"Okay, tell me what's got you so fired up," Casey said, interlacing her fingers in front of her.

"I got two hits on victims whose murders match the kills we're looking for."

Casey's eyebrows shot up. "I'm listening."

"Have you checked your news feed today?"

"Unfortunately, no. I've been buried. I was going to scan it while I swallowed my first meal of the day. Why?"

"Because Karly Listor was killed last night. Our guy did it."

Casey's jaw dropped and she automatically grabbed her iPhone and scrolled through the news. "I don't believe this," she said. "She was even more high-profile than Chris Maher. And you're sure about the signature kill?"

"Positive." Ryan stressed that fact and then went on to tell Casey about the second hit, the one where the victim was an upstate New York psychiatrist. "I plan on researching this Dr. Clarke later. I'll also add Jake Flanders to the mix, especially since he and Karly Listor were killed in the same town. But right now, I'm focused on the more obvious similarities between Listor and Maher. I'm way out of my league. Do you think we can call Hutch and ask if he'd give us some insights? We'll leave out the sketchy parts of how I managed to get my results."

Casey nodded, unblocking her number and pressing Hutch's direct line.

He answered right away. "I'm guessing this isn't a summons for a repeat performance."

"I wish, but no," Casey replied.

"Could it possibly be about Karly Listor's murder?"

Casey didn't pretend. "Yes. Ryan and I need an ASPD expert. I know you're buried in work, but could you possibly break away for an hour? Now would be ideal."

Hutch chuckled. "No pressure there. But, yeah, give me a while to finish what I'm working on. Then I'll head on over." A pause. "I don't want to know anything I don't want to know."

"Of course," Casey assured him. "That goes without saying."

"Good. Then I'll make it as ASAP as I can."

"Hutch?" Casey stopped him before he hung up. "Please make whatever *legal* preliminary inquiries necessary. We need you totally up to speed when you get here."

"I'd planned to do just that—right after we ended this call."

"Then I won't keep you."

Offices of Forensic Instincts
Main conference room
Tribeca, New York
2:45 p.m.

Hutch propped his hip against the oval table, flanked by Casey and Ryan, who were standing on either side of him. He perused the documentation Ryan had provided—scrubbed squeaky clean before his arrival.

"Pretty interesting stuff here," he commented, his brow furrowed in concentration. "First off, Ryan, I think you're right about this sociopath resenting powerful figures, especially if they've been condescending to him. It's possible that he's met his victims, but my guess is, probably not, at least not before he killed them. Listor was more than vocal, both on the airwaves and via the internet. She reduced him to a groupie in her comments. That would be enough for him. Maher is another story. A food blogger, no matter how successful, wouldn't fire him up enough to kill. Nor did Maher have the same level of wealth as Listor, assuming wealth is also a trigger."

Hutch clearly had another motive in mind. "So let's take a different approach. Maher wasn't the target, his father was. Daniel Maher is a wealthy superstar, something that screams power. It's possible that anything—something he said in an interview, even something he conveyed in one of his movie roles—made your guy feel demeaned. That would fuel his rage. Seeing this through, the obvious tactic would be for him to try to get to Daniel Maher, which would be next to impossible."

Casey pursed her lips. "So he'd do the next best thing. He'd punish Daniel Maher by killing his son, hoping it would destroy Daniel. Which, in many ways, it did."

"Exactly," Hutch said. "Ryan, find out what movie project Daniel Maher is currently or most recently involved in. If that movie is available, watch it from beginning to end. Watch trailers, too. Then go on to the hype and publicity surrounding it—interviews, TV appearances, you know the drill. Look for anything belittling he said or did, right down to the kind of character he played. Could be his family role or his career choice. Sorry, I know this is time-consuming."

"Maybe not," Casey said. "Emma and I went to Daniel Maher's place and interviewed him after Chris's murder. He's desperate to find his son's killer. He said he'd help us in any way he could. Maybe another visit would help. Maybe he'd supply us with everything we need in one fell swoop. This time, I'd ask Claire to come with me, to channel her energy in the hope of sensing something—anything."

"Careful, Case," Hutch said, turning to look Casey in the eye. "As viable a theory as I'm proposing, it's still just a theory. None of this is proven. So you'll have to come up with a good reason to ask Maher for what you need without revealing anything."

Casey nodded. "Plus, I don't want to further torment the poor man by implying that he's responsible for his son's murder. I'll think of something."

"Good," Hutch replied.

Ryan was rubbing his chin. "But what about Jake Flanders? He doesn't fit any part of this theory. He was poor, jobless, and completely unknown, outside of his family. Now, out of the blue, he's killed in the same town as Karly Listor. I'm just not seeing the connection."

"I'm willing to bet there isn't one—at least not the kind you're looking for," Hutch replied. "Flanders was just in the wrong place at the wrong time. Your sociopath probably made a first attempt to kill Listor. I don't know why he backed off, but something got in his way. Check out the dates—see if Listor had anything going on the night Flanders was killed. And whatever it was, it made the killer unable to follow through on his plans for Listor. That would really push him over the edge. It would explain his road rage, an attempted outlet for his unsatisfied fury."

"Wow," Casey murmured. "You're saying he had no intention of killing Flanders, but when Flanders tried to overpower him on the parkway, our killer went crazy. His rage exploded into something so big that he lost all control and just went after Flanders."

"Yup." Hutch nodded. "He probably brutalized that poor guy even more than usual, he was so over-the-top. This isn't uncommon behavior for a sociopath—transferring their fury to a random victim when prevented from getting to their real target."

"That's why I can't link Flanders to any of this." Ryan blew out a breath. "This antisocial personality disorder stuff is not only complex but it's scary and overwhelming. I've dealt with murder, but I never got into the killer's head. No wonder Claire gets so drained."

Casey arched a brow in his direction. "Remember that the next time you're about to mock her talent."

"Point taken."

Hutch was still scanning the printouts. "I see you did your due diligence on Dr. Clarke, as well."

"It's not as thorough as it will be, but I wanted to put something together for you to look at."

"You covered all the basics," Hutch replied. "Name, addresses—both work and home—career history, family, close friends and colleagues, professional reputation, and areas of psychiatric treatment at the time of his murder."

Ryan nodded. "They're not delved into yet, just pretty much bullet-pointed. Also, I have to dig up Clarke's outside interests, see if he had any prison record, and determine whether he had any bad habits like gambling or drugs."

"Do that, but don't waste too much time on it. I don't expect you'll find anything of interest. Based on our current theory, I'd guess that Dr. Clarke was a person of power in the killer's mind. Psychopathy is one of Clarke's areas of expertise—I see that both in his career history and up until his death."

"You think he was treating our killer?" Casey asked.

Hutch wiggled his hand. "It's possible. But I doubt it; guys like your killer don't really sit for analysis like that. I suspect that reading articles Clarke wrote or topics he spoke about—assuming he did—was enough. We don't know how renowned Clarke was. Ryan, you've got to get hold of anything he wrote or published. Check news sources, blogs—the whole shebang. The reason I'm saying this is because, if I'm right, the killer never actually met any of his victims, excluding Jake Flanders, who was an anomaly. He either listened to them on radio talk shows, read their articles, scrutinized their blogs, or even watched them on TV. He was obsessed with them and infuriated by them. Meeting them wasn't part of his plan. Killing them was."

"Where does Aimee factor into all this?" Ryan asked. "She doesn't fit the profile of any of the victims."

"No, she doesn't," Hutch acknowledged. "Then again, I doubt your guy has targeted her to be one of his signature kills. Why would he? No power, money, or air of condescension."

"But what about the clear message he left at her mutilated apartment?" Casey asked in exasperation. "He's clearly trying to scare her, practically to death."

"I agree," Hutch replied. "But that's not the same thing as killing her. My guess is that she's more of a threat to the mob than to him. For all we know, they hired him to keep an eye on her. That could be for many reasons. If it's tied to CannaBD, they could be afraid that she knows something she doesn't realize she knows. If not, maybe they're worried that Rita passed along confidential information to her. Suppositions abound. But if any of them apply, she's a loose end, one that bears keeping an eye on. Remember, this assassin works for the mob, too, not just for himself."

Casey's eyes flashed. "All I know is that we've got to stop him."

Hutch gave her a small smile. "And you will. I have faith."

31

Offices of Forensic Instincts
Main conference room
Tribeca, New York
Wednesday, 8:32 a.m.

Casey sat in her usual spot at the head of the conference room table with her phone on speaker, as Claire, Ryan, and Patrick settled themselves around the table. She'd Slacked them last night, asking them to be there for an 8:30-a.m. meeting. Knowing they'd all be prompt, she'd timed her phone call with their arrival.

"I've got Emma and Marc on speaker," she told the others. "This way, we can all hear each other's updates simultaneously, so no repetition is necessary."

"Great," Ryan said.

"You first, Marc," Casey said. "I have a feeling our update is going to take a lot of time—it's pretty big."

"No problem." Marc went on to report that "Emily" and "Zachary" had made great progress on day one and were soon headed out for day two. They'd visited four colleges and had walked away with three confirmations of Ryan's theory. The fourth person had politely ignored their phone because Emma was sitting there.

"Score!" Ryan said with a grin, taking a second to pump the air.

"Good news," Patrick said.

"It sure is." This time, Emma chimed in. "Also, I confiscated a few personal items from the three suspects' offices, Claire. I hope they'll help."

"Thanks, Emma," Claire said with a smile. "I'm sure they will."

"That's it from our end," Marc said.

Ryan turned to Casey. "Can I ask Marc a quick favor before you get into it?"

Casey gestured at the phone. "Sure. Go ahead."

"Name the favor," Marc said.

"I'm sure you read about Karly Listor's murder."

"Yeah, I'm sorry about that, but she made more than her share of enemies with her outspoken comments."

"Our sociopath did it."

Marc was silent for a moment. "You're sure?"

"Very. Still, I want solid confirmation. Could you call your friend at the Hartsville PD? He'll give you the details I already know but want firsthand proof of."

"I'll do it as we drive," Marc assured him. "And I'll get back to you as soon as I have the info we need."

"Thanks. That'd be great." Ryan sat back in listen mode.

Claire and Patrick were both staring at him.

Casey stepped in. "As I said, there's a lot that each of you needs filling in on. Karly Listor's murder is only part of it."

She went on to explain everything, occasionally glancing at the notes on her iPad. She focused heavily on Hutch's analysis, advising the team that she'd shared all her notes on Slack.

They all opened their laptops, logged in, and began to read.

Casey gave them time to absorb what they were learning.

Patrick raised his head. "This is quite a lot to take in. Have you contacted Daniel Maher?"

"Yes. Before you guys got here, I called him on his private line. I told him I have some additional information and that I need his help."

"Sorry to interrupt," Emma said from the other end of the line. "But since none of you is clued into the entertainment world, I'll jump-start this for you. Daniel Maher's new movie will be released to theaters in a week. It's called *The Cost of Evil.* Obviously, it's not available on DVD or on Netflix, so you'll still have to go to Daniel to get an advance copy. If our psycho hasn't been able to get his hands on it, Daniel's last movie, which was released thirteen months ago, was *Trapped without Hope.*"

"Well, I missed the boat on all that." Ryan frowned at what he considered to be a rare error on his part. "I should have checked this out. But I've been so inundated… Anyway, I'll watch the two movies tonight from soup to nuts and supply you all with notes. I'll find the trailers. I can also—"

"No you can't," Casey interrupted. "You've already got too much on your plate. I already made the appointment with Daniel. He's expecting us. Claire and I will ask him for both movies, together with all the publicity surrounding them—online interviews, TV appearances, and whatever else he has. I think I have a way of pulling this off without clueing him in."

Claire nodded but shot Casey a quizzical look.

"I want any insights you have or any energy you pick up on," Casey said, answering her question. "So you'll be accompanying me. Okay?"

"Of course," Claire replied.

"Great. Just so you know, I told him Emma is out of town and I'm bringing another colleague with me. We have an eleven-o'clock appointment. Once we accomplish what we need to, we'll grab a sandwich and head straight out to CannaBD."

Claire inclined her head. "You want me to see if I sense any energy there that could help us figure out our killer's identity."

"That's exactly what I want, assuming the killer has any connection to CannaBD."

Claire frowned. "It'll be difficult if we split up. I know Marc was supposed to go with you and that you two were going to divide up the interviews."

"Change of plans," Casey said. "We'll do this together. If we don't get to every single employee, so be it. I'm willing to bet that if there's negative energy there, you'll sense it right away. And we'll go where it leads us. We'll start with the key players who are Aimee's equals in different areas—Oliver Steadman and Kimberley Perkins."

"We're going to have a busy day."

"Me, too," Ryan informed them. "I'll be spending the day in my lair, seeing if I get any other hits on my search for victims and doing more in-depth research on Dr. Roger Clarke. I'm also hoping that some of the burner phones' records come in."

He paused, choosing words that were as "layperson-understandable" as possible. "I'll be concise so I don't bore you to tears. I woke up one of the sleeper bots I have inside the T-Mobile network. I've been sending it instructions to obtain information I want, erasing my tracks along the way. What I get back won't be totally comprehensive, not until I have the full data on all eight burner phones."

Patrick accepted that with a nod. "Oh, and Marc, I could use your help analyzing the bank records. I'm working on them now and getting closer to the answers we're looking for. But since you and Emma took off, it's been a slower process."

"No worries," Marc said. "Emma and I will be home tomorrow, Friday morning at the latest. I'll be right with you, until Ryan gives us our marching orders."

"My gut tells me we're getting close," Casey summarized, seeing Claire nod her agreement. "Close to figuring out both the mob guy and the sociopath. I'm just worried about Aimee. If we're closing in on the killer, he could be closing in on Aimee." She turned to Patrick, who answered her question before she asked it.

"She's on pins and needles. She and Travis have been constantly texting about her moving in with him. I know you told her it would be a while, but that isn't stopping her from asking me if I've made the necessary arrangements yet. I've stalled. I'm pretty sure that, at this time, you don't want her living anywhere but at the brownstone. And I agree with you."

"You're right about how I feel. I want her close to the brownstone at all times."

"That's going to go over well," Emma said sarcastically.

Casey sighed. "I hate to upset her. But we can't get lax, not when so much is going on. It's only been a few days since her apartment was viciously destroyed. And the killer has been active since then. I don't want her exposed, even with Patrick's security team in place."

"I agree," Marc replied immediately. "You also need to speak to her this morning about your plans to visit CannaBD today and to give her your impressions when we return. Pick and choose what you tell her about the rest of our findings."

"I will. But she deserves an update, however partial."

"Yes, she does."

Ryan was scowling. "No matter how guarded we are about what we say, she's going to freak out. She's been very strong since the break-in, but that's not going to hold up when she hears the psycho is escalating. I'm with Casey and Marc. I vote to keep her here—protected and with her hysteria in check."

"I agree," Patrick said. "I guess that's what was keeping me from rushing through the process of getting her set up there. As things stand, I can shift the team I was putting in place and have the guys move back to the brownstone."

"I'm completely on board with all of this," Claire said. Seeing the flicker of guilt cross Casey's face, she added, "Even though it's smart to keep Aimee here, I know you feel upset about keeping her from Travis. Long shifts at the hospital or not, he should be able to see her."

"Why can't he?" Ryan asked. "She can't go there, but there's no reason he can't come here." A corner of his mouth lifted. "Let's call it *unmarried conjugal visits*."

Welcome laughter bubbled up in Casey's throat. The comment was *so* Ryan.

"Our security here is the tightest of anywhere," she said. "So let Aimee arrange some visits from her boyfriend." Her lips twitched again. "Unmarried conjugal visits."

Ryan grinned back. "They can hang a sock on the door so we won't bother Aimee during those times."

"Okay, Ryan, we've got it." Casey wasn't letting this get out of hand. "So clearly we're unanimous on Aimee continuing to stay here."

"Should I tell her?" Patrick asked. "It's me she's been asking."

Casey shook her head. "I'll do it. I'll tell her about our CannaBD visit, about giving her a late-day update, and about compromising without endangering her by asking her to stay at the brownstone but urging her to invite Travis here. I think that'll ease her angst, at least about seeing her boyfriend. The rest—she's going to steel herself for something unpleasant. Unfortunately, I can't tell her not to."

***

9:45 a.m.

Casey poked her head into the brownstone's kitchen to see if Aimee was eating breakfast. She hadn't been in her room, so this was the next best guess.

Sure enough, Aimee was sitting at a stool at the counter, drinking coffee and half-heartedly nibbling on some toast. She looked up when Casey came in.

"Hi." She studied Casey's face to see if she had any news for her.

"Hey." Casey poured herself a cup of coffee and slid onto the stool next to Aimee's.

"Why do I know I'm not going to be happy with whatever you're going to say?"

"Probably because you're not." Casey took a sip of coffee and then set down her mug, turning to face their client and supplying her with the information she needed to hear. "For starters, Claire and I are making a return trip to CannaBD this afternoon. As I told you, we need to interview as many people as we can. I need a certain comfort level before I write off the idea that there's any connection between your company and your predicament. Of course, I'll fill you in on the results as soon as we get back." A pause. "I'll also have a few other pieces of information to share, but that's also going to have to wait until later."

"Why?" Aimee asked.

"Because we need to assimilate more facts. We'll update you this evening."

Aimee sighed. "Fine. I've learned not to argue with you."

"As for Travis," Casey continued, carefully explaining why any idea of moving into his place was going to have to wait. She concluded on the cheerful note that the team agreed that Travis should be allowed to visit Aimee here.

"Unmarried conjugal visits?" Aimee started to laugh, as Casey had hoped she would. The tension breaker was essential. "I love the idea. Tell Ryan that I'm impressed with his creativity." She paused. "Things are escalating, aren't they?"

Casey wasn't going to lie. "Yes. That's why we want you here."

Aimee's fingers tightened around her coffee mug. "I'll prepare myself," she said quietly. "I've grown a backbone, but that doesn't mean I'm not scared to death."

"We promised you we'd solve this investigation *and* keep you safe. We'll do both." Casey squeezed her hand. "Just hang tight."

32

East 84th Street
Manhattan, New York City
Wednesday, 10:55 a.m.

Claire didn't so much as blink when she and Casey arrived at Daniel Maher's staggering fifty-story skyscraper. She'd been through this uber-rich neighborhood many times on her way to and from Central Park. In addition, even though her parents had cordially asked her—and her so-called gift—to leave when she was eighteen, Claire had grown up in a sprawling mansion in affluent Grosse Point, Michigan. So wealth didn't impress her. She was much happier with her simple lifestyle where she could be herself.

Her eyebrows did lift when she saw the thin line of media still perched around the building's front door.

"They haven't given up and gone away yet?" she asked Casey incredulously.

"Actually, the majority of them did," Casey replied. "You should have seen this place when Emma and I first arrived. It was mayhem. We could barely see the entranceway, there were so many reporters and bloggers. Guards and police officers were posted everywhere. They had to shove us through the doors to get in."

"Ouch." Claire shook her head. "I'll never understand media hounds. Never."

"We don't have to, at least not right now," Casey said, already heading toward the front doors.

Claire quickly caught up with her, and together they went through the less-arduous process of announcing themselves, both to the guards and, afterwards, to the front desk.

A few minutes later, they were in the elevator, climbing to the thirty-seventh floor and Daniel's four-bedroom apartment.

They knocked on the door of apartment D.

Once again, Malcolm Evans, Daniel's personal assistant—a.k.a. bodyguard—greeted them at the door.

"Ms. Woods, Ms. Hedgleigh, please come in," he said, politely gesturing for them to do just that.

Casey wasn't surprised that she had no need to introduce Claire. Clearly, Malcolm Evans had memorized the name and had probably done some cursory research on her.

Daniel Maher came right out, his hand extended. He'd aged even more than he had when Casey had seen him a week and a half ago.

"Ms. Woods, I'm so relieved you called me. I'm hoping that means you've made progress in finding Chris's murderer." He turned to Claire, shook her hand, as well. "It's nice to meet you, Ms. Hedgleigh. I wish it were under happier circumstances."

"I understand," Claire said with genuine sympathy. "I'm so sorry for your loss."

"Thank you." Daniel gestured, once again, to the sofa in the sunken living room. "Please, have a seat."

They complied.

"Please call us Casey and Claire," Casey urged him, remembering the exchange from the last time when he'd insisted they call him Daniel.

He nodded. "Very well. Casey and Claire." He looked around as if he'd forgotten something. "I apologize for being such a poor host. What can I offer you?"

Casey waved away the offer. "Nothing, thank you. We'll get right down to the reason for our visit."

The pained relief that crossed Daniel's face tore at Casey's heart. And she wasn't about to make it easier, given what they were going to ask of him with no explanation at all.

Claire sat quietly, letting Casey take the lead. In the interim, she cleared her mind, let the energy flow.

"We've learned more about the killer," Casey told him as gently as she could. "It's caused us to further investigate everyone in Chris's life and dig even deeper into theirs. That means we need a few things from you."

"Name them."

"We need an advance copy of *The Cost of Evil*, together with any advance publicity you have. In addition, we'll need the same for *Trapped without Hope*, simply because it's been out for a year and is already on DVD, so the average person can watch it."

"I can give you copies of both now, and Malcolm can compile all the applicable publicity material and transmit it to you within the hour." Daniel rose, then paused. "I have to ask, why would my new and most recent films have anything to do with Chris's death?"

"We don't know that they do," Casey hedged. "But you're a longtime superstar. You showed Emma and me the publicity photos Chris made for you and told us he handled your online presence. I'm assuming he did even more, like promoting you on his blog." Casey crossed her fingers.

Thankfully, she got the answer she'd hoped for as Daniel gave a pained nod. "He did. As I told you last time, I'm pretty much computer illiterate." Another pause. "I'm not stupid. I realize you're leaving gaping holes in your explanation. I have to ask, can you elaborate, even just a little?"

"Not at this time." Casey wasn't about to lie to him. "We'll tell you everything, as soon as we can. For now, just know you're helping us greatly. And Daniel, we *will* catch Chris's killer."

***

11:45 a.m.

Back in the car, Casey turned to Claire even before she called into the office. Claire had been utterly silent since they'd left Daniel Maher's apartment, her eyes downcast and her lips pursed as they descended the elevator. Casey recognized the signs of Claire going through her process and being troubled by some aura or insight. So she'd left her alone.

But now that faraway look was gone—although the distressed expression remained—and Casey carefully reached out to her.

"Something upset you," she said. "What was it?"

Claire rubbed her temples with her fingertips. "Conflicting energies, all struggling to be heard. The core of those energies is one of pure sorrow. Horrible to endure and painful to sense. Then, ribbons of guilt woven through the sorrow. Deep-seated guilt that won't go away."

No matter how much of a reach it was, Casey's trained mind went straight to a never-considered possibility. "Guilt based on what?"

Claire gave a quick shake of her head. "Not what you're suggesting," she replied, having obviously explored that particular aura. "Daniel Maher is a good man. The grief and the guilt are intertwined, experienced by a father who's not only lost his son but who feels as if he let him down and that he wasn't there when he was needed."

"Then what's eating away at you?"

"There was a third energy that overshadowed both the others."

Casey sat up straighter, sensing that this was going to be significant. "Which was?"

"A powerful aura of hatred and violence. It appeared as a halo around the other emotions, and yet it was intense enough to force them into the background."

Casey processed that. "The killer?" she asked.

"Yes," Claire said with utter certainty. "Hutch was right. That sicko's target was Daniel. Murdering Chris was retaliatory punishment." She shuddered. "That horrifying aura. Every time it's inside me, my entire soul recoils. And I just can't make it go away."

She uncapped a bottle of water and took a deep swallow. "Let's get out of here. I don't think I can take much more."

***

12:20 p.m.

Once Claire was doing better, she and Casey grabbed a sandwich and drove off, heading for CannaBD. Casey immediately called Ryan and Patrick and gave them a full update.

"Claire was living inside all this," Casey concluded. "She's badly shaken."

Ryan cleared his throat. "You okay, Claire-voyant?"

"Not really," Claire answered honestly. "But at least we know that Hutch was right. The rest—I'll have to revisit it, like it or not."

"For now, try to clear your mind," Patrick soothed. "You sound pretty spent. Are you sure you're up to the visit to CannaBD? It can wait a day."

"I suggested the same thing," Casey said.

"No." Claire shook her head. "The sooner we find this animal, the sooner Aimee will be safe. And selfishly, the sooner I can be free of this torture."

They all knew that voice. Claire wasn't going to be swayed.

Ryan cleared his throat. "I'll watch the new movie and the previous one from beginning to end just as soon as you give them to me. I'll look closely for everything Hutch advised."

"Good," Casey said. "Concentrate on anything belittling Daniel says or represents in his role. Daniel's muscle man is compiling all the publicity for both films—trailers, interviews, TV appearances—whatever Daniel participated in plus whatever others posted about his performances. He promised we'd have all that within the hour. So continually check our inbox and save all the attachments on Box."

"Done," Ryan replied. "A few things from my end. Marc got back to me. With a little persuasion, his buddy at the Hartsville PD confirmed the details of Karly Listor's murder. It was a dead ringer to Chris Maher's."

"No surprise there," Casey said.

"Yeah, and no surprise that our pals at NYPD Homicide gave us a call to check in—or rather, to check up—on us. They're pretty clueless, other than the basics, and they're making sure we're not doing anything naughty to solve this investigation before they do—which would be in, like a few months, using their ineffectual means and relying on a miracle."

Casey scowled at the smug note in Ryan's tone. "Ryan, what did you tell them? And *how* did you tell them?"

Ryan chuckled. "Not to worry, boss. I was respectful and reassuring. I told them we've made no great strides and have no viable evidence—made worse by the fact that we don't have access to their case files. I topped it off by asking if there were any clues they could share to help us protect our client. They, of course, blew me off, and I hung up, pleasantly and humbly."

Casey's brows rose. "I'm impressed. It's not like you to be so tactful. I'm proud of you."

"Yeah, well, don't be," Ryan replied. "I wanted to puke."

"But you did what you had to," Claire said. "I'm proud of you, too. And if it makes you feel any better, you're not the only one who wanted to puke. I almost emptied the contents of my stomach in the lobby of Daniel's gazillion-dollar skyscraper."

"Okay, I feel less alone." Ryan's quip was underscored with lingering concern for Claire.

"I'm fine, Ryan." As usual, she read his mind. "And this great veggie wrap is providing necessary sustenance. I'll be in full form by the time we get to CannaBD."

"Just take care of yourself," Patrick said in his usual fatherly manner.

"I will."

"Oh, and Casey," he added, "I'm starting to see patterns in these bank statements. I could use another pair of eyes. I want to make some headway by the time Marc and Emma get back."

"No problem," Casey replied. "But first we have to figure out how much we're going to tell Aimee and then have that meeting with her that I promised."

33

CannaBD headquarters, parking lot
Elmton, New York
Wednesday, 2:10 p.m.

Casey was bristling with irritation when she and Claire pulled out of the lot.

"Talk about a waste of time," she said, veering onto the road. "Unless you picked up on something that you kept well-hidden from me, we made this trip for nothing."

Claire shrugged. "More or less. Especially with Oliver Steadman home sick. Based on Aimee's description, I really wanted to meet him."

"Somehow, I doubt he was sick. Way too coincidental. Nick told his entire staff that we'd be visiting today, wanting to speak to each of them."

"No arguments here," Claire said. "Oliver was not only absent, he made sure to lock his office door. So there was no chance for me to get inside and pick up on any of his energy."

Casey scowled. "Gee, another amazing coincidence. This guy is clearly hiding something. We'll have to find a way to track him down and confront him outside of work. Because there's not a snowball's chance in hell that Nick will ever agree to a third meeting." She paused. "You said 'more or less.' What did you mean?"

"I meant that I got a wave of energy off of Nick Colotti. He was practically vibrating with tension, anxiety, and apprehension." Claire's eyes narrowed in thought. "And a filament of darkness I just can't place."

Casey zeroed in on that. "You think he's involved in what's happening to Aimee?"

"I think it's possible. But that dark energy is muddied, so I can't place exactly what his role is."

Casey digested that. "Whatever it is, it might explain my feeling of being watched when I was in his office."

"That's entirely possible," Claire replied. "Nick Colotti is a very complex man with a lot of layers."

"All this would explain why he was so unnerved by you," Casey said, attempting to connect some dots. "Obviously, he'd done his research. Before he even shook your hand, he demanded to know if you were a psychic. And when you calmly explained to him that claircognizance is a metaphysical gift that allows you to sense energy without knowing how or why you received it, he flat-out dismissed it, saying he was a scientist and didn't believe a word of what you were saying. He was downright hostile. I hadn't seen that trait in him before, nor did Aimee mention it."

"Well, it was there now," Claire replied. "Plus, I couldn't help but wonder why he was so aggressive and rattled if he thought claircognizance was pure nonsense."

"Clearly, he doesn't. Leading us to the reality that he was scared to death of you. Scared that you would pick up on that dark energy you're describing."

"So now what?"

"Now we get back to the brownstone, try to get Marc and Emma on the line, and bring everyone up to speed. After that, we've got to plan our talk with Aimee, which I promised her would happen tonight. We can begin by telling her our perceptions of this latest CannaBD meeting. We need her input, and it will also provide a good jumping-off point for us to get into what's going to be a brutal conversation."

***

Offices of Forensic instincts
Tribeca, New York
Wednesday, 5:10 p.m.

The FI team had met, including Marc and Emma, who'd connected via phone. They'd all caught up and gotten on the same page.

Marc and Emma were still batting close to one hundred percent and were planning to come home tomorrow. Ryan had watched *Trapped without Hope* in its entirety, as well as checked out all the pieces of publicity Malcolm had forwarded with regard to that movie. As Emma had described, Daniel Maher had played a brilliant CIA agent who crushed criminal masterminds whom he obviously considered to be lesser-than. All the publicity followed that lead, including the TV interviews with Daniel, in which he threw his weight behind the premise of the film.

"If the new movie and the publicity behind it are anything like this one was, we sure as hell have our killer's motive for going after him," Ryan had summed up. "I also did more digging into Dr. Clarke, and he definitely fits the bill for one of the killer's targets. He has extensive experience and writes articles and speaks on ASPD in a scientific way that our killer would not appreciate. I'll give you more details when everyone's home tomorrow."

"That works." Casey relayed everything from her and Claire's two meetings today and supplied their impressions.

Lastly, Patrick discussed the pattern he was following with Rita's bank statements and assured them that, with Casey's input later tonight and Marc's professional eye tomorrow, he believed they'd finally be getting somewhere.

"All good," Casey said, eager to get to the main point of the meeting. "In less than an hour, Patrick, Claire, and I have to sit down and provide Aimee with some kind of updated explanation. She's our client and this is her life. We can't hide everything, not anymore. So what do we tell her?"

The whole team rehashed the options, and by the time they hung up, they'd come to a consensus.

It was time to share it with Aimee.

***

7:05 p.m.

Casey held the team meeting with Aimee in the brownstone's small conference room, bringing in sandwiches and trying hard to make things as relaxed as possible.

It wasn't going to work.

Aimee sat straight-backed in a tub chair, interlacing her stiff fingers on her lap. "I appreciate your trying to make things easier for me," she said, taking in the food and beverages. "Unfortunately, I don't think that's possible. So, please, let's get down to the facts. Much as I understand this is your investigation, I also know this is my life. I need to know what's going on."

Casey nodded, taking the lead. "For starters, Claire and I visited CannaBD again today, as you know. On the whole, there were no red flags—except two. First, and most glaring, Oliver wasn't there. He knew we were coming, yet he abruptly called in sick. Despite your dismissive attitude toward his oddities, I think this bears looking into."

"So you're going back to CannaBD?" Aimee asked.

"No." Casey shook her head. "We're going to have to find a way to confront him outside of work. Not only because he's purposely staying far away from us but because Nick would never agree to it." Casey went on to describe Nick's anxiousness, as well as his hostility when he was faced with Claire's gift.

Aimee frowned. "That doesn't sound at all like Nick."

"I'm sure not. But something is upsetting him, and it concerns us and this case. I didn't mention it to you before, but the first time I met with him, I had the distinct feeling I was being watched. Something's just not right there. We'll find Oliver Steadman and get some answers. And we'll further investigate Nick himself if it comes down to it. We know the basics. Maybe we need to know more."

Casey met Aimee's gaze. "Remember, don't mention a word of this to Nick. We need him unaware and off guard."

"I haven't mentioned anything to anybody. I don't intend to start now." So far, Aimee looked nervous but not terrified. "What else do you have to tell me?"

"Ryan's done some deep research in several areas. Ryan?" Casey gestured for him to run with it.

Again, carefully, so as not to step on any land mines, Ryan told Aimee about the pattern he'd established in their killer's targets. Like last time, he stuck to the strangulation and the left-behind college football glove and omitted the truly grotesque parts. "It looks like he has a thing about power and money—both acquiring them and killing for them."

Aimee inclined her head and gave him a quizzical look. "I have neither of those."

"We don't think he's targeting you for a kill," Claire said quietly.

"Then for what?"

Patrick cleared his throat. "He's taunting you for some reason. He wants to scare you out of the picture. Our guess is that you're a threat to whatever it is he's involved in."

Aimee pushed for more. "Enough of a threat to torment me but not to kill me? Something is missing from that explanation."

"We don't know everything yet," Casey told her, feeling good that she could at least be honest about something.

"But I have a possible link that might explain things." Ryan took over the explanation again. "It's about Rita."

Now Aimee looked upset. "You already told me she was taking bribes from parents to get their kids into colleges that were above their abilities."

"That's not the full extent of it," Ryan said. "We thought those burner phone calls were from parents. We don't anymore. We believe that Rita had a network of college professionals who were working for her—in schools all over the tristate area—and that those professionals were doing exactly what she was doing. Only in their cases, they used her tactics, collected those payoffs, and provided Rita with a cut of their earnings."

He saw Aimee's face go white, but he gave her the rest of what the team had agreed upon, after which they could pick up all the pieces together.

"And we don't think the buck stopped with Rita. We think she had a boss who was pulling the strings. He might have blackmailed Rita into doing this or even threatened her or anyone she cared about."

"Someone like me," Aimee whispered, tears gathering in her eyes. "That's why she was so worried about me when she told me she was dying. She was afraid that whatever animal she was working for would harm me, even after she was gone."

"We're pursuing that premise," Ryan concluded.

"And the fear works both ways," Casey added. "Rita was afraid for you. But her boss was afraid she'd talked to you, told you even a little about what was going on."

"Enough to make me a threat," Aimee concluded. "Not enough to kill me but to try to scare me into silence and to keep a close eye on me." She ran both shaking hands through her hair as the ultimate reality sank in. "Oh my God," she breathed. "That's the link here. Whoever's in charge of this, they hired the serial killer to trash my apartment, as well as to kill Rita and Chris Maher—plus all the other victims you've discovered. Those victims must have overstepped their bounds. And my life is hanging by a thread because whoever this psycho is, is close to me in some way. Close enough to keep an eye on me."

"Your life is *not* hanging by a thread," Casey countered without denying Aimee's ultimate realization. "You have us to protect you. That's why we're keeping you at the brownstone, rather than letting you stay with Travis. Our security is airtight. Also, as you can see, we've made a lot of progress. We're getting much closer to our answers—and to the killer."

Aimee's jaw set. "And the person behind all this? Have you gotten any closer to them?"

Casey didn't as much as glance at the team. They'd made a firm and unanimous decision *not* to tell Aimee anything about the mob. That would push her over the edge, and they still had no concrete evidence to support their theory.

"We're pushing hard on that," Casey said. "We have no answers yet. But we will. And that will bring down the house of cards."

"Not on the killer." Aimee was no longer the same naïve girl the team had first met. Life had changed that. "It seems to me you have two branches of the same investigation—the person pulling the strings and the sociopath who's killing people. Even if you figure out who's behind this, there's no assurance they'll name the killer."

"We see it the same way," Claire told her. "Which is why we're covering all our bases. Once again, we're asking you to trust us."

Aimee swallowed hard. "I have and I do." She stood up, her fingers digging into the sides of the tub chair as she did. "I appreciate your candor. But I need some time alone now. So if you'll excuse me…"

She didn't wait for an answer.

She just left the room.

34

Offices of Forensic Instincts
War Room
Wednesday, 10:45 p.m.

Casey and Patrick had spent the past hour in the War Room, with Patrick filling her in on what he'd accomplished, or the first steps he'd taken to accomplish it.

He'd taken the personal extension college numbers Ryan had separated out and applied them to the last six months of Rita's bank records, searching for a pattern between Rita's deposits on or near the dates of her conversation with the college staffers who reported to her. In that same vein, he'd tried to find a pattern between the same deposits and the timing of the burner phone calls.

"That's quite a daunting task for one person," Casey had said. "I might not do as good a job, but I'd be happy to be a Marc stand-in."

"I wouldn't say that, but I do appreciate the help," Patrick replied. "As you can see, there are reams of paperwork to go through to establish an ongoing pattern. The preliminary analysis Marc and I did when the bank records first came in was done without any foundation. We were shooting blanks. Now at least we have something to work with."

Several hours later, they'd still just touched the tip of the iceberg. Patrick was handling the college tie-in, and Casey was handling the burner phones' links—both to Rita's deposits.

"The pattern is there," Casey said, sitting back and rubbing her eyes. "But locating every link is draining."

Before Patrick could reply, there was a tentative knock on the door.

"Yes?" Casey called out, wondering who besides her and Patrick were still in the brownstone, up and about.

"It's Aimee," came the response from the other side of the door.

Casey walked over and opened it. "Everything okay?"

Aimee nodded. "I'm so sorry to interrupt you. And I know that it's short notice. But Travis just finished his shift and…" Her gaze flickered to Patrick. "I was wondering if you could possibly make arrangements with your security team for"—her lips twitched—"an unmarried conjugal visit."

"Tonight?" Patrick frowned. "It's after one in the morning."

Casey rolled her eyes. "She's a big girl, Patrick. Can it be done or not?"

Patrick looked sheepish. "Sorry. Force of habit. I have two daughters in their early twenties. Anyway, yes, I can make it happen. I'll alert my team and they'll do what's necessary." He held up his index finger. "There's one condition. I want Travis at the door in an hour, while Casey and I are still here. The security code for our Hirsch pad is confidential, plus I want to be sure you're safe until the door is shut and locked behind you and Travis."

"Of course." Aimee looked like she wanted to hug him. "Travis will also leave first thing in the morning, as early as you say—after someone on the team has arrived," she added hastily. "But he won't interfere with your workday…"

Casey held up a palm to stop her. "Quit while you're ahead. Patrick already said yes. I know him and how protective he is. Keep talking and he'll come up with a reason to change his mind."

Aimee made a zip-up-her-mouth gesture.

"We'll let you know as soon as things are in place," Casey said. "Now go ahead and text Travis the good news. I'm sure he'll be elated."

After Aimee had scooted off, Casey shut the door and turned to Patrick. "Looks like we're taking a break from our work."

"Give me a minute." Patrick called John and laid out the situation.

He hung up and turned back to their work, stifling a yawn.

"You're exhausted," Casey said. "And you still have to supervise Travis's arrival. My eyes are burning, and I have a crushing migraine. Let's pick this work up tomorrow."

As she spoke, Patrick's cell phone rang.

He glanced down at the screen. "It's Adele," he said, referring to his wife.

"Hi, honey," he greeted her. "Before you remind me that I'm four hours late for our dinner, I apologize. Casey and I are working on something pretty intricate, and I completely lost track of the time."

Casey pointed at the door. "Go home," she said in a quiet undertone. "I'll handle Travis's arrival. Besides, Marc will be home by midday, so you'll have your true counterpart to take over where I left off."

She raised her voice to a normal level. "Hi, Adele," she called out. "Mea culpa. I kept Patrick slaving away. But I'm shooing him out the door now."

"Hi, Casey," Adele called. "No problem. I was just checking in."

Casey smiled at Adele's tolerant response. She was a lovely, kind woman who was accustomed to her husband's absurd hours—much worse, she claimed, than during his years at the FBI.

Patrick glanced quizzically at Casey. "Are you sure?"

"Very sure. Besides, I probably have a few not-so-nice texts from Hutch. I was supposed to be home around ten." She grinned. "Close but no cigar. I'll call him and explain." Standing up, she began arranging the reams of paper to continue analyzing first thing in the morning. "Good night, Patrick. See you at nine. Just shoot me a quick text giving me the go-ahead on Aimee and Travis. And good night, Adele. Enjoy your late, but hopefully not burnt, dinner."

***

Forensic Instincts
Third-floor "guest room"
3:35 a.m.

Aimee and Travis lay quietly on the sofa bed, her head pillowed on his chest, his lips in her hair.

"That was the best unmarried conjugal visit ever," Aimee murmured.

"The best *what*?" Travis asked, pure puzzlement in his tone.

She smiled. "That's what Ryan called this when he was persuading the team to let you visit."

Laughter rumbled in Travis's chest. "I like it. So we'll dedicate our first unmarried conjugal visit to Ryan. He was the catalyst for the end of my cold showers."

Aimee sighed. "It shouldn't have to be this way. Thanks to that fucking serial killer, I feel as if I'm in actual solitary confinement."

"I wish you'd stay with me." He blew out a breath. "But I understand why you can't. You need maximum protection—and that means being here."

Aimee kissed his chest. "Thank you for understanding." Her hand balled into a fist against his skin. "Even with these restrictions, I feel empowered. That bastard wanted me to melt down and back off. He was positive he could make that happen. Well, he couldn't. I'm still in the game, and I'm not throwing in the towel. So I won this round. I plan to win the whole damn match."

Travis was quiet for a moment.

"What if destroying your apartment isn't all he has planned for you?" he asked tentatively.

Aimee swallowed, hard. "I've thought of that, many times. But no matter how frightened I get, I'm not letting fear destroy me. He's *not* going to kill me. Forensic Instincts won't let it happen. And *I* won't let it happen. I've come to realize I'm a lot stronger than I thought."

Travis blew out a breath. "I'm proud of you. But I'm also still worried. Please don't get too cocky. And don't let your guard down."

"I won't," Aimee said softly. "Your support means the world to me. But I'll be fine. FI's going to find this psycho, and I'll do whatever I can to help them. I wish I could tell you more. But I can't. Just know that I'm fully and safely on board."

She paused. "Let's not talk about this anymore, okay?"

"More than okay." Travis rolled her beneath him. "In fact, let's not talk at all."

35

Offices of Forensic Instincts
Tribeca, New York
Thursday, 11:35 a.m.

Despite the fact that Casey had told Patrick to come in at nine, he was there at a little before seven, as was Casey. They were both eager to resume their tedious applications so they could find firm and consistent patterns to the two links to Rita's bank records.

"All these banking transactions were deposited in cash," Casey said, noting aloud what was becoming more and more obvious.

"Yup." Patrick nodded, his forehead creased as he continued their process. "Cash is a favorite of criminals and, particularly, of the mob. Offshore accounts are not that common. They have safes and hiding places at home. I remember one of my FBI friends was working on a squad investigating the Tarillo family. He and his team finally got what they needed on one of the capos. When they made the arrest, they found a million dollars under his mattress."

Casey whistled. "Wow. So Rita's payoffs were chump change to whoever hired her."

"Probably," Patrick agreed. "Rita was smart. All the deposits made are under ten thousand dollars. That's the best way for her to stay under the radar and away from investigations. She was well taught."

Before they could continue, Yoda announced, "Marc and Emma have returned to the brownstone." Almost simultaneously, Emma called out, "We're home. Where is everyone?"

Casey's lips twitched. "That's our Emma. I should have planned a welcome home party."

She walked over and opened the War Room door. "We're coming," she called back.

Claire joined them on their way down, eager to see what Emma had brought her.

They reached the foyer at the same time as Ryan bolted up from his lair. Normally, he blocked out any noise when he was working. But this was his theory, and he wanted to be there to hear the final verdict.

Marc grinned. "What a greeting. Madeline is going to have to step up her game."

Casey rolled her eyes. "Your wife adores you, Marc. I doubt we can compete."

"You're right, you can't." Marc rolled his overnight case to the corner alongside the coat rack and parked it there. "But I have to say it's good to be called by my name again. I was starting to think I *was* Zachery."

"You gave us a final update last night," Ryan said, for once not in the mood for banter. "But now it's time for details."

Marc rolled his eyes. "Can we at least go up to the conference room, where Emma and I can pour ourselves some coffee and sit down? In case you haven't noticed, we're barely in the door." He glanced around. "Plus I want this discussion to stay private—at least for now."

"It was so awesome," Emma breathed, her entire face aglow. "I felt like Nancy Drew."

She didn't even bother putting down her backpack. She paused only long enough to wave a large paper bag around. "We stopped for sandwiches. No one here ever eats and I'm starving." She was already headed to the staircase.

"Yeah," Marc muttered. "*We* stopped for sandwiches."

The whole team chuckled and then followed Emma up the staircase. Marc joined them, heading up to the second floor and the main conference room.

They each grabbed a sandwich and a cup of coffee or tea. Then they took their seats around the oval table and waited for Marc and Emma to fill in the blanks.

"There's not a lot you don't know," Marc said. "Ryan was dead-on. Each faculty member had a different job and pay grade. But they had one thing in common. They were all living way above their means. You could see it in the way they dressed, the way their offices were decorated, even in the pricy knickknacks on their desks and cabinets."

Ryan was puffed up like a peacock. "Did they freak out when you asked about Rita?"

"Big-time," Emma supplied. "I thought a few of them were going to wet themselves. Every single one of them reacted—and not in a happy way."

"And the blaring fax machine sound was successful, too," Marc added. "Their phone numbers all rang on command, and no one looked anything but annoyed at the interruption."

"Interruptions that were ideal for me." Emma unzipped her backpack, groped around inside, and pulled out a bulging collection of Ziplocs.

She glanced at Claire, then carefully slid each individual Ziploc over to her. "Personal items from each office we visited, all labeled by name, department, and school."

Claire eagerly scooped up the bags. "You're a lifesaver, Emma. I'm sure I can pick up different energies from these. Maybe some of them will help us move forward."

"Good job, you two," Casey said to Marc and Emma. "A trip well spent. And more than enough proof for me."

"Good job, them. Great job, me," Ryan said, still beaming. "Sometimes I astound even myself."

"Frequently," Marc muttered. "Although this time kudos are in order. You knocked this one out of the park."

"Yup. And I'm psyched. Because once we have all the banking data you three are acquiring, and once I get back all the call logs from Rita's cell phone, we'll be able to confirm everything except who Rita's boss was. We'll tackle that next—it'll be my responsibility."

"You have a plan?" Casey asked.

Ryan grinned. "I *always* have a plan. Usually with backups. I'm working on them now."

Casey pushed back her chair. "Then I say we all get back to work. Marc, obviously I want you analyzing Rita's bank records with Patrick. Since Ryan needs this info ASAP and three heads are better than two, I'll be joining you. Patrick and I were starting to see a pattern in the evidence. But we have months of transactions to go through. I think all three of us should have at it."

"Say no more." Marc gobbled up the rest of his sandwich and finished his coffee. "Fortified and ready."

"My lair awaits." Ryan shot off a mock salute and headed toward the door.

"One sec," Casey said, stopping him. "You're on major overload. A chunk of what's now being researched is also going to be on you. I have a way to lighten your load and make Emma very happy in the process."

"Tell me." Emma was sitting up straighter now. "I was already sinking into a major depression, thinking I wasn't getting anything juicy to do."

Casey's lips twitched at Emma's dramatic reply. Then she said, "I want you to take over Ryan's job of analyzing Daniel Maher. Get the two

DVDs from the lair. I know that Ryan already watched *Trapped without Hope*, but a second pair of eyes is always helpful. More importantly, there's still *The Cost of Evil*, which is not yet released and which Ryan has yet to watch." Casey paused to reiterate Hutch's instructions of what to look for.

"Pay special attention to scrutinizing all the trailers and other publicity that Daniel forwarded to us," Casey continued. "That's crucial, because there's every chance the serial killer hasn't yet seen *The Cost of Evil* but has tuned in to all the talk shows, interviews, advance reviews, websites, and blog opinions that are doubtless splashed everywhere."

"Daniel's not-yet-released movie." Emma was practically vibrating with excitement. "I'm all over this."

Ryan was grinning. "Come on down to my lair and I'll hand over the two DVDs. I took notes on what I saw and read, which of course you have access to. And, thanks, to you and Casey, for giving me some breathing room."

"My pleasure." Emma was already right behind him. "Lead the way."

Claire rose, as well. "I'm off to my yoga room with this mountain of Ziplocs. The sooner I open myself up to the different energies, the sooner I can, hopefully, provide some insights."

Casey crossed her fingers. "Good luck." She turned to Marc and Patrick. "War Room, here we come."

***

Forensic Instincts
War Room
Thursday, 4:45 p.m.

Marc had joined Casey and Patrick, picking up where they left off, analyzing patterns in the evidence. With his input, things had moved along at a rapid clip.

The pattern in the bank records that Casey and Patrick had begun to see became increasingly more prevalent, as they matched the cash deposits with phone calls to and from the burner phones.

"There's no doubt that Rita's deposits were made soon after her calls to and from all eight burner phones," Marc said, rechecking the data that had become more and more consistent. "That suggests that all eight burner phones belong to one person. Which is no great surprise."

Casey nodded. "The deposits, as Patrick and I saw, are all under ten thousand dollars—just under the radar. What I don't understand is why the amounts are all different."

"My guess is that all the jobs yielded different levels of profit," Patrick deduced.

"Yeah," Marc agreed. "And because of that, Rita must have been giving different cuts to different people. The more extensive their assignments were, the more she had to pay. Same with the number of people used. More pros require more cash. She had to work it out so she kept large amounts for herself while keeping her people happy. Thus, the varying deposits. Also, take note of the fact that, not only are all the deposits made *after* the burner calls, they were also made *before* the college calls. Rita was paying herself before breaking out the amount for her colleagues."

"Smart," Casey said. "She made sure to take care of herself first."

Marc was looking thoughtful. "This procedure isn't innate knowledge, not to someone who'd been a university employee for most of her life. She was taught and taught well. Her boss is a seasoned pro."

"With the mob," Casey supplied.

"That was my take from the onset," Patrick replied. "It pieces things together nicely and strengthens Ryan's theory."

Casey glanced from Patrick to Marc and back. "At this point, I need a consensus, since we've been at this for four-plus hours and have covered months and months of records, yielding supportive results. Do we have enough to take to Ryan?"

"Yes," Patrick said without pause.

"A second yes," Marc agreed. "Ryan needs this evidence ASAP. We have more than enough to give him. If he needs us to go back even further, we will. But my guess is that he'll want to run with this."

"Then it's unanimous," Casey said. "I'll post all this data now. Then, I'll head down to Ryan's lair and fill him in. Other than the burner phone tracing he's doing, this should finish up his research and move things forward."

36

Ryan's lair
Thursday, 5:35 p.m.

Ryan sat at his desk, rubbing his temples. He was tired and impatient. Hell yeah, he was psyched by the conclusions Casey had just reported to him, even more so because she, Patrick, and Marc were all in complete agreement about them. Another huge chunk of the puzzle had been solved, including the fact that, as he'd guessed, all eight cell numbers were owned by the same criminal.

Now he needed those damn call logs. He had to figure out the ID of Rita's mob connection. And since the team knew less than nothing about him, the fastest way to accomplish their goal was to physically locate him.

Ryan's sleeper bots were working backwards, starting with the cell phone numbers and querying the cell tower records to determine which ones interacted with each cell phone. Once Ryan knew the relevant cell towers, he'd need to assemble, compress, and then exfiltrate all the data from those towers on the prescribed dates: time stamps, durations, any and all data that might help him determine the speed and direction of the burner phone as it moved away from one tower and closer to another. Was the caller traveling by car or by foot? Did they stop along the route?

Once those answers materialized, Yoda would be able to transform the data into simulated videos—videos that would show the path taken by the cell phones and their operator. The simulation would show the streets and roads taken, the stores on either side, and the cell phone owner's movement as he progressed along the route. From there, Marc and Patrick would be able to visit those businesses, ask the store managers for copies of their security camera videos on the dates in question. And if fortune smiled down on them, they would catch a glimpse of the cell phone owner's face, or at least the make, model, and license plate of the car he was driving.

Ryan had already completed the long and tedious task of researching algorithms to transform the incoming cell tower data into a time series of GPS coordinates. With that having been accomplished, it was now a waiting game.

***

Ryan must have passed out at his desk, sheer exhaustion having taken its toll.

The silence was broken by Yoda, who announced, "Ryan, the first batch of cell tower data has arrived. It covers four of the burner phones. Would you like me to generate a Google Earth animation showing the movement of each cell phone as an overlay on the base map layer?"

Ryan jolted awake, totally alert and excited. "Absolutely, Yoda, as quickly as possible."

Thirty minutes passed before Yoda said, "Your animation is ready."

Ryan leaned forward and previewed the animation.

"I can already see patterns here," he said. "The starting-stopping motions, along with the time intervals between stops, indicate a drive, not a walk. There are specific streets at specific times when the calls were made. Also, the different cell phones seem to be switched off when one is in use. I have to assume that the owner is blocking all attempts at being caught."

"Excellent observations and theories," Yoda replied. "But what I've compiled is only a partial view. We can't create a detailed and complete picture until we have the remainder of our data."

"I know." Ryan propped his elbows on his desk, his mind racing. "But I'll have plenty to do to keep me busy. Now that we know some of the relevant cell towers, it's time for me collect all the data I can."

"I believe I can be of service," Yoda said. "I can assemble, compress, and acquire all the data from those towers on the prescribed dates."

"Great." Ryan was almost as pleased with Yoda as he was with himself. "I need time stamps, durations, and any other data that might help determine the speed and direction of the burner phone. I'll work with you. Between this research and your Google Earth animation, we can form a pretty detailed analysis of our target's traveling routes."

Ryan paused, glancing impatiently at his computer monitor. "I'm hoping that, since this data just arrived, the rest will quickly follow suit. Then we can incorporate all eight cell phones into one big picture."

"There's no guarantee that the remaining information will arrive tonight or even tomorrow," Yoda replied. "I comprehend that you feel a sense of urgency, but I must remind you that it's not based in fact."

Ryan rolled his eyes. "Gee, thanks, Yoda."

"You're welcome, Ryan."

Not for the first time, Ryan wished he'd created his almost-human AI system with a sliver of emotional intelligence. But he'd thought very differently back then—before Claire. If he wanted any nonscientific feedback, she was the one he'd have to turn to. And right now, she was closeted in her yoga room with no time for interruption.

"My algorithm is in place," Ryan said. "We'll use it to work with what we have until the remaining cell tower information from the other four numbers comes in—whenever it does," he added, fully aware that Yoda was incapable of picking up on the sarcasm. "At that point, you can isolate and repeat your process with the new data, culminating with creating a second Google Earth animation. I'll study that while you combine the data and create a composite animation showing all eight cell phone numbers."

"That's a sound plan," Yoda responded. "We'll be able to watch the full video simulation showing the locations of each cell phone and its time progression while moving."

"Let's go for it."

***

Claire's yoga room
8:05 p.m.

With shaking hands and terrified awareness, Claire re-zipped the final Ziploc that Emma had given to her and tried to breathe past the pounding in her chest.

She was drained, but her body wasn't registering that fact. Nor was it attuned to the fine beads of perspiration trickling down her back, dampening her forehead. Her physical being had been a vessel for the past few hours, and it remained as such as she fought her way to the surface.

She'd handled every one of the college employees' personal items. Each one held different energies, none of which mattered in the long run.

Because, in the end, there was only one smothering presence that had dominated Claire's metaphysical connections, just as it had from the day the FI team had taken on Aimee's case. She couldn't escape it, and it was growing more powerful with each passing day.

The killer.

***

Ryan's lair
9:20 p.m.

Finally, the announcement Ryan had been waiting for.

"The second collection of cell tower data has arrived," Yoda told him. "It covers the final four burner numbers."

"Yes!" Ryan pumped the air, nearly leaping out of his chair.

"I expected that you'd be pleased. I'll immediately finish the composite Google Earth animation you requested."

Ryan was nodding vigorously. "Do that."

Another thirty minutes passed.

"Your animation is complete," Yoda said.

"Great, Yoda. I'll study it while you combine the data and formulate a comprehensive map including all eight cell numbers. At that time, I can apply my algorithm to transform all the incoming cell tower data received into a time series of GPS coordinates. We'll be able to watch the full video stimulation, following the locations of each cell phone and its time progression while moving."

Ryan was already scrutinizing the new map Yoda had created and comparing it to the first. The same alternations between cell phone numbers in different locations—cell number one in one spot, after which it vanished. Then cell phone five—same thing. Ditto with all the other eight numbers.

"This son of a bitch really doesn't want to be found," Ryan muttered. Even as Yoda completed all he had to do combining, compressing, and exfiltrating all the new data, Ryan jumped ahead, mentally joining the two animations and, like a jigsaw puzzle, piecing them together.

"We're going to catch you, you bastard," he said between clenched teeth. "Count on it."

***

Forensic Instincts' main conference room
Friday, 1:25 a.m.

The entire team gathered around the oval table, gazing intently—and exhaustedly—at Ryan. Even Hero was stretched out, snoring, at Casey's feet. But Ryan had Slacked them forty-five minutes ago, practically demanding an immediate, urgent meeting and requesting that they all be in the main conference room ASAP. And here they all were.

"This had better be good, Ryan," Marc muttered, looking unusually grouchy. "I hadn't seen Maddy in almost three days. You're not the only one here with a sex life."

Ryan had the good sense to look sheepish. "Sorry, pal. I didn't mean to mess up your homecoming. If this weren't urgent…" He broke off, glancing around the table. "Was *everyone* home?"

Casey took a swallow of coffee, arching a brow in his direction. "Is that so unusual at one thirty in the morning?" She waved away her own question. "Actually, yes, it is. Especially when we're getting so close to solving a life-threatening case. As it turns out, I was here, working."

"So was I," Claire said. She looked drained and haunted but was doing her best to hide it until Ryan finished his update.

"Me, too," Emma said, nibbling at a candy bar. "I was rewatching Daniel Maher's movies. I've seen each of them twice, including the newest one, which I had to catch up on by scrutinizing it once and then again. I was compiling notes."

"And I was still in the War Room, double-checking to see if there were any details we'd missed, plus getting a security update from John," Patrick said.

Casey took that all in, then looked back at Ryan. "It appears you're not the only one who was burning the midnight oil."

"Well, I'm the one who's going first," Ryan said. "I've been pacing the floors since I Slacked all of you."

Casey sobered, sensing Ryan's urgency and feeling the excitement he was exuding. Clearly, this was going to be something big and meaningful. "The floor is yours."

Ryan didn't even bother sitting down. He just stood behind his chair, practically vibrating with energy. "All the cell phone tower data is in—and that's on all eight phone numbers," he informed them. "Yoda and I have been working half the night assimilating the data and creating the Google Earth animation you're about to see. Open your laptops."

Everyone complied and, following Ryan's instructions, found the video animation he was referring to.

"As you can see, our simulation has isolated each of the burner numbers, carefully connecting one phone number to the next and revealing a host of different routes the owner's taken over the past several months," Ryan explained. "I've highlighted the most frequently traveled ones. Given the stopping and starting times, as well as the speed with which he's moving, I concluded that he's constantly driving, not walking."

"I see that arrival and departure times are also designated," Casey said, studying her screen.

Ryan nodded. "A key point to note: the frequent routes drop off entirely in Central New Jersey. So my guess is he either lives near there or his boss does. As a result, he goes off the grid."

"And becomes untraceable," Patrick agreed, his forehead creased in thought. "A completely viable assumption." He looked up at Ryan. "You did an exceptional job here."

"Thanks," Ryan replied. "But now it's time for you and Marc to do the legwork."

Marc nodded, all grouchiness having vanished. "We'll have to retrace the burner phones' routes, first with drive-bys and then on foot. We'll be looking for CCTV or surveillance cameras along the way. We'll start with the most frequently traveled routes, taking note of the stops most likely to yield us results."

"I can hack the outdoor video surveillance like traffic cams if you need me to," Ryan offered.

Patrick shook his head. "Let's use that as a last resort. Marc and I will start by parking, probably in a centrally located gas station lot, so we can cover as much area as possible. We'll canvass coffee shops, restaurants, retail shops. Hopefully, the owners will let us review their video surveillance records so we can try to find a vehicle, a person, a face that pops up more than once. If we don't get a hit by then, we'll have to broaden our search, doing the same with lesser-traveled routes."

"I've made it a little easier for you," Ryan said. "I asked Yoda to create an MP4 file and install it on both your iPhones. This way you'll have access to all the video footage you need without having to drag along your iPads or laptops."

"That's great." Marc was already checking out his phone. "We'll start at seven a.m. if that works for you, Patrick."

"The sooner the better." Patrick's eyes twinkled. "This way, the diners and early-morning businesses will be open, and you'll get to finish your night with Madeline."

A corner of Marc's mouth lifted. "I appreciate the understanding."

As psyched as Casey was, she was staring at Claire, seeing what bad shape she was in.

"Claire?" she prodded gently. "What's happened?"

Claire sighed, dragging a hand through her hair. "Nothing monumental with the items Emma brought me. I mean, they all screamed guilt in one form or another, but I could barely focus on them. His presence dominated everything. He's getting closer and more fixated on Aimee and now on us."

"The killer," Casey said.

Claire nodded. "It took me an hour to breathe normally and start to come back to myself. He blocks out everything else. And he's going to strike soon."

Ryan clearly felt bad that he hadn't noticed Claire's demeanor. "Sorry, Claire-voyant," he said. "You've obviously had a bad time of it."

"It's not just how bad it was," Claire replied. "It's the shifting emphasis, of course to Aimee, but now to us. He knows how involved we are. He doesn't plan on leaving us out of his sick plan. I don't know how or when, but he's coming after us. I have visions of each of us being choked to death, knives protruding from our thighs."

"Is that your fear talking or your metaphysical insights?" Emma asked, eyes wide with terror.

"My fear," Claire clarified. "But it could very well become a reality."

"Which would make the headlines, big-time," Casey said. "And that would shoot his ego up sky-high, given how high-profile we are." A quick glance at Patrick. "I know how much of John's team is tied up with safeguarding Aimee. Would it be possible for him to put added security on us?"

"I'll contact him as soon as we wrap up," Patrick said.

"*The Cost of Evil*'s movie trailers are pretty gruesome," Emma inserted into the conversation. "Daniel plays a bone-chilling killer who's after a despised lifelong nemesis he can't seem to one-up and wipe out. The interviews and the trailers themselves clearly show him in an escalating pattern of killing people who stand in his way, yet still being ineffective in his end goal—I'd guess those things alone would majorly piss off a serial killer who thinks he's infallible."

"More evidence that Daniel Maher was the initial target in his son's murder," Casey said. "We've got to focus on both these threads—tracking the mob leader and finding the killer before he finds us."

She rose. "All of you, go home and get some sleep. The next few days are going to be brutal."

37

Offices of Forensic Instincts
Kitchen
Tribeca, New York
Monday, 7:10 p.m.

Patrick took a healthy swallow of whiskey, setting down his glass tumbler and turning to Marc, who'd just done the same. Both men were rumpled and frustrated, their eyes red-rimmed from lack of sleep.

"This sucks," Ryan announced, striding into the room and grabbing a beer from the fridge. "I knew this would take time, but you've been on this for three days. Where the hell is this guy?" He shook his head even as he spoke. "That's a ridiculous complaint, especially coming from me. I created this program. I knew it would take hours of time, interviewing people and watching weeks of video footage. And in all fairness, three days is nothing. Sorry."

"Don't be," Marc said. "We're disgusted, too. We've talked to a slew of cooperative business owners—in Manhattan, Westchester, and New Jersey. We've watched weeks of their video cams. And we're just not seeing the same car or driver twice."

"It'll happen." Patrick was ever the voice of reason. "Marc, you and I have both done our share of surveillance. It's frustrating and endless. And this is more complex than just tracking down an average criminal. We don't know his ID or anything about him or his habits. We *do* know that he's taking great pains to stay invisible."

"You're right." Marc blew out a breath. "I think Ryan's impatience is starting to rub off on me."

That made Ryan smile. "It's good for you to have a flaw or two. Perfection is highly overrated."

"Shit, this is maddening," Marc said. "But I don't care if we have to visit every store, eatery, and gas station along the routes Yoda zeroed in on. We're not stopping until—"

Marc broke off and they all stopped talking when the kitchen door swung open and Aimee stepped inside.

"Subtle," she said. "Very subtle. I wasn't listening in, although maybe I should have been." A quick glance at Patrick. "Where have you and Marc been all weekend? Or are you going to blow me off?"

Marc shook his head. "No. We're not. We've been trying to track down the guy who was Rita's boss. But that's hard to do when you know little to nothing about him."

Aimee eyed him thoughtfully. "You must know something. You're not the types to shoot blind. But I won't ask about your methods. I'll only ask how close you are."

"We're not sure—yet," Patrick replied. He wasn't happy with the situation with Aimee. She was getting far too restless to suit him. "But you have to sit tight. We're close enough to know that we have to move carefully. When we find this guy, as well as the killer, we have to hit bull's-eyes. There's no room for mistakes."

Aimee paled a bit but nodded. "I understand, and it freaks me out. But I have to believe it's all going to be over soon, and I'll be able to get on with my life." She paused. "I've started searching for apartments online. I'm not looking anywhere even close to Washington Heights—the memories are just too awful. But the day this nightmare comes to an end, I'll be visiting my list of prospects—step one in starting over."

She helped herself to a yogurt and a spoon and then gave the team a group wave. "I'll be in my room, slaving away at my laptop. Without my work, I think I'd lose my mind entirely. That'll be step two—getting back out there to visit college campuses and to see my colleagues at CannaBD. Even dealing with Oliver looks good about now."

She left the kitchen, the door swinging shut behind her.

"Dammit," Patrick muttered. "Aimee is another reason we'd better wrap this up fast. She's not going to stay put forever. Human nature is funny. Her place was destroyed in the most horrific way possible—but it happened over a week ago. Impatience is starting to surpass fear. Not good."

Marc opened the fridge, took out two more yogurts, and handed one to Patrick. "Let's review the last few weeks' footage. Then we'll go home, grab some sleep, and hit the streets again at dawn."

***

Formen's Diner
Woodfield, New Jersey
Tuesday, 11:45 a.m.

Marc and Patrick were sitting in a booth, eating their burgers. Neither of them was particularly hungry, but eating lunch here was a thank-you to the diner's manager for providing them with yet another two weeks of camera footage. Yoda's simulation had labeled this a stopping point three times. It was enough to focus on, since Marc was hooked on the theory that this diner was close to either the mob guy's home or office. This was the fringes of Central New Jersey, and the video animation never proceeded farther than this. It was just too much of a coincidence.

While he and Patrick ate, they reviewed the latest video footage in silence.

Abruptly, Marc sat up straighter, eyes narrowed. "Yes-s-s," he muttered.

"What is it?" Patrick asked from the other side of the booth.

Marc turned his iPhone around so Patrick could see it. "That sedan parked there." He pointed mid-lot. "I've seen it before—same parking lot, same diner—maybe twice, maybe three times, just like Yoda's routes indicate."

Patrick peered closely. "I see a side view of the car. No plates and no owner. We've seen hundreds of cars. Are you sure?"

Marc nodded. "Yup. Maddy and I get a kick out of attending auto shows. We can't afford most of the cars, but it's cool to see the latest and the greatest. I remember when this particular model was released. It captured both our attention. It's a Mercedes-Maybach S-class, their most expensive and, I believe, newest model. That particular color is called ruby black—not a typical color for any other manufacturer. So, yes, I'm sure."

Patrick grinned and he and Marc bumped hands.

"It's only step one," Marc said. "We have to find the corresponding footage and confirm that I'm right. Then we have to narrow our search down to this particular make, model, and color vehicle."

"It's a hell of a lot better than looking for a needle in a haystack." Patrick was already standing, grabbing the check the waitress had left for them, and tossing a generous amount of cash on the table. "Let's get back to the brownstone. We've got a lot of reviewing and comparing to do."

***

Offices of Forensic Instincts
Tribeca, New York
Tuesday, 1:20 p.m.

Marc and Patrick walked in and went straight to the War Room.

They were setting up when, about two minutes later, Ryan opened the door and joined them. "You found something." His tone was laced with excitement.

"Sure did." Marc told and showed Ryan what he'd spotted.

"Oh, yeah." Ryan was already settling himself beside them. "I want to be in on this. And not just to pat myself on the back, although you both know how much I love doing that. But three heads are better than two. We'll find that other footage."

They'd barely gotten underway when Casey and Claire walked in.

"I heard the commotion," Claire said.

"As did I." Casey looked more than hopeful. She looked certain. "You found something. There's no way you'd be back here if you hadn't. Plus, I feel the anticipation in the air."

Marc retold his story.

"Great work." Casey was already approaching the table. "I'm on board to help."

"Me, too." Claire arched a teasing brow at Ryan. "You're going to be unfit to live with, aren't you?"

To everyone's surprise, Ryan shook his head. "Not yet," he said. "When we hunt down that son of a bitch and catch his serial killer, *then* all deserving compliments will be received." A quick flash of a grin. "Humbly, of course."

Casey rolled her eyes. "Of course."

4:45 p.m.

"I got him," Casey said with great satisfaction. "Ten days ago, ten thirty a.m., in a slightly different spot in the diner parking lot." She pointed. "You can't see as much of the car as you can on the first video footage, but it's enough."

"Sure is." Ryan was leaning over her shoulder. "The front end of the car. He's parked ass in. Different cell numbers again?"

Casey nodded. "Different from each other and different from his other trip."

Patrick frowned. "We still don't have a solid pattern. He eats there on different days and different times. Judging from what we've seen, weeks can pass between visits, and so far, his routes to get there have been completely unrelated. I say we stay here and keep looking. If we haven't found another sighting by whatever time we quit, then Marc and I will go for a stakeout early tomorrow morning. But those can be endless. And the clock is ticking."

"I agree," Marc said. "We're not losing any time by following Patrick's suggestion. Let's go at this until we drop from exhaustion. If we find nothing, he and I will park ourselves across the street from the diner at seven a.m. and wait."

38

Formen's Diner
Woodfield, New Jersey
Wednesday, 8:45 a.m.

After pulling a true all-nighter at the brownstone, the team still hadn't zoomed in on any more footage that showed the Mercedes in it. So, as planned, Patrick and Marc had each grabbed a shower and a change of clothes and headed straight back to the diner.

They arrived just before seven, situating Patrick's sedan diagonally across the street from the parking lot. Neither of them was in the mood for conversation, plus they had work to do. Each of them was reviewing the videos they'd taken from willing CCTV operators over the various routes the eight burner phones had taken. Marc was revisiting those from Westchester, and Patrick was going back over those from the pertinent sections of Manhattan.

Back at the brownstone, the rest of the team was hard at work, continuing where they'd left off an hour earlier. As Ryan suggested, they stuck to the frequent routes that ran through northern New Jersey to the tip of Central New Jersey in the hopes that any of the CCTV footage Marc and Patrick had obtained from store owners would show the car they were hunting down.

Nobody was coming up with anything.

After reading Ryan's latest glum text, Patrick turned to Marc. "This doesn't feel right. Staking out a `maybe' for heaven knows how long when we have a killer closing in—I have a bad feeling about this."

"Yeah, so do I." Marc looked up from his screen. "Suggestions?"

"I suggest giving up this sit-and-wait nonsense." Patrick pointed at a half dozen routes on Yoda's map. "All these are in Manhattan. I realize that Manhattan is ridiculously overcrowded, but I think we should revisit various stores, gas stations, and restaurants near the stops made by our guy along those routes. There were a large number of stores we couldn't get to. Let's give it another go."

"I'm all for it," Marc agreed as Patrick turned on the car and released the parking brake. "We can always come back here at the end of the week and recheck the latest footage. But right now, we're spinning in neutral and wasting our time. Let's go."

***

Midtown Manhattan
Wednesday, 3:10 p.m.

Marc and Ryan had done hours of canvassing, getting both gracious receptions and doors shut in their faces. Now, they were back in the car, sticking to a slow perusal of Midtown—specifically, West Forty-Seventh Street and Ninth Avenue. Their target had traveled this route four times over the past month, Ryan had just reported. And his sedan had been caught in two of those trips.

Both Marc and Patrick were perched at the edge of their seats, easily watching the vehicles that were crawling along West Forty-Seventh Street, thanks to construction that was causing gridlock.

"I never thought I'd be grateful for traffic," Marc said.

"Neither did I," Patrick agreed. "Except that, if we don't get lucky soon, I'm going to have to find a parking lot so we can travel by foot."

As he spoke, Marc shot up and pointed out his passenger seat window. "There he is."

Patrick followed the direction Marc was pointing in and then vigorously nodded. "Six cars up in the right lane. I'll move up as fast as I can."

Marc was already getting his iPhone ready. "I'll get a photo of the plates and, hopefully, one of the driver."

Luck was finally with them. The left lane moved a little faster than the right, as the drivers eased around the jackhammer blocking the right lane. Four car lengths later, Marc was able to make out the plates.

"Jersey plates," he said as he took a bunch of photos.

They continued to approach the sedan.

"Just a little more," Marc muttered.

They pulled slowly alongside the Mercedes. One occupant. A dark-haired man of middle age in the driver's seat, chatting on his cell phone.

"Bad boy," Marc said, leaning forward, his cell phone just peeking up through the passenger-side window. "Doesn't he know that non-hands-free talking while driving is against the law?"

He snapped off a few shots, then waited for the best angle possible and repeated the process.

"We got you, you bastard," Patrick said, seeing the triumphant expression on Marc's face. "Now text those photos to Ryan, and let's get back."

***

Offices of Forensic Instincts
Ryan's lair
Wednesday, 3:45 p.m.

Ryan bolted out of his chair. "Hell yeah!"

He printed out Marc's photos, first magnifying them into super-size. He Slacked the rest of the team with the news and then got down to tracking the license plate.

He was barely underway when Casey burst in.

"Sorry, but you're not getting solitude, not this time," she announced. "We're invading the lair." Claire, Emma, and even Hero—who'd sensed the hyper-charged atmosphere—practically flew into the room behind her.

"Here." Ryan handed Casey the photos. "Take a look at these while I'm digging up all I can."

The team was all super-psyched, leaning over Ryan's shoulder as he worked. Normally, he would have bristled. Not this time.

Claire reached over to touch the photos Casey held. She pulled away as if she'd been stung. "That's him," she said softly.

Ryan turned to gaze at her. "You okay?"

She gave a shaky nod. "He's everything we feared and more. We've got to bring him down, even if it means alerting the NYPD to the situation. That's how dangerous he is. And the killer"—she shuddered—"I can feel his evil emanating from this man—the man who hired him."

"I hear you," Ryan replied. "But I want to try tackling this alone—not for long," he added, seeing Claire's reaction. "I promise not to be a cowboy, Claire-voyant. If we need the cops, we'll involve them. Okay?"

Claire nodded.

Ryan turned back to his desk, stopping his work just long enough to patch in Patrick and Marc. "Now everyone's right here with me," he said.

"Good," Marc replied. "We won't interrupt you until you tell us something."

Everyone else followed suit.

A half hour later, Ryan said, "Dammit. Nothing at all on these plates. I've done everything, including hacking the New Jersey DMV. Zip."

"My guess is they're stolen," Patrick replied. "Not really a surprise."

Ryan grunted. "Then it's on to facial recognition. No one is *that* invisible."

An hour later, he'd proved himself wrong.

"It's like he and his fucking Mercedes-Maybach S-class don't exist," Ryan said. "No police record. No appearance in national newspapers or on social media. No record of his vehicle purchase at any of the New Jersey car dealerships. Abso-fucking-lutely nothing." Ryan ran a hand over his face. "I'm not giving up, not by a long shot. I'm going to find this guy."

Casey laid a palm on his shoulder. "You're not giving up and neither are we. It's after five o'clock and none of us has eaten much in days." A quick glance at Emma. "Would you mind ordering a couple of pizzas? We'll bring the photos up to the kitchen and keep at it."

"No problem." Emma was already punching the phone number of their usual takeout place into her iPhone.

"More than a couple," Marc corrected. "We're home. We'll meet you in the kitchen."

Ryan was reluctantly rising to his feet, leaving his desktop and grabbing his laptop. "Yoda, keep working this. I must have missed something."

"Very well, Ryan," Yoda replied. "But I do believe you've been very thorough. Nevertheless, I'll widen the vehicle search to neighboring states and find obscure sources of social media."

"Thanks."

They all trekked up to the kitchen, Casey carrying the photos, and then hovered around the kitchen nook. Ryan immediately got back on his laptop, starting a new and different search. Casey spread the photos across the countertop. She wished she recognized this man.

The pizzas arrived, and everyone dug in. Ryan wasn't his usual chow-down self. He nursed his first slice, clearly frustrated and determined.

Aimee walked into the room, sniffing. "Do I smell pizza?"

"You sure do." Casey gestured at the boxes. "Help yourself."

She caught herself as she spoke and began swiftly gathering up the photos. But she was too late. Aimee had already spotted them before Casey could safely tuck them away.

No one missed the bright light of curiosity that sparked Aimee's gaze. Mentally chastising herself for her own carelessness, Casey knew this one was on her to handle.

She steeled herself for a barrage of questions she had no idea how to answer.

But when Aimee did ask her question, all their jaws simultaneously dropped.

Brows drawn, she glanced at the few photos remaining on the countertop and asked, "Why are you so interested in Nick's dad?"

39

You could have heard a pin drop in the room.

Ryan reacted first, swiveling around on his stool to stare at Aimee. “Are you telling us that all these photos are of your boss’s father?”

Aimee nodded. “Victor Colotti,” she supplied. “He’s the one who funded CannaBD and is still our main investor. He also owns a liquor distribution company—along with a bunch of other businesses—and makes sure our product gets on as many shelves as possible—in bars, restaurants, and liquor stores. He’s boosted our sales big-time. What is it about him that you want to know?”

Casey recovered first. “We’ve been checking out anyone and everyone you might have been in contact with. And we spotted him near CannaBD and had no idea who he was. We were actually going to ask you if you knew him. And now we know.”

Thankfully, Aimee accepted the totally fabricated explanation, because she nodded and helped herself to a slice of pizza.

“Victor doesn’t come around often, but we’re all on our best behavior when he does. He’s a very formidable man—friendly but intimidating.” Aimee chewed and swallowed. “I was scared to death that he’d make Nick fire me when everything with Rita first went down and I talked to the police for the first time.”

Casey and Marc exchanged an imperceptible glance.

"Fortunately, he didn't," Claire said.

"I think that's because I didn't mention CannaBD in my police interview. He did insist on staying in the loop. So I've kind of been on edge about that, too."

Claire nodded her understanding. "Are Nick and his father close?" she asked in that soothing tone that put people at ease.

Aimee shrugged. "Nick checks in with him a lot. But I don't really know how tight they are. Nick is a pretty private guy, so he doesn't talk about personal stuff with the team. Does that matter?"

"Not really," Casey said offhandedly. "Just curious. Because you never mentioned Victor Colotti before."

"I rarely see him. He pops in occasionally to see how the business is doing. That's about it."

"Okay," Casey said. It was time to let it go. No point in arousing Aimee's suspicions. They'd do their own research, find out what they needed to.

"Eat up." Casey gestured toward the pizza boxes. "Emma always orders enough for twenty people. Whatever's left over we grab for lunch. So there's more than enough."

Aimee grinned. "I remember from last time." She helped herself to a second slice and then headed for the door. "I'm going to shower and get ready. Travis and I have an unmarried conjugal visit at seven. Thanks for making it happen, Patrick." With that, she left the kitchen.

Once her footsteps disappeared from earshot, the whole team stared at each other.

"Nick Colotti's father?" Ryan shook his head in self-deprecating disbelief. "How could I have missed that? I checked Nick out thoroughly. I knew he had a father who had helped him fund CannaBD and was still investing in it. But there was no evidence of—"

"Stop blaming yourself," Casey interrupted. "Victor Colotti made himself invisible. Do you actually think he'd leave evidence that could be found by researching Nick?"

"True." Ryan turned back to his laptop and started pounding away at the keyboard. "Yoda," he called. "Get me everything, and I mean *everything*, you can on Victor Colotti. He's Nick Colotti's father. Lives in New Jersey and owns and runs a liquor distribution company plus a whole lot more."

"I'm on it, Ryan," Yoda replied.

"So am I," Ryan said. "There are photos of him stored in the cloud. That's about all I can tell you or give you at this point."

Marc was squinting thoughtfully. "Casey, maybe you should shake the apple tree a bit."

"Call Nick, you mean," Casey said. "I think that's a good idea. I'll thank him for being so cooperative, tell him how impressed I am by his staff, and say how much I'd enjoy meeting his father—the guy who helped him launch the business."

"That'll be enough to send him through the stratosphere," Emma said.

"Yeah, it will," Ryan agreed. "But give me until morning before you make that call. I want to get everything that *does* exist on Victor Colotti and his businesses that I can before he realizes he's been made and slams those doors shut."

Casey nodded. "Not a problem. The business day is over, and I don't want this call to be so obvious. If I call after nine a.m., at least he won't have his guard up on the first ring."

"Just after he hears your voice," Claire said. "You're going to have to walk a very thin line. Then again, that's some of what you do best."

Patrick's wheels were turning. "It's best for another reason. Travis will be with Aimee all night. That'll keep her busy while Ryan does his research into her boss's father. She's already curious enough. We don't need to slow Ryan down by playing hide-and-seek to keep things under wraps."

"You're right." Marc was nodding his head. "I think we should all jump on the bandwagon and help Ryan as much as we can. He might be doing the heavy lifting, but all of us are capable of doing peripheral research. It may be a long shot, but let's see what we can come up with."

"Done," Casey agreed. She handed Ryan a box with a half-eaten cheese and pepperoni pizza in it. "Go back to your lair. You're most comfortable and most effective there." She gave the team a rueful look. "Sorry, guys. Another night of little sleep. We can take turns running home for a quick shower and a mini catnap. But that's it."

***

Ryan's lair
10:03 p.m.

Casey knocked on the door and walked in. "Your turn," she announced. "Claire has been sitting in her yoga room, trying to get as much energy as possible from those photos of Victor Colotti. She's wrapping up. So it's break time."

Ryan was staring at his screen.

"Yoda and I have put a lot together," he told her. "Colotti senior also owns a restaurant and a catering business. He services large home parties of super-rich people. People with college-aged kids."

"His income source," Casey concluded. "Make sense. Parents frantic to get their kids into a great school, who can afford to pay anything to accomplish that. Colotti makes that happen—and gets paid a fortune in the process." She paused. "That's where Rita must have come in. She fudged records, did whatever needed to be done to get those kids admitted. And she had colleagues in different schools who were paid to work with her and accomplish the same results in their respective schools."

"Exactly." Ryan bobbed his head up and down. "I'm getting into checking out his restaurant and catering business. That'll tell me more."

"Not now, you're not." Casey stood firm, swiveling his chair around. "Go home with Claire. Yoda can handle this alone for a few hours. Right, Yoda?"

"Yes, Casey. I have a great deal of material to work with. I'll have more answers for Ryan when he returns."

"Great." Casey literally dragged Ryan out of his chair. "Goodbye, Ryan. Security detail will be at the door in a minute or two to pick you up. John's arranged for them to do door-to-door service while we're under protective watch."

He rolled his eyes at her. "Damn, you're persistent. Fine. I'm going. But if there's anything I should know…"

"There won't be," she assured him.

"Then okay."

"Meet Claire in the foyer and wait."

***

Forensic Instincts foyer
10:08 p.m.

Claire was standing in the doorway when Ryan came up from the lair.

"Hey," he said.

"Hey yourself." She studied him for a moment, seeing her own buried-in-work look on his face.

He returned the appraisal. "You look like you're about to collapse," he said.

"You look worse."

His lips curved. "I can't argue with that. My brain is about to explode."

"I hear you." Claire paused, watching his face with keen insight. "Ryan." She put a gentle hand on his arm. "Maybe you should head home alone. Security can go to both our places, no problem. This way, you can have some time alone to unwind."

Ryan looked down at Claire's hand on his sleeve, and that odd feeling squeezed inside him again—more prominently this time, given how high his adrenaline was running.

"No." He shook his head. "I want you with me. At my place. Now."

Claire's brows lifted at the very different kind of urgency she heard in Ryan's tone. Then, she nodded. "Of course."

They sat in the back of the car together, oddly quiet for the two of them. But Ryan's fingers curled around Claire's until they reached his apartment building.

"Thanks, Gary," he said, opening the car door.

"Not a problem. I'll be nearby. Just text me when you're ready to go back."

"Great."

Ryan waited until he and Claire had climbed the stairs to his apartment, gone inside, and locked the door. Then, he turned to face her.

"Let's go to bed," he said without preamble but with sober intensity.

Wordlessly, she headed for his bedroom.

Ryan followed suit, leaning in his doorframe and watching as Claire tossed her jacket on a chair and pulled off her yoga clothes. With that utter grace she possessed, she crawled into his bed and waited. Just like she belonged there. Which she did.

Holding her gaze, Ryan stripped off his clothes and climbed into the bed beside her.

"I'm here," Claire said softly, sitting up to press her body against his and to wrap her arms around his neck. "And I need this, too."

That was all Ryan needed to hear. He had no idea how much Claire had already perceived. It didn't matter. It was there and it was real.

He pulled her under him, touching her in light, caressing strokes, and shuddered as she wrapped her legs around him, drew him inside her.

He sank into her body, shutting his eyes as sensation swamped him. He didn't move—not right away. Instead, he lay perfectly still, just savoring the wonder of their joined bodies.

When he did move, it was at Claire's urging, her arms tightening around his neck and her body shifting restlessly under his.

Ryan's resolve shattered and his promise to himself to make this slow and tender evaporated. He gave in to the urgency that always dominated their lovemaking—an urgency that had been there from the start. Only this time it was different, wild and frantic, but different.

At the very pinnacle of sensation, Ryan raised Claire's arms over her head and intertwined their fingers, pressing their joined hands deeply into the pillows. Her breathing ragged, Claire opened her eyes, and their gazes locked as they went over the edge together.

Afterwards, Ryan stayed where he was, his mind and his body awash with something he'd never before experienced and never imagined he would.

"I'm in love with you, Claire."

The words were easy to say because the feelings had been there, unsaid and stupidly unrecognized, until now.

Tears welled up in Claire's eyes, trickled slowly down her cheeks. "I've been fighting my love for you even harder than you were fighting yours for me. It's scary and it's profound and it changes everything. But, Ryan, I love you. I have for a very long time."

Ryan lowered his head, kissed her with an emotion he needed to express. Him—emotional.

He rose up, his thumbs caressing her cheekbones, and grinned, thinking about how much he'd changed. "Two confirmed loners, never allowing themselves to need another person. There goes another scenario down the tubes."

Claire smiled, looking a little giddy. "Two loners who are polar opposites in so many ways."

Ryan's dimple flashed. "We'll still kill each other at work. But, ah, when we come home." He paused, raised his head, and, in true Ryan form, jumped to the next phase that most couples contemplated for months. "I want to live together. But how do polar opposites decide whose place to move into?"

Claire brushed his damp hair off his forehead. "I don't really think there's a compromise for that one."

"Am I going too fast?"

"Not a drop," Claire assured him. "It's just that… well, look at your place. It's a minimalistic techno-center. I love being here, but…"

"But you need the soothing surroundings of your yoga retreat." Ryan's wheels were turning. "Half time in each?"

"Now *that's* an offer I can't refuse." Claire's smile was infectious. "Besides, your bed is roomier. That's a definite plus."

Ryan laughed. "Consider it done. Hell, this night has gone from miserable to incredible."

"There is one bit of bad news," Claire said, straight-faced.

"Uh-oh. What's that?"

"We have another half hour of R and R left tonight. And I have no intention of letting you sleep."

"Really?" Ryan pulled her over him. "Then let's celebrate this devastating piece of bad news for the entire half hour."

40

Forensic Instincts
Thursday, 12:15 a.m.

Ryan was whistling when he and Claire stopped on the second-floor landing and headed to the conference room. Sure enough, the whole team was gathered around, doing research and planning out the next day.

"Hey," Ryan greeted them. "We're back. Casey, you and Marc are up. Tell Hutch and Madeline we say hi."

Casey looked up and eyed him thoughtfully. "You're whistling... and surprisingly cheerful. I thought you'd be a bear when you got back."

She stopped, glancing from Ryan to Claire and back.

"Ah," she said. "Finally."

"Finally what?" Emma demanded. "Did Yoda turn up something I don't know about?"

"I'm going down to check on that right now," Ryan replied. "But not to worry. He and I will have dissected Victor Colotti in record time. I'm super motivated." Before the team could ask any more questions, Ryan gave them their answer in his customary straightforward manner. "Claire and I are in love."

Emma squealed and Patrick and Marc grinned.

"What a surprise," Marc said in that dry way of his.

Casey rose and gave each of them a hug. "It's about time you saw what all of us have seen for months. We're so happy for you."

"Thank you," Claire said, rolling her eyes at Ryan.

He looked totally at sea. "What?"

"I'm going have to get used to everything in my life being an open book." She smiled. "But you've managed the turnaround. So I'm up for the challenge."

"What turnaround?" Ryan demanded. "I've always told it like it is."

"Says the man who never mentioned to me he had a sister, much less an entire family," Claire retorted.

"Ah, it's good to see that things at work will still remain stormy," Marc said, folding his hands behind his head and leaning back, as if he were readying himself to watch a theater production.

Ryan frowned. "Okay, you have a point," he said to Claire. "But other than my private life, I've always been open."

"I *am* your private life," Claire reminded him.

He threw up his hands. "Fine. You win. But you're the one who changed me. Now I feel like being open about everything."

"Lucky me."

Casey rapped her knuckles on the table. "Play nice, children. We've got a case to solve."

Ryan blinked, abruptly returning to earth and snapping to attention. "Anything significant to report, Yoda?"

"I've made some progress on Victor Colotti's catering business," the AI system reported.

"I'll be right down." Ryan winked at Claire and headed for the door.

"Oh, and Ryan?" Yoda said.

Ryan paused in the doorway. "Something else?"

"I'd like to offer my sincere congratulations."

The entire team looked at each other, wide-eyed, and then burst out laughing.

"Thanks, Yoda," Ryan said. "I guess I did program you with some humanity, after all."

"I've had periodic updates," Yoda reminded him.

"True." Ryan's eyes were still twinkling. "As I've changed, so have you. Good for us both. See you downstairs."

The team was still laughing as Ryan exited the room.

***

Ryan's lair
12:20 a.m.

Ryan slid into his chair and swiveled around to face his laptop and monitors.

"Okay, Yoda, tell me what you've got."

Data started appearing on Ryan's screen as Yoda spoke.

"Victor Colotti owns a restaurant, a catering business, and a liquor distribution company," Yoda reported. "He launders money directly through his seemingly legitimate restaurant business, as well as takes in enormous profits from the parties he caters. My research uncovered a list of such parties over the past six months. And they share several factors."

Ryan was staring at his screen. "All the owners live in extravagant mansions," he surmised. "They're also filthy rich, middle-aged, and have high school kids with high expectations of enrolling in the best colleges in the country."

"Precisely."

"Nice work, Yoda." Ryan was all ready to proceed.

"There's something else—something I believe will please you."

"Go on."

"Look at your left screen. In my follow-through, I also found a list of upcoming parties that Victor Colotti's catering business is about to handle—three, in fact, over the next two weeks. One is tomorrow—pardon me, it's after midnight—tonight."

"I see it." Ryan pumped the air. "You're brilliant, Yoda. With Casey calling Nick tomorrow, this couldn't be more ideal. I'll suggest to her that we tighten the timing. She should call Nick at the end of the day. He'll then call to warn his father. Which will throw Victor for a loop, either at the party or as he's driving to it. Too late to cancel, especially since he wants that money. But even if he cuts it short, Patrick will have security detail parked nearby, ready to tail him. My guess is that Victor will be such a wreck that he'll blow out of there ASAP and go straight home."

"Or perhaps to warn his own boss?" Yoda suggested.

"Uh-uh." Ryan shook his head. "That will be one ugly meeting. Victor knows what's at stake, and he'll want to plan carefully before he takes any step that might end with a bullet in his head."

"I understand, Ryan. I'd suggest telling Patrick to have his security detail be cautious. Obviously, if Victor Colotti should spot him, the entire Forensic Instincts team would be in danger."

Ryan's jaw tightened. "We're already in danger, Yoda, and we have been since we took Aimee on as a client. But now? The moment Casey makes that call to Nick, and he calls his father, Victor Colotti will realize he's been made—by us."

***

Colts River, New Jersey
Friday, 3:50 p.m.

Victor was at his desk, scanning his computer to review tonight's guest list. As always, he'd gotten the list from the hostess, claiming he was checking to see if there were any conflicts or issues. Translated, that meant he was making sure there weren't competitors' names on the list, other families he'd catered bigger and better parties for or families who boasted a more viable candidate—son or daughter—to get into the top-notch school that was the first choice of tonight's hosts. You'd think they'd already know that kind of stuff. But, nope, being rich didn't necessarily mean being smart.

To Victor, those lists opened up doors for him. He used them to research the other families so he could tactfully determine other avenues to pursue—friends or family of the guests. He wished he could just contact the guests themselves, but that would destroy the relationships he currently had. On the flip side, some of the guests came directly to him, usually during the party, and asked for his help, no matter what the cost. Those new clients were fair game, and he never turned them away.

It was a delicate balance, but he'd learned to walk the tightrope well, and always to provide the appropriate calming responses necessary.

Now, he sat back, confident that he had everything under control. And not just the parties. His life.

Two weeks had passed since the horrible chain of events that had started with his lunatic killer violently desecrating Aimee Bregman's apartment and culminated with that bone-chilling threat from Sal.

Everything had been quiet since then.

Victor wasn't stupid. He knew that Sal was keeping an eye on him. And he knew that his serial killer was still celebrating his victory, scaring Aimee right out of her apartment and into Forensic Instincts' nurturing arms. Their team obviously didn't know anything damning or they would have done something by now. So all was contained.

He was starting to feel that knot in his gut ease up a bit, and he was starting to get back to business as usual. Much of that was thanks to Linc. Because of his research, a bunch of college kids had been bailed out of trouble. There had also been an increasing number of lucrative house parties. And, of course, CannaBD was selling like wildfire, which meant major profits for him.

Just to be safe, he'd let another few days pass, after which he'd check up on the psycho and make sure his next target was far removed from Victor's operation.

For now, he had to get ready for a party.

***

Offices of Forensic Instincts
Main conference room
Friday, 4:45 p.m.

Casey sat, poised at the head of the table, ready to make her call. The rest of the team was gathered around her, waiting eagerly to hear Nick Colotti's response. Patrick's security guy, Larry Sanders, was already parked near the mansion where the party was being held, watching and waiting for Victor's arrival.

Controlled and confident as always, Casey paused, her finger on the *recents* setting on her iPhone. "I told Aimee we were having a closed-door meeting," she told the team. "She got it. But just in case she gets curious, I locked the door, and I'm ready to switch over from speakerphone at a moment's notice."

"It won't come down to that," Emma said. "If I hear her anywhere close by, I'll text her and say I'll meet up with her as soon as we're done. She'll either think I'm going to tell her something or that I want to gossip and chat. Either way, she'll leave us alone."

"Smart." Casey glanced around. "So we're good?"

Nods and "yups" all around.

"Then it's a go." Casey pressed Nick's number and put the call on speaker.

"Nick Colotti," he answered in an unhappy tone. Clearly, he'd recognized Casey's number. But running from her would only make him seem guiltier.

"Hi, Nick," she said cheerfully. "I just wanted to call and thank you for all your cooperation in our investigation."

You could actually hear the relief at the other end. "No problem," he replied. "I'm glad I could help. How's Aimee? We haven't talked in a couple of days."

"She's hanging in there." A smile brightened Casey's tone. "You're lucky to have her. Not only is she smart but she's a delightful houseguest. She's turned all of us on to CannaBD beer."

A bark of laughter. "Marketing, even now," Nick said. "Yeah, she's great at what she does."

"She's hinted that you'll soon be branching out into other drinks—like wine. We'll be all over that."

"When the project is completed, I'll send you a free case."

"Your father won't mind?" Casey asked innocently.

Silence.

"Why would my father mind?"

"Well, he is your key investor. And he's involved in your day-to-day operations, just as he is with all his businesses. A clever and resourceful man, on all fronts. We've learned so much about him over the course of our investigation. You must be very proud."

"I… am." Nick sounded as if he had marbles stuck in his throat.

"I'd love to meet him one day," Casey continued. "I'm always impressed by successful entrepreneurs. They build their businesses from the ground up and always find ways for them to thrive, no matter what it takes. As I said, he's a fascinating man to research." Casey broke off. "Sorry, I didn't mean to go on like that. I really just wanted to say thanks. Hopefully, you'll be getting your employee back—in person—very soon."

"Great," Nick said. He was clearly torn between shutting down and probing further. He opted to keep his mouth shut.

"Hope to talk to you soon," Casey said. "Goodbye."

She punched off the call.

Ryan grinned. "Well, you sure poked the bear. I wonder how long it'll take him to get to his father."

"That's an interesting question," Patrick said, glancing down at the text he'd just received on silent. "According to Larry, Victor arrived fifteen minutes ago with his catering truck right behind him. His Mercedes-Maybach is visible from where Larry's positioned. Larry says he's got a great view and eyes on all the comings and goings."

"The party isn't officially starting for an hour," Marc reminded them.

"So we wait," Casey replied.

41

CannaBD
Elmton, New Jersey
Friday, 5:03 p.m.

Nick was a wreck.

He locked his office door, went straight to his desk, and squatted down so he could reach the bottom drawer. After working the key out of his pocket, he inserted it and slid open the drawer. Quickly, he glanced out his inside office windows to make sure no one was around. Then, he pulled out his "Linc" burner phone. Linc had been his father's nickname for him ever since childhood, when they'd spent hours together playing with Lincoln Logs. And a pseudonym certainly served as useful now in adulthood, given what they were involved in.

Tonight's party was being held in Millsbridge, New Jersey—probably the most affluent town in the state. The drive from Colts River took a little over an hour. Maybe Nick would get lucky and catch his father before he went in.

He dropped into his desk chair and pressed the button to his dad's burner phone—the one used only for Linc.

It went straight to voice mail.

Dammit, Nick thought. *He must be directing traffic as his team sets up. Well, I don't care what the hell is going on or what I interrupt. I'll call and text every five minutes if I have to. But I'm getting through.*

It took forty-five minutes, with Nick praying that his dad hadn't already launched into party mode without checking his messages, before Victor returned his call.

"Talk to me," Victor said in a tight voice. "You left me six voice mails and sent me a dozen texts. You never do that when I'm working. Something's wrong."

"Very wrong," Nick replied. "Are you standing in the middle of a crowd of people?"

"Of course not. I'm in the bathroom. What is it?"

Without preamble, Nick told his father the entire conversation with Casey Woods.

"*Son of a bitch*!" Victor growled between clenched teeth. "She's playing you, knowing you'll reach out to me." He forced himself to calm down. "My investment in CannaBD isn't a big secret, but I don't exactly publicize it. So where is Forensic Instincts getting their information?"

"You know the answer to that," his son replied.

"Aimee Bregman."

Nick blew out a breath. "What are you going to do?"

"I need to think," his father replied. "How much does Aimee really know about me and how much of this is Forensic Instincts going on a fishing trip? There are details of my life that are buried deep. Digging them up is virtually impossible."

"Yeah, those are the same details you won't share with me."

Victor felt a stab of guilt. "I doubt that's going to be the case for much longer. I'm sorry, son."

"Don't be. I already have my suspicions. I'm sure I won't be surprised. And remember, I'm smart and I have a level head, along with an organized mind. I can talk this through with you. Together, we'll figure out how much Forensic Instincts knows and the best way to handle them and Aimee."

"You're a fine man and I hate to fuck up your life," Victor said. "I'll do my best to protect you. And the talk would be great. I don't want to overreact and go off half-cocked, making a bad situation worse. I want to calmly think this through. And you're the best person to help me do that." He paused. "I won't be home until late. I don't want to have this conversation in the car, while I'm driving. I need to concentrate."

"I'll be awake," Nick assured him. "Where's Mom tonight?"

"Out with her friends, probably gossiping about the best way to get me to buy her that ginormous ring she's been hinting about all week."

Despite his anxiety, Nick chuckled. "It'll be hers by next weekend," he predicted.

"Probably."

"Anyway, I'll give her a call around ten, just to shoot the breeze," Nick said. "It's been a while, so she'll be thrilled. It'll put her in a good enough mood that she won't pout when you lock yourself in your office again."

"Smart idea." Victor glanced at his watch. "I've got to get back. This is prime schmoozing time."

"No problem." Nick felt better. He always did when he was actively *doing* something rather than being an ostrich with his head buried in the sand.

"Talk to you later," Victor said. "And thanks. You're the best."

***

It was after eleven when Victor drove away from the Millsbridge estate, a large check in his pocket. As always, he'd buried the college entry fee in his catering bill, which he'd later run through his restaurant business.

He'd make a whopping profit and no one would be the wiser. And if life allowed it, he'd surprise Frances with that huge rock she wanted.

But he had to be realistic.

What Linc had told him was more than unsettling. It was downright scary. He had to figure out just how much that investigative team actually knew. Aimee had obviously told them enough to make them suspicious. She'd probably mentioned how displeased he was about her police interviews and how he wanted to stay on top of any dealings she had with the NYPD. She could definitely describe him. Had she overheard him talking to Linc at the office? Anything was possible. But during his rare visits to CannaBD, he and his son almost always stuck to business profits and long-term plans for the company's future.

Almost always.

He dragged a hand across his damp forehead, fighting back the panic.

It was Rita's death that had brought Aimee to Forensic Instincts. They'd obviously done a thorough investigation—made more widespread by Chris Maher's murder, thanks to his fucking sociopath of a killer. To the police, it looked like Aimee was the last man standing from that meeting at Fielding's Bar. But again, no amount of police questioning or Forensic Instincts' sniffing around could implicate him. Who he was, who he worked for were buried far too deep to unearth.

Somehow, he didn't feel appeased. Casey Woods and her team must suspect him of *something*. Or they wouldn't be taunting his son in order to get to him. What the hell had Rita told Aimee Bregman? Had she unburdened herself when she found out she was dying? He doubted it. It would only put Aimee in more danger. Still, when she steered Aimee away from Chris Maher, had she dropped bread crumbs about the college scam—enough bread crumbs to put Aimee on the right track? Had something about the scam come out during the shouting match between Rita and Chris at Fielding's Bar?

Victor swallowed bile. He was driving himself crazy, going around in circles and finding no answers, only more reasons to panic.

He needed to go through the possibilities with Linc. It was the only way to formulate a plan to fix things, to protect his whole family.

The alternative was unthinkable.

***

Larry followed Victor's car from the house straight onto the parkway, staying far enough back and shifting lanes in the thin stream of traffic in order to remain unseen. Given how late it was, Victor was making good time. Larry wished there were more traffic within which to conceal himself. But it was Friday night, close to midnight, on a suburban parkway that was either congested or bottlenecked during weekday rush hours. Now, it was pretty much smooth sailing.

About forty-five minutes later, Victor pulled over to the right lane, signaled, and exited the parkway. Larry knew this was a toll exit, so he held back a minute, waiting before he followed. He emerged just as the Mercedes left the toll booth. Now things would get trickier. An affluent area with quiet, winding roads. He'd have to be careful.

He paid the toll and then continued along, keeping a healthy distance between himself and Colotti.

Thirteen minutes later, Colotti slowed down and turned onto a cul-de-sac, where each mansion was more breathtaking than the last. Larry glanced at the sign. Rolling Crest Terrace. He stayed put as Colotti veered onto the street. He counted to twenty and then followed.

It was a split second too soon.

Victor saw the black sedan in his rearview mirror just as he turned into his driveway. He cursed himself for being so deep in thought that he hadn't noticed it before. He always looked over his shoulder, always sensed when he was being followed. This was the wrong damn time to become careless.

He slowed down, lowered his front window, held out his hand, and gave his pursuer the finger. Let the asshole know he'd been spotted.

Victor then accelerated and pulled straight into the garage.

Fucking Forensic Instincts. And fuck him for being such a jackass.

Victor heard the car turn around, tires squealing as his pursuer took off.

This night just can't get any worse, Victor thought, resting his head against the steering wheel.

He was wrong.

42

Colts River
Saturday, 12:38 a.m.

Larry pulled off the parkway at the first possible alcove, parked, and turned off his headlights.

Like the consummate professional he was, he pulled out his phone, texted Colotti's address to Patrick, and followed up with a phone call.

"Nice work," Patrick greeted him, putting him on speaker.

"Not so nice." Larry didn't spare himself. "I pulled onto Colotti's street a split second too soon. I was made."

"You're sure?"

"Oh, yeah. He made sure I knew. He flipped me the bird out his car window. I got the hell out of there ASAP. But the damage was done. Sorry, Patrick, I really screwed up."

Casey saw the expression on Patrick's face. He was a perfectionist. He was about to blow Larry away.

"It's not the end of the world, Larry," she interceded. "I'm sure Nick already alerted his father to the fact that we're sniffing around him. The fact that we're tailing him wouldn't come as a shock. So he now realizes we know where he lives. That's not as important as the fact that we do know."

Larry blew out a breath. "Thanks for stepping in before Patrick could decimate me. But he'd be right. Even though I'm less accustomed to the suburbs than I am to the city, I should have acclimated. You want me off the case, Patrick?"

Casey shot Patrick a warning look.

He sighed. "That won't be necessary, Larry. Just up your game." He ended the call.

"You were too soft on him," Patrick bluntly told Casey.

"I don't think so," Casey shot back. "He's a great member of our security team. He made a mistake. It happens to all of us. Don't cut him off at the knees for that."

"Casey's right, Patrick," Marc said, fully aware that he and Casey were the only ones Patrick would take that from. "Light traffic, late night, rich town with houses set acres apart, and quiet local roads. It's not like being swallowed up in Manhattan traffic where you've got maneuverability and coverage."

"I guess you're right." Patrick's jaw softened a bit. "Now what?"

"Now we let Victor squirm," Casey said. "He has no idea what we know and what we don't. He's in trouble. The walls are closing in on him. He has a superior to report to. That could be fatal. Let's just wait a bit, do our research here and quietly."

"I'll take his address and run with it," Ryan said. "Let's see what data I can get off of it. And I'm not finished digging into his businesses. Maybe I can turn up his boss on my own."

Claire arched a brow. "Do you plan to bring down the whole mob?"

He grinned. "With my skill? Anything's possible."

***

Victor's home office
Colts River, New Jersey
Saturday, 1:05 a.m.

Victor dropped onto the sofa across from his desk, pausing only to pour himself a drink before calling his son.

"Hey, Dad," Nick answered the phone. "You okay?"

"If you call being tailed by Forensic Instincts to your own home being okay, then I guess I'm doing fine."

"They…" Nick swore under his breath. "You didn't spot them until it was too late?"

"Nope. I was a careless idiot. I was too busy working through my problems to notice the tail until he was practically at my front door."

"So he got your address."

"Oh, yeah."

"All right, let's stay calm," Nick said. "What can they find out about you with your address that they couldn't dig up before they had it?"

"I don't know." Victor downed his drink, then paused to refill his glass. "I'm not a professional investigator, and I know how good Forensic Instincts is. I don't have any accounts tied to the house, if that's what you mean. The purchase was quiet, but I'm sure it was recorded and filed with the town. The town has nothing other than that on me. No one does."

"What about your captain? I'm sure he's got a hell of a lot. How pissed off is he going to be about all this?"

Dead silence.

"You know?" Victor asked at last.

"Oh, come on, Dad, you're always telling me how smart I am. It didn't take a genius to figure it out." Nick gave a humorless laugh. "So, you can stop worrying. I'm in a lot deeper than you realized."

"Yes. You are." Victor took another swallow of bourbon. "But knowing and doing are two different things. You're an accessory, at worst."

"I don't care what I am, as long as I'm helping you. So let's go over everything—and I mean *everything*—and come up with a viable plan."

As Victor was about to speak, his "Sal phone" rang.

"That's him," he said to Nick, sounding like a prisoner about to receive his lethal injection.

"Go ahead and answer. Let him talk. You just listen, hear how much he knows and what he has to say."

Victor rose. "I'm putting you on mute."

"Why?" Nick demanded.

"Because I'm still protecting you, no matter how smart you are. You don't know as much as you think you do, and I'm going to do everything in my power to keep it that way." Victor squared his shoulders. "Stay put." He pressed the mute button over his son's protests.

He walked over to the phone, crossed himself, and answered. "Hey, Sal."

Sal didn't return the greeting. "You lend new meaning to the word *asshole*," he said in a lethally quiet voice. "Letting your son lead them straight to you. Being followed and never noticing. Want to send a full dossier on all of our operations to Aimee Bregman and Forensic Instincts?"

Victor squeezed his eyes shut. "I'll find a way to fix this."

"No. *I'll* find a way to fix this. You still don't get it, do you? You're in deep shit. That means *I'm* in deep shit. I should have listened to my gut and taken you out weeks ago." Sal paused long enough for visions of that to sink in. "But as it turns out, I'm glad I waited. I need you to do something. Do it right, and I *might* let you live. *Might.*"

Victor knew better, but he had no choice but to comply. "Tell me what you want me to do, and it's done."

"How much does your son know about you?" Sal asked. "And don't lie to me."

Dear God, Victor thought, squeezing his eyes shut. *How I prayed this day would never come. Sal is dragging Linc into this.*

He took a final stab at preventing it. "He knows about the college scam. I've never told him another thing."

"The murders?"

"He only knows they happened. Nothing about my connection to them. He's my son, Sal. I purposely keep him shielded from that part of my life."

"Well, that's over." There wasn't a shred of compassion or understanding in Sal's voice. "He's about to get involved."

Without waiting for a reply, Sal issued his orders.

Victor flinched as he listened. "Sal…"

"Say another word and there's a bullet with your name on it."

He disconnected the call.

Victor stared at the cell phone for a long time before putting it down and heading back to the sofa, where he'd been talking to Linc. He felt like a dead man. And he was soon going to be, whether he pulled this off or not. He knew the mob. They didn't forgive or forget. But no matter what, he had to protect Frances and Linc. They had a chance at a life. The mob would hover around Linc for a while, make sure he was out of the picture. Once they were convinced, they'd go away. Frances they'd know was never in the picture. In their eyes, she was a mobster's wife, uninformed and uninvolved. She'd inherit his money and be happy, naively believing in whatever accidental death Sal came up with.

Wearily, like a man twice his age, he lowered himself to the sofa and unmuted the phone.

"I'm here," he told Linc.

"What happened?" his son demanded.

"Nothing good. Nothing…" Victor's voice cracked as tears filled his eyes, began trickling down his cheeks. "I need you to do something," he choked out. "So listen to me."

"Dad, you're scaring me." Linc had never heard his father cry. "Are they going to… *do*… something to you?"

"What's important is, I won't let them do something to you or your mom. So you have to do exactly as I say."

Linc was shaking, but he didn't argue. "Okay, I will. What is it you need me to do?"

Victor fought back the emotions consuming him and gathered the strength to lie to his son one last time.

"First thing in the morning, I need you to call Aimee Bregman and get her to come to CannaBD at ten a.m. I realize she'll be suspicious of you, but you must find a way to get past that and make it happen. It's my job to be there, to convince her to shut her mouth and fire that team of private dicks she hired."

"And if she refuses?"

Victor's silence was deafening.

"Dad?"

"Listen to me," Victor said. "After that phone call to Aimee, you're done—for good. When Aimee arrives at CannaBD, get the hell out of there. You know nothing other than the fact that I asked you to set up a private meeting with Aimee."

When Linc spoke again, he sounded fiercely determined. "I understand what you're saying—and what you're *not* saying. I don't plan on letting anything happen to you. I'll make this work."

Victor shut his eyes, wishing he could undo things, wishing he would live to see Linc's successes, his wife, his children. But none of that was meant to be.

"Thank you, son," he said quietly. "Call me once Aimee's there and you're not."

He hung up and bowed his head.

"May God forgive me," he whispered.

43

Offices of Forensic Instincts
Tribeca, New York
Saturday, 8:45 a.m.

Casey sat at the conference room table, legs crossed, sipping a cup of coffee and feeling restless. Something was eluding her, a piece of the puzzle that was just out of reach. The kill pattern. It had something to do with the kill pattern. But what?

She wasn't going to stop racking her brain until she figured it out.

Emma sat across from her, also drinking coffee and stress-eating a large bagel oozing with cream cheese, for once, in silence.

Ryan was leaning against the coffee station, a miserable expression on his face. Aside from learning a few insignificant details about Victor Colotti's restaurant business, he was still coming up empty. He'd switched over to his research on the serial killer, even going so far as to magnify the visuals of Victor's car in the hopes of spotting a passenger. Not only was it a total bust but Ryan knew he was just grasping at straws by doing it. Mobsters didn't drive around with their hired assassins.

Claire was standing quietly near the windows, tense and uneasy, having tossed and turned all night, consumed by the growing sense of evil that was closing in on them.

Marc had arrived right behind Casey and was now on his iPad, reading Casey's notes about what Hutch had said about the killer. Hutch was the best there was at his job, but Marc was also former BAU, and maybe he'd spot something in Hutch's analysis that the team hadn't.

Patrick had come into the conference room five minutes after Marc. He'd obviously gotten over his annoyance at Larry, because he reported in that he'd instructed Larry to shower, change, and switch cars before heading back to Colts River. Since situating himself right outside Colotti's house would be stupid, Patrick instructed Larry to drive to the closest main street and hide his car amid a cluster of trees. It was a long shot, since Patrick doubted Victor was going anywhere, but a long shot was better than no shot.

Now, Patrick heard a *bing* and glanced at his iPhone for the twentieth time. "Same news from Larry," he said. "Colotti hasn't pulled onto the main street all morning. Rolling Crest Terrace is a cul-de-sac, which means there are no other ways out. And no suspicious visitors, either. That's easy to discern since it's a quiet street on a quiet Saturday morning."

"He's probably closeted in his house, either running through his options or talking to his boss, dealing with the fallout from that," Casey said.

Hero's head came up as someone knocked at the door.

"It's me," Aimee called from the other side of the door. "Sorry to bother you, but it's important."

Casey and Marc exchanged glances. What now?

"Come on in," Casey called back.

Aimee stepped inside and glanced around, seeing them all in respective locations. "I'm glad you're not having a meeting. Normally, I'd respect your privacy. But I've got a business emergency I have to deal with."

Casey was immediately on high alert. "What kind of emergency?"

"Nick called a few minutes ago," Aimee said, visibly upset. "He's having a major meltdown, and I don't blame him. We have a new business investor, Jason Williams, whose financial commitment to CannaBD is surpassed only by the backing of Nick's dad. Jason's contract with Nick was attorney approved on both sides and practically signed on the dotted line. All of us, well, not so much Oliver, but the rest of us were ready to pop the cork and bathe in champagne. Now there's some technical issue that needs to be resolved ASAP, before we lose Jason as an investor. Nick practically begged me to come in, just for an hour. Kimberley and Oliver will be there, too. I have to go, Casey. This is my work home we're talking about. I have to do whatever I can to help save this deal."

She paused, stiffening as if to prepare for a fight. "I told Nick I'd be there at ten."

Aside from the suspiciously coincidental timing, two names waved red flags in Casey's mind: Nick Colotti and Oliver Steadman. Nick because of his questionable dealings with his father, and Oliver because he was still on the suspect list.

"Please, Casey," Aimee begged. "I can't be under lock and key every minute. This is my boss and my colleagues. It's my responsibility to be there."

Despite her concerns, Casey couldn't really argue with that. Aimee was dedicated. And this emergency could be on the up-and-up. Maybe there was a way to make this work.

"Okay, Aimee—*with* stipulations," she added before Aimee could become giddy with a sense of independence.

"Ryan," Casey instructed. "I want you to do a thorough search on Jason Williams and his imminent investment in Canna BD. I want everything there is, on the man and on the deal."

"Done." Ryan was already headed to the door, actually grateful for something meaningful to do.

Casey met Patrick's gaze and spoke to him directly in front of their client, so Aimee would recognize the importance of this.

"Patrick, I want two cars appended to the rear of Aimee's Honda CR-V," she said. "Yours and John's. John is your number one guy. And *no one* gets by you."

Patrick's eyes narrowed, although he nodded. "I'm not happy about this."

"Nor am I," Casey agreed. "But Aimee's right about her commitment to her job. So she'll do it our way, or no way at all."

Without hesitation, Aimee nodded. "Be as cautious as you need to be. I accept your stipulations. Just let me do my job."

"No deviating from the rules," Casey warned.

"None. I'll just do my business and leave."

Casey nodded. "Then go get ready."

***

Driving to Elmton via parkway
Saturday, 9:45 a.m.

Aimee shifted lanes, well aware that Patrick and John were each within several car lengths of her, moving in and out of traffic. Rush hour wasn't a concern—it was way past nine, and it was Saturday. Still, Patrick had opted to avoid the FDR Drive and taken the Saw Mill Parkway instead. A direct run and, despite the annoying tolls, a fast-paced route where drivers would be moving along at a rapid enough pace to be concentrating on the road, not the other drivers.

Ryan had done his homework on Jason Williams and his upcoming investment in CannaBD and reported that the man was both highly intelligent and aboveboard and that the investment deal was indeed about to be finalized.

So all systems were go.

Aimee glanced at the clock on her dashboard and anxiously shifted to the left lane, which was flying along, unhappy because she realized she'd be timing it close. Using her Bluetooth, she called Nick.

"Where are you?" he asked, sounding frantic.

"On the parkway," she replied. "I just wanted to let you know that I might be a couple of minutes late. It took me awhile to convince Forensic Instincts to let me go."

"How late?"

"Maybe five minutes if you count parking and walking to the building."

"Okay." Nick calmed down, although he still sounded jumpy. "The rest of the team is already here. But we'll wait."

Aimee felt a twinge of guilt. "Sorry."

"No problem. I know you're living in Fort Knox right now. Is security following you to make sure you're safe?"

The question made Aimee uncomfortable for some reason, so she kept her answer vague. "I'm sure they are. There wasn't time to discuss it. I just got in my car and took off."

"Thanks, Aimee." A pause. "I'm really sorry."

Nick sounded as if he truly felt badly for dragging her in, given the circumstances.

"Not to worry," she replied. "I'm almost at the exit."

Patrick hadn't liked this arrangement from the start. His concern mounted the closer they got to CannaBD. John was going to park across the street from the building. Patrick planned on parking in the lot, backing into a spot that was hidden behind the huge green trash collection bin. Squatting on the driver's side of the front seat, he'd be able to see both the lot and the door, but no one could see him.

The plan would have been foolproof.

Except for the fact that the killer was already inside.

Aimee practically jumped out of the car, locking it and striding quickly toward the building. She glanced at her watch. Only three minutes late, including the walk. She didn't glance around to see if Patrick and John were in place, otherwise she might have noted that the only two cars in the lot were hers and Nick's. Then again, Kimberley lived close by and often jogged to work. And Oliver was antisocial enough to park on the street to avoid mingling with the others once the business day was through.

She blew through the doorway and headed straight to Nick's office.

He was sitting at his desk, white-faced, his body oddly twisted.

"Nick?" Aimee glanced around the empty room. "Where is everyone?"

At that instant, she realized Nick's arms were tied behind him.

She started backing away, instinct screaming that something was very wrong.

"I'm so sorry, Aimee." Nick looked terrified.

Nick's fear was contagious, and, wordlessly, Aimee backed up faster.

In the doorway, she collided with an obstacle—a man, who, before she could turn around or scream, locked his left arm around her neck in an iron grip.

"Hello, Aimee."

44

Aimee knew that voice.

"Tr— avis?" she choked out, her throat already constricting.

Travis barked out a laugh. "I wish I could see your face right now. It would heighten the pleasure. Ah, well." He moved forward, shoving her into the office and into one of the two chairs in front of Nick's desk. He kept his arm locked around her throat, his elbow pressing down on her shoulder so she couldn't move.

He dropped the gym bag he was carrying onto the floor. With his free hand, he grabbed Aimee's right hand and twisted it behind the back of the chair.

Aimee gave a sharp whimper of pain.

Travis ignored it. For his own purposes, he released his grip around her throat—only long enough to swiftly accomplish what he needed to.

He grabbed hold of her left hand and roughly curled it behind her, as well. Holding her two wrists together, he reached into his pants pocket and pulled out a zip tie. He cinched it tightly around her wrists.

The pressure on her windpipe gone, Aimee screamed and began bucking to get free.

"Sit still," Travis ordered. "Otherwise, I'll do it for you. In fact, the thought of that is very appealing."

His lethal words made Aimee go still.

"Smart girl."

He leaned over just enough to pick up the gym bag, straightening so he could plunk it down on Nick's desk. Unzipping it, he extracted, one by one, a rope, a butcher knife, and a college football glove. The knife and the football glove he placed neatly on the desk. The rope he grabbed hold of, tucking it beneath his arm as he took a moment to pat Aimee down.

"Wired?" he asked, then answered his own question. "Nope. Good. But feel free to continue screaming for as long as you can. Even your superhero security team can't hear through these concrete walls."

He let those words sink in.

Silence.

He went back to work. He wrapped each end of the rope around first his left hand and then his right. He gave the finished product a tug and smiled, pleased with the amount of tension he felt and knowing the level of pressure he could now apply.

Still smiling, he twisted the rope around Aimee's neck and tugged.

Aimee gasped for air and reflexively began to struggle again.

Travis jerked her body back, hampering her attempts to break free. "This isn't going to be quick," he told her. "So stop fighting me. You'll just exhaust yourself trying, and it's not going to work. Besides, I have too much to say before I squeeze the life out of you."

"What are you doing?" Nick burst out. "My father is coming to meet with Aimee. He told me to get her here and then leave."

Travis barked out an eerie laugh. "Is that what he told you? You're even stupider than I thought. No, Nicky, I'm here to finalize some business, starting with little Aimee here."

Nick's eyes widened with realization. "You're going to *kill* her? You can't do that, especially right in the middle of—"

"I can do anything I fucking feel like doing," Travis responded, with an odd glint in his eyes that Aimee couldn't see but Nick could.

"Your father ordered me to do it elsewhere so you'd be spared. But how could I resist the pleasure of choking and mutilating Aimee in the place that would bring you—spoiled little rich boy—and your arrogant bastard of a father down? Not a chance. I'll make a new life, but you'll both be in jail for life, or dead." He shrugged. "Don't care. But I'm proud to say that I did a great job of framing you and your daddy for Aimee's murder. Plus, you, Nicky, have also assumed the role of the serial killer who horrifies the world and leaves his signature kill on all his victims."

Nick looked as if he were going to be sick. "What do you mean?" he managed.

"Just what I said. You're not the only one who's good at hacking. With a little assistance from a pro, I created a whole new identity for myself years ago. Time to rinse and repeat. Anyway, I digress. You're going to serve a lifetime sentence. Your father will be right there beside you. With a good lawyer, he could lessen his time by ratting out his colleagues. Regardless, he'll wind up dead, either in prison or out. The mob will see to that. On the other hand"—Travis indicated Nick's cell phone—"you could call your daddy now, tell him what's going on, and he'll race right over here. That way, I could be merciful and kill you both instantly. Or rather, officially, *you'd* die at your enraged father's hands, and *he'd* die by suicide. As I said, your choice." He patted the pistol he kept in his jacket pocket.

Nick recoiled and shut his mouth.

Travis's lips curled. "Think about it."

He shifted his attention back to Aimee. "Now where were we? Ah!" Using his hip, he swiveled Aimee's chair around until it faced the vacant chair beside it. He rotated the noose around her neck until the ends were locked in front of her throat and used his foot to maneuver the empty chair ninety degrees. He sank down into it, making sure he was eye to eye with Aimee. He saw the terror in her eyes and his body tightened with excitement.

"Scared?" he taunted. "You should be. You said a lot of nasty little things about me and my skills when you were curled up against me. Pity. I actually liked you—and the sex wasn't bad, either. But no one"—he leaned forward until his lips brushed Aimee's ear—"*no one* talks about me that way."

He tightened the noose until it was cutting into her flesh, but not tight enough to be lethal.

The reality of asphyxiation set in. Aimee went wild, her feet pushing at the floor, her hands fighting the zip tie so she could get free. When that failed, her entire body went rigid, and she started shaking uncontrollably.

Travis had felt that reaction many times. But this time he was watching as well as experiencing it. And this was Aimee. That made it more arousing than the others had been, and infinitely more satisfying.

Save maybe for Rice. Killing him had been a high like no other. A life for a life.

Travis stared at Aimee, releasing his grip just a fraction. He wanted her to process every word he was saying.

"Still think you're smarter than me, little girl?" he mocked. "Still think you and that Scooby Doo team can bring me down?"

Aimee shook her head from side to side. *Please keep talking*, she prayed. She'd insisted that Patrick be patient. But she knew he would only wait so long. And that's how long she had to keep herself alive.

"Why… new… life…?" she croaked, grateful that Travis had loosened the noose enough so she could get out a few words.

"Because Travis Bishop was sloppy." That odd light came into his eyes. "Travis Grady is extraordinarily brilliant and methodical." His voice dropped, and there was a bone-chilling sound to it. "Just two personal kills. You. And that son of a bitch Rice, who murdered my brother." Once again, he pressed his lips roughly against her ear, and she could feel the abnormal thrill vibrating through him. "An eye for an eye, little girl."

Out in the car, Patrick eased his weight enough to keep full strength in both legs. He peered around the parking lot, decidedly uneasy. Aimee had told him about the parking and jogging habits of her colleagues. And it had only been ten minutes since she walked through the door. He had to hold back a little longer, fight his feeling that he was making a big mistake by doing so.

Casey had spent the last hour frantically poring over articles on antisocial personality disorder. Unfortunately, Hutch was unavailable or she'd be talking this through with him. But as it was, she was on her own.

She'd read the same information over and over again, learned a little more each time, but nothing clicked with what was bothering her.

She was about to move on to the next article when a Q and A question caught her eye:

Q: Do sociopaths have any feelings at all?

A: Yes, when it suits them to.

Casey sat up straighter. She'd already read, ad nauseam, about high-functioning sociopaths' lack of empathy and genuine inability to deeply care about another person. But what if they *chose* to care?

The deviation from the killing pattern.

Casey's mind snapped back to the mutilation of Aimee's apartment. Why had the killer deviated from his usual pattern? Why just scare Aimee, hoping she'd back off? Why hadn't he killed her, the way he had all the others?

Because what he'd done was softer than killing her. Because on whatever level he was capable of, he cared. He'd certainly said so, and meant it, throughout their interview.

Casey snatched her cell phone, furious at herself for taking so long to snap this puzzle piece into place. She was a behaviorist, with a keen ability to read people and their tells. This bastard had found a way to elude her.

No time for self-chastising now.

She couldn't type those three words fast enough.

"Please, let me have gotten to him on time," Casey prayed as she put down her phone. "Please."

She raised her head. The whole team was staring at her, especially Claire, whose palms were pressed to the window and who was growing more and more white-faced with every passing moment.

Casey saw the expressions on everyone's face and responded.

"It's Travis. He's our sociopath."

"Yes," Claire concurred, looking ill but, at the same time, as if a great cloud of confusion had been lifted from her mind. "And he's got Aimee."

Patrick heard the *bing* and read the text before it had stopped sounding.

Travis has her.

He was out of the car, readying his Glock and racing toward the building in a heartbeat.

"Now where was I?" Travis asked, ignoring Aimee's weak, lingering attempts to free herself. They both knew it wasn't going to happen. But Aimee needed him to think she believed that it could. If she went limp, he'd know it was a setup.

"Please… don't… do… this," she squeezed out.

"It has to be done."

"Why…?" Tears slid down her cheeks.

"Two reasons," he replied. "One, I'm being paid a shitload of money to take care of you. And two, because you pissed me off, demeaned me, made yourself better than me. You're not even my equal. And stop being so melodramatic. It's irking me."

"But—"

"Enough!" Travis shut her down, rising to plant his feet so he could use all of his weight to choke her until every breath was gone from her body. "Now you're boring me. You're pathetic."

Aimee felt herself fading away.

"Goodbye, little girl." Travis pulled with all his strength, soaking in the pleasure as he watched Aimee die.

"Let her go!" a voice boomed out.

Travis snapped around in surprise.

Two shots blew through his head, piercing his skull and penetrating his brain, as Patrick double-tapped him. His body jerked wildly, and the rope slipped through his fingers as he fell to the floor, dead.

Aimee collapsed, coughing and gasping for air.

Patrick holstered his weapon and strode into the room and over to the mini fridge. He yanked out a bottled water and wrenched off the cap. Then, he went to Aimee. Squatting down, he pulled a tactical knife out of his boot and carefully cut the zip tie binding Aimee's hands.

"Drink this," he said gently, propping her up and holding the bottle to her lips. "Slowly."

There were black spots swimming before Aimee's eyes, but she complied, coughing violently in between sips of water. Vaguely, she saw John walk past them, pistol raised, and one-handedly cuff Nick, ignoring the zip tie already binding his wrists.

Eventually, Aimee pushed away the water, sucking in one breath after another. Her fingers came up to touch her bruised throat, and she began shaking and sobbing uncontrollably.

"It's over," Patrick told her quietly. "He can never hurt you again."

"Dear… God," she managed, rocking back and forth. "How could I… not have known?" She coughed again. "How could I not…?"

"Sociopaths make sure you don't." Patrick kept it short and sweet. Longer explanations would come later.

He looked over at John. "I'll contact the team now," he told him. "Once you're driving, call NYPD Homicide. Fill them in on what happened here. Have them coordinate with the local police departments, here in Elmton to take Nick in for questioning and in Colts River to arrest Victor Colotti."

"And Aimee?" John asked.

"I have to stay here and answer the cops' questions. Take Aimee to the hospital to be checked out. Then bring her back to the brownstone. She needs time. The cops can talk to her later—and I'll be sure to tell them that when they show up at our door." He stopped talking and indicated with his eyes just how bad Aimee was. Her crying and shaking had ceased. She was holding her throat and staring at Travis's dead body, the blood beginning to pool around him. She'd gone deadly still as shock set in.

John nodded.

Patrick gave Aimee's hand a paternal squeeze. "John will take you back to the brownstone. I'll be there as soon as I talk to the police."

John gently lifted her into his arms, carrying her like a small child. "It's okay, honey," he murmured. "We're going home."

45

When Casey's cell phone sounded, the whole team was grouped around the table, tense and waiting.

Casey grabbed the phone and put it on speaker. "Patrick, we're all here."

"Aimee is safe but still in shock," Patrick reported. "Also in pain. Travis was choking her to death when I burst in and shot him. He's dead. He left me no choice. Nick is involved with his father's dirty business dealings, including today's setup. Right now, he's handcuffed to a chair, gaping at the dead body. So, he's not going anywhere. John is calling the NYPD to coordinate with the locals and arrange to have Victor Colotti arrested and Nick taken in for questioning. Also, John is taking Aimee to a local hospital to get her checked out. Then he'll bring her back to the brownstone. He's already on the road. I'm going to be here for quite some time answering questions for the Elmton police."

Casey's phone beeped, signaling an incoming call. John's number displayed on the caller ID.

"Patrick," she interrupted. "That's John calling. I have to take it. He might have an update on Aimee's condition. Keep me posted between interrogations."

"I will."

Casey switched to the other call. "John, we're all on the line. Patrick just gave us an overview. How is Aimee?"

"Fair," John replied carefully. "I wanted to stop at the hospital, but she refused."

"I'm fine," Aimee whispered, her throat still raspy. Her hollow tone conveyed how deeply traumatized and numb from the ordeal she was.

"We'll have our doctor here by the time you arrive," Casey responded. "She can check you out so you don't have to deal with a hospital."

"I think that's a good idea," John said, discernably gauging how much Aimee could handle hearing. "I spoke to the NYPD. They'll be sending detectives to both Elmton and to Colts River."

"You and Patrick covered all the bases. Nice follow-through."

"Casey?" Aimee's weak, raspy monotone came through the speaker. "His name wasn't Grady. It was Bishop. Have Ryan check that out." She paused, coughing and wheezing. "He said Coach Rice killed his brother."

Casey stared at the phone, her shock manifesting in silence.

"Thank you, Aimee," she said aloud, masking her surprise. "You're a very brave woman."

"Thank you—for everything."

"I'm signing off now, Casey." John's voice made it clear that Aimee had had enough.

"See you soon." Casey ended the call.

"Poor thing," she said, turning to the team. "It's clear from the gravelly sound of her voice that the son of a bitch was well into choking her."

"Now it all makes sense," Claire murmured. "The conflicting auras I was picking up on, being torn between it being a mob hit or a personal one. It was both."

Ryan was typing angrily on his keyboard. "It might make sense to you, but it doesn't to me. I did a full background check on Travis

Grady..." His voice trailed off. "I was researching the wrong man. How could I have missed something so obvious?"

"Not obvious," Marc said. "For you to miss it, he had to have used a pro to create a whole new ID for him—one you weren't looking for."

"Travis Bishop." Ryan wasn't so quick to forgive himself. "Yoda, put up a full screen. I want to see everything we've got on Travis Grady, just as a means of comparison. And then work with me. I want to get under the hood. We need to find this invisible Travis Bishop and find out everything about him. Starting with his brother's name and the cause of death."

"Yes, Ryan."

The Grady data appeared on the screen. Address, driver's license, passport, workplace. All the information matched up with what he'd told Casey in their interview. His place of birth also checked out, as did his military record. And all his social media platforms matched his persona.

Ryan dug deeper, scowling as he did. "Marc's right. The ability to create this level of a whole new, impenetrable ID is the work of a seasoned pro," he muttered. "He's made it near impossible for anyone to break down this wall. But I'm not anyone. I'm finding this bastard." He went back to pounding at the keyboard.

"Ryan," Claire said. "Focus on the victim."

Ryan stopped and turned to face her. "Who—Rice?"

"Yes. This is about him. Check out his life, his career. I worked that case. I got all kinds of weird, contradictory auras. Dig deeper into him. I think that will lead you to Travis Bishop."

"Okay." Ryan didn't question her. He just switched screens. "Yoda, keep working on Grady to Bishop. I'm moving on to Rice."

"I'll continue, Ryan," Yoda replied.

Ryan pulled up Peter Rice, deceased football coach at Brightington University. "The basic rundown I've already done. You've told us and the local police that he was stealing from the mob. There's no proof of that, of course. But I'm accepting it as fact. Personal life—nil. All about his job. With regard to that, I've got mixed reviews. He was a beloved football coach, but a demanding and intimidating one. He drove his players and won a dozen championships."

Ryan's brows drew together in thought. "That information came from articles written after his death. Let's go back to before it." Ryan's fingers flew over the keyboard as he pulled up articles, both from local newspapers and from the Brightington school news.

"Nothing on Rice, at least not directly," he reported. "But lots of stuff about his star quarterback"—Ryan broke off—"Hank Bishop."

"Travis's younger brother," Claire said, looking more certain by the minute.

Ryan kept reading. "Apparently, the poor kid blew out his knee, was unable to continue playing, and lost his football scholarship. He was about to be tossed out when he was killed in a car accident. The autopsy revealed a shitload of drugs and booze in his system."

Once again, Ryan turned to Claire. "Murder?"

"No." She shook her head. "Not in the legal sense."

"You're saying that Rice drove him into the ground and ultimately to his death."

"That's what I'm saying."

Ryan quickly brought up Hank Bishop and scanned his bio. "Born and raised in Reed, Alabama," he read. "Star quarterback in high school. Got a full-ride Division 1 scholarship. Coming from a dirt-poor family, this was the opportunity of a lifetime. A first-rate college education with a shot at the NFL. He'd be the first in his family to go beyond high school."

Ryan continued scanning the news clip. "Well, if we wanted any further proof, here it is. Mother: Ada. Father: unknown. Brother: Travis."

He gave Claire a triumphant look. "You're amazing," he said.

"All data on Travis Bishop ceased to exist a decade ago," Yoda announced. "But before that, he was very much alive. Check your left screen, Ryan."

Ryan raised his head and read. "In and out of trouble since elementary school. Spent time in juvie for beating up and threatening other kids. Was seen and got great enjoyment snapping the necks of small animals. At sixteen, he was kicked out by his mother and promptly enlisted with the army."

Casey pursed her lips. "So some of it was true," she murmured, reading about Travis's military career and his training as a medic. "He just picked and chose threads of reality to weave into his new identity. Sticking to the truth is easiest to remember."

With that, she glanced around. "Let's close the door on Travis Bishop. He's dead. Now we know the dual reasons why. Let's look ahead, because we now have bigger fish to fry. Not only have we solved the case and rescued Aimee from right under the NYPD's noses but we infiltrated a mob family. The police are going to be all over us, and not happily. We'd better get our stories straight. As for Aimee, we're not letting them near her until she's able to handle it. She was almost choked to death by a man she thought cared about her. I'll physically stand between the NYPD and Aimee if they try to get past our front door."

46

Offices of Forensic Instincts
Main conference room
Noon, three days later

The entire team, sans Casey, were gathered around the oval table, nibbling at their pizza slices and waiting for word from their boss. Casey had gone upstairs a half hour ago to check on Aimee. Even though their doctor had said that Aimee's injured windpipe and bruised throat and neck would quickly heal, the FI team was still keeping a close watch on her.

The unpleasant altercation with the NYPD was behind them. It hadn't been pretty. The NYPD was livid about everything—FI's investigation, the possible illegalities associated with it, the lack of communication between FI and their homicide department, and of course, FI's taking on a mob soldier.

Casey had calmed the detectives down, reminding them that FI had kept them in the loop about everything they'd been hired for—Aimee's safety and, of course, anything new about Rita Edwell's alleged death. The significant and newsworthy events, the FI team had just stumbled upon when interviewing Nick Colotti. And the full truth had just exploded over the past twenty-four hours, when they'd learned that Nick Colotti, on orders of his father, had manipulated Aimee and summoned her to CannaBD headquarters, where the entire violent scene had taken place. The FI team had never met Victor Colotti and had only just learned he had mob connections.

The NYPD was smart. They knew Forensic Instincts. And they were more than certain that there was a hell of a lot more to the flimsy story than Casey was providing. But there was no proof that FI had done anything illegal. The few facts they'd provided checked out. And Aimee Bregman, who the detectives had finally managed to interview yesterday, corroborated FI's story one hundred percent.

The cops had given up and gone away.

They had more than enough to feel good about. It had been the NYPD that made the major arrests, starting with Victor Colotti and leading to his captain, Salvatore Orsatti. From there, they'd uncovered the college entrance scam and ultimately—and most importantly—cracked the Tarillo family wide open. They'd also brought to a close the heinous reign of a serial killer, unearthed all his murders, and given peace to the families of his victims.

Their work would be commemorated, and all the press conferences they held would be rife with medals and promotions.

If the media and the fans of FI spun it differently, that was their right to do. FI remained respectfully silent.

Now, Casey walked into the conference room, giving the team the thumbs-up. "Aimee has some color in her cheeks. She's talked to her parents, who are flying in today to be with her and even to help with the apartment hunting. CannaBD might be history, but Aimee's already had job offers from three New York City companies. Oh, and Emma, she's scarfing down three slices of pizza."

Emma grinned from ear to ear. "I knew that would break her. After eating nothing but tea and toast for three days, there's nothing better for a growling stomach than an `everything pie.'"

"Great," Ryan said, reaching over to grab a few slices of his own. "Now that we know that everything's good, it's time to stop eating like birds. Time to chow down."

They all laughed and followed suit.

As they finished and gathered up the paper plates to toss, Ryan noticed that Claire was smiling to herself.

He walked over to her, looking distinctly pissed off. "I usually put that smile on your face," he grumbled. "I don't like it coming from somewhere else. So, unless you're fantasizing about us, I want to know why you look so damn happy."

Claire gave him a beatific smile. "Because that's how I feel."

"Why?" Ryan demanded.

Before Claire could respond, Yoda announced: "Fiona McKay has arrived."

"Huh?" Ryan blinked in surprise.

The rest of the team was now looking at him.

"I had no idea Fee was coming over," he said. "She never barges in when we're solving a case."

"The case is solved," Claire reminded him. "And she isn't barging in. I invited her."

Now Ryan looked not only confused but irked. "This isn't another jewelry party, is it?" he demanded. "Because she's lucky I'm still wearing the chain she gave me last time. Yeah, it's cool. But I don't do jewelry."

"Yes, we know." Laughter bubbled up in Claire's throat. "But don't worry. That's not why she's here."

"Then why?"

"Because you and I are completely open about our private lives now," Claire answered sweetly. "And we have news to share with her—news she's been dying to hear for a long time. I called her because she's my friend. But she's also your sister, so I thought you'd want to be there."

In a rare show of public affection, Claire took Ryan's hand and linked their fingers together. "Come on, Mr. Emotional. Time to tell Fiona that we're in love."

ACKNOWLEDGMENTS

My gratitude to all the professionals who generously offered me their time and expertise and who helped me make AT ANY COST the best book I could create:

James McNamara, Retired Supervisory Special Agent, Behavioral Analysis Unit, FBI and former Marine Infantry Officer

FBI Special Agent Anthony L. Zampogna (retired)

First Grade NYPD Detective John DiCaprio (retired)

NYPD Lieutenant Ralph A. Manente (retired)

FBI Special Agent in Charge Jim Nelson (retired) and a recognized expert on the subject of Organized Crime

FBI SSA Chance Adam, Balkan/Eurasian Operations Unit in Criminal Division

FBI Chief of Organized Crime Section at FBI HQ Matt Heron (retired)

FBI Supervisory Special Agent Michael Ross, Organized Crime Section, FBI Headquarters (retired)

FBI Supervisory Special Agent Lou DiGregorio (retired)

FBI Special Agent Marty Towey, Lucchese squad (retired)

And last, but truly first, my innermost team:

LP, for being the quintessential gem of an editorial partner

Amy Knupp, Blue Otter Editing, who somehow misses nothing and makes every book as flawless as possible

Ted Polakowski, who fine-tunes every minute detail with the utmost of care

My wonderful, one-of-a-kind family, all of whom are part of both the creative process and the cheerleading process!